Ladybug

By

Sean Mikell

∞INFINITY
PUBLISHING

ISBN 978-1-4958-0187-7
ISBN 978-1-4958-0188-4 eBook

Published December 2014

INFINITY PUBLISHING
1094 New DeHaven Street, Suite 100
West Conshohocken, PA 19428-2713
Toll-free (877) BUY BOOK
Local Phone (610) 941-9999
Fax (610) 941-9959
Info@buybooksontheweb.com
www.buybooksontheweb.com

Prelude

The French colonized Indochina in the mid-1800s and for the next hundred years successfully governed the country and oversaw its rich agrarian economy. Rice fields, rubber plantations, and lush mango groves dotted the landscape while French culture permeated its cities and town.

In mid-1940, the Japanese-Sino War was in full swing and the Japanese occupied China as far south as the Indochina border in addition to the Island of Hainan in the Gulf of Tonkin.

In September 1940, the Japanese launched an amphibious attack on Indochina's east coast. It was supported by ships and planes from aircraft carriers and bases on Hainan Island. Within hours after the onshore assault, columns of Japanese infantry swooped down over the country's northern border as far south as Hanoi. Within days, the Japanese had successfully blockaded all rail and water routes preventing the shipment of fuel and armaments from Indochina to occupied China.

For the next ten months fighting continued between the Japanese and the French for control of the southern half of the country. Finally, in July of 1941, one hundred forty thousand Japanese troops invaded the South and won complete control of the country. Japanese forces occupied Indochina until the end of World War II.

Following the war, the French returned to Indochina and recovered control of its government and economy. Once again, the country flourished under the French, as exports of rice and rubber fueled it's expanding economy. Just as before the war, it became a country of rich merchants and wealthy plantation owners. Hanoi and Saigon were once more centers of commerce and culture.

In 1950, Communist leader Ho Chi Minh organized a resistance force aimed at reclaiming his country from the French. He led a small band of fighters who had fought bravely alongside the French against the Japanese just a few short years earlier. After a bloody four year war, his Vietminh forces finally drove out the French in 1954. During the war, China and the USSR supported Ho Chi Minh and provided him with money and military assistance. The US supported the French but provided very little in the way of financial and military aid.

Vietnam is located in Southeast Asia, occupying an area of 127,848 square miles. It borders China in the North, and it's 1250 mile eastern coastline borders the Gulf of Tonkin in the North and the South China Sea in the South. Its Southern peninsula, known as the Mekong Delta, has approximately 800 miles of coastline which borders the Gulf of Thailand.

The Mekong River separates Vietnam from Laos and Cambodia along its western border. The country runs a North-South distance of 1,025 miles. It is only 50 miles wide at its narrowest point where the coastal city of Da Nang is situated.

It is a country of dense forests, rolling hills, and tropical lowlands. South of Saigon, the Mekong River discharges into a vast swampy region known as the Mekong Delta. It occupies 14,000 square miles of low level plain no more than ten feet above sea level at its highest elevation. It is crisscrossed by a maze of putrid canals and rivers. Twenty five percent of the Delta is cultivated, making it one of the richest rice growing regions in the world. The other 75% is covered by dense jungle and snake infested swamps.

Early in the Indochina War, President Eisenhower told the US Congress, "We will make substantial resources available to assist the French in their military effort to defeat the Communist Vietminh aggression." In the following months, Eisenhower began sending money and munitions to the French.

In January of 1954, Eisenhower sent twenty five B-26 medium bombers to the French base at Dien Ben Phu along with spare parts and 200 mechanics to support them.

By the end of March 1954, French forces continued to suffer huge losses at Dien Ben Phu and their Northern outposts. In spite of the influx of US military aid, they lost all their airfields and they had to parachute reinforcements and new supplies. The Vietminh continued major victories as they encircled Dien Ben Phu and its outlying outposts. The war was going very poorly for the French and their allied supporters.

In the French's final battle with the Vietminh at Dien Ben Phu, President Eisenhower sent a flight of B-29s from Clark Air Base in the Philippines to bomb the communist insurgents. It was a case of "too little – too late", however, and the Vietminh swarmed the French fortress and won the final battle. By the end of the war, China had recognized "The Democratic Republic of Vietnam" as a Communist country with its capital city in Hanoi.

Following Ho Chi Minh's victory, the country was split into two regions by the "Geneva Convention of

1954". The Convention set the 17th parallel as the border between the Northern and Southern Regions. This was seen as a temporary measure pending a democratic election to unify the country under one leadership. Ho Chi Minh made Hanoi his North Vietnam capital. Once again, his communist government was backed by China and the USSR. The South Vietnam capital was Saigon and it was led by Ngo Dinh Diem and his democratic party. It was backed by the United States.

Within months after the new North/South arrangement, Ho Chi Minh began an aggressive program of land reform. His Vietminh forces swooped down below the 17th parallel, taking over plantations and villages and leaving a wide path of rape and destruction.

Ho organized his Northern forces as "The Peoples' Army of Vietnam" (PAVN). At the same time, residual Vietminh forces in the Mekong Delta organized a band of guerilla fighters and called them the "Vietcong". They were very successful in recruiting vast numbers of Vietcong fighters from the local population. The Vietcong became the most vicious, cruelest, and inhumane of all the fighters in Vietnam and, in many cases, did not wear uniforms.

Fighting escalated as the North and the South fought for control of the country. Diem's strategy was a forceful takeover of North Vietnam with his "Army of the Republic of Vietnam" (ARVN). Ho Chi Minh's strategy was different. His goal was to fight until his opposition no longer wanted to. His Vietminh and Vietcong forces were battled hardened from the four year war with the French. To achieve a final victory, he would rely on the war weariness of Diem's South Vietnamese army.

President Eisenhower quickly saw South Vietnam as a counter revolutionary force to repel Ho Chi Minh's Communist aggression. He began sending vast sums of money and military equipment to Saigon. However, Diem put these resources to use by oppressing anyone who opposed him. He raged an "Anti-Communist" campaign and executed thousands of Buddhist Monks, college students, and anyone suspected of being a communist. The Diem Regime's first priority was to protect itself from its own insurgents, and then to carry the fight to the Vietcong and the Vietminh. There were three unsuccessful attempts to assassinate Diem in 1954.

Despite the corruption in Diem's government, Eisenhower chose to continue his support to Saigon. He felt strongly that Diem's forces would ultimately be able to push Ho Chi Minh's armies back to Hanoi and then overthrow his communist government.

Without approval from Congress, Eisenhower started sending handfuls of Green Berets into South Vietnam to train Diem's fighters. To get around Congress, he called these men "advisors" although they frequently fought alongside the South Vietnamese regular army.

The bloody civil war raged on during 1955 as the US cadre of advisors increased to nearly 250 Green Berets. There was little awareness in the United States of its escalating involvement in Vietnam.

In 1955, thirty thousand North and South Vietnam fighters were killed and deaths of civilians on both sides reached nearly 80,000 since the civil war had began a year earlier. Air Force Technical Sergeant Richard Fitzgibbon became the first US casualty of the war. By early 1956, four hundred US advisors were embedded in South Vietnamese army units.

Fighting continued to escalate during the year and by December there were nearly 600 Green Berets embedded in Diem's ARVN forces. US casualties were reported to be ten killed and twenty six injured in 1956.

In January 1957, General John O'Daniel headed up a temporary US command post named MACV (Military Assistance Command Vietnam) at the Grand Hotel in Saigon. Secretary of State John Foster Dulles told Saigon that MACV would be limited to 350 people with the primary function of managing US military assets. Meanwhile, Eisenhower continued to deploy Green Berets as military advisors. In February, an assassin fired a shot at President Diem as he arrived on foot for the inauguration of the Ban Me Thuot Economic Fair. The shot missed Diem, but his Secretary of Agrarian Reform was seriously injured.

As the US involvement in the Vietnam War escalated, it became clear that there was a serious deficit in military intelligence. After two years of stand down following the Korean Armistice, the US intelligence community was seriously hampered by cutbacks in personnel and equipment. The CIA struggled to place skilled operatives on the ground in Vietnam, while the NSA pressured the Army, Air Force, and Navy to step up their communications intelligence production. The Vietnamese language, with its seventeen different dialects, posed seemingly insurmountable barriers to radio intercept operators. Major US universities were called on to offer Vietnamese language training to intercept operators and analysts.

In February 1957, the NSA opened an office at MACV headquarters in Saigon to coordinate its military radio intercept operations. At the time, the three services operated a handful of land based intercept sites in South Vietnam, Taiwan, and the Philippines. Meanwhile, the Navy and the Air Force manned a limited number of airborne radio intercept sorties off the coasts of China and Taiwan.

Chapter One

Northwest Zero Two

Saturday, February 23, 1957

Northwest Orient Flight Zero Two swung around to the left, as it backed away from International Gate 6 at Tokyo Haneda Airport. The long aft section of the extended Super Constellation bobbed gently up and down as it's propellers changed pitch and pulled it forward onto Taxiway Delta. It was a typical gloomy overcast morning in Tokyo as Zero Two taxied slowly in the direction of Runway One Niner for its departure to the south.

Patches of light rain blew against the side window where Air Force Lieutenant Myles Garrison was sitting. He was fortunate, he thought, the way things had worked out. Commander Banta had allowed him to proceed immediately to Saigon after his stint in Arlington instead of taking a leave in the States. Enroute he'd managed the time necessary in Tokyo to clear up some very sad personal things.

Now, with that finished, he'd be able to get down to work in Vietnam. He knew he needed to do this no matter what, and would have paid his own way to Tokyo if the Commander hadn't come through. Now he was heading to Saigon, emotionally and physically drained, but finally beginning to feel some peace after the horrendous past few days.

He had been waiting for his flight since six in the morning when the Dai Ichi Hotel shuttle dropped him off at the International Terminal. He'd had a light breakfast at one of the airport kiosks before proceeding to the Northwest

Orient ticket counter for check-in and boarding pass. Now, settled down in a window seat over the left wing, all he had left to do was endure the nine hour flight to Manila, change planes, and then continue on to Vietnam.

The last leg of his trip would be a three hour hop across the South China Sea direct to Saigon. He was looking forward to his new accommodations in the Grand Hotel and starting up Blue Cover. There was plenty of work ahead but that was fine, after all the hard work and long days he'd put in at NSA Headquarters in Arlington.

He was tired and hoping for sleep once in the air. As the Super Connie continued its monotonous journey along Taxiway Delta, he leaned his head against the window and his eyes tracked raindrops slowly edging their way down the glass toward the rear of the plane. The raindrops continued their relentless path, eventually joining together to form a quivering puddle at the base of the window.

The Northwest senior stewardess welcomed the passengers and announced emergency procedures. Myles watched as she strapped on a yellow life jacket and imitated blowing in the inflation tube. She made it look simple, but he wondered just how easy it would be in a real emergency. He imagined himself helping the elderly man across the aisle as the ocean came pouring in through the bulkhead. She finished by pointing out the four emergency exits and requesting the passengers check their seat belts.

Finally, the Connie rolled onto the runway, turned left, and came to a full stop. The airframe shuttered as its engines revved up to full power. Then it accelerated down the runway and in a few seconds was in the air.

He watched the gray landscape pull away as the Connie gently ascended through three, four, five thousand feet, and into the morning sunshine.

At cruising altitude, the seat belt sign went off and he could see the stewardesses pulling their carts out of stowage and loading them up with drinks and snacks. In a few minutes, the stewardess who had made the announcements parked her cart next to his row. She took a few seconds to scan a document taped to the side of the cart.

"Lieutenant Garrison, I'm Nancy your flight attendant. May I get you something to drink?"

"Well …. Nancy …. let me see," Myles hesitated.

"I'll have a Bloody Mary please."

"Coming right up."

He glanced up at the blonde stewardess as she served up two Bloody Marys.

"Thank you."

"Certainly sir. I'll be serving breakfast in about an hour. If you need anything else, just let me know."

"Thanks again. No this'll be fine."

Two Bloody Marys would be just what he needed to bring on some sleep.

After a while, Nancy cleared his tray and held out a menu.

"I'm sure your breakfast is wonderful, but I'll skip it if you don't mind. I had something earlier and now all I want is some sleep. Could you bring me some eye shades please?"

"I understand. Sorry you'll miss breakfast. Would you like a glass of champagne before your nap?"

"No thanks, the Bloody Marys did the trick."

Nancy brought him eye shades, ear plugs, pillows, and a blanket.

"Oh …. thanks …. I think this is a nine hour flight. How about waking me an hour before Manila. Then maybe I might have something. OK?"

"That'll be fine. Have a nice sleep. Just one thing though, we refuel in Taipei in about five hours. Should I wake you then?"

"Yes please, that would be great. I've never seen Taipei …. in fact I've never been to Taiwan. Thanks."

Myles pushed his seat back all the way and, with his eyes and ears covered, nested his head deep in the pillows scrunched between the seat back and the window.

In a few minutes he fell asleep.

Suddenly, he was awakened by somebody violently jostling his shoulder.

"Myles, may I join you?"

A tall dark man in a black suit stood there holding a drink.

"What? I'm trying to sleep …. sir," he raised his voice at the "sir". He was surprised and angry.

"Please Myles, may I sit here?" the tall stranger said, as he gestured to the open aisle seat.

"Just a minute here …. I don't know you or what you want, but no, you may not sit here," Myles shouted back, as he slammed one of his pillows down on the empty seat.

Without saying anything. the stranger turned and disappeared up the aisle.

Myles tried to go back to sleep but couldn't get the incident out of his head. He pushed the call button.

"Can I help you sir?"

It was Nancy.

"I hate to bother you Nancy, but some crackpot just came by and offered me a drink. I didn't take it, and then he asked if he could sit by me. He was in a black suit and looked like an Oriental of some kind. He even knew my name. You know anything about that?"

"No I don't. Let me check it out. I'll see if I can spot anybody matching that description and ….."

Myles interrupted, "He went up to the front of the plane."

"OK, I'll take a look."

She was back in a few minutes and took the open aisle seat.

She whispered, "Myles, I didn't see anybody like that. There were two Orientals up there but they weren't in suits or dress shirts. You said he was in a black suit?"

"Tall, Oriental, in a black suit, white shirt, and black necktie. You think he could have changed clothes in the lavatory?"

"That must be, but if he did I didn't see him. Why don't I bring you another drink and maybe you can get some sleep. I'm guessing it was some guy trying to make your acquaintance and then you scared him into changing clothes. You know a handsome young American Officer might be tempting. I wouldn't worry about it. You want that drink?"

"No thanks. I'll try to get some sleep. Don't forget to wake me when we get to Taipei. Thanks for your help."

"See you in Taipei," Nancy said, as she got up and returned to the front of the cabin.

Once again he pulled on his eye shades and crawled under the blanket. He fell into a deep sleep and started to dream.

Russia performs atmospheric nuclear test; Morocco gains independence; South Vietnam President Diem announces new constitution; Rebellion occurs in North Vietnam defying Ho Cho Minh's plan for land redistribution; Israel captures Gaza; 200,000 Russian troops put down anti-Stalin revolt in Budapest; President Eisenhower defeats Adlai Stevenson to win second term; Elvis Presley's "Hound Dog" tops the charts; "Wizard of Oz" is televised for the first time; "Lil' Abner" opens on Broadway.

Chapter Two

Victoria Tea Room

Saturday, November 17, 1956

Myles' dream took him back to a gray cold Saturday afternoon. He was heading to Tokyo on the afternoon train to pick up the suit he'd ordered from his friend, Morita-san the tailor. Tomorrow would be his twenty-third birthday, finally, after being stuck on twenty-two for what seemed forever. The past week he'd gotten promoted to First Lieutenant and received a commendation from the National Security Agency. He was feeling good.

As the train slowed for its approach into Tokyo Station, he pushed back from his window and watched the travelers gather up their things and ready themselves for the station.

The rain had stopped and he decided to walk the eight blocks from Tokyo Station to Morita-san's shop.

He exited the South Terminal and headed west on Sotobori Avenue. He knew the neighborhood like the back of his hand. After four blocks, Sotobori crossed the north end of Ginza Avenue where the twelve story Seibu Department Store was the outstanding landmark. From there, Ginza headed south for fifteen blocks of restaurants, shopping, and entertainment.

He glanced up at the Seibu as he walked through the Sotobori-Ginza intersection. Four blocks further west on Sotobori, he reached Morita's tailor shop.

"How does it feel?" Morita asked as he helped Myles slip into the grey flannel jacket. In the mirror, the jacket was a perfect fit. There were still pins on the sleeves and collar, and some white stitching along the lapels and bottom seam. Other than that, the jacket looked great and felt perfectly comfortable.

"This is great, Morita-san," Myles replied. "Let's try on the pants, and if that's good you can take out the pins and stuff. I'm going to wear this great looking suit to get some dinner and then take the train back to Shiroi. It's in between paydays, and I can't afford a weekend in town. Maybe next time you can come have a drink with me."

"Yes, I will for sure. Thank you," Morita said, as he manipulated one of the lapels. He liked his Air Force friends. "I take out pins now. Suit is ready."

"Thanks, Morita-san. I'll take real good care of my new suit," Myles said, as he extended his hand in appreciation. "I'm pretty sure I'll see you next week and maybe have Brent and Manahan with me. We'll go out for a drink over at the Opal."

On Tokyo weekends the Opal Coffee Shop was a favorite spot for Myles and his friends from the 21st Radio Group. It was conveniently located on the Ginza, just two blocks south of the Seibu on the same side of the street. It was an easy walk from Tokyo Station. In a city of six million, it was a safe haven. Besides that, the beer was reasonable, the food was good, and everybody spoke English.

Outside back on Sotobori, Myles looked at his watch. It was still only four o'clock so there was time to have a drink, get some dinner, and catch the nine o'clock train back to the base. He wouldn't mind the half mile walk from Matsudo Station back to Shiroi Air Base, even though it would be dark and cold.

Fashion Floor, Mitsukoshi Department Store

Customers were filing out now from the Saturday afternoon fashion show at Mitsukoshi Department Store. A small group of models were in the midst of changing back into street clothes. Yoshiko Moryama was the last to show and was changing back into one of the outfits she'd shown earlier. Mariko, the fashion coordinator, had given her permission to borrow the suit.

"Yoshiko-san, why you wear pink in November?" her friend Myami asked sarcastically.

"Very simple, Myami-san, pink my favorite color and it beautiful suit?"

"Yes, yes, it is. So you keep wearing pink. Maybe next time white suit in winter. That mean snow. Right?" Myami tried to save face.

"When you see snow, you still see pink. So sorry," Yoshiko responded, as she finished stuffing personal things into her hat box.

"Sayonara," she called out to those remaining on the floor, as she headed to the escalator on her way out of the store.

"Sayonara," they answered in chorus. They liked her immensely. She was a favorite for sure.

Out on the street, she decided to take a taxi to Tokyo Station and catch an early train to Yokohama where she lived with her parents. As a taxi pulled up, she decided instead to stop somewhere for tea. She asked the driver to take her to the Victoria Tea Room.

Victoria Tea Room

Myles left Morita's shop and turned right in the direction of the Victoria Tea Room. It was a short walk, just three doors away on Sotobori.

The Victoria was another favorite spot for the 21st Radio Group, but it was definitely for more formal occasions like a special date or a visiting parent. The lobby was lined with pink marble and polished brass. There was an elegant mahogany reception desk just inside, always with a beautiful girl in evening gown to greet the guests.

As he entered, he felt good in his new suit. This evening he didn't recognize the hostess, but there she was just as beautiful as expected in her turquoise evening gown. Sequins and seed pearls shimmered in the soft pink light and her Chinese collar was just smooth enough and straight enough to frame her lovely young face.

"One please, it will be just me. Oh .... and will you please hold this package for me?" he asked, keeping his eyes glued on his beautiful hostess.

"Of course, sir," she said, as she reached for his package.

Soon a young man in a tuxedo appeared and led him to a small table next to a row of booths. In a few minutes, a waitress dressed in a tuxedo shirt and black tie arrived.

"May I take your order sir?"

"Thank you. I'd like your menu and would you bring me a Sapporo beer please," he spoke slowly and was very careful to reciprocate her wonderful manners.

"Certainly sir."

She turned, and walked back along the row of booths toward the kitchen area.

In a few minutes she returned with a bottle of Sapporo and a half full lager glass of the amber liquid.

"Would you like to order, sir?" she asked.

"Yes please. I'll have a club sandwich and a salad with house dressing."

He handed over the menu, as he glanced out the window at the cold grey late afternoon sky.

"Yes sir," she said, as she topped off his glass and turned back toward the kitchen.

Myles sipped his beer and his thoughts wandered back to events over the past week. On Wednesday, Major Hickson had called the 21st together to announce his promotion. Then on Thursday, the Major called a surprise meeting to announce his NSA award. Jim Larsen from the NSA Liaison Office made the presentation, praising Myles for his work on breaking a Chinese Air Defense encryption code. It was definitely a good week and he felt a little humbled by the string of events.

Just as he put down his glass, he glanced over to a booth several tables away. His thoughts about last week quickly faded. He was seeing the most beautiful girl he could ever have imagined, and there she was, sitting alone just a few steps away.

She was wearing a two piece pink linen suit and a white silk blouse with a Chinese collar. Her shoulder length ebony hair parted down the middle and fell along side her high cheekbones and ivory skin. Her dark eyes tilted slightly toward her temples. To Myles, she seemed not much over twenty years old. There was a small hat box underneath the table next to her legs. She sipped tea and was having some pastries from the dessert cart.

The waitress attended to her several times, bringing fresh tea and chatting softly. Another waitress stopped by to speak. She seemed very popular with the waitresses. She had the sweetest most genuine smile he had ever seen.

Time was running out. So far, he'd not been able to make eye contact with her. She was finishing her tea and reaching for a tiny beaded white clutch on the seat beside her. He had to make a move .... now or never. As he moved his plate aside he noticed a white thread wrapped around a button on the sleeve of his new jacket, and instantly he had a plan. He gently extended his right arm.

"Miss, could I bother you … just for a second?"

He put on his most innocent smile and turned on every bit of charm he could muster. She turned toward him with just a trace of a smile. Now's the time, he thought, I have her attention.

"Could you help me with this string on my button please?" he asked.

Her smile broadened and she started to giggle. "You have button problem?"

"Well, yes, my tailor left this string on my button," he said, pointing to the troubled button.

"I can do," she replied.

She scooted aside in the booth and motioned him to sit by her. He pushed his chair back and carefully stepped over to the booth.

"May I sit by you here?" he asked.

"Please here," she said, gesturing to the open space beside her.

His heart was pounding and he could barely keep his hand from trembling. She carefully held his arm and with her other hand began to manipulate the string. His body was against her as she worked on the button. Finally, the string yielded and she proudly handed it over.

"Thank you very much," he said, placing the string in his coat pocket.

"You welcome," she replied.

He somehow managed to communicate that he was about to leave the restaurant and would she allow him to see her out? She nodded and, much to his astonishment, held out her hand for him to help her from the booth.

Ginza

They stopped at the reception desk where Myles retrieved his package. He took her hand and helped her down the two steps to the sidewalk.

At a loss for the correct Japanese, he somehow managed to invite her to walk with him back up Sotobori in the direction of Ginza Avenue. She accepted and they started out on their walk, he with his package and she with her hatbox.

At the Sotobori-Ginza intersection she paused for a moment.

"We turn to right please. OK?"

"Yes, we walk to the right and go down Ginza," he found himself answering in broken English.

He was beside himself. Here she was, inviting him to walk with her down the Ginza. What could be better?

Together, they gazed upon the full glory of the Ginza stretching out before them as far as the eye could see. Ginza was Tokyo's version of Times Square and Broadway combined. It went on for nearly a mile of animated signs and colored neon lights on both sides.

In a bold move, he gently placed his hand on her shoulder and held her back for a second.

"My name is Myles. What is your name?" he asked, not knowing what kind of reaction he'd get.

"My name, Yoshiko."

"Yoshiko, is such a pretty name. You speak very good English. Where did you learn that?"

"We study English high school. I like very much. Thank you. I have birthday today. You surprise?"

"Oh yes, I am surprised and very pleased."

She didn't reply. OK, he thought, her English is good, but not that good.

They were quiet now as they continued their walk along the Ginza. Across the street on the left was the Seibu Department Store and then, just beside it, the famous Nichigeki Music Hall, Tokyo's version of Radio City Music Hall.

There were lots of things to enjoy on the Ginza. By now, he was carrying both his package and her hat box. A few blocks down the Ginza, she spotted the Sushi Oki sushi restaurant across the street. Without saying anything, she tugged at his sleeve and urged him to cross over at the next stoplight. Through the window they watched the sushi chef arrange razor thin slices of raw tuna on tiny cakes of sushi rice.

She explained sushi in great detail which cleared up a long standing mystery for him. Then, equipped with a knowledge of sushi, he got up enough nerve to ask her for a date next weekend for sushi at Sushi Oki. Frankly, all he expected was maybe a giggle at best. But no, she bowed and graciously accepted. She squeezed his forearm and they turned to continue their walk down the Ginza. Soon, Myles took her hand. There was no resistance.

By this time they had walked all the way down the Ginza as far as the Kabuki Theater. They stood there together, staring at the gaudy posters of men dressed in wild Kabuki costumes.

"Train," Myles said. "I think we should go to Tokyo Station."

"Yes, we go train. We take taxi?"

"Here, stand by me," Myles said, as he took her hand.

They stood together waiting for an empty taxi.

They learned a lot about each other during their Ginza stroll. It was an odd conversation considering her broken English and his broken Japanese.

She was born this day in 1936 which meant she was twenty years old as he had guessed. She lived with her parents in Yokohama and commuted to modeling assignments in Tokyo. She had no brothers or sisters.

After high school she attended a two year fashion academy in Yokohama and landed a job with a model agency in Tokyo. She worked mostly in fashion shows at the big department stores. The pink suit she wore today was borrowed from the Mitsukoshi Department Store in Shimbashi, where she had done a showing earlier in the day.

As for Myles, he was born November 18, 1933 in a little town in Iowa. He had one younger brother, Matthew, who was sixteen. Myles graduated from Notre Dame in 1955 with a Masters in Mathematics, and immediately took a commission in the Air Force. He trained for a year in communications intelligence with the National Security Agency in Arlington, Virginia, and was assigned to Shiroi Air Base in June.

Ladybug

As they stood waiting for a taxi, Myles spotted a boutique not far away. Without saying anything he pulled her into the shop and started pointing out some gold jewelry. Without her noticing, he deftly slipped a thousand yen note to a clerk standing nearby and took a cloisonné *Ladybug* pin from the counter.

Once outside the shop, he hailed down a seventy yen taxi for their trip to the train station.

"Tokyo Station please," he addressed the driver.

Inside the taxi, he took her hand and gently squeezed *Ladybug* against her palm.

"Happy birthday, Yoshiko."

She grinned broadly, and then frowned.

"No, no Myru-san. I cannot ……"

Completely ignoring her explanation, he took *Ladybug* from her fingers and gently pinned it to the lapel of her pink jacket. Her resistance faded to gratitude.

"Thank you very much, Myru-san."

They exited the taxi and she led him into the terminal.

"Myru-san, stop now."

She took him by the arm and slowed him to a stop.

"Saturday, we meet South Terminal taxi place ten morning. You understand?" she asked.

"Very good," he responded. "The South Terminal taxi stand at ten o'clock Saturday morning. That will be very good."

"Sayonara, Myru-san, have safe trip," she replied, as she lovingly fingered the *Ladybug* pin on her lapel.

With that, she turned and, not looking back, walked away and disappeared into the crowd.

As he sat in the Tokyo-Matsudo train, he leaned back, closed his eyes, and thought about what a really special day this had been. He raised his arm to check the wonderful stringless button.

The trip from Tokyo to Matsudo went by quickly. He exited the train at Matsudo, unaware of the cold and the lateness of the hour. He started out on his half mile walk to the Shiroi main gate with the utmost of pleasure. He was already looking forward to next Saturday.

The next day, he couldn't get Yoshiko off his mind. He took his boy scouts to Sunday Mass and then to lunch at the base snack bar. The rest of the day passed pretty much as usual except for his constant memory of the previous day. He wondered how Yoshiko had spent her Sunday.

Monday, November 19, 1956

He got up earlier than usual Monday morning. He was fully energized and ready to get back to work. Frozen grass crunched beneath his feet as he trudged alone across the parade ground in the direction of the compound.

He'd only been at Shiroi Air Base for six months, but already he had developed an appreciation for the base and the work being done there. It was the perfect location for its intelligence mission. It was secluded and easy to protect. It had no airfield and only about thirty plain grey buildings. It was not found on any map or chart and there were no external signs identifying the base.

All of the clandestine intelligence work took place in the "compound". Like the other buildings on the base, it was painted gray with no external signs or markings. It was the largest building on the base, occupying an area roughly the size of a football field. Other than its size, its only distinguishing features were its twelve foot high chain link fence, and an array of odd shaped antennas sprouting from the third floor roof.

The National Security Agency had been the landlord for the past three years. It was shortly after the Korean War Armistice in 1953 that the Agency took ownership from the Air Force. The compound housed the NSA Far East Liaison Office and was headquarters for six Air Force, Army, and Navy communications intelligence units. Combined, the three services operated forty-six radio intercept sites scattered around the Far East from Korea in the North, to Vietnam and Singapore in the South.

Myles' Air Force unit was the 21st Radio Group. It was the newest to join the others in the compound, but already it controlled five remote intercept sites in Okinawa, Taiwan,

South Vietnam, Thailand, and the Philippines. Like the other forty-one sites, the mission of 21st Radio's sites was to intercept non-friendly military radio traffic.

He was at his desk before any of the others arrived. He sipped coffee and leafed through his incoming messages and a short stack of overnight intercepts. Shortly after eight, Major Hickson stopped by his desk.

"Lieutenant Garrison, congratulations again on your promotion. How about lunch at the Officers Club to celebrate? Think you can work it in?"

"Yes sir," Myles replied with a huge smile. He liked and respected the Major.

"Good, I'll stop by your desk at noon."

Minutes later, First Lieutenant Roy Brent tapped on Myles' shoulder.

"Lunch with the old man eh!" Brent cajoled.

"Well, yeah! Can't turn down a free lunch. It's for my promotion. I'm sure you got a free lunch for yours. Right?" Myles answered, not defensive in the least.

"Good work," Brent said, as he returned to his desk.

Myles glanced back in Brent's direction. 21st Radio was not a big operation. Its ten enlisted men and five officers worked in one large room. Each was either an analyst or a linguist or both. The ten enlisted men were at least in their second tours. All were Sergeants with experience in communications intelligence and some had served in the Korean War. The officers had the same training and experience as the enlisted men, the only real difference being an ROTC or OCS commission. Myles' promotion last week rounded out the officer group to five First Lieutenants.

It was an open arrangement. Each man had a desk, a typewriter, and a file cabinet. Officers' and enlisted men's desks were intermingled and arranged in clumps according to their mission. Each man had space for wall maps behind or next to his desk.

In the front left corner of the room, there was a long table where the daily courier pouch was opened. Lieutenant Wentz and Sergeant Wideman were in charge of sorting the material and delivering it to the four teams of analysts.

Two small offices were arranged at the top of the room. One was for the commander, Major Ira Hickson, and the other was for the first sergeant, Master Sergeant Marcus Barney.

Myles shared floor space with Sergeant John Johnson. Their mission was analysis of Chinese and North Vietnamese radio traffic intercepted by detachments in Taiwan, South Vietnam, and the Philippines. Every working day, they processed over forty pounds of radio logs intercepted from more than thirty enemy transmitters. The other three teams had similar workloads.

At the end of every day, each of the four teams shipped raw intercepted traffic along with their analyses to NSA Headquarters in Arlington, Virginia. It was up to the teams to assess the urgency of any new intelligence, and then alert Arlington immediately by high priority encrypted message.

It was an unusually large volume of intercepts this morning, due mainly to an upsurge in Vietcong activity in the Mekong Delta. As usual, Myles and Johnson divided up the logs and chatted back and forth when anything significant turned up. Several times during the morning each of them got up to add colored pins to the wall charts.

Around noon, Major Hickson stopped by Myles' desk.

"Myles, are you still interested in my lunch invitation? I'm ready whenever you are."

"I am ready, and I'm looking forward to it," Myles replied.

Gusts of cold wind pushed at the two men as they made their way across the frozen parade ground on their way to the Officers Club. Once inside, Major Hickson led the way to the dining room and to his favorite corner table.

After a delicious lunch of the Club's signature bean soup and Reuben sandwich, the two men pushed back and began to sip their coffee.

"Thanks for a great lunch, Major," Myles said. "I'd like to reciprocate some time."

"Thanks for your offer Myles, but you don't need to. This was for your well deserved promotion. I still remember when I made First Lieutenant back in 1950. It was Korea and it was pretty rough. Anyway, I got promoted in minimum time like you, so I know the feeling."

Major Hickson shook Myles' hand.

"Thank you, sir," Myles replied.

"I tell you what, Myles. Why don't you join Peggy and me at the club for Thanksgiving dinner on Thursday? I think she's planning on two o'clock. We'll have drinks and turkey. Anybody you'd like to bring?"

"Well, thank you, sir. I'll enjoy seeing Peggy again. No, I don't have anybody. You know we don't have many possibilities here on base sir. School teachers and nurses are just about it and there's a long waiting line for them."

"Great, we'll see you on Thursday then."

"Thanks for inviting me, sir. I'll be looking forward to two o'clock on Thursday," Myles replied. "Thanks again for the great lunch."

Back in the office, the Major asked Myles to come see him in about an hour to tie up some loose ends. Meanwhile, Sergeant Wideman had placed a new stack of intercepts on Johnson's desk.

"Got anything new on Hainan Island?" Johnson asked, as he gave Myles half of the new traffic.

Last week, they had added a second blue pin on Hainan Island in the Gulf of Tonkin. The North Vietnam coastline bordered the Gulf, and the Chinese island of Hainan served as the protectorate for North Vietnam. Adding a second squadron of Mig 17s to this tiny island was a serious expansion of North Vietnam's air defenses. Myles had alerted the NSA immediately when he and Johnson gleaned the information from a string of encrypted messages between Hainan and Hanoi.

"Not so far, but you can be sure we'll be seeing more. One thing we need to do is ask Taiwan to stay on that frequency full time. I don't want to take a chance on their scanner missing anything. Let's have them put one of their manual positions on it full time," Myles replied.

"Good idea. I'll take care of that right away," Johnson said, as he reached for a pad of blank message forms.

"Thanks. I'll see you in a little while. I have an appointment with the Major," Myles said.

"See you after that," Johnson replied.

Myles knocked on the Major's closed door.

"Come in Myles."

Major Hickson was expecting him.

The Major was seated at his desk almost hidden behind stacks of papers. With five officers and ten enlisted men reporting to him, he was constantly swamped with incoming and outgoing messages and reports, and an unending stream of requests and advice from the NSA. He delegated as much as possible to Sergeant Barney, but Barney had only recently transferred into the group from Germany. For a while he would be busy getting to know all the enlisted men and their work assignments.

"Myles, that work you did on Chinese air defense was outstanding. Jim Larsen over at NSA couldn't thank me enough. He said your analysis will become a regular part of ACOM Group's protocol."

Myles was very familiar with NSA's Asian Communist Group and knew people in the Air Force and Navy sections. It pleased him that they appreciated his work.

"He says they're asking if we could do the same for North Vietnam's air defense structure. What do you think of that?" the Major asked.

"Well sir, I guess anything's possible. I would really need to look at that. Johnson's a damn good linguist but he's also an analyst. We would probably need to bring in another linguist and another two analysts. Besides that, our five sites don't have near enough intercept capacity. We would need to add at least another five or six positions and target another fifteen or so transmitters. 29th Radio down at Clark Field in the Philippines might relocate some of its assets, and Naval Security Group airborne might be brought in," Myles responded.

"Well, Myles, that was a very professional answer. I think that lays it out plain and clear. Be prepared though, my guess is we're going to get orders along those lines. You know how fast things are heating up down there. The Joint Chiefs already have six hundred advisors down there training the South Vietnamese army. It's only a question of time before things get really crappy. BCOM reported just this morning that Ho Chi Min is setting up ground defenses on his supply trail along the Laos and Cambodian borders. I expect somebody's going to pay a visit to Arlington before too long. Hope you like Washington. Got any favorite restaurants in Georgetown?"

"As a matter of fact, I do. I'll be glad to go if I'm needed back there."

"Thanks, Myles. I'll let you know if anything comes down the pike. That's all for now."

The Major picked up a stack of papers.

Myles returned to his workspace. For a few minutes he stood by his wall map and studied the Mekong Delta. Then he spoke to Johnson.

"Look at this sergeant."

Myles circled the Delta with his finger.

"How'd you like to be in the middle of this?" Myles asked.

"Well, it's a pretty dangerous place to be. The swamps and villages are saturated with the Vietminh and the Vietcong. It that's not enough, did you know there are more snakes per square foot than any other place in the world .... and almost all of them are poisonous. There are even snake farms where they grow snakes for local restaurants. We had a few rattlers in Texas but nothing like that. I hate the Vietminh, the Vietcong, and the snakes," Johnson replied.

"That's what I thought you might say. I'm glad you agree. There are times when I think we should just get the hell out of there and let Ho Chi Minh have the whole country .... but then I think about those poor people. Our intercepts just tell us what the military is up to. We really don't know how many women and children are being raped and murdered every day. I hope our CIA people are embedded in the countryside. Maybe they're doing something about it."

"You're right in thinking that way Myles. There's no question we need to stop Ho Chi Minh and maybe even make him a war criminal. I think we're doing the right thing and I hope you and I might make a difference. How about a beer after work?" Johnson asked.

"Good idea. I'll meet you at the bowling alley around six," Myles answered.

"Great. I might get there a little before you. I'll save us a table," Johnson replied.

Later, after a couple of beers, and a lot of conversation about more pleasant things, the two men headed back to their dormitories.

Tuesday, November 20, 1956

Around eleven the next morning, the office was quiet except for the faint sound of ruffling papers and the clanking away of a few typewriters. Sergeant Wideman had just finished delivering all the morning's intercept logs when suddenly the office door flung wide open without any warning. Two Air Policemen rushed inside and stood at parade rest.

"We need everyone to be calm and to remain at their desks," one of the AP's blurted out.

Everyone in the room stopped and obeyed the command. Then a man in civilian clothes came in and brushed past the two men. He went directly to Major Hickson's office and knocked at the door.

"Come in," the Major answered, not knowing what was happening.

The civilian entered the office and closed the door behind him.

"Major Hickson, I am Stephen Braum from the Judge Advocate General's office here on the base. We have your office on lockdown. I have two AP's out there. We need to talk," the civilian said.

"Mr. Braum, we do need to talk. What you're about to say better be good," the Major said.

"Sir, Jim Larsen in the NSA Liaison Office has reported an incident to JAG. It might be nothing, but if it is something it could be very serious. Just take a seat, Major."

Braum sat down in front of Major Hickson's desk.

"Sir, is it necessary to scare the hell out of my men? Can't you just pull your people out and then you and I talk?" the Major asked.

"Sir, they need to stay. This might not take long. They need to stay so that no paper work or documents get concealed or destroyed," Braum said.

"OK. So get on with whatever you need to do," Major Hickson retorted.

"It has been reported that one or more documents are secretly delivered to this office once a week. The material is Top Secret but it is of such a nature that it should not be in this office, or be connected with 21st Radio in any way. It is not known who receives the documents, what is done with them, or what is their final disposition. Do you know anything about this Major?" Baum asked.

"Absolutely not. I've never heard of such a thing. Please feel free to look around and search everything. There's nothing like you describe here nor has there ever been," the Major said.

"Fine. I'll have my men make a quick search."

Braum left the office and spoke to the first AP.

The APs hurriedly walked around the big room and looked at every exposed piece of paper. They didn't speak to the men who silently sat at their desks. In about twenty minutes the search was over and Braum and the two APs were gone.

Major Hickson was stunned by the whole episode. Shortly after the visitors left he addressed everybody from the front of the room. He wasn't sure what to say or how to explain the event. He simply told them about Baum's statements, and then followed that by saying it was a false alarm. He urged the men to ignore the whole thing and get back to work.

In a few minutes Myles went over to Roy Brent's desk.

"Roy, what do you think about all that?"

"Myles, I've never seen anything like that before. All I can say is I hope there's nothing to it. I'll just assume it's a false alarm."

"Me too," Myles answered and he went back to his desk.

Myles and Johnson spent the rest of the day studying the new traffic. Once or twice, they got together and decided to place a few new pins. Nobody seemed to let the incident bother them very much and it was work as usual for the rest of the day.

The next day passed by quickly. Johnson had come up with some new intel on South Vietnam President Diem. It didn't look good for our advisory forces down there. Diem was playing them off against his regular army, the Army of the Republic of Vietnam, and publicly making them the scapegoat for all his problems. Arlington had to be notified immediately anytime our forces were jeopardized in any way. Johnson had sent off a flurry of Emergency Messages to BCOM, warning them of the situation.

Thanksgiving was really a great day. Myles joined the Hicksons for an enjoyable Thanksgiving feast at the O-Club. The Major continued his celebration of Myles' promotion and award by covering the bill. Peggy added her congratulations in the form of a hug and a kiss on the cheek. All the while, Myles managed to keep his most recent personal life out of the discussion.

Friday, November 23, 1956

Friday finally arrived. Just like Monday, Myles got to work an hour early. By a quarter to eight, others started straggling in and heading for the coffee pot which he so graciously had fired up. Johnson brought Myles a fresh cup.

"What's going on this morning Myles?" Johnson asked.

"Well, how about translating these?" Myles handed him a stack of intercepts from South Vietnam. "Might be about Diem."

"I'll get right on it."

Just then, Myles felt a tap on his shoulder. It was Major Hickson with Sergeant Barney at his side.

"Lieutenant Garrison, how about giving Sergeant Barney a ten minute tutorial on the Vietnam situation?"

"I'll be glad to. Here Sergeant, sit here where you can see my wall maps."

"Thanks Lieutenant, please call me Marcus."

"That'll be fine. I'll just begin with a brief history. The French occupied Vietnam since the Second World War. In the early fifties, Ho Chi Minh organized an army to kick out the French and take his country back. Well, he succeeded. In 1954 he won his final battle at Dien Ben Phu and kicked the French out of Vietnam for good. It never got much publicity, but President Eisenhower sent B29s up from the Philippines to help out the French but it was hopeless. So far so good?" Myles asked.

"Great," the Sergeant said, as he shifted slightly in his chair.

"After that, Ho Chi wanted to take over all of Vietnam and make it a communist country. But there were problems. South Vietnam was more democratic and resisted a communist takeover. To resolve the differences, the Geneva Convention declared the seventeenth parallel as a temporary dividing line between the North and the South until elections could be held to install a national government. That was 1954. There was never an election and there's been a civil war between the North and the South ever since."

"OK, I guess that's where we come in, right?" Barney asked.

"Exactly. Last year, Eisenhower started sending money and weapons to South Vietnam along with some military advisors. As of now, we have nearly six hundred advisors down there. That's pretty much it, Sarge. I'm almost finished. Do you have any questions?"

"No, I don't think so. I think I know the rest of the story. Our mission is to operate radio intercept sites in Southeast Asia to provide intel to the NSA. Right?"

"Sergeant, you got that right. We gather intel on Korea, China, and Vietnam. NSA appreciates our work. I see it's almost quitting time. We can talk more after you've been with us a little longer."

Myles was eager to finish up.

"Myles, thanks so much. I appreciate your patience."

With that, the two men stood up and shook hands. Sergeant Barney turned and headed back to his office.

"Hey Myles, I got your translations. Want to take a look? Sorry to say, not much new here. It just confirms some of the stuff we got last week," Johnson said, as he handed over his translations.

"Thanks, I'll put it in my backlog. I'm skipping lunch today. I've got some catching up to do," Myles replied.

Just before quitting time Major Hickson stopped by Myles' desk.

"Myles, great job you did with Sergeant Barney. He couldn't stop talking about your Vietnam briefing. He said to thank you again. I told him you're a good man and we got the right team working on Vietnam."

"Thanks Major. Glad to help," Myles answered, as he finished locking his desk and filing cabinet. "Johnson and I are heading over to the bowling alley for a cool one. Care to join us?"

"Gosh, I wish I could but Peggy's expecting me. Have a great weekend and behave yourself," the Major finished the conversation.

Later at the bowling alley, Myles and Johnson had their beers and discussed the weird events that took place earlier in the week. Following Major Hickson's advice, they decided to assume the intrusion by the APs was a stupid mistake.

*The US has 600 Special Forces advisors in Vietnam;
Holland and Spain withdraw from Olympics to protest
Soviet aggression in Hungary; US tests first aerial
hydrogen bomb over Bikini Atoll equal to 10 million tons
of TNT; US first class postage stamp is $0.03; Tommy
Dorsey dies; US Supreme Court declares segregated buses
illegal in Montgomery, Alabama; Nikita Khrushchev
utters phrase "We will bury you."; Floyd Patterson
defeats Rocky Marciano for heavyweight championship;
DNA molecule is photographed for first time; "The Price
is Right" debuts on NBC; Videotape first used on TV.*

Chapter Three

Ginza

Saturday, November 24, 1956

It was a chilly morning as Myles walked to Matsudo to
catch the Tokyo train. He waved to the farm ladies and
children, knee deep in rice paddies. They waved back with
bundles of rice plants in both hands, and their wide
brimmed hats down their backs. He was wishing everybody
well this morning.

Ten o'clock sharp and, as expected, the train pulled to a
stop in Tokyo Station exactly on time. Myles was out of the
car in seconds. Following the signs, he headed to the South
Terminal gate wasting no time.

"Myru-san, over here," Yoshiko called out as she stood
by a waiting taxi.

He was breathless from his halfback gallop down the sidewalk and from his first sight of her, as beautiful as he remembered.

"Yoshiko-san, stay there, here I come."

He gave her a good hug around her waist and urged her into the taxi.

"Climb in, I'm right behind."

Yoshiko instructed the driver in Japanese, "Go to the Ginza please. I will tell you where to stop."

"Yoshiko-san, I am happy to see you again. You look very pretty today in that Chinese dress."

She smiled and put her hand on his arm.

"Thank you Myru-san. It Mitsukoshi dress. I wear yesterday in show. I borrow."

"I missed you. How are you?" he asked.

She put her hand on his arm. He figured that meant I'm fine how are you.

"Where are we going?" he asked, hoping for a clue.

"We go Ginza have surprise, OK? Just a minute."

Once again, she put her hand on his arm.

"Driver stop here."

The taxi pulled over in front of a row of shops about half way down the Ginza. Like last week, she had her hundred yen coin ready. He helped her out onto the sidewalk.

"Thank you Myru-san. We go here," she thanked him, pointing to the Ginza Camera Shop, a few steps away.

Inside, the manager was showing a camera to a customer at the back counter and didn't notice them coming in.

"We wait here," she said, as she pressed him against a side counter.

Finally, the customer bought the camera. The manager was about to thank him all the way to the front door when he spotted the two of them. He instantly broke into a wide grin and came rushing to Yoshiko with arms fully outstretched.

"Yoshiko-san, come here please."

He completely enveloped her in a huge bear hug. She was barely visible in the mass of arms and body. Myles held back. He knew this must be true love of some sort.

Finally, she freed herself and stepped back from the gorilla's reach.

"Now, stop, stop, please Uncle Masuda-san. This my friend. His name Myru-san."

Myles got all that and was beginning to get the drift. Her Uncle Masuda owns this camera shop, and a very nice one at that. She is his favorite niece and they don't see each other very often. Now he would need to be on his best behavior to win his trust and friendship.

"Now, Myru-san, this my uncle, Masuda-san," she introduced Myles to Masuda, bowing slowly and deeply. She made this a very clear and proper meeting.

The two men shared a warm solid handshake. Myles liked him so far, but could only hope the feeling would be mutual. Yoshiko seemed pleased and stood at attention alongside.

"Very pleased to meet you Mr. Myles. Are you in business here in Japan?"

"Well, sir, actually I graduated from college not long ago and now I am an officer in the US Air Force. I am stationed at Shiroi Air Base," Myles spoke in slow careful English.

"Wonderful, and how did you become friends with my niece?" he maintained a cautious smile as he spoke.

"Well, we met last Saturday," Myles said, trying not to appear nervous. "We met at the Victoria Tea Room. It was by accident."

Uncle Masuda frowned.

Yoshiko grasped the situation.

"Actually Uncle Masuda-san, we sit close in tea room and he pick up napkin I drop on floor. He very polite."

"Oh, I see. Thank you Myles for being so thoughtful. May I call you Myles?" Masuda replied, his frown melting into a smile.

"Absolutely sir. Your English is excellent by the way," Myles said.

Yoshiko was pleased things were going so well.

"Oh, and Myles give *Ladybug* for birthday. Very cute, you think?" she pointed to the *Ladybug* pin as she spoke.

"Your birthday. I totally forgot your birthday. How old are you now? Never mind I remember."

Now it was Uncle Masuda getting nervous.

In a strategic maneuver, Masuda took his niece by the arm and led her around the store. They spoke in rapid fire Japanese, way beyond Myles' speed of comprehension. Finally, Masuda placed two cameras on the glass counter, a Canon and a Nikon, the two best cameras made in Japan. Yoshiko picked up the Nikon and handed it to Myles.

"This number one camera, Myrsu-san. Nikon S-2 type. Thirty five millimeter, very simple use. I like very much. You like too?"

"Yoshiko-san, this is really nice and I would like to buy it for you. You need a camera for sure. But, it must cost at least a hundred thousand yen and that's too much for my Air Force pay."

"Myrsu-san not worry. Uncle Masuda-san loan camera."

"Yoshiko-san, loan, loan, we cannot do that. I might break it or lose it. Anyway, I couldn't take it to the base. Somebody might steal such a fine camera."

"Myru-san, please no excite too much. He say loan camera for long we want ….. even hundred years."

She was hoping they could finish the discussion, load some film in the camera, and head back out onto the Ginza. It was a beautiful late Autumn day and she wanted pictures.

"Well, OK then. We will borrow the Nikon, but only for two weeks. We will take a lot of pictures by then. OK?"

Out on the sidewalk, they continued their walk down the Ginza in the direction of Sushi Oki with Yoshiko proudly swinging the new camera from her shoulder.

Sushi Oki

She stopped Myles three times on the short walk to Sushi Oki. Each time she saw something, she commandeered a likely looking pedestrian to frame and snap with Myles at her side.

He wondered just how the pictures would turn out. Guess he'd find out next Saturday. Now he had a reason for another date.

"Yoshiko-san, we go to Sushi Oki now, OK?"

"Yes, yes, Sushi Oki. "

They entered hand in hand with the borrowed Nikon hanging properly on her left shoulder near *Ladybug*. Myles helped her up onto a stool.

"Thank you Myru-san. Now have sushi," she reassured him.

She dove headlong into a serious discussion with the sushi chef. Finally, she extended her hand over the counter for a contractual handshake.

"We have four course sushi. You like," she said to Myles.

Sounded good to Myles, but then he hoped she hadn't spent his week's paycheck. He'd had sushi before and knew it could be a little pricey, and a Ginza location is definitely top of the line.

"Yoshiko, I'll have a beer please."

"No, no, Myru-san, we have sake. You like very much."

Very shortly the chef placed a beaker and two cups in front of them. Yoshiko poured the warm sake and pushed a cup near Myles. She raised her cup. "Campai."

Myles followed with his cup. "Campai."

It was really delicious sake, better than he'd ever had before, even at the Japanese party at the Officers Club.

Like the sake, the sushi was the best he'd ever tasted. Whatever the cost, it was worth it. He even enjoyed the raw blowfish.

Eventually, they finished the last course of salmon caviar and the last cup of sake. Yoshiko assured Myles that they had enjoyed the best that Sushi Oki had to offer.

Fully satisfied, the couple walked through hanging beads and out onto the sun splashed Ginza. It was two o'clock.

"Myru-san go Seibu Store now?"

"OK, we walk to Seibu but we rest the camera, OK?"

With her arm around his waist, she started him back up the Ginza toward the Seibu Department Store. It was five blocks, but Myles liked the idea of walking off the raw fish and rice. Besides that, the Opal Coffee Shop would be just a few blocks away so he could show her where he and his friends hung out.

In a few minutes they came to the Opal. It was a small place with plate glass windows across the front. It was dim inside, but one could see tables and booths and a small group of customers. Hostess Fumiko greeted them at the door and started showing them to a booth.

"No, no, Fumiko-san, we are just visiting. This is my friend Yoshiko-san."

Fumiko bowed and was obviously impressed with Myles' new friend. As they turned to leave, a voice came from a nearby booth.

"Hey Myles, who's your friend?"

"Hey, guy, what's up?" Myles replied.

With that, Bob Davison jumped up and started to introduce himself to Yoshiko. Myles stopped him in his path.

"Yoshiko-san this is my friend Lieutenant Davison."

Davison bowed and then moved toward Yoshiko. Once again, Myles stepped in and delivered a decisive block. He wanted to make sure his message was clear.

Yoshiko bowed gracefully, but not too low.

"Please to meet you," she said, softly.

She was polite but not too polite. She sensed that Davison was not that good a friend.

"We're leaving now. If any of the guys come in, please say hello. Maybe we'll see you later at ....," Myles stopped in the middle of his sentence. "Actually, we're not sure where we'll be. Anyway, good to see you."

The last thing he wanted was to have Davison come stalking.

Except for bumping into Davison, he was glad that Yoshiko got to see the Opal. Now they had a meeting place, if they ever needed one. As they left, he glanced back one last time. Fumiko and Davison were scurrying through the swinging door back to the kitchen.

After a few blocks, they came to the Seibu Department Store. It was an impressive sight. Between the sixth and eighth floors there was a huge twenty foot tall clock. It was a traditional Ginza landmark. Every hour it chimed a program of classical music that could be heard many blocks away.

"I in show here like Mitsukoshi," Yoshiko said. "It good place but no borrow dress sometime. We go inside."

She took him on the escalator all the way to the top floor, pointing out all the departments along the way.

She knew the store like the back of her hand. It was his first time in a big Japanese department store and he was impressed. It reminded him of Macys.

Coming back down, Yoshiko escorted him off at the sixth floor. She took him by the hand and pulled him over to a low stage in the center of the room.

"Myru-san, this fashion department. I do show here," she proudly announced, as she hopped up onto the stage. Myles looked around to take it all in. It was a beautiful setting. Overstuffed chairs and sofas surrounded the small stage and there was a gold podium just off to the side. The gold blended perfectly with the plush lavender carpet and the pastel furniture.

"This is beautiful, Yoshiko-san. I am proud of you," he said, as he helped her off of the stage.

"Over here Myru-san, I change dress."

She pointed to a side entrance bordered with gold braided tapestry.

"Yoshiko-san, I am very proud of you. I hope some day I can be here to see you model and buy some clothes."

Just then an elegant lady in a gray suit appeared from nowhere.

"Kazuko-san, how are you?" Yoshiko called out to the elegant lady.

"Yoshiko-san, I am fine thank you very much. Why you here today?" elegant lady replied.

"I here with my friend. This Myru-san. He very best friend."

Kazuko-san bowed, then extended her graceful arm. Myles wasn't sure if he should kiss her hand or shake it. He guessed she wasn't sure if he was European or American. He revealed his nationality by softly shaking her hand.

"Myru-san, very pleased to meet you."

"And you, Kazuko-san, you have a very nice place here."

"Oh, thank you. We are proud of Yoshiko-san. She models western clothes very nice. Maybe you come sometime?"

"I will for sure. Yoshiko-san, should we leave soon, it is nearly four o'clock."

"Yes, yes, thank you Kazuko-san, but we go now. I see you next time. I look forward," Yoshiko acknowledged. "Sayonara."

"Sayonara," Kazuko bid them goodbye.

Back out on the Ginza, they paused and looked up and down the sidewalk, both wondering what was next. She leaned against his shoulder.

"Mai, we go rest someplace?" she asked.

"I think that is a good idea?" he reassured her. "We will go to my club."

"Thank you. We go. I like you very much Mai."

Was he hearing right? She switched from Myru-san to "Mai." He knew this had a special meaning. In Japan, it was common for lovers to invent pet names as a sign of intimacy. Now he was "Mai" and she liked him very much..

A taxi pulled to the curb. He helped her into the back seat and scrunched in beside her.

"Fifth Air Force Officers Club please?" he asked, not sure the driver would understand.

The driver nodded three times and pulled away from the curb.

The Fifth Air Force operated a downtown Tokyo Officers Club for Air Force, Army, and Navy officers stationed or transient in Tokyo. Myles and the other officers from Shiroi would go there for drinks or maybe have dinner and take in a show.

Yoshiko was excited as they approached the club. It was a five story brick building just a few blocks from the Imperial Palace. There was a wide portico in front with a circular drive rising from the street up to the entrance. Wouldn't you know it, Myles thought, here comes Mr. Nikon.

Yoshiko hung out the window and snapped a few wide angle shots, making a special effort to include the Fifth Air Force Officers Club sign. He figured good ole Uncle Masuda would be developing all these pictures next week.

The taxi came to a stop at the front door. Two fine looking Japanese doormen in morning coats greeted the cab and swung open both rear doors.

Myles scurried around the back of the cab and rescued her from the doorman. He cupped his hand under her elbow and escorted her into the main lobby. He stopped for a minute to explain all the amenities. He ushered her around most of the main floor, showing her the formal dining room, the night club, the shops and the guest lounge. He explained how he could stay in the upstairs hotel for a very low price.

Now it was time for relaxation as he had promised. In the lounge, they settled into two huge leather chairs next to a small mahogany butler's bench near the great fireplace. This November afternoon was not cool enough for a fire, but it was a cozy setting for the two of them.

"Are you comfortable, Yoshiko-san?" Myles asked, as observed her struggling to situate herself in the deep leather chair.

She was having trouble managing her fitted Chinese dress with the revealing side splits.

"It OK, Mai."

They relaxed for over an hour, sipping on one drink and talking about everything from her job to his family back home.

"Yoshiko-san, should we have some dinner before we catch our trains? We can eat in the dining room if you like. They have mostly American food."

"Mai, so sad we must go. Opal Coffee Shop? We get Japanese food there. You say you like go there. OK?"

"Good idea."

He patted her on the back and motioned for the check.

As they were picking up her coat, Myles suggested he use a three day pass next weekend so they could see more of Tokyo and not be rushed. He suggested he get a room at the club for Friday and Saturday nights.

"Good idea, Mai. On Friday I show at Seibu where we go today. You come see show. You not buy clothes, only see me.""

"OK, that will be our plan for next weekend then."

He asked the attendant to call upstairs and make his reservation. She promptly picked up the phone and, just like that, he had a room reserved for next Friday and Saturday.

As they started down the curved walkway, low and behold, coming straight toward them, were Roy Brent and Daniel Manahan.

"Myles, Myles, what the heck are you up to old man?" Brent called out. "Fancy meeting you here, and why are you leaving so early. The night's young. And who is this lovely creature?"

As with Davison, Myles immediately went on the defensive.

"Now, guys, behave yourselves. Watch your manners please. I would like very much to introduce you to my good friend Yoshiko-san. Yoshiko-san, these are my good friends Lieutenants Brent and Manahan."

As expected, they moved toward her, but Myles was ready to pounce.

"Very pleased meet you. Myru-san say you very good friend in Air Force and stay Shiroi like him," she said as she went into a deep bow.

"Myles, you should bring Yoshiko to our Christmas party. I have the Ryoko Hotel in Shinjuku for Saturday, December 22. I'll tell you more about it back on base, but Yoshiko is definitely invited," Brent said.

"Thank you very much. I please attend Christmas if Myru-san invite me."

She put Myles on the hot seat.

"Of course, once I get the details."

He knew Yoshiko would want to go. He just needed to work it out.

The taxi dropped them in front of the Opal. He was ready this time with his hundred yen coin.

Fumiko was still on duty.

"Welcome back to Opal. How about that booth?" she said, pointing to the back of the room.

"That's great Fumiko-san, we've had a busy day. So a little quiet time and something good to eat would be nice. We just came from the Officers Club."

After a supper of miso soup and fried soba, they thanked Fumiko and went outside to get a taxi. In a few minutes they arrived at the South Terminal. Before coming to a stop, Myles asked the driver to wait at the curb before getting out.

"Yoshiko-san, we have a plan for next weekend. I will come Friday and stay at my club Friday night and Saturday night. I think you should have my telephone number in case your work gets busy and you must change our plan. Is that OK?" he asked very slowly and carefully. He retrieved one of his Air Force cards and pointed to his phone number.

"OK, Mai. I call if cannot see you Friday."

Myles paid the driver and helped her out onto the street. He straightened the Nikon on her shoulder. They posed motionless for a few seconds, then she raised her face and they kissed. Then they kissed again.

"Sayonara, Mai."

She turned and walked into the crowd.

"Wait, wait, Yoshiko-san," Myles shouted, as he raced after her.

For an instant he panicked, but there she was, waiting for him, getting knocked about by the human traffic.

He gave her a soft hug, then stepped back and took her right hand.

"I'm so sorry. What time should we meet next Friday?"

"Oh, I forgot too. We meet at South Terminal taxi place ten Friday Morning. OK?"

"Yes. Ten o'clock. See you then. Sayonara."

Sunday, November 25, 1956

The next day Myles went to church with his Boy Scouts to hear a special sermon dedicated to our fallen warriors in Korea. The exact number wasn't given but he knew it was around 38,000. Fighting ended in 1953.

As he listened to the sermon, he couldn't help being moved by the scope and depth of the tragedy. He wondered if we might be headed into another quagmire in Vietnam.

Major Hickson and Peggy were at the service and Myles suggested they sit with him and his scout troop. He seated them alongside the scouts in the front row.

The Major had been involved in the Pusan Peninsula retreat, and suffered shrapnel wounds in his back and frostbite in his feet. He married Peggy soon after he returned to the States in 1952. Peggy was a wonderful wife.

Myles could see why the Major wasted no time tying the knot when he got back from the war. They had no children. She was full time looking after him and doing volunteer work for the Officer Wives Club and the Welcome Wagon.

After the service, Peggy invited Myles to join them at the Officers Club for the Sunday buffet, but he needed to stay with his boys. They were meeting in the base gym for award ceremonies, and then they were treating him to some campfire cooking.

"Thanks for the invitation," he said. "May I have a rain check on that? I'm eating some boy scout cooking today."

"Sure Myles, and thanks for letting us sit with you. It was a little tough on the Major. You know he had friends over there that didn't come back."

"I know. Major, see you tomorrow back at the office."

He gathered up his scouts and headed over to the base gym. He was looking forward to passing out merit badges and then helping build a campfire in the middle of the parade ground.

Monday, November 26, 1956

It was another cold gray morning as Myles trudged across the parade field toward the compound.

At he sat at his desk organizing his work, he felt a hand on his shoulder. He froze for an instant to play along with the game.

"Good morning my friend, how'd it go Saturday night?"

It was Roy Brent offering him a steaming black coffee.

"Thanks for asking. I'm glad you guys got to meet Yoshiko. She was really impressed. Thanks for the coffee. Excuse me I need a little cream and sugar for a change."

"No, no," Brent said, as he reached for the cup.

"Please, let me wait on you today. You're probably worn out."

"No, as a matter of fact I feel fine. There wasn't anything to tire me out except for a nice long walk along the Ginza. I take it you approve of Yoshiko."

"Approve? What are you saying man? She was beautiful. We're looking forward to seeing her at the Christmas party. Where'd you meet anyway?"

"Well, it was just by chance. A week ago Saturday, I was alone in the Victoria and so was she. I couldn't resist introducing myself so I took a chance and, well, it just worked out. So Saturday was really our first date."

He scooted his chair up to his desk.

"Thanks for the coffee, Roy. I need to dig into this stack of stuff."

Around eleven o'clock, he got up and stretched to clear the cobwebs. Brent, Manahan, and Davison had desks just behind his along the wall. They each had their own set of wall charts and a tall filing cabinet much like his arrangement.

He decided to have lunch at the snack bar so he could stop by the Base Exchange. He needed new business cards and a box of cigars.

On his way out, he stopped at Brent's desk.

"Roy, have you thought any more about the AP search last week?" Myles asked.

"Well I've tried to put it out of my mind but I'm still wondering about it. I asker Major Hickson about it earlier but he couldn't tell me anything. He said the NSA Liaison Office filed a complaint with the Judge Advocate General. Hell, I didn't even know there was a JAG office here at Shiroi."

"There is? That's news to me. Where is it?" Myles asked.

"You won't believe it. It's in the same building as the base theater. There's just a Colonel, a Mr. Braum, and a clerk. Guess there's not much for them to do in a place like this. Anyway, I think it was a false alarm. I think the APs and the search was just a show of strength meant to warn us. You don't have any secret documents do you Myles?"

"Not on your life. I hope this will be the end of it. I'm going over to the Base Exchange. Anything I can get for you?"

"No thanks. See you later," Brent answered.

It was a few minutes past twelve as he stepped through the front door. He was surprised to see Peggy Hickson sitting alone with an open briefcase on her table.

"Myles, over here," Peggy called out.

"May I?" Myles asked as he pulled out a chair.

"Of course. Sit with me and order some lunch."

"What are you up to Peggy?"

"Well, I'm getting ready for my meeting with the Welcome Wagon. I'm president this year. We're having a special meeting to get ready for three new families. Two Lieutenants and a Captain are coming in next week with their wives, no kids, just wives. They're Army so I guess the Army's beefing up their staff."

"Yeah, I guess so. I can't predict the future but I think you might see more people coming in before too long. Think you can handle that?"

"We can handle that and a lot more. By the way, the Major's real pleased with your work, Myles. You must be doing well."

"Peggy, he's been real good to me. Thanks for mentioning that. Sergeant Johnson deserves most of the credit though and I've made sure Major Hickson and Sergeant Barney know that."

"Myles, if I ever get the chance, I'll repeat what you just said about Sergeant Johnson."

"Thanks, I appreciate that. Am I holding you up from your meeting?"

"I do need to be leaving soon. My meeting is at twelve-thirty," Peggy answered.

"Good .... but there is something I'd like to share with you," Myles said.

Myles wanted Peggy to know about Yoshiko.

"What is it Myles?" she asked.

"I tell you what. It's something that can wait. I'll let you go for now. I need to go to the Base Exchange to get my promotion cigars," Myles changed the subject. "We'll talk again soon. Good luck at your meeting."

He helped her from her chair and walked her to the door.

After his stop at the Exchange he headed back to the office with a box of Golden Nuggets.

By four o'clock, the office air was saturated with cigar smoke and he'd passed out fifty cigars. Major Hickson and Sergeant Barney each took a handful for later. He was glad to oblige since both of them had helped with his early promotion.

He didn't get a lot done on the first day back at work. He picked up on an air defense drill near Shantou, when four Mig 17s scrambled in the direction of a phantom bogey. From just that little exercise, he was able to get their call signs for the day and their scramble and radar frequencies.

He also noted that the scramble took only three minutes and forty-five seconds from alarm to wheels up which was much better than before they upgraded from Mig 15s. He sent the information to the 26th Fighter Interceptor

Squadron at Clark Field in the Philippines which had just upgraded from F86s to F100s. He copied BCOM in Arlington and 13th Air Force Headquarters at Clark. They needed to know what their counterparts were doing.

That night, after a couple of beers at the Officers Club with Brent and Manahan, he retired to his room and wrote letters to his Mom and Dad, and little brother Matthew

Tuesday, November 27, 1956

The courier bags were unusually heavy this morning. Tuesday was the day when all the weekend bags from the detachments finally made it to Shiroi. Lieutenant Wentz and Sergeant Wideman worked feverishly to get all the traffic separated and dropped on the appropriate team leaders' desks. As Wideman dumped the contents from Detachment Three's pouch out onto the table, something unusual popped out on top of the pile. It was a tattered yellow business envelope, separate from the larger packages. From its position in the pile, he figured it must have been stuffed into the bag first and then the regular packages piled in on top of it.

It was addressed simply to 21st Radio with no other markings on front or back. There was no classification markings. For a moment he wasn't sure what to do with it. The address was handwritten with what appeared to be a dull pencil and was barely legible. He set it aside until he finished sorting and delivering all the other traffic. He took the envelope back with him to his desk and started thinking about it. Normally, he would have given a piece of unidentified mail to Sergeant Barney, but for some reason he felt he needed to think this over.

Finally, he decided to deliver the envelope to Myles, since normally most of Detachment Three's traffic came from South Vietnam. He went over to Myles' desk and stood there for a second holding out the envelope.

"Myles, so far I haven't shown this to anybody. It was in the pouch from Detachment Three at Tan Son Nhut so I guess it might be meant for you and Johnson," Wideman said, still not sure if he was doing the right thing.

Myles took the envelope.

"Thanks Sarge. I'll take a look at it and then decide. I guess for now, I'll ask you not to mention it to Lieutenant Wentz or anybody else. It is unusual. Have you ever seen anything like this before?"

"Never. All the traffic we get is always stuffed into large Top Secret packages from each detachment. See .... all this says is 21st Radio .... at least that's what it looks like. It's hard to make it out. Back in the States we'd call it junk mail."

"Strange. I'll let you know later what this is ..... that is, of course, if you have the need to know. Thanks," Myles said. "That all for now?"

Myles watched as Wideman returned to his desk. He examined the envelope for a minute. The hand written address was barely legible as Wideman had described. He held it up to the ceiling light and saw what looked like a small piece of paper folded once over itself. The yellow envelope seemed to be the ultra thin vellum which used to be used for overseas air mail. He decided not to open the envelope and, instead, take it into Major Hickson.

It was nearly lunchtime, and Myles decided to wait until later to see the Major. He folded the envelope once over itself and stuffed it into his pocket. He decided not to show the letter to Johnson. He figured the less exposure to this .... the better.

Around two o'clock, Myles decided to see the Major. He knocked once and stood back from the door.

"Come on in Myles," the Major invited him in.

"Major, how did you know it was me?" Myles asked.

"Well, you're the only person that knocks only one time. Take a seat."

Myles pulled the envelope out from his pocket and handed it to the Major. The Major accepted the envelope.

"Sir, this was in Detachment Three's pouch this morning. It was just loose in the bag. It's simply marked 21st Radio. I thought you might want it," Myles said, hoping to see the Major open it and get an explanation.

The Major didn't seem surprised. He tore the envelope open and unfolded the note. From where he was sitting, Myles could see three or four hand written lines in the same dull pencil script as the address. The Major quickly read the message and then stuffed it and the envelope into his shirt pocket.

"Did I do right, Major?" Myles asked. "Was it something for you?"

"Well, I'll tell you Myles. It is for me but nothing I was expecting. Detachment Three is at Tan Son Nhut, right?"

"Yes sir. They've got five manual Morse positions and two radio teletypes. They're in an old school house hidden away on the southeast edge of the base. They monitor about fifteen Vietcong transmitters, mostly in the Mekong Delta. I can't figure how that got into their pouch," Myles answered.

"Well, I'm surprised. I don't know either. I need to do some thinking for now. Just keep this between ourselves. I might or might not talk to you later about this. If you see any more of these envelopes please get them to me right away. I guess that'll be all for now. Thanks Myles."

"I will. I guess that was all I had for now sir."

Myles stood up and left the Major's office.

As he walked back to his desk, he noticed Johnson standing at the wall map inserting pins. He detoured over to the map.

"Hmm .... let's see what you got there?" he asked Johnson. New pins were highly significant. Pins indicated over ninety percent reliability on whatever they identified.

"Look here," Johnson said, as he pointed to three red pins about halfway between North Vietnam and South Vietnam. "We've located three new PAVN transmitters. It's the first time we've ever heard from them, so they must be no more than two or three weeks old. They could be part of the main communication network from the North to the South."

"That's great news. If we could lock in on that trunk line we could listen in on everything coming down from Hanoi. How about going over the traffic with me in the morning. This could be really big. Where the intercepts come from?" Myles asked.

"Detachment Two at Clark," Johnson answered.

"That's a little surprising, don't you think? I'm surprised they've got the range for that distance. That must be ..... what .... nine hundred miles from Clark? Those must be powerful transmitters. Your hunch might be right. That would mean they could relay communications from Hanoi directly into to VC receivers in the Delta. Let's talk in the morning. I'm staying over a little tonight. I've got some catching up to do," Myles said.

"See you in the morning," Johnson answered.

Myles worked until six-thirty and barely managed to get to the dining hall just before closing. Later that night, the strange envelope lingered in his thoughts as he dozed off to sleep.

Wednesday, November 28, 1956

Around nine the next morning, Johnson looked over at Myles.

"Boss, you still want to see that traffic on the new transmitters?"

"I do, but let's do it later. I left things in a mess last night. Let's get together around eleven, OK?"

"See you at eleven. That'll give us a chance to see what's new from Detachment Two this morning," Johnson answered.

"Sounds good," Myles replied, wondering if another surprise might be in Detachment Three's pouch.

Around ten, Sergeant Wideman delivered the morning Vietnam intercepts. He didn't mention anything special as he placed the stack on Myles' desk.

"Business as usual?" Myles asked, as Wideman started away to another desk area.

"Nothing exciting today," Wideman answered.

Myles and Johnson met for an hour and went over all the intercepts that revealed the three new mid-country PAVN transmitters. They agreed that Detachment Two had done an excellent job in pulling in those long distance transmissions. Myles decided to commend them on their good work. Before quitting time, he sent a message to the Commander of Detachment Two.

TOP SECRET

PRIORITY   **PRIORITY**   **PRIORITY**

1/28/56

TO: CMDR DET 2; 21ST RAD, CLARK

RE: COMDR HQ 21ST RAD, SHIROI; CHF BCOM, ARL; HQ NSA LIA, SHIROI

DE: GARRISON/JOHNSON 21ST RAD, SHIROI

EXCELLENT WORK PULLING IN DISTANT FREQUENCIES FROM CENTRAL VIET. YOUR POSITIONS TWO AND THREE VERY PRODUCTIVE. NEW INTEL GLEANED VERY VALUABLE WITH ULTRA HIGH CONFID LEVEL. AS ALWAYS MAINTAIN VIGILANCE. PLEASE ADVISE YOUR NEEDS.

AR 1130H

TOP SECRET

Thursday, November 29, 1956

Shortly after eight Myles got a phone call.

"Lieutenant Garrison, please come see me .... right away if you can," The Major sounded serious.

As far as he could remember, this was the first time the Major had ever called him on the phone. He spent a few minutes wondering what was up. Why a phone call? He was puzzled .... maybe it was the envelope. He headed for the Major's office.

"Come on in Myles. I called you on purpose. I didn't want to rattle the troops by coming to get you. I'd rather keep this low key for now. Anyway, I've got some NSA news. The Liaison officer wants to change your assignment. Have a seat."

"Is this about the AP incident Major .... or the yellow envelope?"

"No. I'm hoping the AP incident is behind us. No, it's about Vietnam. But before I get into that take a look at this."

He opened a plain Manila folder and handed Myles a short stack of documents.

"Major, should I be seeing this?"

The first page was marked Top Secret Lantern in bold red letters. Off to the side, it read Eyes Only.

"Go ahead and read the first page. Then we'll talk about it."

"Yes sir."

Myles read the page and looked up at the Major.

"How'd you get this Major? Is this something you should have?"

Myles couldn't help thinking about the APs last week and the JAG issue.

"It's OK Myles. I know what you must be thinking after last week. Trust me. This is something separate from all that. This came from Comsec. You got any friends in Communications Security Myles?"

"No, sir."

"Well, actually you might. Comsec has people embedded in every branch of the intelligence community. All you need to know is that this came from Comsec somewhere in Saigon. But that's off the subject, at least for now," the Major continued. "What do you think about the first page?"

"Well it's from Ngan Me Nhu. It says he is Chairman of Agrarian Reform under President Diem and it's to Charles Wilson, Secretary of Defense. It tells about a promise Dulles made before he retired to send 350 Flood Control Specialists to MACV. There's a time line for this. Oh ... here it says rabbit season is open in Saigon Province. Then he says he wants some special things but he doesn't say what. And rabbit season .... do you know what that means, sir?"

"I'm not sure. This is the first time I've seen that reference. Just a guess .... but I think it means more that shooting rabbits," the Major answered.

"Is it about killing people sir?" Myles asked.

"Could be .... I guess we'll find out more later. I'll give you a few minutes to look over the rest of the pages, but first let me tell you about your new assignment."

Myles put all the pages back in the folder and placed it in his lap. He couldn't help worrying what this was all about.

"Here's the deal. Your concern about things heating up in the Delta has gotten Arlington all worked up. BCOM's adding more people and they want more support from the field. So we need to scale up our effort along the lines of your recommendations."

Just then .... a knock on the door.

"Come in," the Major responded.

"Oh, excuse me," Sergeant Barney said, as he stood in the doorway.

"Come on in Marcus. Myles and I are covering something you ought to know about. Take a chair."

The Sergeant sat alongside Myles and was ready to listen.

"I was just telling Myles how BCOM is adding people to get more intel on the Vietcong. ...."

Sergeant Barney interrupted, "BCOM .... what's that? You guys got to get used to treating me like a virgin on anything Far East."

"Myles, I guess you didn't cover the NSA with Marcus. How about filling him in?"

"Yeah, well, the NSA, I guess you know what that stands for, right?"

"I'm not that stupid. But BCOM, I don't know."

"OK, the two sections we work for in the NSA are ACOM and BCOM. ACOM is China and BCOM is Vietnam. I think those are the missing pieces of the NSA puzzle for you Marcus," Myles decided to go with first names since the Major set the stage.

"Thanks Myles. Now as I was saying, Arlington has been paying a lot of attention to what we've learned about the North Vietnam military with our limited volume of intercepts. So they want to get more of the same, a lot more. To make a long story short, they want you and Johnson pulled off China and put one hundred percent on Vietnam."

"Major that's great news. I feel we can really do some good," Myles spoke, as he straightened up in his chair.

"OK. I think things will start to happen fast. Next week the Chief of BCOM in Arlington, will make a swing through Japan, Taiwan, the Philippines and South Vietnam. One of her stops will be here at Shiroi, and while she's here she wants to see you."

"She, did you say she?" Sergeant Barney interrupted.

"That's right. Navy Commander Sheila Banta heads up BCOM. I hear she's sharp as a tack and tough as an old catcher's mitt. Myles, you and Johnson will still report to me, but she wants a direct line."

"I understand, sir. Will there be any travel involved?"

"Not right away. I think the biggest change will be that you and Johnson will manage all the Vietnam traffic. You'll be turning over all your Chinese stuff to Lieutenant Davison.

"But sir, we need much more Vietnam traffic. Will this be worth it?" Myles expressed concern, knowing that their assets were limited.

"Commander Banta's promised me we'll be getting help. I don't know how much help we'll get or where it's coming from …. but she's promised. If you need more manpower you'll get whatever you need."

"Thank you, Major. I'll be looking forward to next week. By the way, my timing isn't too good. I've got a three day pass this weekend?"

"That'll be fine. You might not get another three day pass for a while."

"Thanks Major. Marcus, are you following all this?"

"I'm fine Myles. I don't know what I can do, but I'll help in any way I can. When will Sergeant Johnson learn about his new assignment?" Sergeant Barney asked.

"If it's all right Marcus, I'll cover this with him after we finish here. He'll be thrilled to hear the news," Myles said.

"That'll be fine, if it's OK with you Marcus," the Major said to Sergeant Barney.

"I'll follow up with him later," the Sergeant replied.

"I guess that will be it for now," the Major said.

Everyone stood up and they all shook hands.

"Myles, stay for a minute," the Major signaled to Myles.

"Yes sir," Myles said, as he handed over the folder.

"Keep the Eyes Only file just between you and me. We'll talk about it again after Commander Banta's visit next week."

"Yes sir."

Myles sensed a tenseness coming into the Major's voice.

"Major, that yellow envelope I gave you yesterday .... is that connected to any of this?

"Yes. That's all I can say. You can go back to work now."

Myles finished out the day a little stunned by the peculiar session he'd had with Major Hickson and the changes in his assignment. He was worried about the documents and being pulled into something that he couldn't even talk to Roy Brent about. He left work a little early and headed straight to his room to pack for his trip to Tokyo in the morning.

Fidel Castro's invasion force lands on Cuban coast; Britain and France pull out of Egypt; Japan becomes member of the United Nations; Roger Vadim's film "And God Created Woman" is released; Trans-Canadian Air Lines crashes in British Columbia killing all 62 on board; Suez Canal crisis causes petrol rationing in Britain; Wilt Chamberlain plays his first college basketball game; Assassination attempt on South Vietnam President Diem fails, Secretary for Agrarian Reform injured; No Nobel Peace Prize awarded for 1956.

Chapter Four

Three Day Pass

Friday, November 30, 1956

The long awaited day finally arrived. Myles pulled his suitcase down from the overhead and nestled it between his feet and the seatback up ahead. The train was slowing now as it approached Tokyo Station. In a few minutes he'd be out the gate and looking for Yoshiko.

Very shortly, the two joined up at the taxi stand by the South Terminal gate. They hugged and kissed over and over again before climbing into a taxi. It had only been six days but one would have thought it had been a year.

"Yoshiko-san, I've missed you very much. How are you today?"

She touched his arm.

"I miss you too, Mai."

The driver was waiting for his instructions.

"I have my suitcase here, should we go to the Officers Club and get me checked in?"

"I tell driver," she replied.

In a few minutes, the taxi turned into the circular drive and stopped near the entrance.

"Yoshiko, we will go inside to get my room."

He paid the driver and helped her out onto the sidewalk.

Inside, the hostess remembered her from the previous Saturday. They chatted for a few minutes and Myles suggested they go to the coffee shop while he checked in.

"Thank you, Mai, I see you soon. Your friend take care me."

The two girls headed for the coffee shop, while Myles took the elevator to the second floor. He was back in few minutes.

He spotted them in the coffee shop at a small table near the entrance. She and the hostess were still talking and getting acquainted. It was an elegant place ..... white tablecloths, silver service, and flowers. Myles sat down and thanked Yoshiko's new friend for seeing about her.

"Yoshiko-san, there are some things we might want to do this weekend. Would you like to have my ideas?"

"Yes, what you think Mai?"

"First, are you still working in the show today at Seibu?"

"Oh, Mai, no. That show for me cancel. So we totally free."

"OK. There is a USO floor show tonight here in the club. It will be American singer Joni James. It starts at eight o'clock and I can get a reservation. Or, there is an Elvis Presley movie at the Nichigeki Music Hall. It is called

"Love Me Tender", like the song. I think it is his very first movie."

She liked the idea of the movie. Elvis was immensely popular in Japan and she was a big fan.

"Mai, I like movie tonight. But, I like first take you Ikebukuro. You know that place?"

"I've heard of it. It's way out in northwest Tokyo isn't it?"

"Yes, fifteen minute train from Tokyo Station." Myles was really interested in what she was about to come up with.

"I work Mitsukoshi Store in Ikebukuro all week, not today. I no go home Yokohama each day, I stay apartment in Japanese hotel Mitsukoshi rent for models. So that where I staying tonight and tomorrow night too. So, I want take train to apartment at Ikebukuro and pick up things. You want come with me?"

She sounded so sincere, he could hardly refuse.

"Of course, that's a wonderful idea. I've never been to Ikebukuro."

Fifteen minutes later, she took him by the hand and led him out of Ikebukuro Station.

The area around the station was definitely not like downtown Tokyo. It was like a small country town. The main streets leading from the station were paved, but most of the side streets were unpaved gravel. Mitsukoshi Department Store was just across the street from the station.

In the area around the store there was a collection of small shops and restaurants, a bicycle shop, and a gas station.

Still leading him by the hand, she turned left at the first corner and up a side street. She pulled him to a stop.

"Here Mitsukoshi apartment for models. We get camera and things. OK?"

They entered a small courtyard behind a low concrete block wall. There was a small fountain and a still pond surrounded by two cherry trees and a small willow tree. At the doorway, they kicked off their shoes and slipped into white cotton slippers.

"Good morning," a little old lady, maybe sixty or seventy years old, greeted them at the door. She bowed as low as she possibly could, without upsetting her center of gravity.

"Good morning O-basan. This my friend Myru-san."

Another round of bowing followed.

"Welcome Myru-san. Please come inside."

"Mai, O-basan is manager. She very good to me."

Yoshiko ushered Myles up a short flight of polished wood stairs and down a narrow hallway. The wooden floor had a satin sheen, polished by years of stocking feet and slippers. There was one sliding paper door on either side of the hallway. The door on the left was open and she invited him inside.

It was a Japanese room like he had seen in pictures. The walls were framed in cream colored rice paper and the floor was tightly woven rice straw. In one corner there was an open closet with a futon rolled up inside.

An open suitcase was on the floor with an assortment of clothes piled along side. He recognized the lavender dress and purple shoes from last week and, of course, there was Mr. Nikon.

"What you think apartment Mai? It very small but can walk easy to job at Mitsukoshi."

"This is really nice. I like it very much."

"Oh, look," she said.

She walked to a vacant corner concealed by a curtain. She pushed the curtain aside revealing a tiny bay window jutting out over the courtyard. It was outfitted as a small kitchen with a sink and a two burner hot plate. There were three empty shelves under the counter.

"Mai, this kitchen," she broke into a giggle. "See place for dishes."

"I like this very much. Do you rent by the day or by the week?" Myles asked.

"When I have job, Mitsukoshi pay by week. O-basan very happy. Japanese toilet end of hall. No bath, only toilet."

"Well, where do you take a bath?"

"Another street there Japanese bath house. I go there. You go too sometime?"

"Well, maybe?"

She started going through her suitcase.

"I put make up in hand bag and we go Tokyo. Oh, I show you Mitsukoshi. Please take camera, Mai."

They recovered their shoes, bid O-basan sayonara, and headed back out onto the gravel street.

They toured the Mitsukoshi Department Store, saw the studio where she worked, and met some of her friends. It was a lot like the Seibu, just a smaller version.

Back in Tokyo, they started walking down the Ginza to visit Uncle Masuda and drop off the film from last Saturday.

Masuda spotted them coming through the door and rushed up to greet them. There was a great hug for Yoshiko and a strong handshake for Myles.

"Masuda-san, it is so good to see you again. How are you?" Myles spoke first.

"Oh, I am fine thank you. What are you two doing today?"

"Uncle Masuda-san, I have present."

Yoshiko placed four rolls of exposed film on the glass counter.

"How long we get?" she asked.

"Next Saturday of course. How is the Nikon doing? Would you like to change it for another kind, maybe a Canon?"

"No, we have Mr. Nikon member of family. Right Mai?"

"We love the Nikon with the wide angle lens and easy to operate," Myles chuckled, mimicking Yoshiko.

Yoshiko excused herself to go to the back of the store where Masuda kept an American bathroom for his customers. He felt it was something special that he could offer to pull customers in off the Ginza. It must work .... Myles thought .... he's got a good business. Maybe I should open a camera store on the Ginza someday.

After visiting Uncle Masuda, they walked for a while and then lined up at the Nichigeki to see "Love Me Tender" as planned.

They loved the movie. Debra Paget played opposite Elvis. Myles had to explain the Civil War to Yoshiko. No matter how hard he tried, he just couldn't make her understand why Americans were killing Americans.

After the movie, they went back to the Opal for soba and tempura. They asked about Fumiko not being there but couldn't get a straight answer. It seemed to be an unscheduled day off. Back out on the sidewalk, Myles hailed a taxi for the short trip back to Tokyo Station.

On the way, she kicked off her shoes and snuggled up to Myles with her head on his shoulder. They didn't speak.

After dropping her off at the station he stayed with the taxi for his ride back to the Officers Club. It was a sad parting for both of them. It didn't seem right. He clutched the Nikon close to his chest as he watched the night lights pass by on his way back to the Club.

Before they said goodbye, they agreed he would take the train to Ikebukuro in the morning and have breakfast with her in the Mitsukoshi Grill.

Saturday, December 01, 1956

Myles got his wake up call at eight and ordered coffee service. He hadn't slept very well. He couldn't stop thinking about Yoshiko alone on the train. She was fearless .... he thought .... but just the same he felt uneasy about her being alone like that, attracting a lot of attention on the train and in the stations.

After breakfast, he walked down the single flight of stairs to the lobby and picked up the Saturday Stars and Stripes to read on the train.

He dropped his key at the desk and was heading to the front door when he spotted an attractive blond Naval officer coming out the coffee shop. Could she be Commander Banta, he wondered? She might be staying at the Club over the weekend before heading out to Shiroi. He figured there was nothing to lose as he approached her.

"Ma'am, would you be Commander Banta by any chance?" he asked.

She stopped in her tracks and swung around. She looked very smart in her Navy blue uniform with eight ribbons across her chest. He guessed she might be in her late thirties.

"Yes, I am," she replied, a little surprised.

"I'm sorry to bother you ma'am. I am Air Force Lieutenant Myles Garrison from 21st Radio at Shiroi. Major Hickson, our commander, informed me you'll be visiting us next week."

Just then, a Navy Lieutenant appeared, probably after paying the tab at the Coffee Shop.

"Yes, I'm so glad you stopped me. I'm looking forward to seeing you. This is Lieutenant Peabody. He's traveling with me."

"Good to meet you Lieutenant. Is there anything I can do for either of you? I'm staying here at the Club on a three day pass."

"Lieutenant, is there anything we need?" the Commander asked.

"Not that I can think of. Lieutenant Garrison, please call me Bill. Commander Banta has friends in Tokyo and we're going to see some of them today. She's giving me the night off. If you're not doing anything, maybe we can have a drink."

"That'd be great, Bill, I'd love to but I already have a commitment for tonight. I'm really sorry. And you should call me Myles. There's a neat little place not far from here where a lot of our guys go for drinks. It's safe for you to go there. Just ask a taxi to take you to the Opal Coffee Shop. Everybody knows where it is."

"Thanks Myles, for looking after Bill, I was worried about leaving him to fend for himself tonight. This is his first trip to Tokyo. I look forward to seeing you in a few days."

"Same here, I have to be going now. You guys take it easy."

Myles was tactfully trying to get away.

Before leaving, he bought two bouquets of flowers in the lobby gift shop. Then he caught a taxi to Ikebukuro.

It was nearly twelve-thirty by the time he got to Ikebukuro. He was concerned about being late. He was supposed to be there for breakfast. Twelve-thirty was more like lunchtime.

He found his way out of the station and up the gravel road to the apartment. Yoshiko and O-basan were sitting on the front doorstep.

He held up the two bouquets as a peace offering, but all he got was a couple of faint smiles.

"Mai, you very late. We worry."

"I am so sorry girls. I tried to hurry but I had to speak to some people about my job."

He kicked off his shoes and motioned Yoshiko up the stairs, bouquet in hand. O-basan was right on their heels with an empty vase.

"Yoshiko-san, I am so sorry. I got up early, but in the lobby I met a Navy Commander who I will see next week. I had to speak to her."

"Her, you say her?" Yoshiko was surprised.

"Yes we have lady officers, too, and she has a high rank in the Navy."

"How you like my dress today, Mai?"

She decided to move on, now that he knew he was in trouble.

"What a beautiful dress. Is it borrowed from Mitsukoshi? I see *Ladybug* there on the collar."

"No, Mai, Uncle Masuda-san give birthday money I buy myself. I glad you like."

She punched his arm. "*Ladybug* like too," she said, pointing to the pin, high up on her collar.

"OK, here we are on Saturday. We missed breakfast. Should we go have lunch now?" Myles suggested.

"We go have noodles," she said, as she was getting her things together.

She slid the door closed and Myles followed her down the hallway.

They walked down the gravel road heading out of the neighborhood. Myles had to steady her when she stumbled in her high heels.

After a lunch of steaming hot noodles and tempura vegetables they decided to check out some of the neighborhood shops. Eventually, they ended up at the Mitsukoshi. Yoshiko bought a scarf to match her new dress and a necktie for Myles.

It was late afternoon by now and they agreed to go back to the apartment. Her new shoes were starting a blister.

O-basan was nowhere in sight when they got back and they quietly snuck upstairs. Inside she helped him out of his jacket and hung it along with her coat in the futon closet. She knelt down and unrolled the futon.

"Here Mai, we lie down," she whispered softly.

They stretched out on the futon with their heads and shoulders inside the closet. She was close to him now and he was careful not to move. He sensed a certain tenseness in the silence, but it was not uncomfortable.

Quietly she rolled to one side and put her arm over his chest. He could feel her heart pounding and the warmth of her body and the sweet smell of her hair.

"Mai," she whispered softly. "I love you very much. I ...."

"Yoshiko, I love you."

He slipped his hand over her back and unzipped her dress. She didn't resist.

They made love for what seemed like hours on end. Finally, they slept .... with her arm over his chest and her head tucked under his chin. They slept that way until ten o'clock the next morning.

Sunday, December 02, 1956

The morning sun came streaking in through the corner window. Myles held Yoshiko close as he stroked her hair.

"I love you my darling Yoshiko."

She scrunched up as close as she could.

"I love you, Mai."

They slowly dressed, in between hugs and kisses, and generally made themselves presentable, should O-basan come knocking. They talked about their plan for the day and agreed another excursion to the noodle shop was in order. Myles was beginning to think about his hotel reservation and what to do about getting back to the base.

After some discussion, they figured the best thing would be for him to go back to the Club for his suitcase and then go straight back to Shiroi.

Then, next Friday, there would be no sense in him staying at the Club. Instead, when he got off work he would take the train all the way to Ikebukuro. She would be there to meet him at the apartment around seven o'clock. That was the plan.

After a huge lunch of miso soup and fried soba, she put Mr. Nikon to work one last time. She prevailed on the noodle chef to take their picture hugging each other over empty noodle bowls. Then it was time for him to go. He pushed away and gave her one last hug before heading out the door to catch a taxi.

"Sayonara, Mai," she bid him goodbye, for now.

He took a taxi to the Officers Club. Two o'clock on Sunday afternoon in Tokyo was a quiet time. Millions of weekday occupants were at home in the suburbs enjoying the weekend with their families. Yoshiko, as well, was still in Ikebukuro enjoying herself more than if she'd gone home to Yokohama.

The taxi deposited Myles at the Officers Club front entrance. He was crossing the lobby, when he spotted Bill Peabody slouched in an overstuffed chair taking a snooze.

Commander Banta was nowhere in sight.

He didn't disturb him, as headed to the elevator. In a few minutes, he was back downstairs, standing at the reception desk. Bill Peabody was up now and standing alongside Commander Banta, both in civilian clothes.

"Good morning, Commander."

"Good morning, Myles," Sheila Banta said. "We're using first names today. You're looking mighty spiffy. Got a date today?"

"Sheila, are you sure that's OK?" Myles wanted reassurance.

"Myles, when you get to know me, you'll learn I'm really a down to earth girl. Sure, today it's Sheila."

"Well, Sheila, no date today. I'm heading back to Shiroi."

"Too bad, you could've joined us in Tokyo. Bill explored the night club scene last night, thanks to Brent and Manahan. He ran into them at the Opal. They got him back to the hotel before two though .... that was his curfew."

"Good. What's on your agenda for today?" Myles asked.

"We'll be tourists today. How was your date last night?" He was hoping she wouldn't ask.

"Thanks for asking. I had a very respectable date with a beautiful respectable Japanese girl. There's not much social life back at the base."

"Great, you'll have to tell me about her sometime," the Commander replied.

"Fine, I'd like to. Well, if you guys don't mind, I think I'll catch a taxi and head for the train station."

"See you in three days," the Lieutenant waved goodbye.

Monday, December 03, 1956

It wasn't easy settling down to work on Monday morning. The weekend with Yoshiko stayed fresh on his mind and he couldn't forget the situation with Major Hickson and the documents. He was tempted to confide with Johnson about everything, but he decided the timing was not right and it wasn't worth the risk.

Around ten o'clock, he asked Johnson to sit with him and review the progress they'd made in the past few weeks. Johnson assembled a stack of intercepts and rolled his chair over next to Myles.

"Myles, look at this," Johnson said, holding up the intercepts. "This is all new stuff we got from Taipei. We wouldn't have gotten nearly this amount of traffic without that dedicated manual position we asked for. I'm working on a summary of the past week's gleanings. I should have it finished later today."

"That's great. The summary is a good idea. We'll have it for Commander Banta when she gets here on Wednesday. Let's see what you've got."

"Good idea," Johnson said, as he spread a few of the intercepts out on Myles' desk.

"I see what you mean about the Taipei intercepts. Are you having any trouble with the translations ..... and how about the encryptions?"

"Translations and encryptions .... no problem. Look at this. I've got all the call signs and tail numbers of that new squadron of Mig 17s. And here are the maintenance reports. With the tail numbers and maintenance reports, we can predict their operational readiness on a daily basis .... maybe even on an hourly basis. And these are personnel reports. Here is a list of all the commanders in Hainan and most of Hanoi's coastal air defense units."

"Good work. Try to have your summary ready today. We'll use it to get ready for the Commander," Myles said, as he patted Johnson on the back.

"Myles, there is something else. Here is a pile of intercepts from a new VC transmitter just south of Saigon. It's from Detachment Three. It's really strange."

"I see. I don't recognize that station. Who is it?"

"Well, that's just it. They're calling themselves, Region. It's a strange call sign. Not only that, this is the first time we've ever gotten unencrypted English language intercepts from the Vietcong."

"This is strange. Let me take a look."

Myles reached for the intercepts.

"Here you go," Johnson said, as he handed over the intercepts. "These are all from Region to Pathway. We don't know who Pathway is either."

"This is too good to be true. The gist of these is the strength of an Infantry Regiment fifty miles north of

Saigon. It even describes their defenses .... and, did you see this?" Myles handed one of the messages back to Johnson.

"Yeah. It says they are staging for a surprise attack on Tan Son Nhut. It even gives the time and date. What do you make of it?"

"Well, either this is a huge mistake .... I mean plain text English and all those details, or something else," Myles said.

"Something else. What do you think?"

"I think this looks like an extremely clumsy attempt at C and D. I really think that's what's going on. I think it's a setup."

"C and D ..... Cover and Deception, yeah, that must be it. This tells me they know one helluva lot about us and our intercept sites and they expected we would read this," Johnson added.

"I think that's it exactly. The new transmitter was probably set up just for this purpose. One thing bothers me about this though. From the grammar, it sounds like they have a fluent English speaking agent, or even an American. Look, here's some slang you don't ever see the VC using. I'm guessing they expect us to pass this along to MACV. Then, MACV would pass it on to the nearest ARVN unit. It would be a real nasty ambush," Myles said.

"OK, what we going to do boss?"

"Well, we are not going to pass it to MACV. Let's just keep collecting everything from Region and ask Detachment Three to try to fix its location. I'm hoping they can triangulate with some of ARVN's mobile radios. Let's not report this to BCOM either .... not just yet. We need more information. Have you seen anything from Pathway?"

"No, not yet," Johnson answered.

Later in the day Myles and Johnson finished their work and started readying their files in anticipation of Commander Banta's visit on Wednesday.

Tuesday, December 04, 1956

The next day turned out to be relatively quiet. The volume of intercepts was unusually low for a Tuesday. There were no more Region intercepts from Detachment Three. Myles continued to watch for more yellow letters but there were none since that one a week ago.

Major Hickson had not spoken personally with Myles since the yellow letter and secret documents day. Roy Brent spent a lot of time during the day talking with the teams and prepping them for any questions from the Commander. Lieutenant Wentz and Sergeant Wideman drew housekeeping duty to get ready for the visit. Wideman even coached everybody on how to neatly fold their burn bags.

Around four o'clock, Brent stopped by Myles' desk.

"Myles, are you guys ready for tomorrow?"

"We're ready .... right Johnson?"

"We are as ready as we'll ever be," Johnson answered back.

"Good. Myles, do you have a minute?" Brent put his hand on Myles' shoulder.

"I do. Should we talk?"

"I think so. How about walking with me back to the BOQ after we close up shop?"

"That'll be fine. Let's meet at the front gate so it's not too obvious," Myles said.

It was almost dark as the two of them started out from the gatehouse.

"Myles, I just want to know if you're doing OK. You know, with the Tokyo situation and all that .... and are you still worried about the AP search?"

"Roy, the Tokyo situation is fine ..... couldn't be better. Yeah, I'm still worried about the AP thing. Is there anything you're not telling me?"

"Well, actually there is. I'm worried too. After the Commander Banta visit let's spend a little time in the conference room. I guess that's safe enough. But, yeah, I am worried. Let's go have a beer at the Club."

That was how the day ended. One beer somehow turned into five beers and a lot of tension was released. They were ready for the Commander's visit tomorrow.

Wednesday, December 05, 1956

Commander Banta and Lieutenant Peabody arrived at ten o'clock. Myles looked up from his work when he heard them come in. He jumped up to greet them as they stood by the door.

"Commander Banta and Lieutenant Peabody, welcome to 21st Radio. Here, I'll take you in to meet Major Hickson. He's just around the corner."

Myles started them walking toward Major Hickson's office.

"Let me point out a few things along the way. First of all, what you see here is our entire headquarters. I'm sure you know we oversee five intercept sites in Okinawa, Taiwan, South Vietnam, Thailand, and the Philippines."

Commander Banta cut him short, "We're up to speed on all that Lieutenant. I'm going to ask for a group meeting later so I can meet all your folks. For now, please just show us Major Hickson's office."

"Yes ma'am. We've all heard a lot about BCOM and this'll put a face on it," Myles replied, as he knocked on the Major's door.

"Come in ..... just a minute," the Major said, as he opened the door and stood aside. "Please, come in Commander."

"Commander, I understand you and Major Hickson haven't met. I can assure you he's the best CO we've ever had."

"I'm fully aware of that. How do you do Major Hickson? This is Lieutenant Peabody."

"Come on in Commander. You both please have a seat. Lieutenant Garrison, please get Sergeant Barney."

"Yes sir."

Myles scurried across the hall and in a few seconds produced Sergeant Barney.

"Sergeant Barney, I'm pleased to finally meet you. I've heard so much about your work in Korea, and congratulations on your Silver Star. You saved your men from being overrun by a hoard of screaming gooks. You're a brave man."

"Well, thank you ma'am. My real reward though, was seeing those men live to see another day. You know, six of them were killed a week later in a rocket attack."

"I didn't know that. I'm so sorry. And you, Major, you are a hero too. How's the shrapnel and the frostbite .... and how's that young bride of yours, Peggy isn't it?"

"The wounds are completely healed over. Thank you. Peggy is doing fine. I was so lucky she came along just when she did. I really think she brought me back as far as I am today."

The Major continued. "We hear a lot of good things about BCOM back there in Arlington. Anything we can do to help, please don't hesitate. Myles, would you like to leave us for a few minutes?"

"Yes sir." Myles went back to his desk.

"Commander, I've asked the men to get together at eleven. I understand you'd like to say a few words and then meet with Lieutenant Garrison privately," the Major said.

"Eleven is fine. I'll see Lieutenant Garrison after lunch If that's all right."

"Fine. Is there anything you want to cover with me first?"

"Yes, if you don't mind. I want to explain why we need more intel on Vietnam. This will take just a minute."

She paused for a moment, and then continued.

"Ho Chi Minh is building up his forces along the Ho Chi Ming trail from North Vietnam all the way down to the southern tip of the Mekong Delta. There are a hundred thousand Vietcong fighters in the Delta gearing up for an invasion on Saigon. There's another hundred thousand PAVN troops in the midlands. Our fear is a giant pincer movement trapping Saigon and our base at Tan Son Nhut in the middle. That would be a game changer from which we'd never recover. It would be bloody beyond comprehension. We could lose all our advisors and maybe a half million South Vietnam soldiers and civilians. To make things worse, we're expecting President Diem will be assassinated in the next month or so. Now you see why we need more intel?"

"Absolutely! Are you going to cover this in your presentation?" the Major asked.

"I'll cover most of it. Whatever I leave out you can cover with them later. They need to know."

She paused and continued.

"The other reason I'm here today is to talk about assignment changes. You got the word we want Garrison and Johnson to be put on Vietnam full time. Well, there's a lot more than that. But for now, let's just say they'll stay here in Shiroi for the time being and we'll be getting them more assets. I'll make that announcement at the group meeting after I put out the same information I just gave you. Can you give me Lieutenant Garrison's time in grade as First Lieutenant?"

Major Hickson was caught off guard, "Well, Commander, he just got promoted a few weeks ago."

"Too bad, I have plans for him. I can't tell you just what until I've had a chance to speak with him. That's what I'll be doing this afternoon."

"I like Myles, he's a damn good man. I'd hate to lose him, but that's entirely in your hands Commander. Are you ready to talk to the troops?" the Major asked.

"Yes, let's get started," she said, as she and the Lieutenant rose from their chairs.

The Major introduced Commander Banta and Lieutenant Peabody to the group. He asked all the officers and enlisted men to introduce themselves.

After the introductions and some background by the Major, the Commander took the floor. She updated the situation in Vietnam in much the same way she had covered it with the Major and Sergeant Barney.

She went on to describe her role as Chief of BCOM and its twenty six subsections. BCOM's mission was communications intelligence for North Vietnam. All of Shiroi's Vietnam intercept assets were under her control.

"Now that's the status quo," she concluded. "But I can promise you that we'll be adding a lot more intercept capacity in the very near future. I know where it'll be coming from but I can't tell you today. You'll hear about it .... maybe next week."

She turned to Lieutenant Peabody. "Lieutenant, I'm not speaking from notes. Is there anything I've left out?"

"No sir. Only one more thing might be useful. Why can't you give a time line for the new assets?"

"I can give you a time line. It is ASAP. Oh, I forgot to mention that the President is sending in five thousand special forces in March. So just watch for the fireworks."

"How about us? We getting any help?" somebody asked.

"No, not for now."

"This is off the subject, but we understand NSA will be moving its headquarters from Arlington Hall to Ft. Meade. How's that going?" Lieutenant Wentz asked.

"Well, it's a busy time to be going through this move. But yes, the Ft. Meade building is about three fourths finished. We hope to move from Arlington in the third quarter next year. Looks like 1957 will be a busy year for all of us."

There was a brief spell of silence.

"I know it gets tough sometimes, but please keep up your good work. Major if it's OK, I'd like to break this off for now. There are still a few things I'd like to cover with you in private."

"Certainly, thank you men. You can go back to work," the Major broke up the meeting.

"Commander, should we go back to my office, or would you like to take a break?"

"Yes, thanks. How about showing me the way to the head?"

The pair headed down the hall.

After lunch the Commander and the Major huddled in his office for fifteen minutes. Then the Major sent for Myles.

"Myles, please come in. We'd like to speak to you."

Myles sat down near the Commander expecting, finally, to get the straight scoop.

The Commander spoke up. "Myles, I think you know what's coming. We've talked all around it this morning, but now we're getting down to brass tacks. The situation is simple. Some of this you might already know. But that's OK."

"Yes ma'am," Myles replied.

"We want you one hundred percent on Vietnam. All the sites, present and future, will feed into you and Sergeant Johnson."

"Excuse me, Commander; I haven't had a chance to speak with Myles about Johnson," the Major interrupted.

"OK. You and Lieutenant Garrison can fill him in later. Sergeant Johnson is our most proficient Vietnamese linguist and a number one analyst. He's already been getting all the Vietnam copy. He'll continue to work with you Myles. I guess you are good friends."

"Yes, I've known Johnson for the past six months, actually since I've been here at Shiroi. I'm pleased to have him. You know he was just a farm boy from Texas and they plucked him out of basic training early and sent him to Harvard for a year to learn Vietnamese. He understands several dialects and speaks almost without an accent. We work well together," Myles answered.

"Yes, well that's the way it'll be from now on. Also, starting today, Lieutenant Davison will take over all your

Chinese work. He's a good man. So beginning tomorrow it'll be all Vietnam for you and Johnson. One other thing, we're bringing you and Johnson to Arlington for a week in BCOM. Your traffic will just have to pile up while you're gone. Lieutenant Brent will screen everything and keep you up to date."

"Thank you Commander for choosing Sergeant Johnson and me for this. When do we leave for Arlington?" Myles asked.

"Next Monday. That will be December the tenth. The two of you will report to Tachikawa for military transport straight through to Andrews Air Force Base. You gain a day crossing the date line, so you will report to Arlington on Tuesday morning. You both will stay at the Air Force dormitory in Suitland, Maryland. I've arranged for you to use a staff car while you're there. Any questions on that?"

Myles thought for a minute.

"No ma'am. We'll both be looking forward to seeing you in Arlington."

"Well, that's about it, Major. Lieutenant Peabody and I ….,"

Just then the phone rang. The Major picked up.

"Lieutenant Peabody, it's for you," he handed over the phone.

"Yes, this is Lieutenant Peabody."

There was a long pause.

"I understand. Hold on," he handed the phone to the Commander.

"Yes, Commander Banta."

She listened intently for a few minutes.

"Affirmative. Thank you," she said, as she hung up the phone

She turned to the Major. "Major, may I use the conference room for a minute. I need to speak with Lieutenant Peabody in private."

"Of course," the Major replied. "Take as long as you need Commander."

Lieutenant Peabody closed the door behind them.

"Bill, here's what that phone call was all about. Let's sit for a minute."

She motioned him to sit close.

"I didn't recognize the voice, Commander. Who was that?"

"Well, that's not important for now. Here's the deal. We need to break off our meeting here and the rest of our tour. We need to get back to Arlington immediately. We'll go to the Embassy from here. I need to speak with some people. I'll fill you in during our car ride back to Tokyo. But for now, we should stop all conversation with Major Hickson and any of his people. We'll just say goodbye and that's it. Clear?"

"Yes ma'am. Is that all?"

"Yes, let's go and tell Major Hickson goodbye. Oh .... and ask for our car to be brought to the front gate. You up to driving? You remember the way back?"

"I'll be fine."

The Lieutenant led the way back to Major Hickson's office.

"Major Hickson, were aborting the rest of our plan for today. Something's come up and we need to leave for Tokyo right away."

The Commander gathered up her notes and stuffed them in her briefcase.

"Certainly Commander. I hope it's nothing serious. I'll take care of getting your car to the front gate. Can I have Lieutenant Garrison show you both out?"

"We know the way Major. Please excuse us to your men. And …. please thank them again for everything. We've got to go."

The Commander nodded to the Lieutenant and they started toward the door. In a minute they were gone. The Major hadn't even had time to wish them a safe trip.

In a few minutes, Commander Banta and the Lieutenant were out of the gate and on their back to Tokyo. After negotiating traffic through Matsudo, the Lieutenant looked over at the Commander.

"Commander, can you tell me now what this is all about? All I got from the phone call was that there was a delay at Fort Meade and the consortium was meeting. Then I was asked to put you on the phone. Why are we aborting the rest of our trip?"

"I will tell you, if you stay focused on your driving. That call was from someone in the Director's office. Consortium is a code word meaning an extremely dangerous situation exists. We've known for a few months that there is a major breach of security in BCOM. Before we left Arlington, I met with the Director's task force and was told they had a solid lead on the source. They said the source might be somebody in my group and there might be more than one culprit"

"It's not me Commander. I can assure you of that," the Lieutenant quickly spoke up.

"We know that Bill. You've been thoroughly vetted. In that phone message, the combination of the words "delay", "Fort Meade", and "Consortium" told me to break off all communication with Major Hickson and everybody in his group. That was a pre-arranged code. So we need to get back to Arlington immediately to handle this."

"But Commander, Garrison and Johnson are coming to Arlington next week. You were planning to tell them all about Beehive."

"I know. We'll handle it somehow. I'm meeting over the weekend with the task force. Just so you know, they're calling the task force, Crossbow. What time is our plane tonight?" the Commander asked.

"We fly out of Tachikawa at eight o'clock. With three refueling stops we should get to Andrews around six tomorrow night."

Out of sight, Lieutenant Peabody was counting on his fingers.

"Good. I don't know how you're going to fit in with Crossbow yet. I'll let you know on Friday. Just stick with your driving for now. I'm going to do a little reading."

She pulled a stack of papers from her briefcase.

Back at Shiroi, the sudden change in plans had Major Hickson thinking about what to do next. He decided to speak with Lieutenant Davison on his change of assignment. He dreaded having to tell him about the change. He would obey orders, of course, but he will be most unhappy about having to pick up behind Myles.

The conversation went pretty much as expected. The Lieutenant accepted the news without any objections, although the Major knew he was boiling inside.

That night at the Officers Dining Hall, Myles sat with Brent and Manahan. They had a lot to digest that evening besides the meat loaf.

"Myles, I hope the hell you're back from Arlington in time for the Christmas party. Maybe you can do a super job and get your tail back here," Brent said.

"Yeah, please do," Manahan piped in. "I want to dance with that girl."

"Don't worry, Johnson and I will do our best. Let's see, if we check in at Arlington on Tuesday the eleventh, we'll shoot for getting out of there by the following Wednesday."

Thursday, December 06, 1956

The next morning Myles went directly to Davison's desk.

"Bob, I need to give you all my Chinese work. I guess Major Hickson covered that with you. When are you going to be free to start talking? I'm ready anytime you are."

"Well, boss, give me a half hour to enjoy my coffee. Then I'll let you know when we can start."

"Fine Bob, just let me know. I'll be working at my desk."

Davison was not enchanted with the idea of taking over the Chinese work. He knew Myles had just gotten a commendation, so at least for a while, more glory would be hard to come by. Myles knew he felt that way and was sorry for his bad attitude.

Around two-thirty, Davison placed himself in the empty chair beside Myles' desk.

"Myles, I've been looking at your wall map. Got anything to add to what's up there.?"

"There are some things. In the morning, I'll turn over a stack of documents that will account for what you see on the chart. And before I leave today, I'll give you all my air defense call signs and frequencies."

"Good. When will we talk again?" Davison asked.

"Ten o'clock in the morning. Johnson and I are leaving first thing Monday morning so we need to wind up by noon."

"OK, Myles."

Davison returned to his desk.

Friday, December 07, 1956

It was nearly ten and once again, Davison plopped himself down in the chair by Myles' desk.

"Ready to get started?" Davison wasted no time showing a little arrogance.

"Right. I have an outline here of what I think we need to cover. First ……."

"Wait, did you say what you think we need to cover?" Davison put an emphasis on the word "you". "How about what I think we need to cover?"

This time he put the emphasis on "I". "I figure we've got two hours to do this, then you'll probably leave for one of your long lunch breaks. Right?"

"Wrong. I really want to help you here. You've been given this assignment and whether you like it or not it's in your lap. Just stuff your smart ass remarks and let's get started. Oh, by the way, Sergeant Petersen will be your Mandarin translator. He'll be a great help. Of course, I'll only be gone for two weeks."

"Only two weeks, yeah. Bet you'll bust your ass getting back here to your little sweetheart. Remember I met her at the Opal?" Davison said, as he broke into a wide grin.

"Bob, I'm going to start talking and you can listen or not. When I'm finished, I'll be finished. That's it. Take it from me, I recommend you get your shit together. I happen to know you have two and a half years time in grade as

First Lieutenant. If you ever want to make Captain, this will be the best opportunity you'll ever get. Understand?"

"Myles, I'm a little hung over today from casino night at the club. Guess I'm a little edgy. I'm sorry for that remark about your girlfriend. She's not to blame for anything. Let's get going with this."

The two of them finished their briefing around one o'clock. Myles helped Davison carry the stack of papers back to his desk. He glanced around the room which was mostly empty from lunch break.

Now that Davison was out of the way, his plan was to skip lunch and head over to the NSA office to get travel orders and travel pay. Then around three, he'd meet with Johnson to give him his orders and money, and brief him on the trip. After that, he'd finish up his own work and get out of the office by four-thirty. It wouldn't take him long to pack a bag and head off to Tokyo.

A few minutes before three, he corralled Johnson and gave him his paperwork and cash.

"Johnson, here's all you'll need. I've read the orders. A car will pick us up outside our quarters at three-thirty Monday morning. Have everything packed in your B4 bag and make sure you have your orders and money. Uniform will be dress blues. In your bag, pack one complete extra uniform, a civilian suit, some dress pants, sports shirts, and a warm-up jacket of some kind. A pair of civilian shoes would be good if you can squeeze them in. I know I sound like your mama, but you said you weren't used to travel. OK?"

Johnson reached for his orders and the two hundred dollars travel pay.

"Oh, that's OK Myles. Yeah I did say that. Thanks for your help anyway. I'll be ready Monday morning."

"Good. As for me, I'll be packing the same way."

"That all? Anything else I should know? What kind of plane will we be on?"

"The orders don't say but I'm guessing it'll be a C121 from Tachi. If that's the case, there'll be two stops on the way to San Fran .... probably Wake Island and Honolulu. From San Fran to Andrews .... I don't know .... probably one stop."

"I'd forgotten what a hassle that trip is. Do they serve booze on the plane?"

"You're kidding right? Of course not. There'll be plenty of box lunches though .... dry sandwiches and hard apples."

"That's OK. We can make up for it in DC. That's what the two hundred bucks are for, right?"

"Hell yes. We'll figure out a good way to spend it. See you Monday morning."

Johnson hustled back to his desk and Myles could see him talking with the other Sergeants telling them about his trip. One last thing was to check in with Major Hickson.

"Come in."

Myles entered.

"May I sit for a minute Major?"

"Of course, take a seat. Ready for your trip? I've seen you covering things with Lieutenant Davison. How'd that go?"

"Yes, well, Johnson and I are ready for the trip. We've got orders, money, and all that. Guess we won't see you until the Christmas party. As for Davison, well he's as ready as he'll ever be. He should be OK."

"Great. Myles, I know what's going on between you and him. Don't worry about it. He really is a good man. He's had a few glitches along the way which have slowed down his promotion, but he's only paying for his own actions, or I should say, inactions. He's got a chance here for a new beginning and I hope he steps up. You've been really patient with him and I respect you for that."

"Thanks Major. There's really no bad blood. He's just a little cranky sometimes. I'm sure he's got his own set of issues to deal with. I wish him luck."

"Myles, there's something I need to cover before you leave. I haven't talked with you before now because I wasn't sure how to handle this. Anyway, here's the thing. Commander Banta and I had a few private minutes together before she left on an emergency. She told me about your new assignment and she was going to cover it with you Wednesday afternoon. I know you're a little rushed for time so I'll condense it for you."

"I have time Major. Don't worry about that."

"Fine. When you and Johnson get to Arlington, Commander Banta will tell you about a new BCOM program. We've all known that the three services' intercept capabilities are seriously obsolete. The equipment is old and unreliable and there is a shortage of analysts and linguists. Well, what she's doing is organizing a new branch of BCOM which she's calling Project Beehive. She's having ten intercept vans built with state of the art everything, including new Doppler direction finding equipment which will locate transmitters within ten meters."

He continued. "Beehive will be run totally by BCOM personnel. There'll be no involvement with the Air Force, Army, and Navy, except for coordination of course. She'll be dividing the vans up into five units of two vans each. So this'll be a totally new concept. The vans will be very mobile and can be moved around by Sikorsky Skycrane helicopters. You with me so far?"

"So far .... so good," Myles replied.

Myles was eager to learn more.

Now, one big difference with Beehive is that the vans will be placed as close up to the enemy as possible. They'll be equipped with weapons and explosives for self protection and destruction if it comes to that. It's going to be a dangerous operation. She wants you and Johnson to be part of Beehive. It will be voluntary. She won't order you to do this," the Major paused.

"That's all I can say for now. Please keep it to yourself until you hear it from the Commander next week, but now you have a heads up. I'll let you go and get ready for your trip. By the way, Peggy wishes you a safe trip."

"Thank her for me Major."

"Just one last thing, Myles. There's a rumor you'll be bringing a Japanese girl to the dance. If that is true .... please be careful. You don't want to lose your clearance."

"I am bringing a Japanese girl. But she's nothing special, believe me. Just a date. Don't be concerned. If that's all, sir, I'll be taking off a little early. I need to take care of some personal things."

"Wait, Myles."

The Major pulled the Manila folder from his top desk drawer.

"This will take just a minute."

"We have time Major."

"Commander Banta doesn't have any knowledge of this. You should keep it entirely to yourself. You must not tell anybody about this. You should remember what you've read on page one all the while you're in Arlington. Keep your eyes and ears open for anything that might connect to it."

Then the Major tore the folder and its contents into four pieces and stuffed them into his burn bag.

"You won't get to see the rest of the pages but when you get back there will be more. Don't worry about that girl friend business. Have a great trip. We'll all be anxious to hear about your assignment and the changes coming down the pike."

Myles hurried back to gather up his papers and to say goodbye to Brent and Manahan. He made a special stop at Davison's desk and extended his hand.

"Take care Bob. I'm leaving the Chinese Communists in good hands. See you in a couple weeks."

He looked over at Johnson.

"See you early Monday morning my friend."

"See ya," Johnson replied, as he waved Myles out the door.

He was finally free. He got back to the BOQ as fast as his legs could carry him and started stuffing clothes in his overnight bag for his trip to Ikebukuro.

International Criminal Police Organization "INTERPOL" is founded; IBM introduces the "305 Ramac" computer which was first to use disk storage; Bob Barker debuts as host of "Truth or Consequences; Asian flu epidemic first appears in China; Eiffel Tower repaired from fire on top level earlier in the year; "Dear Abby" first appears in syndication; Grace Kelly, Bing Crosby, Frank Sinatra in "High Society"; United Artists releases "Invasion of the Body Snatchers"; The Four Lads tops charts with "Standing on the Corner".

Chapter Five

Furniture

Friday Evening, December 07, 1956

The Ginza Line Express pulled into Ikebukuro station on time at seven o'clock. It was already dark as Myles hurried down the sidewalk past the Mitsukoshi and turned left up the gravel road. At the last minute, he realized he'd forgotten to bring a house warming gift, but then he had found his way back and that was the main thing.

Just like last Saturday, Yoshiko and O-basan were perched on the top step at the front door. No sooner had Myles stepped through the stone gateway, when Yoshiko ran toward him and gave him a really big hug. She kissed him hard.

"Mai, I miss you this week. We so happy see you, O-basan and me. How was train ride? Did you eat? You bring suitcase?"

"Yoshiko-san, I am happy to see you and O-basan. Yes I have my suitcase with clothes and no I have not eaten."

With that, Myles stepped forward and scooped them both up in a giant bear hug. They giggled and tried to squirm away. O-basan promptly snatched up his bag and proceeded up the stairs. Myles and Yoshiko hugged and kissed again. Then they followed O-basan, shuffling slowly, and carefully, in their cotton slippers.

Upstairs, Myles noticed a soft orange light emanating from the open door to the apartment. Yoshiko pulled Myles back to a stop.

"Mai, close eyes please."

She placed his hands over his eyes.

"OK, I cannot see. What?"

She slowly led him down the hall coming to a stop at the open door. She turned him in the direction of the light.

"Now, you see. OK?"

He gasped with surprise. There, staring him in the face, was a high four poster double bed, fully made up with a New England bedspread. A small table sat at the left of the headboard between the bed and the little kitchen space. A small lamp graced the table, resting on a frilly white table cloth. A straight wooden chair stood against the wall between the futon closet and the kitchen area. Over on the right side of the room there was a small dressing table with a mirror and a tiny padded bench. The whole scene looked to Myles like something out of a New England tour guide.

"Yoshiko-san, oh my gosh, this is beautiful. Where did this come from?"

"Mai, you like? Now we have home for you every week. You think?"

"Well, yes, much better than the club for sure."

"Mai, Uncle Masuda-san buy for us surprise. Now unpack clothes and we go get Japanese food. I have surprise too. OK?" she said, as she pushed his arm to emphasize her point.

Well, he thought, there goes the arm punch. I was beginning to miss that. Oh, and there was *Ladybug,* perched high over her left collar. He was starting to feel at home.

He pulled off his necktie and changed into a red pull over sweater. As he was changing, he watched Yoshiko going through a row of dresses and jackets in the futon closet. She changed into a brown Chinese high collar split skirt dress, a lot like the lavender one she had worn before. Once changed, she carefully transferred *Ladybug* to her new outfit.

"We go now Mai, you want eat, you hungry?"

"Yes, I'm right behind you."

He was amazed at how quickly she was adapting to English in their conversations.

It was nearly eight o'clock and it had turned cold. Myles' sweater felt good and he put his arm around Yoshiko's waist as they walked up the gravel road. Out on the main street, she led them in a different direction from the noodle shop.

"Mai, here surprise. Is kushi katsu restaurant."

There were no tables, only a large horse shoe shaped counter. Four chefs manned the area inside the horse shoe, taking care of drink orders and cooking the kushi katsu. Yoshiko ordered two beers.

"Mai, this place everything on sticks," she explained. "You order how many sticks and get different kinds. You will like very much."

It was just like she said. She ordered twelve sticks for the two of them. Each stick was about eight inches long and had a different combination of tempura tidbits. It was totally delicious. She showed him how to place his empty sticks in an empty beer mug. After they had eaten and finished their beers, they were presented with the bill based on the number of empty sticks. Myles gladly paid the bill. He liked this place.

They realized it had turned much colder as they stepped outside. They snuggled each other on the walk back to the apartment and it was good to get back. O-basan had turned on their gas heater and it was warm and cozy inside.

Once inside, he sat in the straight chair and urged Yoshiko to sit up on the bed.

"Yoshiko, now please tell me about all this furniture."

She struggled with the English but managed to convey the circumstances. She said Uncle Masuda had decided it was time for her to move out of her parent's home and find a place near her work in Tokyo. He told her he had seen this time coming and that he felt this was the time. He knew she was in love with Myles and it did not look like a temporary thing. He also knew her father would never accept Myles. She would never be able to take Myles to Yokohama and introduce him to her parents. Her mother would be fine but her father, never.

"So, Masuda-san pay for one year rent this place. Mai, he love me very much. He like father. OK?"

"Well, that's very nice. Was this part of your birthday present?"

"Yes, he say happy birthday. He buy furniture. So two day ago, he send truck with furniture and put here. Yesterday I no work. I go to Yokohama and pack suitcase. I tell my Mama-san I now stay in Ikebukuro. So that is whole story. OK?"

Myles understood the whole story.

"Yoshiko, I am so happy for you. I am so happy you have such a fine uncle. Does he know that I stay with you here?"

"Mai, I tell him you be here on weekend and maybe some more time. He only want me be happy, so now he happy too. He trust you. He know you good person. So, that is story and here we are. We live here together very happy."

"Yoshiko, you did all this without talking to me. Why do you think I will be coming here all the time?"

She looked solemn. She didn't speak. She sat with her hands in her lap. He could see tears welling up in her eyes. She buried her head in her hands and started sobbing.

He jumped up and sat by her on the bed. He put his arms around her and gently rocked her back and forth.

"Yoshiko, darling, please stop crying. Please, I want to talk to you."

It took a while, but she regained her composure and turned to look directly at him.

"Mai, I so sorry."

"Yoshiko, I love, I love you. It is OK. We'll be here together from now on, OK?"

He pulled her to him and kissed her gently about her eyes, smoothing away the tears. He kissed her lips and she responded ever so softly with a long lingering kiss.

"Now, let's be happy, Yoshiko. We have a nice place here to live in. I can come on Friday and go back on Sunday. We will have a nice time."

"Oh, Mai, I so happy. I thought you hate me and go away."

"Oh, no. Everything is fine. Do you know it is almost ten o'clock. I think we should go to sleep in our new bed. Don't you think?"

"Yes, yes."

She jumped up and went over to the futon closet, like her old self.

"Here Mai, I buy this present at Mitsukoshi today."

She handed him a beautifully gift wrapped package.

"Thank you very much," he said, as he tore open the wrapping and unfolded a beautiful amber colored silk robe. He stood up, put it on, and spun around.

"You very pretty man, Mai. It fit perfect."

"Now I have present too."

She went to the futon closet.

"Now close eye please."

She slipped on a light blue silk robe decorated with orange and yellow flowers.

"Yoshiko, that is beautiful."

They undressed in front of each other. There was no shame or awkwardness. Clad in their new robes, they crawled into their new bed in their new apartment. That night, in that place, they were in Heaven.

Saturday, December 08, 1956

It was nearly ten o'clock when they awoke. Myles desperately wanted coffee but, of course, there was none. First thing, he thought was to go to the Mitsukoshi today and buy a coffee pot, some cups, and maybe a few dishes. That would be one part of the day's plan for sure.

After a while, they dressed and decided to go out for lunch and do a little shopping. Lunch, of course, was at their favorite noodle shop. As they sat with their soba and green tea, he thought it would be a good time to talk about his trip. He figured this would not be good news and was prepared to kiss away more tears.

"Mai, you should go trip to America. That your job and you go. No worry about me. I have apartment now and job. I OK for you to go. I happy you are going with friend Johnson to protect you. Uncle Masuda-san will watch over me too. You not worry."

"Yoshiko, I am so proud of you for being so strong. Yes, I must go, but I will be back in time for the Christmas Party, I promise."

"OK, when you come back? We make plan."

"Let's see. I really think I can get everything done and come back to Ikebukuro the Friday after next Friday. Then we will go to the party in Shinjuku the next day. I will need a tuxedo. Do you think I can measure for a tuxedo today at Mitsukoshi and then get it on that Friday?"

"Yes, we order tuxedo today. That good plan. I borrow evening gown from Mitsukoshi for party, or you want me wear Japanese kimono?"

"Oh my gosh, you could do that? You could wear a kimono?"

"Yes, I borrow that too. But you know kimono not good for party. Cannot dance in kimono."

"Right, on second thought I'd like to show you off in a slinky evening gown, maybe black or white, you know, low cut with lots of sparkling things, and maybe a crown on your head."

"Oh Mai, the gown good idea. I know exactly. But crown on head, no, no, you silly."

"OK, I know you will be beautiful no matter what," Myles reassured her.

So they now had a plan for the party weekend. They finished lunch and decided to head straight on over to the Mitsukoshi for their errands.

They bought a fine GE coffee percolator at the Mitsukoshi. After shopping for a few other things, they were tired and stopped in the tea room next door to the noodle shop.

"Oh, Yoshiko, what about our pictures? Are they still at Uncle Masuda's shop?"

"Yes he has pictures. We forget pictures this week. We have when you come back. OK?"

"Sure. Pictures in two weeks. Should we be getting back now?"

There was no need for supper that night. They were well fortified by their soba lunch, and tea and cake later in the afternoon. They went to bed early and quietly talked about the first time they met.

Sunday, December 09, 1956

Sunday morning came bright, clear, and cold. Myles made coffee in the new percolator and instructed Yoshiko on its proper use. She made tea for herself.

They decided on lunch at the Mitsukoshi tea room and then Myles would leave from there to go back to the base.

After lunch, she walked him to the station. They walked slowly and deliberately.

At the station, she was anxious to make the separation.

"Sayonara, Mai. Have good trip."

They embraced and kissed. As she pulled away, he reached inside her coat and put his hand near her left breast. Now everything was right, he thought, he could leave knowing that **Ladybug** was just where she was supposed to be.

Monday, December 10, 1956

Dark and cold was the only way to describe Shiroi Air Base at three-thirty on a cold winter morning. Myles pulled himself up from sitting on his B4 bag as he spotted a blue staff car coming around the corner.

"Good morning, thanks for the ride. I am Lieutenant Garrison and we'll be picking up Sergeant Johnson."

"All set Lieutenant, I have it here. Johnson is in Building 22 so that's where we're headed next. I am Airman Coaltrain. I'm pleased to meet you sir."

"Good. You've got it nice and warm in here Coaltrain. Thanks."

Very shortly, Airmen Coaltrain swung the car off the street into the Building 22 parking lot. Myles could see Johnson in the headlights standing near his B4 bag.

"Feels good in here. Airman, I am Sergeant Johnson. Let's get this show on the road."

After an hour's drive to Tachikawa and another two hours processing orders, they were finally on their plane taxiing to the active runway. As Myles had predicted, it was a Constellation all right, but not an Air Force C121 version. He was pleased it was a chartered Far East Air Lines plane which was outfitted much nicer than the Air Force version.

Both of them slept the first leg of the trip. They landed at Wake Island for lunch in an open air sheet metal building. There was just enough time for Spam and powdered eggs. The long walk back to the plane was good exercise.

The rest of the trip went pretty much the same ..... long flights and short breaks. Taking into account the time change and crossing the international date line, they were on the ground at Andrews at ten Monday night ….. the same day they left Japan.

"Myles, I don't get it, here on the same day we left. How's that work?"

"Johnson, as smart as you are, you should be able to figure it out. It's simple. We crossed the International Date Line between Midway and Samoa and that sets the calendar back one day. On the way back we lose a day. So it all evens out."

"Oh yeah, I knew that," Johnson replied, as they walked out of the main exit.

Outside, Myles identified himself to an Air Policeman standing by an empty staff car. He signed for the keys while Johnson loaded their bags in the trunk. In a few minutes they were on their way to Suitland Hall.

"Nice car Myles. Know where you're going?"

"I know my way pretty well around this place. You know I spent four months here going to school in Arlington. First thing we'll do is head over to the Air Force dormitory at Suitland. Once we get settled, we'll go out for a really nice dinner. I'll make sure you get some booze. OK?"

"Good plan," Johnson answered.

There was practically no traffic on the way to Suitland. They got there in less than thirty minutes and finished checking in by eleven. Before leaving for dinner, Myles checked with the Officer of the Day and picked up a plain white envelope. It was a letter of welcome from Commander Banta with driving instructions to Arlington Hall. There was a map showing BCOM's location on the second floor of the main building.

They had a nice dinner at a nearby Hot Shoppe as Myles had promised. A big steak and a few drinks was just what they needed for some good sleep and help getting over the time change.

Tuesday, December 11, 1956

They left for Arlington early the next morning to allow time for some sightseeing. They drove past the Capitol, the Smithsonian, the Washington Monument, the White House, and Arlington National Cemetery. It was worth the extra time. Johnson had never been to Washington.

A little before eight o'clock, Myles led Johnson down the main hallway on the second floor. Unmarked double doors sealed off the end of the hall. The entire building was Top Secret and none of the interior doors were marked. The badges they brought with them from Shiroi were good for all areas.

Inside the double doors a female Navy Petty Officer greeted them. She looked at their orders and had them sign the visitor roster. Commander Banta had name tags waiting for them. The Navy Petty Officer led them down a short hallway and into a conference room.

Commander Banta was standing at the head of a long table and was involved in a discussion with two Naval officers. Six civilians were seated at the table. All of them were males and appeared to be in their late twenties.

The Commander noticed them entering the room and quickly rushed over to greet them.

"Lieutenant Garrison, so good to see you. Sergeant Johnson, I remember you from Shiroi. You had some good questions, thank you."

"Thank you Commander, how's Lieutenant Peabody?" Myles asked. "I don't see him here,"

"He's fine. He works over at ACOM so you might not be seeing him today. I'll tell him hello for you though. He's still talking about how Lieutenants Brent and Manahan took such good care of him in Tokyo. Maybe you can see him over the weekend."

Once everybody was seated the Commander spoke.

"May I have everybody's attention. I apologize but I must leave you all for a few minutes. Please introduce yourselves and I'll be right back."

Outside the conference room, she stepped across the hall to her private office and closed the door behind her. Lieutenant Peabody was standing near her desk.

"Bill, they are here. I'm sorry I haven't had a chance to fill you in on our Crossbow meetings over the weekend. We are ninety-five percent certain they are clean so we're going ahead with plans for them in Beehive. When you meet them later, just behave normally. We still have a serious problem and it might involve Major Hickson and some of the others in 21st Radio. We might know more by the weekend. I'm going back into our meeting now. Just go back to business as usual until you hear from me."

"That's good to hear Commander. I like those guys. I'll wait to hear from you. Good luck with your Beehive group this week."

"Thanks. I'll be in touch later."

The Commander showed the Lieutenant out of her office and then headed back to the conference room.

With everybody seated at the table, the Commander stepped up to the podium. She took a few minutes to formally welcome everybody to the meeting.

"Now, before we start, I want each of you to study the faces of everybody in this room. You should memorize all names and faces by the time we break for lunch today. Any questions so far?"

One of the civilians raised his hand.

"Will there be a quiz?"

Muffled laughter filled the room.

"No, no quiz .... unless you want one."

She paused briefly and then continued.

"First of all, you ten people have been handpicked for an extremely sensitive .... high priority .... top secret assignment. Effective today, you are BCOM Team B26A. Your work assignment is Project Beehive. We will spend four days this week and three days next week learning what Beehive is and some of the details of your assignment. Normally, I would ask if any of you have any reservations or doubts you should speak up now. But I'm not going to do that. You're here and nobody's going home early. So let's not have any more silly remarks. You haven't been given an agenda for the next seven days because I reserve the right to change the schedule at any given time."

She stopped for a brief moment and looked around the room.

"I'm going to start out this morning with the reasons for Beehive. Sergeant Johnson will you switch off the lights please? I have some slides," she explained.

She spent the next hour reviewing the current situation in Vietnam. She began with the Vietminh victory over the French in the final battle at Dien Ben Phu in 1954 and finished with the current civil war between the North and the South. One of her last slides was an organization chart of the North's forces which included the Vietminh and the

Vietcong in the Mekong Delta and the PAVN juggernaut coming down from the 17th Parallel."

She gestured for Johnson to turn the lights back on.

"You are all experienced analysts working on Vietnam projects so you know the level of intel you've been providing NSA. No doubt you are all proud of the work you've been doing. Well, I am here today to tell you that the quantity and quality of your intel has been pitiful. I am also here today to tell you that it's not your incompetence that's in question. The military has not upgraded their Comint resources since the Korean War. Most of their sites are located in safe comfortable areas where intercept quality is poor. Their equipment is old and unreliable. In plain words they've gotten fat and lazy."

She continued, saying that all this needed to change, and quickly, if we were to have any chance of keeping the North from taking over the South. She said the NSA was in the process of changing to meet the new challenges in Southeast Asia as well as around the world.

"A year from now, practically all of our operations will be consolidated in a new facility at Fort Meade, Maryland. We're adding a considerable amount of new equipment and people, including a Cray XL1000 Super Computer in the second basement. I plan on giving you a tour of Fort Meade during this session if there is time. Any questions so far? Do you need a break?" she asked.

There was no response.

"Good. One thing I forgot to mention about Vietnam .... as of today, North Vietnam is way ahead of us in communications intelligence. They have sixty two intercept sites going as far South as the Mekong Delta. They have over two thousand linguists who speak and understand

English. Many of these are intercept operators at the sixty-two sites. They also have about five hundred cryptanalysts. So you can see how far behind we are. Right now, today, we have only twenty-four qualified linguists in Vietnam."

She stopped again and was hoping for questions.

"Commander, on the move to Fort Meade .... will Arlington Hall be shut down after the move?" one of the civilians asked.

"No, we'll keep Arlington open. In fact, we might actually keep part of BCOM here. I'm thinking about keeping B26A here. Anything else before I go on?"

No show of hands.

"OK then. What we're going to be doing in B26A is creating a new network of radio intercept assets in Vietnam .... not operated by the military, but by the NSA. We are having new intercept vans built with far superior equipment. We'll start with five vans operating in five regions. One region will be the coastline of North Vietnam. That will be a van placed on board a destroyer which will picket up and down the Gulf of Tonkin. Three will be in the area south of the 17th parallel. And one will be located in the heart of the Mekong Delta. This afternoon we'll talk more about these placements. Any questions?"

Once again, no show of hands.

"OK, I'll continue. The ten of you here today will be in command of the five regions with me as your chief. So you can see this will be a totally new operation, totally run by the NSA. The Director has given me a lot of freedom so far, but you can be certain he will be following Beehive very closely. He will be responsible for keeping the Joint Chiefs current and providing us with a list of customers in the intelligence community. Question?"

She spotted a hand.

"Commander Banta, I'm taking notes and I see a pile of handouts on the side table. Will we have vault space for our working papers?" one of the Naval Officers asked.

"Yes. When you leave today please stop by Petty Officer Davidson's desk. She'll show you the vault and assign each of you a shelf. Anything else?"

No questions. Everyone was too intrigued to let her stop for any more questions. They all wanted to hear more.

"OK then. You have just heard a part of the big picture. After lunch we're going to move to the auditorium where we have a demonstration van set up."

The rest of the day, the Beehive team spent going over the van prototype. They each had a chance to sit at the intercept positions and listen to recorded Vietnamese radio traffic. There were three voice positions and three Morse positions. Besides the radio positions, there was a KW6 encryption console, and a low frequency long range radio transmitter. There was also a Doppler radio beacon direction finder with ten meter resolution.

There was room in the van for six intercept operators, two linguists, a radio operator and an officer in charge .... ten people in all. The van also had a food locker, a refrigerator, and a double bunk. Even with that many people and that much equipment the van was not cramped. The van was heated and cooled by a heat pump. An electric generator was mounted on one end of the van which held enough diesel fuel to power the van for forty-eight hours.

They worked until six o'clock at which time the Commander dismissed them until eight the next morning.

Myles and Johnson were bushed as they headed out to the parking lot. It was already dark when they got to the car and it was getting cold.

"Well, is this anything like you expected? I watched you today and you were really concentrating. I could see you were impressed with everything, especially the van," Myles said.

"I was. I can't wait to find out just what our job is going to be. I could work in one of those vans if I had to. By the way, did you see the wall cabinet marked Emergency? Was that fire extinguishers?" Johnson asked.

"Yes, two fire extinguishers, plus a whole lot of guns and ammo. The vans will be located as near as possible to enemy positions .... maybe within a mile or two. But the main items will be explosives to destroy the van and everything in it, in case it is captured. I can tell you now, there will be people killed in these vans. This is going to be serious business."

Myles wasn't scaring Johnson. He just wanted to be truthful.

"Damn. To answer your question, no this isn't what I expected. I really just figured they would teach us some new encryption systems, and maybe some new traffic analysis methods. I am totally blown away by all this. Why do you think they picked us?" Johnson asked.

"I think we just have the right experience," Myles didn't have a good answer.

"Well, I guess you're right. How about stopping at that Hot Shoppe for supper on the way back to Suitland?"

"Let's do it," Myles agreed.

They had a great meal at the Hot Shoppe. Myles reminded Johnson that they each had two hundred dollars to spend. Johnson was beginning to enjoy his expense money. He had three Rolling Rocks.

Wednesday, December 12, 1956

Morning dawned cold and clear. It felt good to get to Arlington Hall and feel the warmth of the conference room. They both had plenty of Hot Shoppe coffee under their belts so they were revved up and ready to take on the day.

"Good morning everybody. You all sleep well? I hope you're adjusted to the time change. We've got another busy day. There's coffee on the back table. Help yourselves anytime you want. Will someone bring me a black coffee please?"

Johnson was the first one to the coffee pot and presented the Commander with her coffee.

"Thanks Sergeant. Today we'll talk about the five regions in more detail and then I'll announce your assignments. After that, things will start to fall in place. Tomorrow and Friday, we'll run through some scenarios as a training exercise. Over the weekend we'll catch a plane to Dallas to visit the factory where the vans are being built. Then on Monday and Tuesday we'll break into our five teams and develop our strategies and talk about where we'll get the people to staff the regions. Any questions before I begin?"

Myles raised his hand.

"Yes Lieutenant."

"You will probably cover this, but I'm wondering how many vans will be allocated to each region?"

"Thank you, Lieutenant. We will start with only one van in each region. They will be delivered in March to Tan Son Nhut Air Base in Saigon. Five more vans are under construction and they will be delivered in May or June. The actual schedule will depend on how well the startup goes. That answer your question?"

"Yes ma'am. Thank you," Myles acknowledged.

"One other bit of housekeeping before we get started. Next Wednesday everybody will get travel orders. Unless something changes, you'll all be leaving Andrews early Thursday morning."

She paused for a moment and sipped her coffee.

"So, thanks to Lieutenant Garrison's question, we now know that each region will start out with one van. So let's move on. Here are the placements of the first five vans. Sergeant Johnson, the lights please?"

In the darkened room she put up a slide showing a map of Vietnam.

"Here are the first placements."

She used a pointer to locate five colored flags. The first flag was in the Gulf of Tonkin.

"The destroyer USS Maddox will patrol the coast of North Vietnam with our van on board."

Then she moved her pointer in a circle encompassing the northern region of South Vietnam.

"Vans will be just south of the 17th Parallel on the East coast, the Central region, and the Laotian and Cambodian borders. The fifth van will be south of Saigon in the center of the Mekong Delta. All of these placements are very near enemy troop staging areas. We expect to be able to intercept ninety percent of their radio traffic. The Maddox will patrol within line of sight of seashore gun batteries and gunboat bases. The land based vans will be so close to the enemy you'll be able to smell them. All of them will be in serious harm's way."

She placed the pointer on the table and continued.

"Now, I have your assignments. You've been brought here in pairs for a reason. Each pair is being assigned to manage one of the five regions. Here's the breakdown."

The Commander continued by reading off the names of the five regions and the teams responsible. She placed the two Naval Officers in charge of the USS Maddox. Then she named the three civilian teams responsible for the three northern land based sites.

"And finally, in the South, Lieutenant Garrison and Sergeant Johnson will be responsible for Blue Cover which will place its first van right here in of the center of the Mekong Delta.. So that's the layout gentlemen. Any questions?"

Sergeant Johnson raised his hand.

"Yes," she said, as she turned in his direction.

"OK, each of the teams gets one van to start up their region. You showed us where these first vans will be located. When each team gets their second vans, how will they be placed?" the Sergeant asked.

"Tell you what. I'll tackle that question after lunch. So let's break for now."

After lunch the Commander stepped up before the group.

"First order of business is to address Sergeant Johnson's question about where the second wave of vans will be located. All I'm prepared to answer today is that they will be as close to the enemy as possible, in places where intercept quality is good. I wish there were more high spots in the Mekong Delta, Sergeant, but we'll see what we can do."

The rest of the day the Commander expanded her discussion to include additional details on the vans. A lot of questions came up on the exact timing of the first placements. There was also a lot of interest on security measures since the vans would be so close to enemy positions. Around five o'clock the Commander decided to break for the day.

"If there are no more questions let's call it a day and I'll see you in the morning. Don't forget to lock up your notes. Have a nice evening."

Everybody began shuffling their notes and getting ready to leave.

"Lieutenant Garrison will you please see me for a minute?" she asked.

Myles signaled for Johnson to wait for him.

"Myles, I want to invite you and Johnson to dinner at my apartment. If you accept, this will be off the record and a private matter between the three of us. Can you handle that? Of course, if you have other plans, I understand."

The Commander was trying to be discreet.

"Commander I can speak for Johnson. Thanks for inviting us. We'll look forward to it. Just tell me the time and place."

Myles realized how highly irregular this was. He couldn't imagine why she would be doing this. Singling the two of them out from the rest was a risky thing for her to do.

The Commander drew Myles a map and suggested they be there around seven o'clock, and dress comfortably.

Wednesday Evening

Back in the dorm, Myles asked Johnson to drop by his room.

"Well Johnson, guess we'll be high cotton tonight. Are you nervous?"

"You bet. Sure you can't say I got a headache and go by yourself?" Johnson pleaded.

"Hey, can you imagine me showing up alone on the Commander's doorstep? Sit down, I want to show you something and then we should be changing clothes. We don't have a lot of time."

Johnson plopped down on the single bunk. Myles handed him a yellow sheet of paper.

"This came in today. The Petty Officer gave it to me when we left the conference room. Take a look."

It read:

ZPTIJ LPDBM MFETI GJOFC BSOFZ QJTTF ETFOE FVB

"Well, boss, it looks like a simple encryption system but there's not enough characters to really tell. What is it?"

"You're pretty close. It is a simple substitution .... but with a slightly different twist. Roy Brent and I invented it for our personal use. We call it the Inflation code. You just substitute each letter with one letter higher in the alphabet. It is so simple I can read it by just looking at it. Here's what it says," Myles slowly read out.

YOSHIKO CALLED SHE FINE BARNEY PISSED SEND ETA

Johnson looked puzzled.

"What is this?"

"I want to share something very personal with you. Since we're going to be together most of the time from now on, you should know about this. Something might come up and I want you to be prepared. This is a really personal matter but I know I can trust you."

He paused and then continued.

"Brent knows about this and this message was meant to protect me."

"Myles, you can trust me a hundred percent," Johnson reassured him.

"Thanks. I know you mean it."

He felt good having Johnson as a friend. He went on to tell him the whole story of Yoshiko, right up to the message from Brent.

"Myles, I'm so happy for you. I can't wait to see this girl at the party. Are you getting into trouble? I mean, your security clearance, your job, and all that. How's this going to play out?"

"It's so simple really. We will just continue to date and have a good time. You'll be very impressed when you meet her. No, I'm not getting into trouble. After a while the magic will wear off and we'll break off the relationship. I think it'll all work out and no harm will be done. I just wanted you to know about this, just in case something does come up. Don't worry about it. Now let's leave for the Commander's place."

The apartment wasn't far from Suitland. Myles was surprised that the Commander would have picked such a location. From Suitland Hall, it was just a left turn down Suitland Parkway, then left at the Census building, over the Anacostia River Bridge, and then up Pennsylvania Avenue for a few blocks. It was a ten minute drive.

The front door was one step up from the sidewalk. It was between a liquor store and a delicatessen. Myles wondered why a Navy Commander would pick such a place to live. Maybe, he figured, she just likes fine wine and deli food.

Commander Banta greeted them at the door, dressed in tight jeans and a low cut T-shirt.

"Come on in guys. Any trouble finding this place?"

"No, not all." Myles replied. "In fact it was really a simple drive from Suitland. I like your neighborhood."

"Was that a tongue in cheek Myles? Don't be too quick to judge. This couldn't be better for me. I commute against the grain of traffic and I can get to Arlington in twenty minutes. Did you notice my liquor store and deli? Pretty convenient eh?"

"Yeah. I envy you. I see a nice living room, dining room, and kitchen. I'm guessing you've got two bedrooms in the back."

"You got it. This used to be a hardware store. I was lucky to find it. The rent is a lot lower than the fancy high rises in Arlington and Alexandria."

"How about a drink? I'll bet you never had dinner with a Navy Commander before. Right? Anyway, let's forget rank tonight. Please call me Sheila."

"Sheila .... thanks. I'll have whatever you're having. How about you Johnson?"

"Same for me thanks."

They sat with their drinks and exchanged small talk about life in Washington. After a few minutes Sheila excused herself into the kitchen. Myles watched her behind the counter as she stirred the spaghetti and shuffled dishes. Another time, another place .... he thought .... she sure looked cute in T-shirt and jeans.

"Hope you guys like spaghetti. It's my dad's recipe. Otherwise, I'm not too good a cook. Seems like I've always been too busy to learn."

"Well, it smells wonderful. Now I can connect your name, Banta, with Italy. I wasn't sure about that."

"Yes, you're right. I am a blonde Italian. Here let me serve your plates."

For the next thirty minutes, they ate spaghetti and drank Chianti. The conversation ranged from sports to music. Myles was surprised to find out how much the three of them had in common.

"Sheila, that was wonderful. I can tell you truthfully that was the best spaghetti I've ever had. How about you Johnson?"

"Man, I agree a hundred percent. Sheila that was great," Johnson wasn't quite sure about addressing a Commander by first name.

"I'm so glad you liked it. How about moving to the living room. I have some good Amaretto from next door. You guys up to it?"

Very shortly, she joined them at the sofa with a tray of drinks.

"Thanks. That looks good," Myles said.

Johnson hadn't said much during dinner. Being the enlisted man, he just didn't feel comfortable letting his hair down. He didn't feel as sophisticated as the other two, although he had one year at Harvard.

"Oh yeah, that looks great," Johnson added.

The three of them settled down on the sofa. Myles noticed she sat closer to him than to Johnson. In fact just a few inches more and her body might actually be touching his. As it was, the weight of her body caused the cushion to slope down between the two and Myles sensed gravity pulling them together.

"Sheila, please give our complements to your dad for his great spaghetti tutoring," Myles said.

"I will. You know I am the General's only daughter and he loves me so much. He worries that some bum might latch on to me for my Navy pay. He talks to me every week. If I ever get serious about anybody, I pity him. Anyway, there's nobody for him to worry about. I haven't had a real date in over a year."

"Well, Sheila, I think that is just a crying shame. Haven't you met any Admirals here in Washington?" Myles asked.

"Oh yes, but they are either married or have some kind of problem. Anyway, I'm not interested in Admirals. I think Lieutenants might be more exciting. Well, enough of that for now. I do have something I want to share with the both of you. I will be a little out of line as far as secrecy but this place is not bugged so I'm going to take some liberties. So, what I am going to say will be strictly between us. Is that OK?"

"Speaking for the both of us, let me say how nice this has been and how much we appreciate your inviting us. Yes, we will consider what you tell us as strictly confidential," Myles reassured her.

"Good. You're welcome for my invitation. The pleasure was all mine. Now, getting down to business. First, you both will stay at Shiroi until the your van is ready. After that, you will set up a command post in Saigon. Major Hickson will take care of your day to day needs while you're in Shiroi, but you will report directly to me. Is that what you've been expecting?"

"Pretty much, yes, I think so."

Myles looked at Johnson who nodded in agreement.

"Next, there is a question of rank. You are both seriously under ranked for your new jobs. The other four team leaders are two or three pay grades above you guys. The Air Force won't promote either of you because of your low time in grade. So here is what I'm going to do. For the time being you will keep your present ranks. But sometime in the next few months, maybe as soon as two months, I'm going to retire you both from the Air Force. Then I will get you into the NSA and permanently assigned to B26A. Will you go along with that?"

"Well, I guess so. I think we were both planning on an Air Force career? Right Johnson?" Myles glanced over at Johnson.

"Right Johnson?" he repeated.

"Oh, yeah, an Air Force career," Johnson finally replied.

"For you Johnson, I can get you a GS9. That's equal to an Air Force First Lieutenant. And you Myles, you will be a GS12. That would be an Air Force Major. Those ratings will pay the same and give you the same privileges as the Air Force ranks. I hope you're both happy with this. Now, for the rest of your time here you'll continue training as if nothing has changed."

"Well, Sheila, you've given us something to think about. Thanks again for everything. I'm thinking we should be getting back to Suitland. It's nearly nine o'clock."

"I see it's nine o'clock," she repeated. "It is getting late. Let's see, you've been here nearly two hours. Yes, it is getting late."

The Commander escorted them to the front door and walked with them to the car. She said good night and promised to see them in the morning.

Suitland Surprise

It was a short drive back to Suitland. Neither of them said much. There was some small talk about the dinner. They were both a little stunned over leaving the Air Force so suddenly. In the parking lot, Myles suggested Johnson come to his room for a few minutes to talk.

As they approached Myles' room, they saw his door standing wide open. Inside, all the contents of his closet and chest of drawers were strewn about the floor. The bed was turned upside down.

"What the hell is going on?" Myles shouted out. "Johnson, go see if your room is secure."

In a minute Johnson returned.

"My room's OK, Myles. Can you see if anything's missing?"

"I don't know. I'll have to look through my things. Here, help me with this."

Myles started handing clothes to Johnson.

"Just put these things back in the drawers. Then I'll be able to see if anything's missing. No, wait, instead go up front and report this to the Officer of the Day."

Johnson headed up the hall and Myles started hanging up his clothes. Ten minutes later Johnson returned .

"Myles. Lieutenant Jacobs said to inventory your stuff and fill out this report."

He handed Myles a form.

"OK. I've been through everything and nothing valuable is missing. The only things not here are some insignificant road maps and papers. Maybe this was just vandalism. I'm glad they didn't get into your stuff," Myles said.

"Yeah. Do you need any more help with things? Can I help you fill out that form? Can I help make up your bed?"

"No thanks. I can take over. Let's just call it a night. How about stopping by here around six-thirty in the morning. We'll get breakfast on the way to Arlington."

"Sounds good. If there's nothing I can do, I'll see you in the morning."

Rear Admiral Dufal is first American to land airplane at South Pole; Great Britain performs nuclear tests at Maralinga, Australia; Israel paratroops drop into Sinai to open Straits of Tiran; Concrete girder weighing 200 tons crashes killing 48 in Karachi, Pakistan; White Sox manager, Marty Marion, resigns; Celebrations continue into November following NY Yankees 4-3 World Series victory over Brooklyn Dodgers; American actress Bo Derek is born; American golfer Babe Zaharias dies; Gary Cooper and Anthony Perkins star in "Friendly Persuasion"; Kaye Starr records "The Rock and Roll Waltz".

Chapter Six

Arlington

Thursday, December 13, 1956

Johnson stopped by Myles' open door shortly after six-thirty.

"Morning Myles, how'd you sleep after the burglary?"

"I slept fine considering, what happened. You hungry this morning?"

Johnson thought for a moment.

"No, not really. I ate a ton of spaghetti last night. I could do with some coffee though."

"Me too. Let's drive on into Arlington. We can get coffee in the conference room," Myles suggested. "I need to drop this report off at the OD's desk."

"Sounds good to me. Did you find anything else missing? You said last night there were some maps and papers and that was it."

"That was all there was. I do need to turn in this form though. How about warming up the car? I'll be right behind you."

Myles handed Johnson the car keys.

Johnson did the driving and managed to make only one wrong turn.

Eight o'clock sharp and Commander Banta opened the day's business. She was in the process of explaining the agenda when the conference room phone rang.

"Excuse me," she said, as she went to the small table in the corner of the room and picked up the receiver.

She listened intently for a few minutes and then went into a series of "Yes, sirs" and "No, sirs." Then she returned to the podium.

"The Director has made the President, the CIA, and the Pentagon aware of our session this week. He's asked that I interrupt our schedule so I can make a presentation on Beehive in the Oval Office next Tuesday. CIA, Defense, and the Joint Chiefs will be there. Anyway, I am changing our plans to accommodate them. We'll break in a little while so I can take care of some things. I'm going to cancel our trip to Texas this weekend. Instead, we'll move up Monday's and Tuesday's sessions to Saturday and Sunday. That means we'll wrap up early on Monday. I'll have new orders cut so you can fly out of Andrews on Tuesday morning. That won't leave me much time to get ready for the big show, but that's my problem. Any questions?" she asked.

One of the Naval officers raised his hand.

"Commander, is there anything we can do to help you get ready?"

"Thanks but I don't think so. One thing you'll need to do is inform your units that you'll be back two days early. Sometime today I'll give you time to write messages. On second thought, take some time right now. I need to step over to my office."

She hurried out of the room, leaving the group shuffling papers and writing messages. Johnson went to the coffee bar in the back of the room and brought two coffees up to where he and Myles were sitting.

"It looks like we'll be getting home a little early," Myles said. "Sit with me while I draft a message to Major Hickson. You can check to see if I leave anything out. I figure we might get back to Shiroi on Thursday. Remember we have to tack on a day when we cross back over the dateline."

The two men sat together and Myles placed a yellow note pad where Johnson could easily see it. He began to write.

To: Major Hickson, 21st Radio Group, Shiroi.

We return Shiroi estimate Thursday. In office Friday. Please pass message to Lieutenant Brent.

From: Garrison

"Think that covers it?" Myles asked.

"Yeah, that's good. Short, but sweet. Why notify Brent?"

"So he knows we'll be back for the party. He might be counting up the attendance."

In a little while, the Commander returned. She asked Johnson to collect the messages and give them to Petty Officer Davidson to deliver to the message center.

The rest of the day and Friday, the group worked on exercises using recorded North Vietnamese radio traffic. Each two man team was furnished with several hundred translated messages and a list of coordinates identifying radio transmitter locations. Myles' and Johnson's logs contained intercepts from Vietnamese ground forces along the Ho Chi Minh trail and along the Laos and Cambodian borders. They found the work much harder than what they were accustomed to but they did pretty well, enough in fact for a pat on the back from Commander Banta.

Saturday, December 15, 1956

Saturday morning there were more exercises and each team presented their results to the rest of the group. In the afternoon there was a guest speaker from the Pentagon and a visit to the small arms shooting range in the basement. They practiced firing M16s and Colt .45s until their ears were ringing and their shoulders were hurting. A team of Army Green Berets stopped in and made a presentation on escape and evasion. In the question and answer period, Commander Banta gave the group most of the information she had passed on to Myles and Johnson at the spaghetti supper.

Around four o'clock Saturday afternoon, Commander Banta suggested they take an exercise break and return at four-thirty. Myles urged Johnson to accompany him on twenty laps up and down the main hallway. On the last lap they met the Commander coming out of her office.

"Oh, Lieutenant Garrison may I see you in my office for a minute?"

"Sure thing. I'll see you back in the room," he told Johnson, as he followed the Commander into her office.

"Myles, yesterday I got a report that your room was broken into. It said the only things missing were some maps and papers. There were no specifics. I need to know a little more about what those papers were. I have to make out a follow up report. I know it's a pain but please help me out."

"Sure Commander. There were two road maps .... one of Washington and one of Maryland. I really don't need them anyway. I know my way around pretty well. The papers were my travel orders from Shiroi to Andrews, a receipt for my pay, two letters from my parents, two crossword puzzles from the Stars and Stripes and, let me see, I guess that was it."

"OK. You're sure that was all there was?" the Commander asked.

"That was it. Just a bunch of junk .... nothing I can't do without." Myles answered. He wondered why this was so important. He intentionally didn't include the message he'd gotten from Brent. He figured it was irrelevant and none of anybody's business.

The Commander frowned and handed Myles a Manila folder. "Did you forget about this? This among the papers taken from your room. Go ahead and look."

Myles immediately recognized the sheet of yellow paper. It was the encrypted message from Brent.

"Oh, damn, I forgot about this. It's really nothing. How'd you come to get it?"

"How I got it is of no consequence. Here are the rest of your things."

The Commander handed him a folded up stack of maps and papers bound with a rubber band.

"Myles, we're good friends and I'm sure there's a good explanation for skipping over that encrypted message from Shiroi. Want to talk about it?"

"Sure! I just forgot about it. It was just a note from somebody back there in the office. It was nothing, really. It's encrypted in a simple system I worked up. I assure you it was just a personal note."

Myles was beginning to get a little nervous. He wasn't sure what was going on but he did not want the Commander knowing anything about Yoshiko.

"Myles, if it is just a personal note, how about telling me who it was from and what it said. I had my people take a look at it and they couldn't break the encryption. I really doubt it's just a simple personal system. What's the big deal here?"

"Commander, I am entitled to a personal letter. That's all it is. And the system .... it's just what I said. I'm not surprised your people couldn't break the system. There were only twelve groups. I don't think anybody can break a stand alone twelve group encryption .... at least not in two days. If I tell you it was Lieutenant Brent, won't that be enough?"

"No, we do need to know what kind of secrets you and Lieutenant Brent have. There are security issues that could come into play. Are you and Brent homosexuals? Are you and Brent involved in some kind of spying activities? These are just two possibilities. This is really crazy but I do need to know. Please tell me what this is all about. Now that I know it was Brent's message I'll have somebody question him in the next hour."

Myles decided to keep Yoshiko a secret ..... at least for the time being. He was gambling that Brent would protect the secret if he were questioned. This is incredibly stupid, he thought, and all over something as innocent as a girlfriend and a note from a friend.

"Commander, after I get back to Shiroi and have a chance to talk to Lieutenant Brent, I'll tell you what it's all about. It's neither of those two things you mentioned. It's all totally innocent. So, I guess, I'll just have say I'll tell you later."

"Damn it, Myles. Just tell me and then everything will be back to normal. If you don't .... well, I just don't know. Is your answer, then .... you won't talk?"

"My answer, Commander, is there is nothing to worry about and I'll talk to you next week," Myles answered in a trembling voice.

"Fine. I'm really uncomfortable with this. I guess I have only two choices. One is to assume the worst and lock you up and wait until we have a chance to speak with Lieutenant Brent. What happens after that will depend on what the Lieutenant tells us. The other choice is simply to carry on as usual until the truth .... whatever that is .... comes out. What do you suggest?"

"Commander, I say let me go back to my Beehive training and put everything on hold until you talk with Brent or until I get back to Shiroi. I promise you that everything is OK. It's just a personal matter ..... I'd like to keep it personal for a little while. Can you go along with that?"

"Myles, you are certainly convincing. I'll go along with what you said. Just go back into the conference room. Promise me, though, won't send anymore messages and won't mention a word of this to Johnson or anybody else in the group."

"Yes, ma'am. Thanks for your vote of confidence."

Myles was relieved beyond description.

It was nearly six o'clock when the Commander called the group back to order. She clasped the sides of the podium like it was going to fly away. She tried to act normal.

"Since it's so late on a Saturday, I'm going to call it a day. You've had a busy day and I hope you've learned a lot. You might need to rub liniment on your shoulders after your encounter with the M16. The coach said each of you fired over two thousand rounds without shooting each other. Good work. So, if there are no questions, I'll see you in the morning. I'm sorry you're going to miss Sunday Mass."

The Commander dismissed the group.

Myles and Johnson had a quiet Saturday night. Myles was brain numbed after his session with the Commander and didn't feel like talking much. Johnson sensed something was wrong but didn't ask any questions. They had dinner at their favorite Hot Shoppe and went to bed early.

Sunday passed with more exercises and guest speakers. The teams spent more time in the van mock ups and learned how to operate the new direction finding equipment. A technical representative from Collins Radio taught them how to operate the low frequency radio transmitter. Once the vans were operational, the transmitters would be used to communicate over the NSA Criticom radio network. Criticom was set up to instantaneously communicate with NSA, the Joint Chiefs and the White House in case of dire emergency.

By the end of the day, the teams had become totally familiar with the van and it's equipment. The Commander dismissed the group early and promised a very short Monday session.

On the way back to Suitland, Myles stopped at a downtown jewelry store and bought a sterling necklace studded with turquoise carvings. Jewelry wasn't Myles forte, but he and Johnson were both impressed with the piece. It would be his homecoming present for Yoshiko. Turquoise wasn't seen much in Japan, and sort of represented the American Southwest. He was pleased and hoped Yoshiko would likewise be pleased.

Around noon on Monday, Commander Banta thanked the group for coming to her meeting and taking on the challenges laid before them. She told them how important Beehive was and how many millions of lives could be saved by the work of this small group of dedicated people. She said that when they meet a year from now, maybe in Saigon or Manila, there might be some missing faces.

"So, that's it for this time. I'll be leaving now. I've still got lots of work to do getting ready for tomorrow. I'll tell President Eisenhower hello for all of you."

She quickly scooped up her papers and walked past Myles' side of the table as she headed for the door. She put her hand on his shoulder as she brushed past him.

Myles and Johnson had their last travel money dinner and went to bed early. At six o'clock the next morning they checked out of Suitland Hall and drove to Andrews. Myles left the car at the curb where he'd picked it up. He flagged down an Air Policeman and gave him the keys. Within an hour, they were on a plane headed to San Francisco for the first leg of their return trip to Japan.

Back at Shiroi

Major Hickson got Myles' message first thing Monday morning and passed the information to Sergeant Barney and most of the crew. He made sure Brent saw the message.

Tuesday, December 18, 1956

The next morning, Brent realized that he really hadn't gotten the details about the party out to all the folks. They knew about it in general terms and had the date fixed on their calendars, but there was more information they needed to know. He thought he'd send out a memo.

21st RADIO CHRISTMAS PARTY

Saturday, December 22, 1956 Ryoko Hotel, Shinjuku, Tokyo

Our first annual Christmas Party (Dance) will be held as above. Here is the plan.

At nine o'clock Saturday morning a special base bus will depart from the Officers Club. Everyone should bring overnight luggage. Dress is casual. The bus will arrive at the Ryoko Hotel in Shinjuku around noon.

A block of rooms will be reserved for us. Each room will have either a double bed or two single beds and a bath. All accommodations will be Western style, including the toilets. The cost for each room is ten dollars for Saturday night. The party starts at six-thirty in the main ballroom on the fifth floor. From the arrival time to party time, everybody will be on their own to shop, sightsee, or whatever suits you. Shinjuku is close

to department stores, shops, restaurants, bars, and night clubs.

If you get lost or need help, the American Embassy is located in Akasaka next door to the Zen Nikku Hotel. Any cabbie will know where it is.

Dress for the party will be black tie. There will be cocktails from six-thirty until seven, followed by a four course dinner, and dancing until midnight. We have reserved a Japanese Glen Miller style orchestra.

At eight o'clock the next morning, there will be a full breakfast buffet in the ball room. Checkout is ten o'clock and the bus will depart shortly thereafter.

There will be an open bar during the cocktail hour and from then on until midnight. There will be Western whiskey, vodka, gin, wine, beer, and cold sake. Around eleven o'clock, the kitchen will set up a small midnight breakfast buffet near the bar with Irish Coffee.

The hotel is owned and operated by the Irobi family who are very good friends of mine. Let's all have a great time. One last thing. The Irobi's have been very generous with the contract for the party. If you happen to meet Mr. or Mrs. Irobi or any of their three daughters, please thank them in the most gracious manner.

Now, this is the part I wish I didn't have to tell. I will need to collect a ten dollar per person cover charge for the party.

I will be not be on the bus Saturday morning, since I need to be at the hotel the night before. So, I will very tactfully collect the cover charge sometime during the evening. Thanks.

Lieutenant Roy Brent.

Brent read his missive over a few times and felt he covered everything pretty well. He planned on passing out copies on Wednesday. He was pleased that there will be a one hundred percent attendance. Based on early feedback, it sounded like most of the guys were bringing dates. Some might even latch onto some of the American school teachers and nurses. Peggy Hickson and Ruby Barney will be the only two wives attending.

Thursday in Ikebukuro

Yoshiko woke earlier than usual. She was eager to finish her last day at Mitsukoshi and then have Friday off to do some last minute shopping before the party. She was hoping Myles would somehow manage to get to Ikebukuro early Friday night.

One thing puzzled her though, what would she do about an evening gown for the party? A kimono was definitely out after talking about it with Myles. Someday she would wear kimono for Myles, but not this time to an American Christmas Party. But she certainly didn't have an evening gown. The Mitsukoshi wasn't able to loan her a gown as she had hoped.

Around noon, an idea popped in her head. Kazuko at the Seibu was a good friend. Would she possibly loan her one of the store's gowns? She would call her in the morning to confirm Saturday's work and then pop the question about the gown.

That would work out fine, she thought. Saturday afternoon after work, she could dress at Seibu and be ready to go straight to the party. Myles could hang around in Tokyo while she was working and then dress in his rented

Mitsukoshi tuxedo at Seibu. To make it easy for Kazuko, she would promise to return the gown on Sunday.

That night she brought in supper for O-basan and herself from the noodle shop.

Friday, December 21, 1954

Around nine the next morning, Yoshiko was on the phone with Kazuko at the Seibu.

(In Japanese)

"Kazuko-san, this is Yoshiko. Thank you for scheduling me for work on Saturday. Can you tell me what the work is? The agency told me it will be a special day."

"I'm always happy to have you here. On Saturday, we have the Officers' wives from Camp Zama for a showing of Spring clothes. We're expecting about twenty or a few more."

"I hope many will come. Spring clothes sounds like lot of fun."

"I'm sure it will be. The color for Spring is pink and the clothes are really exciting. You will be excellent for this line of clothes. The show will go from ten o'clock until one o'clock."

"I'm already looking forward to it. Now, may ask you a personal favor?"

"Sure, what can I do for you?"

"Well, my friend Myles whom you met a couple of weeks ago has invited me to a Christmas Dance at the Ryoko Hotel in Shinjuku Saturday night. It will be a formal party with tuxedos and evening gowns, All people will be Americans from Myles' Air Force. My problem is I don't have proper evening gown and that is my favor."

"Yoshiko, I know what you're going to ask. You know our policy is not to lend out clothes to our models like the Mitsukoshi stores sometimes do."

"Yes, I know but I thought this could be an exception."

"Tell you what. I will make an exception just for you. In fact, now that I think about it, I have an idea."

"Oh, that be fantastic. What your idea?"

"Well, we have a new line of evening gowns that we haven't brought out yet. I'm thinking that after the fashion show, we could set up a special photo shoot for the girls to model the new gowns. Then I could make a special section in the papers in a couple of weeks and also make a special section in our next catalog in January."

"Kazuko-san, thank you for making exception for me. I can return gown for sure on Sunday."

"That sounds great. We'll do the photo shoot and finish up maybe about five o'clock. By then you will have picked out your favorite gown to borrow. What time does your dance begin?"

"Time is six-thirty."

"Great, that will work out just fine. Between five and six we can do your hair and dress you out properly. We can make you beautiful so Myles can be proud of you. After you're dressed and ready, you and Myles can take a taxi to the Ryoko. By the way, I know that hotel very well. The Irobi family are friends of mine and they run a first class hotel. So you will be an advertisement for our clothes as well as you having a good time. We'll loan you shoes and a coat to go with the gown you select."

"Oh, Kazuko-san, how can I ever thank you. I look forward to Saturday so much."

"You are definitely worth such a favor Yoshiko. I will see you around nine-thirty Saturday morning. OK?"

"OK, see you Saturday."

Yoshiko hung up and could hardly contain herself. She wished she could pick up the phone right now and call Myles.

Back at Shiroi

Meanwhile, Brent was pleased with the response to his memo. Even though he didn't expect it, every last one of the guys had paid him their cover charge. Some had said they hadn't gotten their dates yet but were working on it.

Wake Island

Around the same time, Myles and Johnson were about to land at Wake Island before taking off on their last leg back to Tachikawa.

By now, they had both set their watches to Tokyo time and were mentally getting accustomed to the time change. As they neared Wake, Myles looked to Johnson.

"Well, ole pal, it is now one day later. So you see, we're paying back the day we borrowed on the way over."

For the last time, they had a couple of drinks and napped on the flight from Wake to Tachikawa.

The flight was scheduled to arrive at six o'clock Thursday evening.

Friday, December 21, 1956

Tired as hell and groggy from the time zone change, Myles and Johnson rolled into the office a little past eight o'clock.

"Well, welcome back. How's the world travelers?"

Brent was the first to spot them and called out their entrance.

"How was the trip? Glad to be back?" he added.

"Well, I don't recommend anyone do this on a regular basis, at least until we get passenger jets," Myles commented.

"And Sergeant Johnson, how'd you do back there with all the big brass?"

"Oh, no sweat. Wish you guys could have seen me sitting at the conference table with all the big wigs. They even asked my opinion on a few things," he said, grinning from ear to ear.

Manahan piped in.

"Well, now it's back down to earth. Myles, Davison has been asking about you, right Bob?"

"I was just looking forward to showing him what I've been doing on China the past two weeks," Davison spoke up.

"Bob, I can't wait to see your work. Roy, thanks for your message."

It suddenly occurred to Myles .... better shut up about that message.

"Well, Johnson, let's stop in to see Major Hickson and Sergeant Barney just to let them know we're back."

With that, the pair turned and walked up to the Major's closed door. Myles knocked and leaned against the wall beside the door. He was really tired. Johnson stood more or less erect but not without a lot of effort.

"Enter," came the invitation from inside.

"Sit down .... here by my desk."

Conveniently, there were two straight back chairs just in front of the Major's desk.

"Thanks. We're sure glad to be back home. It was an outstanding visit with Commander Banta and the folks at Arlington. But the travel, oh my gosh, it's a tough trip Major," Myles said.

"Tell me about it. I've done it a bunch of times and it doesn't get any easier. One good thing though, we should start flying the new Boeing passenger jets by the middle of next year. That's good news isn't it?"

"Man, that's great news. Johnson and I might be doing a little flying in our new jobs. Would you like us to debrief everything we've learned?"

"No need right now. I've had a complete report from Commander Banta. I know pretty much all about B26A and Operation Beehive. I know you two will be in charge of the Saigon area near the Cambodian and Laotian borders. So get yourselves caught up here in the office. If you've got anything to do on the base today, take any time off you need. Get rested up tonight. You know we got Brent's big bash tomorrow night. Myles, you know Peggy, she's about to drive me nuts. She busted my paycheck buying a new dress and shoes."

The Major snatched a paper from his IN TRAY and handed it to Myles.

"Here's all the details on the party. Do you have dates yet? I don't see how you could, being away this long. Oh, wait, you're bringing a Japanese girl, aren't you Myles?"

"Well, sir, actually I am. Too bad for Johnson though. He didn't get word soon enough so he's out of luck. He'll have to dance with the other dates. I'll volunteer to let him have one dance with my date."

"Oh, thanks Myles, you didn't tell me that," Johnson answered back.

"Well, I'm on record. You have one dance with my date, but I'll be watching you. Major, I officially submit my request for a dance with Peggy."

"Myles, you'll have to see her about that. She's the boss in the family you know. Anyway, I'm glad you already have a date arranged."

"Yes, but I'm mainly just looking forward to the party. And from this, I see there's going to be a four course dinner. I'm looking forward to that. I know my friend Sergeant Johnson here won't mind a good meal. Knowing Roy, it should be real special with wine and all."

"Good, it should be great fun. You guys just do what you need to do today. If you need me, just drop in, otherwise I'll see you both tomorrow morning on the bus. One last thing .... Myles can you stay for a minute?"

Myles ushered Johnson out of the office and then went back inside.

"Myles, do you remember the secret papers I showed you before you left?"

"Yes sir. I've kept it to myself."

"Good! There's a lot more to it now. We need to talk on Monday. It's some scary business. That's all for now. I'll see you on the bus in the morning."

The bus .... the bus .... thought Myles. He was planning on going to Ikebukuro tonight and then showing up with Yoshiko at the party tomorrow night. He wouldn't be on the bus in the morning. Guess he'd better let Roy know so he can take his name off the bus list. He also needed to have a good answer tomorrow night when Major Hickson and the others ask him where he'd been all day.

Meanwhile, thinking of Ikebukuro triggered some wonderful thoughts about Yoshiko. He couldn't wait to see her tonight and give her a big hug and kiss. Better not forget to bring her present.

"Davison, I'm looking forward to seeing how you've done while I've been gone. Can it wait until Monday? I'm really wiped out and I need get to the cleaners and the bank. You ready for tomorrow? Do you have a date?"

"Sure, we'll talk Monday. I do have a date and you won't believe it. I'm bringing Fumiko from the Opal."

"Hey, that's great. She should be a lot of fun. You going to share a room?" Myles asked.

"Of course. You think that will be a problem with the old man?"

"Don't worry about it. Just have a good time."

Myles couldn't get over the change in Davison. Maybe it was that little talk they had before he left. He might actually get to be a friend.

"Myles, do you have a date?"

"Oh yeah, not a big deal though. Actually, you already met her at the Opal a few weeks ago. Do you remember?"

"Remember, how could I forget. That's a real babe, Myles. I can't wait to see her again."

"That'll be fine. Just promise to behave yourself around her. OK?"

"My solemn promise, Myles, but only if I get one dance."

"OK, deal. I've got a few things to do at my desk now. We'll talk business on Monday. I'll see you at the party."

Myles stopped over at Johnson's desk.

"How do you think it went with the Major?" Myles asked.

"I think he was fine. He doesn't know about us skipping out on the Air Force and becoming NSA spooks, right?" Johnson replied.

"Well, Commander Banta said not to tell so I assume he'll find out about it in due time. My guess, it might even be a month or two when the first vans are ready. I think for him all he needs to know is that we are staying here as is, but we will be working on Beehive. Let's just keep it at that. And hey, I'm real sorry about no date for you. I'll make it up somehow."

"No problem. We'll just not mention the Air Force thing to anybody," Johnson said.

"Good. I'm leaving in a little bit to run some errands on base. That means I won't see you until the party tomorrow night. I'll be in Ikebukuro tonight so I won't be on the bus in the morning."

"OK. Take care of yourself Myles."

"Will do. See you tomorrow."

On the way out, Myles reminded Brent he wouldn't be on the bus in the morning. Brent amended his list.

"OK, no bus. I'll be leaving soon for Tokyo. Got to be at the Ryoko tonight to see about things so I'll see you tomorrow about six-thirty. Right?" Brent said.

"Right."

Myles finished up early and after a quick visit to the cleaners and the Credit Union left for Ikebukuro.

Post-War Germany forms own Army; Thirty die in Los Angeles train crash; Dow Jones closes above 500 for first time; Pakistan proclaimed Islamic Republic; "As the World Turns" premiers on TV; 156 day strike against Westinghouse ends; "King Kong" first televised; Red Buttons debuts on TV in Studio One performance; Clashes in Nigeria kill 380; "My Fair Lady" opens at Mark Hellinger Theatre to begin string of 2715 consecutive performances; "Hot Diggity" by Perry Como high on charts; "Around the World in Eighty Days" wins five Oscars.

Chapter Seven

Party Day

Friday Evening, December 21, 1956

It was already dark when Myles walked up the gravel road into the neighborhood. As he turned left at the corner he noticed the lights on in the second floor corner apartment. He was carrying his overnight bag for Saturday night.

As he stepped through the front door, he heard Yoshiko and O-basan talking in the manager's quarters. They were laughing and joking about something. He went over to O-basan's door and slid it open. The two of them were working over a hot plate in the corner of the great room.

"Yoshiko-san," he called out.

"Mai, Mai," she called back, and charged across the room in her bare feet nearly slipping on the woven straw floor.

Without saying anything, she flung her arms around him and starting kissing him all around his face and neck. He held her tightly, not letting go.

"Yoshiko-san, I missed you very much. I am so happy to be home."

"Mai, I miss you very much."

She kept on kissing him.

"Mai, please put bag upstairs and come down here. O-basan is cook sukiyaki so we eat some here tonight. OK?"

She gave him a little push toward the stairway.

"Yes, I'll go upstairs and come right back."

Wow, he thought, what a greeting and what a surprise. Home cooked sukiyaki ..... can't beat that. In the room, he put his bag in the corner and pulled out the gift wrapped present. He placed it in the center of the bed.

Back downstairs, they sat on O-basan's floor eating sukiyaki and sipping green tea. Yoshiko had done just fine living alone in the apartment. She'd worked a lot, mainly at Mitsukoshi, but at Seibu two times. She'd picked up their pictures at Uncle Masuda's shop and discovered three new restaurants within walking distance of the neighborhood. The loneliest time was the weekend when there was no work and not too much to do. In her travels around the neighborhood, she made a lot of new friends in the local shops.

After they finished, Myles was anxious to get upstairs and give Yoshiko her present.

"Well, look Yoshiko, what is that there on the bed?" he tried to sound surprised.

"Oh, Mai, that for me?"

"Of course, a little something from America. Open it now."

She tore open the package and pulled out the silver and turquoise necklace. She held it up to her chest.

"Oh, Mai, it beautiful. It turquoise from American Indians, right?"

"Yes it is. Let me help put it on."

He placed the chain around her neck and fixed the clasp. Then he turned her around and moved back a step or two.

"Wow, that looks really nice," he said.

"Mai, we should dress in our robes, don't you think, then we should look at pictures."

They changed into their silk robes and jumped on the bed. They didn't bother to look at pictures. They made love until midnight and finally Yoshiko rolled over and got the package of pictures from the side table. They settled back against the headboard with the pictures in Yoshiko's lap.

"Now before we do anything and fall asleep Yoshiko, I need to tell you about the plan for tomorrow and the party."

"Ok, Mai, then I tell my plan too."

It took fifteen minutes or so but Myles was able to explain the gist of what would be going on tomorrow night. He explained why they would need to spend the night at the hotel and not come home to the apartment. She got it all, he thought, at least enough to get things started off right.

"Now, Yoshiko, what is your plan?"

She proceeded to tell him about her show at Seibu tomorrow and how he would need to spend the day alone. She suggested he come to Tokyo with her and then hang out at the club or something. He would need to pick up his tuxedo at Mitsukoshi in the morning before they left. She finished by telling him how Kazuko was going to dress her in a fine Seibu evening gown for the party.

"Yoshiko, what a fine plan. Kazuko is a good friend. Now we can look at the pictures and then we should sleep. I think we need to get up early in the morning. We will set the alarm."

"OK, we look at pictures then go to sleep."

They slept soundly until the alarm sounded at eight o'clock.

Saturday, December 22, 1956

Myles came back from down the hall and a wonderful smell of fresh brewed coffee greeted him as he approached the door.

"Mai, I have surprise. We have coffee. I make in new coffee pot."

"Wonderful! Is it ready?"

"Yes, please sit here on bed."

He took a seat on the edge of the bed and very shortly Yoshiko served him a hot steaming cup of coffee. He took a sip of the hot black liquid. It actually wasn't bad. A little strong maybe, but pretty good and it was just what he needed.

"Yoshiko have some coffee?"

"I try."

She poured a cup for herself.

"No, no, I cannot drink. It too strong taste. I make tea."

"Next time, Yoshiko, let's have some milk with my coffee please. It makes it better and I also would like some sugar ...... maybe some cubes. I thank you very much just the same."

It had been winter for two days now and the weather was cold enough so that things in the little window kitchen stayed cool enough not to spoil.

"Yes, I have some milk and sugar for coffee. More please?"

"Well, yes thank you."

How could he refuse? She'd gone to a lot of trouble for him. He imagined her figuring out the coffee pot …. how much coffee …. how much water. It was worth the ten dollars to have morning coffee.

They finished coffee and tea and dressed for the trip to Tokyo. It only took another ten minutes or so and they were packed and ready to go. Myles stuffed the package of pictures in the side of his bag. He thought he might have some free time to look at them before the party.

"You about ready?" he asked.

"Yes. We go now."

She was wearing the same pink suit she wore on the day they met at Victoria. A flood of memories swept over his brain. Man, oh, man, what we haven't done in the six weeks since we first met, he thought. Images flashed through his mind …….. the string on the button, the Ginza walk, the camera shop, Sushi Oki, the Officers Club, the chance meeting of Brent and Manahan, the apartment, the new bed, the Nikon, …….. it had been a wonderful time. Then he remembered *Ladybug* who had been with them since that very first day.

Myles carried their two bags with the Nikon over his shoulder up the gravel road in the direction of the main street and Mitsukoshi. They saw O-basan on the way out and Myles thanked her profusely for the excellent sukiyaki last night. She put her broom aside and bowed so deeply she nearly lost her balance.

In Mitsukoshi, she took Myles to the men's department where he got his tuxedo. He asked if he needed to try it on, but she said no need. The tailor was so good it would be perfect. In the tea room they had steamed rice and cookies for breakfast.

"You like rice for breakfast food, Mai. Not American breakfast food, right?"

"I like it very much."

Actually he liked bacon and eggs better, but for today rice and cookies would be fine.

They finished, gathered up their bags, and headed over to the train station. There was a gray overcast sky and it was getting colder.

"Yoshiko-san."

"Yes, Mai?"

"This is a special day so we will take a taxi. Stop here and I'll hail one down."

"Oh, thank you Mai."

The ride to Seibu took about ten minutes, a lot faster than the train and a lot less fuss. By the time they arrived it was nearly ten o'clock. A chance of snow was predicted for the day. They had talked about that over breakfast and agreed that snow would be wonderful for the party.

Seibu was crowded as they walked past the food section and stepped on the escalator. Up on the fashion floor, Kazuko was chatting with some American officers' wives.

Kazuko spotted them right away and came over to greet them. She reached out and took Yoshiko's hat box.

"Myles, thanks for bringing Yoshiko on time this morning. You can go now and return around six o'clock."

Wow, though Myles, I thought she liked me. That didn't seem like too warm a greeting.

"Yes ma'am .... and........"

Kazuko noticed the surprise on Myles face as she gave him his instructions.

"Myles, I am so sorry for being abrupt. You see it is very busy here right now."

"Oh, that's all right ma'am. I understand perfectly. Yoshiko told me what you're doing for her tonight. Thank you very much. I will make sure your clothes are returned in good shape tomorrow."

"Great. Yes, we are going to give you a beautiful girl to take to your American party. You will be so proud of her. Now ....., seriously, you may go now if you wish."

"Yes, ma'am, and thanks again for everything. Sayonara."

He looked past Kazuko as Yoshiko was being pulled away by another girl.

"Sayonara, Mai," Yoshiko called back as she disappeared into a side doorway.

Myles took his bag, the tuxedo package, and the Nikon and rode the escalator back to the ground floor. He stopped and started to browse around in the food section. Everything looked so wonderful and delicious. Well, not everything! The worst thing he spotted was a tub of pickled eels. The beautiful little pastries more than compensated for the eels though, so much in fact that be bought a little package of petit fours. He was so hungry after that skimpy bowl of rice that he opened the package and ate them all on the spot. The little clerk's eyes opened as wide as quarters and she gasped a little. Crazy American, she thought, he ate them before he got his change.

He hadn't really thought through his plan for the day up to six o'clock. He thought about the Opal which was just around the corner. And then there's Morita-san's tailor shop and the Victoria Coffee House. Or maybe Uncle Masuda's camera store just to say hello and thank him for the bed. That's what he would do. So he started out on the four block walk down the Ginza.

He and Uncle Masuda had a fine visit. Myles thanked him profusely for looking out for Yoshiko during his absence and the wonderful birthday presents he'd given her. Around noon, Myles said goodbye, thanking him once again on his way out of the store.

His next stop was the Officers Club.

After checking his things, he went into the bar and ordered a Bloody Mary. He needed a little time to think through his strategy for the rest of the day. He had about five hours to kill.

Officers Club

The Bloody Mary must have helped, for it was clear now on just what he should do. Brent was already at the Ryoko getting things set up, and the bus was due around one or one-thirty. So, the thing to do was go to the hotel and check in early to get rid of his bag and the tuxedo package. Then he'd look for Brent to see how he could help. That was it. That was the plan.

The Ryoko Hotel looked more European than Japanese. It was set back from the street with a walkway covered by a royal blue awning. The hotel coat of arms was emblazoned on each of the two front doors. A doorman in a long blue coat and top hat held the door for Myles.

The lobby was small for a forty room hotel, but there was a cozy bar in one corner with four stools and three small tables.

"Hello, I am Myles Garrison with the Air Force party. I'd like to check in early please if possible."

The desk clerk might have been one of the family, he didn't know, but she was certainly cute and polite. She was decked out in a classic hotel uniform, a dark blue suit with gold piping and the coat of arms over the left jacket pocket. To top it off, she wore a cute little pill box hat, once again with the coat of arms.

"Certainly sir, will you be wanting one double bed or two singles?"

Her English was impeccable.

"I would like one double bed please and could you make it on the fourth floor? The ball room is on the fifth floor isn't it?"

"Yes, sir, and also the restaurant."

She slid the register over to him.

Myles finished signing the register and got directions to his room on the fourth floor.

By Western standards, it was a small hotel room. Just the same, there was plenty of room to get around the double bed, and there was a small table by the window. There was no television, only a small radio on the bedside table. The bathroom featured a tiny bathtub, the kind you double up your legs in, and a lavatory. The usual basket of amenities was there, toothbrushes, toothpaste, soaps, shampoos, and lotions. All in all, it certainly was worth the price.

It only took him a few minutes to unpack, then he walked up one floor to the ballroom.

"Hey Roy."

Brent was over by the bar in front of a huge picture window. He had an elderly man and woman cornered there, engaged in serious conversation.

"Myles, you're here early. You by yourself?"

"I am for now. I'll pick up my date later. Can I help you with anything?"

"You sure can. Myles I'd like you to meet Mr. and Mrs. Irobi. My good friend Lieutenant Myles Garrison."

The Irobis bowed deeply, then straightened up and Mr. Irobi extended his hand.

"Please to meet you both. Lieutenant Brent tells me you are planning a fine party for us tonight. I am looking forward to it," Myles said.

"Irobi-san, I'll see you a little later. I need to speak with my friend now. OK?" Brent said.

"Myles, let's go sit over there and I'll bring you up to speed on what we're doing here."

Myles followed Brent across the ball room floor. It was an elegant room. The main bar where they had been talking had ten bar stools and six tables decked out in white table cloths with Christmas Tree center pieces. Behind the bar the huge window offered a panoramic view of Tokyo. With no buildings over ten stories, most of the city could be seen quite clearly. Only thing though, it was heavily overcast today so it was pretty much a gray city out there.

Off to the side of the bar, was a long table with two beautiful spring flower arrangements and one huge poinsettia.

On one side of the room opposite the entrance way was another long table with similar decorations. Around the ballroom floor there were twelve four person tables, arranged like the other larger tables. All of the tables had white linen tablecloths and silver place settings. In the corner opposite the main bar there was a raised platform measuring about twenty feet by ten feet and a pile of folding chairs.

Up on the ceiling, there was one of those huge balls with tiny mirrors. Myles learned later that Brent had actually had to go out and buy it. Red, green, and silver streamers fanned out from the ball to the four corners of the room.

Myles and Brent sat at one of the small tables.

"Myles, I'm so glad you're here. I don't think the bus will get here much before two, so you'll be my only helper, at least for a while. So far, what do you think?"

"Roy, this is fantastic. You've really done well. Now tell me how could you do all this for ten dollars a person. Come on now, really."

"Well, we can all thank my Mom. She was so proud of me planning this party she sent me a thousand dollars for a Christmas present. She never would have believed I could do this. She is so pleased."

Myles knew a little bit about Brent's background. His family back in Georgia had owned and operated a canning business for many, many years. In fact, Brent had often told him how his Mom had invented Brunswick Stew and how it had earned the family way over a million dollars. His Dad passed away about ten years ago leaving his mother to run the business. Brent put off college for a year to help his mom. After graduating from Georgia Tech, he went back into the business for a year before taking his Air Force commission. He had finished NSA school about a year ahead of Myles, and was due to make Captain in another month or so. It was no surprise to Myles that his Mom had sent him a thousand dollars, but it was wonderfully generous of him to put it all into the Christmas Party. But then, he was a special guy.

"Roy, you are so generous in doing this. I mean a thousand bucks of your own money."

"Well, you've heard me say many times ..... you only live once. Right?"

"So our ten dollars a person, plus your thousand covers the hotel, the bar, the food, and the band. I'd say you did pretty good. Thanks a lot pal."

"No problem. Now let's start out by putting the place cards at the tables. I've already had them made out from the attendance list."

He pulled a thick envelope from his jacket pocket and placed it on the table. Myles removed a stack of red cards and fanned them out over the white table cloth.

"OK, Myles, let's start by placing two couples at each table. But first there will be six places at the head table. Major Hickson and Peggy, Sergeant Barney and Ruby, and me, of course, with Toyoko. You remember her from the Albion?"

"Yes I do. I like her. I follow you on the head table arrangement. What's next?"

"At the two tables closest to the head table, we'll put the other four officers and their dates. That would be you and Yoshiko, and Manahan and Margaret Holmes, the teacher. Then ...."

Myles interrupted.

"Wait, I'd like Davison at my table if it's all right. He is my project and this will be an opportunity to bond a little."

"Fine, so the first table will be you and Yoshiko, and Davison and Fumiko. Then, how about Manahan and

Margaret Holmes, and Wentz and Emily Clarkson, the teacher, at the second table?"

"Good. That's good," Myles concurred.

"Now we've got to place the ten enlisted men and Morita-san. I invited him since he knows everybody and is a bachelor. Let me just move the cards around here on the table and call off the way I arranged them. Stop me when you want to change anything."

"Sounds, good. You know we have ten enlisted and with Morita-san that makes an odd number. That would be five tables of two couples each and then what do we do with Morita-san and his date?" Myles asked.

"No, it's all right. We have ten enlisted, true, but only eight have dates. That's sixteen persons, two stags, and Morita and his date make twenty. So that's five tables of four. That'll work out. Then add the two tables for four officers and dates and we need a total of seven tables. It all adds up," Brent concluded.

"You're right. Let's lay them out that way. I'd say split up the two stags and Morita and his date."

So they finally worked out the seating assignments. Just as they finished putting around the place cards, Mrs. Irobi entered the room pushing a cart loaded with tall red candles in red ceramic candlesticks.

"Myles, if there's anything you need to do, Mama-san and I can put the candle sticks on the tables. If you want to come back later that'd be fine."

"I'll take you up on that. I might come back up in a little while and take some pictures."

As he turned to leave the room, Myles glanced over toward the bar and the picture window. Lo and behold, it was snowing. Only snow flurries, really, but it was actually snowing. First of the year and just in time for the party and, maybe, Christmas.

"Roy, take a look outside. It's snowing for your party," Myles called out.

Back in his room, Myles spread his tuxedo out on the bed. It was nearly four o'clock now and just a little more than an hour to go. He decided to rest on the bed for a few minutes and then take a walk outside in the snow.

His walk didn't last more than fifteen minutes. His head was getting wet and the temperature felt like it was dropping. He decided to take a taxi and go to pick up Yoshiko.

He got to Seibu around a quarter past five. He stopped by the flower stand in the food section and ordered an orchid to be delivered to Room 404 at the Ryoko. Then he went directly up to the fashion floor. As he stepped off the escalator, he had the sensation of stepping off a cloud into Heaven and seeing an angel. There, in the center of the floor stood Yoshiko, poised on a small stool, with Kazuko and three photographers shuffling around snapping pictures.

She was in a white low cut evening gown glistening with sequins and silk threads. The dress clung to her body as if it were her second skin. A narrow white silk sash wrapped around her tiny waste showing off her perfect figure. Her hair was up in a French twist with a tiny diamond tiara holding down the braid. There were slits from her knees down to the hem on both sides of the dress, showing white satin pumps and a tantalizing glimpse of her shapely calves. The low top was cut perfectly, showing off just the right amount of cleavage.

Most Japanese girls could not wear such a top but she was perfect in it. Her make-up was exquisitely done with

Seibu's expensive brand, maybe by Kazuko herself. Her eyes were absolutely beautiful with dark shadow and liner. And, to complete the ensemble, she wore white elbow length kid gloves. Oh, my angel, Myles thought. How can anything be so beautiful.

As soon as she spied him by the escalator she started waving and smiling, prompting the photographers to stand up and look around to see what was going on. Myles waved back with arms flying high and wide. He was so happy and it was so good go see her happy like this. Seeing Myles, Kazuko immediately rushed over to slow him down.

"Myles, you're early. OK, so you're here. Now we've still got some work to do so please sit down, be quite, and behave yourself."

"Ma'am, is it all right for me to take some pictures for myself?"

He had Mr. Nikon by his side.

"Absolutely not. Do that at your party. Now be quiet."

The photo shoot was finally over and the photographers were packed up and gone. Yoshiko sat by Myles on the sofa waiting for Kazuko to return. He couldn't help noticing how quiet she'd become and she was looking very tired.

"Yoshiko, are you tired? You've had a long day."

"Oh yes, Mai. I very tired. I would like to go home but I must go to party, right?"

"I'm so sorry my darling but, yes, we must go at least for a little while. They are my friends. I promise I will take good care of you and maybe leave early."

Kazuko finally returned carrying a huge garment bag and then she escorted Yoshiko into a side room. They returned in just a few minutes with Yoshiko wearing a beautiful long black velvet coat. Kazuko placed the garment bag and the hat box by the sofa.

Yoshiko was so elegant, Myles thought, like a princess. Then he noticed. There it was on her left coat collar .... *Ladybug* sitting up there as proud as can be.

"Here Myles. She can pack the gown in this garment bag tomorrow. The people tell me it is snowing real hard so be very careful. This coat should keep her warm. Thank you Yoshiko for doing so well today. Have a nice time at the party."

Myles took the bag and helped Yoshiko stand up. She is really tired, Myles thought. She had been on her feet for over seven hours and shown seven dresses plus the evening gown picture taking.

He managed the hat box and garment bag in one hand and held her left elbow as they walked to the escalator.

"Sayonara, Kazuko-san. Thank you," Yoshiko called out.

"Thank you very much Kazuko-san," Myles added.

The Party

It was snowing heavily now and about an inch had accumulated on the pavement. The taxi dropped them as close to the curb as possible, and Myles led Yoshiko into the hotel and up to the front desk.

"Yoshiko, we are already signed in so I'll get the key and we will go to our room."

"Hey Myles," a voice came from the corner bar.

Davison was scurrying over in their direction with Fumiko not far behind.

"Myles, she is beautiful. Yoshiko how are you? Do you remember me and Fumiko?"

Yoshiko managed a smile and extended her gloved hand. Davison cupped her hand in his and kissed her glove.

"Yes, I do remember you. It so good see you again. I so happy to come to party. Can we go to room now Mai?"

"Bob, please excuse us. She is exhausted. She's worked all day at the Seibu Department Store and needs a little rest."

"Absolutely. You guys go ahead and we'll see you at cocktail time."

In the room, Myles hung up the overcoat and helped her onto the bed. She sat there motionless for a minute or so.

"Yoshiko, I want you to lie down and rest. We have an hour before we need to be at the party. OK?"

"Yes, thank you Mai."

Myles placed his arm around her bare shoulders and gently laid her back with her head propped up carefully on two pillows. He placed a small towel over her eyes and gently stroked her cheeks. Then he pulled off the kid gloves and settled her arms at her side. She was sound asleep in less than a minute. He very quietly lay down beside her, held her hand, and closed his eyes.

He didn't allow himself to sleep for fear of oversleeping. Around six-fifteen he gently touched Yoshiko's arm.

"Yoshiko. Time to wake up."

She moved her arm and turned her head toward him. He bent over and kissed her on the lips.

"We must get up now sweetheart. How do you feel?"

"I feel OK Mai, still some tired."

She reached out with both arms for Myles to pull her up.

"May I have water, Mai?"

She's still not feeling very well, Myles thought. Maybe she's got a flu bug. I'll just have to be very careful with her.

He brought her a glass of water and the white orchid he'd ordered earlier. She reached for the orchid first.

"Oh thank you so much Mai. It beautiful. I can wear tonight, OK?"

"Oh yes, here take some water."

After a while, she started to get some strength back and feel more like her normal self. She was actually starting to look forward to the party.

Myles helped her stand and straighten her dress and her hair. He teased her a little, by tugging on her low top. She poked his arm. Now he knew she was more like her old self.

"I not wear gloves, Mai."

"Yes, I think you should. It makes your dress perfect. Pease wear them for me."

With some effort, they managed to pull on the gloves and smooth them out on her arms. Then Myles attempted to attach the orchid to her dress just below the low top but that turned out not to be the right place. Instead, she suggested the put it in a water glass so they could enjoy it in the room later.

"How I look Mai? You happy?"

"Yes, oh yes. You are perfect."

He held her by her bare shoulders and kissed her softly on her lips.

"Now, we go to party," she said.

Myles showed her out the door and they walked to the elevator on their way to the fifth floor ballroom.

It was nearly a quarter to seven and cocktail hour had progressed nicely from the six-thirty starting time. At first no one noticed as they entered the room. They stood there together for a moment with Myles' arm around her waist. The orchestra was playing Moon River and several couples were dancing. The rest were gathered in small groups near the bar area. Suddenly, a figure in a long red silk Chinese dress came toward them.

"Myles, please introduce me to your lovely date."

It was Peggy Hickson.

"Peggy this is Yoshiko-san."

Yoshiko bowed then raised up and extended her hand. Uncle Masuda had taught her that this is the way to do it with Westerners. The two girls shook hands very slowly and softly.

"Yoshiko-san, I am so happy to meet you. Myles, she is so beautiful. How do you know her? I think you've been keeping a secret."

"Well, I must admit, we have known each other now, let's see, we met six weeks ago today."

"I want to know all about how you met, and all about Yoshiko-san. Please come with me Yoshiko-san. OK, Myles? I want her to meet the Major."

"Yoshiko-san, please go with Miss Peggy. It is OK. I will be with you in a minute. I will bring you a sake, OK?"

Yoshiko was confused and uncertain about what was going on.

"It's OK, Peggy. She is a little unsure of herself with all these people. She's very tired from working all day. She's been modeling dresses at the Seibu Department Store. Please go slow with her."

"She's in good hands Myles. Come with me Yoshiko-san."

She held out her hand and gently tugged her away in the direction of the bar. Yoshiko looked back at Myles. He knew what she was thinking.

"Major Hickson, may I introduce Myles friend Yoshiko-san."

Yoshiko bowed, raised up and put out her gloved hand.

The Major stepped back, nearly speechless.

"My, oh my. Yoshiko-san I am so happy to meet you. Thank you so much for coming to our Christmas Party. Is Myles taking good care of you? Can I get you something to drink?"

"I please to meet you sir. Mai is getting sake for me. He take good care of me."

Major Hickson and Peggy were obviously overcome by this beautiful girl with such poise and grace. Peggy had suspected Myles might have been up to something in recent weeks, but had no idea it could be anything like this.

Just then, Brent and Toyoko came over to join them.

"Yoshiko-san, we met one time before," Brent said.

"Yes, yes, I remember see at Officer Club."

She was obviously reassured by seeing a familiar face.

"This is Toyoko-san, and Toyoko-san this is Yoshiko-san. Oh, excuse me Peggy I'm sorry for butting in."

"Roy, that's perfectly all right. It's nice Yoshiko-san remembers you. When exactly did you meet before?"

"Oh, ma'am it was exactly six weeks ago today. We met at the Tokyo Officers Club late one Saturday afternoon. Oh, here comes Myles." Brent was relieved to see Myles coming toward them, drinks in hand.

"Myles, we're just talking to Yoshiko-san here, she is perfectly beautiful tonight Myles and what a beautiful dress."

"Thank you," Yoshiko said, not really knowing what to say.

"Thanks Roy, I must admit I am very proud of her. She worked all day and then the Seibu people made her up and dressed her for the party. She's a brave soul for coming with me tonight. Excuse us Major, Peggy, Roy, and Toyoko-san. I think we'll sit at our table for a few minutes with our drinks. How much longer until dinner?"

"Please do sit for while, Myles. There'll be plenty of time to socialize and dance after dinner," Peggy said, coming to the rescue.

"Yes," added the Major ".... and I want to make a request to dance with Yoshiko-san."

"Sure thing, Major, but only on the condition that I have a dance with your beautiful wife."

Myles and Yoshiko found their table and sat down with their drinks.

"Yoshiko, thank you for being so polite with my friends. Major Hickson is my commander and Peggy is his wife."

"I be very nice to them Mai, and I dance with Major."

During the fifteen minutes or so before dinner was announced, most of the couples made their way to Myles table to introduce themselves and their dates. There were four American girls, two school teachers and two nurses from the base, and four Japanese girls.

"I think the dinner will be good Yoshiko. There will be some wine if you feel like it, and you only eat some food that you like."

She still looked a little frail and he was concerned.

Everyone was having a wonderful time. It was the first time Myles had seen any of these men in tuxedos and they were very elegant. All the gowns were truly beautiful and he wondered how and where they had been acquired. He was proud of his men for their poise and manners. But, he remembered, these aren't ordinary enlisted men. They had been selected for this work in basic training on the basis of exceptionally high aptitude test results. Security Service automatically skims the top one half of one percent for their intelligence schools. Besides that, most of them had one or two years of college before enlistment, and half of them had one year of language training in universities.

Manahan and his American date approached Myles' table.

"Myles and Yoshiko-san, this is Margaret. You didn't get to meet earlier. Margaret teaches fourth grade at the base school. They call her Maggie. And, Maggie, this is my good friend Myles and his date Yoshiko-san."

"Yoshiko-san, do you speak English? I'm so sorry I don't speak Japanese," Maggie asked.

Yoshiko placed her hand on Maggie's arm.

"Yes, I can speak some English. No worry about Japanese. I am so pleased to meet you. How is teaching fourth grade?"

"Well, fourth graders are generally pretty good. Dan tells me you are a model for a department store. Do you model clothes in shows?"

"Yes, I work for agency and work for Seibu and Mitsukoshi Department Stores, and sometimes other places. You have beautiful gown."

Myles noticed Yoshiko was beginning to feel like her old self. He patted her on her shoulder a couple of times.

Everyone was seated now, chatting quietly waiting for dinner. At the head table Brent and Toyoko, the Hicksons, and the Barneys were having a great time.

The tables were elegant with the Christmas Tree centerpieces and the red candles, and the silver service glistened against the white tablecloths. Yoshiko's skin was golden in the soft yellow candlelight and the sequins on her gown sparkled like stars against a white sky.

Finally, the wine was poured and the dinner begun. As expected, Brent had done a superb job planning the meal. The first course was Boluga Caviar and California Champagne. Then there was Sole Veronique and Piesporter Reisling. The entre was Filet Mignon and a 1952 Chateaux Margeaux. Dessert was Crepe Suzette and Chateau I'Quem. It was a fabulous dinner and Brent's thousand dollars had been well spent.

Yoshiko sampled all of the wines and some of the food courses. Her favorite though was the caviar. She would have preferred the sole less cooked, but she tried it just the same. Myles gave her good marks for tasting everything.

Shortly after the last course, Major Hickson approached Myles' table.

"Well, the band is playing and I think it's about time I have that dance with Yoshiko-san," he said.

Yoshiko looked at Myles and he nodded as he helped her stand up from her chair.

As she and the Major danced, Myles went to the head table.

"Peggy, may I have this dance."

"Yes, you certainly may."

She met Myles at the corner of the table and they stepped out onto the dance floor.

In a few seconds Manahan and Ruby and Kent and Maggie joined them, along with three or four other couples.

"Well, Toyoko-san, they saved the best for me. How about it?"

Sergeant Barney took her by the hand and gently escorted her onto the dance floor.

"Myles, Yoshiko-san is precious. So, you met six weeks ago in a tea room. Is that right?" Peggy said.

"That's right. She is something special isn't she?"

Peggy slowed and pulled back a little.

"You in love with her Myles?"

"Yes, who wouldn't be?"

"No, I don't mean like that. I mean are you in love with her? This is Peggy from Chicago asking you."

"I don't know. I guess I am. But it's just a fling you know. I'm enjoying it while it lasts. She'll probably dump me before too long."

The music stopped and Peggy held him in place.

"Next week please figure out a way to meet me for lunch in the snack bar. We need to talk. Christmas is Tuesday, so make it Wednesday, Thursday, or Friday. The sooner the better. Think you can manage that? This is strictly between you and me. All right?"

"Sure, it'll be our Christmas lunch. I'll think of something. Let's just go ahead and make it Wednesday at twelve-thirty and you can count on me to be there. I'll come up with a good excuse. The Major will have no idea."

"Good. That's settled. Now let's have a blast. Better go get your girl away from the Major. He's really taken with her."

Myles danced the next dance with Yoshiko. She nestled her head under his chin against his chest. They didn't speak. They didn't need to.

They danced two more times and then Myles allowed Brent, Manahan, and Davison to share his prize.

Myles made a special effort to get Yoshiko over to Johnson's table. He was with another stag and one of the other couples. On the way he passed Morita and his date. He'd heard earlier about this, but decided not to react. Morita had a guy for a date. Thank goodness they didn't dance. Yoshiko was visibly startled but kept her composure.

"Yoshiko-san, this is my good friend Sergeant Johnson. This is Yoshiko-san, you remember we talked about her."

Johnson bowed, then Yoshiko bowed. She put out her hand but he, instead, gave her a big hug.

"Johnson, I so pleased meet you. Mai tell me about you good friend. Thank you for being his friend."

"Myles, this is one gorgeous girl, and so smart too. I'd ask her to dance but that's not my thing. We never grew up dancing in Texas."

"Oh sure. She's about danced out anyway. We're going to make the rounds and then take off for the night. We're staying here in the hotel. Room 404 if you need me."

"Swell, see you in the morning. Sorry you're going to miss the Irish Coffee."

"Oh, that'll be fine. Please do me a favor. My camera is back on my table. I haven't gotten any pictures so will you please take charge of the camera for the night and take a lot of pictures? It's loaded and ready to go."

"Sure, I'll take care of it. I'll return the camera in the morning."

"That would be great."

Johnson gave Yoshiko one more hug. Myles took her by the hand and walked the entire space of the party room, giving their goodbyes for the evening. He especially thanked Brent for all his work. Major Hickson and Peggy said goodnight and understood them leaving early.

Back in the room, Myles helped Yoshiko with her gown. They crawled into bed and cuddled up under the blanket. She lay over his arm and put her leg and arm over his body. She nudged her head up over his chest and under his chin. Before falling asleep, Myles thought back to last weekend and his encounter with Commander Banta.

He was worried. Brent hadn't said anything about being questioned. That could be good or that could be bad. He fell asleep, finally, thinking about Yoshiko and the party.

Egyptian President Nasser pledges to take back Palestine; Medic Alert Foundation is formed; South Vietnamese President Diem executes sixteen suspected subversives and Vietcong leaders promise reprisal; US seizes US the communist newspaper, "The Daily Worker"; Khrushchev denounces Stalin at 20th Soviet Party Conference; Tunisia gains independence from France; The DeHaviland "Comet" becomes first commercial jet liner; Peter Ustinov's "Romeo and Juliet" premiers in Manchester, England; Sammy Davis, Jr. opens in "Mr. Wonderful" on Broadway; Patty Page's "Alleghany Moon" high on charts; "My Prayer" by The Platters is released; A loaf of bread costs thirty five cents, a hamburger costs twenty cents, and a Coke costs a nickel.

Chapter Eight

The Morning After

Sunday, December 23, 1956

Myles awoke to the muffled sound of people talking in the hallway. Yoshiko was sound asleep, still in his arms the way she went to sleep nine hours earlier. He moved slightly toward the edge of the bed to see the clock. It was just a little past eight, still time enough to let her sleep a little while longer. She moaned almost imperceptibly and moved her right hand up to the side of his face. Is she awake, he wondered, or just playing possum? Well, let her enjoy the extra rest. She deserved it after yesterday.

He heard more voices outside and decided it might be time to get things moving. There would be a breakfast buffet in the ball room and he didn't want to miss seeing everybody before they all left on the bus back to Shiroi. He gently nudged his sleeping baby.

"Yoshiko, Yoshiko, honey. Time to get up."

"No, no Mai. I sleep."

Myles urged her awake and gently stroked her back. They talked about the night before, agreeing it was a wonderful time and she loved meeting all of his friends. They showered and dressed and then headed upstairs to breakfast.

It was nearly nine and the room was filled. Some were seated and some were lined up at the buffet table. Mr. and Mrs. Irobi scurried about the room serving coffee and tea.

"Over here, Myles," Peggy Hickson signaled them over to her table. She and the Major sat alone, almost as if they were waiting for them.

"Good morning," Myles said, as the Major stood holding out a chair for Yoshiko.

"Why don't you go get some food. We just got here ourselves," Peggy suggested.

Myles piled on the food. Everything looked wonderful. Yoshiko was very picky. She took some steamed rice and some lettuce and tomatoes.

"Yoshiko-san, are you not hungry?" Myles asked.

"Mai, I not feel so good this morning. I not eat too much, OK?"

He put his arm around her waist.

"You just take what you want. Maybe have some tea."

They placed their dishes on the table and seated themselves.

"Oh, Yoshiko-san, I'm sorry you can't eat much. Do you feel OK this morning?" Peggy asked.

"I fine, thank you. My stomach not too strong this morning. Thank you. Please no worry."

"Peggy, I'm sure she's fine. Normally, she eats like a horse. You should see her put away sushi. I think yesterday was just a little too much. You know she worked a full day before coming to the party last night. She'll be fine."

"Well, anyway, we sure enjoyed seeing you both last night, and thank you Yoshiko-san for dancing with me," Major Hickson changed the subject.

Before leaving, Myles took Yoshiko by the hand and made the rounds of the room. He took a little extra time with Davison and Fumiko.

"Bob, Yoshiko-san and I enjoyed sitting with you and Fumiko-san last night. And Fumiko-san, you are a great dancer. Bob, we've got to be going. I'll see you back in the office tomorrow."

Davison pushed back in his chair and started to stand up.

"No, don't get up," Myles said, "Have a safe trip back to Shiroi."

"Thanks pal. Fumiko-san and I hope to see both of you again .... maybe at another party."

Myles and Yoshiko moved on to the next table where Johnson was seated.

"Johnson-san, I enjoy seeing you. We meet again soon maybe." Yoshiko realized Johnson was an important friend and she made sure to properly say goodbye.

Back in the room, it was nearing ten o'clock and Myles helped with the packing and rounding up the borrowed gown, hand bag, and coat.

"We should go now Yoshiko. Have you packed everything?"

"Oh, yes thank you. I ready now."

Myles called for a porter and ordered a taxi. He could have managed but he noticed Yoshiko still wasn't too steady on her feet. They checked out said goodbye to the staff.

They dropped the borrowed clothes off at the Seibu and thanked Kazuko once again for all that she had done.

Three inches of snow had fallen during the night. As they drove through snow covered neighborhoods, Yoshiko leaned over and put her head on Myles' shoulder. He took her hand and they didn't speak.

Myles had the driver take them up as close as possible to the front entrance. Before he could even reach for his money, the driver jumped out and opened Yoshiko's door. Then he pulled out the bags and carried them up to the front door. Yoshiko took Myles' hand as they walked through the courtyard.

Upstairs, they slid open the paper door and were greeted by a comforting flow of warm air.

"Mai, O-basan turn on heater. So nice," Yoshiko said.

Myles jumped up on the bed and pulled Yoshiko up beside him.

"Yoshiko, did you have a good time?" he asked.

"I have wonderful time Mai, and I like your friends .... especially Peggy-san."

"And she liked you too very much. Now I need to talk to you now about our Christmas plan." Myles sat up straight and Yoshiko started to pull herself up.

"No, no, please lie down while I talk."

Myles gently placed a pillow under her head.

"What plan Mai?"

"OK. I return to Shiroi tonight. Then, tomorrow is December 24. Do you know what day that is?"

"What day is, Mai?" she asked.

"It is the day before Christmas. You know Christmas?"

"Oh, yes."

"Well, I have to work in my office tomorrow. Then I have a day off work for Christmas. That means I can come to Ikebukuro for one day. OK?"

"But Mai, I work on Christmas at Mitsukoshi for special Christmas show. I no see you then."

"OK. So I won't come on Christmas. How about New Years?"

"Mai, next weekend we have quiet New Year, just you and me here in apartment. My tummy not still so good."

"If that is what you want Yoshiko, that is what we will do. So I will come to Ikebukuro Saturday morning and go back to Shiroi on Tuesday. So we will have a nice quiet weekend. Maybe we can go to a movie and eat sushi instead. That will be fine."

"Thank you Mai. I know you like friends but I like quiet time better. Thank you very much."

He lay back on the bed and put his arms around her. He could sense her going limp in his arms.

He helped her off with her clothes and he pulled off his things. They pushed the bags and clothes aside and crawled under the futon. They slept until five o'clock.

Myles was awakened by the familiar smell of Yoshiko percolating coffee. She was standing by the kitchenette in her flowered silk robe and just starting to pour coffee.

"Oh, Yoshiko, coffee in the evening. How nice. It smells so good."

"I have some tea too, Mai, and O-basan brought some cake and cookies. That will be a good supper for you. Here."

She handed him a dish of cookies.

After coffee, tea, cake, and cookies, Myles decided he should be getting back to the base.

"Mai thank you so much for wonderful time at party."

"You are very welcome. It was a really a nice weekend. I loved showing you to my friends."

They finished unpacking and sorting and Myles got his bag ready to take back to the base. He gently pushed her back on the bed and propped her head up on two pillows.

"Now stay this way, please?"

He kissed her on the lips, and then gently backed away toward the door.

"I will see you Saturday. Sayonara," he said as he slid the door closed and headed for the station.

Monday, December 24, 1956

Myles finished breakfast at the officers' dining hall and started his walk across the parade field. It had snowed at Shiroi too, but now on Monday morning, it was well trampled and there were even some snowmen still scattered around. It was heavily overcast and cold. Maybe there'd be more snow today, he thought, that would be good for the kids out of school and mothers doing last minute Christmas shopping.

The compound looked ominous this dark morning. It seemed especially quiet with no traffic sounds inside or outside the fence. Silent streams of enlisted men and officers slowly made their way through the compound check point.

Who would know, Myles thought, what all goes on inside this silent place. It was connected to every corner of the globe. Voices and electronic data constantly flowed in and out on radio frequencies connecting thousands of ships, planes, and ground stations. At this very moment, Myles thought, conversations between the Kremlin and Peking are probably being instantaneously relayed to Shiroi. Or maybe the NSA site in Ankara, Turkey, mighty be listening in on transmissions from a Soviet bomber and sending them on to ECOM here at Shiroi. Besides instantaneous electronic delivery, over a ton of courier bags would be delivered today stuffed with radio intercept logs, magnetic tapes, and other clandestine documents.

"Good morning, Myles."

Brent had apparently gotten to work early and was the first to greet him.

"Good morning, Merry Christmas, and what a great party you give," Myles responded.

Major Hickson came out of his office wanting to share in the morning greetings.

"Yes, Lieutenant Brent did a fine job, didn't he. Peggy and I are looking forward to next year."

Next year, next year, Myles thought. What about next year. In an instant, all the things going on in his life flashed through his mind. Where would he be? Where would Yoshiko be?

"Well, thank you gentlemen. I'm glad you enjoyed the party. Didn't we have some beautiful ladies?" Brent replied.

"We did, and Peggy liked all you guys in your tuxedos too. Brent could you get the men together at ten o'clock for an announcement?"

"Sure thing. We'll all be in the conference room."

Brent turned and walked back into the great room.

Myles settled down at his desk and pulled a tall stack of papers over in front of him.

"Johnson, can I see you for a minute?" Myles asked.

Johnson came over and sat by Myles' desk.

"What's up boss? I really enjoyed meeting Yoshiko. I can see why you're happy about her. She is so sweet and pretty. Better watch out. I might give you some competition there."

"Thanks. Look here. It's from Commander Banta, you remember, Sheila?"

He held up three stapled yellows pages. It was a decrypted message dated December 22.

"She sent this on Saturday. Let's read it together then you can help me understand it."

EMERGENCY PRIORITY - XMT 22-12-56

FROM CMDR BANTA, BCOM, ARL

TO LT GARRISON, 21 RADIO, SHR

TOP SECRET BEEHIVE

DECRYPT KW-6 LONGHORN

PART 1 – MEETING WITH POTUS ON DEC 17 GOOD. TOP CONCERN WITH SENSITIVITY TO ESCALATION. ALSO CONCERNS WITH BUDGET.

PART 2 – NAVAL COMPONENT WITH ONE SHIP APPROVED USS MADDOX . SECOND SHIP USS TURNER JOY ALSO A POSSIBLITY. ONE VAN PER SHIP. NAVAL START UP ALSO DELAYED WITH FIRST CRUISE SOMETIME LATE NEXT YEAR OR

EARLY YEAR AFTER. DECISION FLUID. NAVY BRASS INSISTS ON CODE NAME DESOTO FOR THEIR PART OF BEEHIVE.

PART 3 – OTHER FOUR COMPONENTS STILL IN BEHIVE AGENDA BUT SCALED BACK TO ONE VAN ONLY 1957. ADDITIONAL VANS 1958. DELIVER FIRST VANS TAN SON NHUT ON OR ABOUT MARCH ONE.

PART 4 – GARRISON AND JOHNSON UR ROLLOVER PLAN STILL INTACT. WILL CONFIRM GS RATINGS SOON AND MORE INFO ON UR BLUE COVER. NO FIRM DECISION ON LOCATION. POSSIBLE CHANGE FROM LONG MEI TO DUAY BAH DEN. REMAIN SHIROI UNTIL ADVISEMENT.

PART 5 – MORE TO FOLLOW. KEEP CONFIDENTIAL UNTIL ADVISEMENT.

"Well, did you take it all in?" Myles asked Johnson.

"Yes, sir. Looks like some delays but we're still on schedule. Guess we'll start out with one van in Saigon area. That about right?"

"That's it as I see it. Have you noticed that you and I are getting all the Vietnam, Laos, and Cambodia traffic?" Myles asked.

"Yeah, looks like we're going to be plenty busy."

"Let's you and me go to the snack bar for a cheeseburger. I'll remind you at twelve. OK?" Myles asked.

"Great, thanks."

"Let's go to the conference room. It's nearly ten," Myles suggested. "I think the Major has an announcement."

Hickson and Barney came out of their offices and stood in front of the group.

"Thanks for all of you coming together like this," the Major proclaimed. "Everybody, please have a seat."

The sound of chairs being shuffled up to the conference table filled the air. Finally everyone was seated.

"Thank you. The first order of business is a big round of applause for Lieutenant Brent for arranging such a wonderful Christmas Party."

Applause.

"Now ...... I'm proud to announce the promotion of First Lieutenant Roy W. Kent to Captain, United States Air Force. That is effective January first so you can shop for your bars and cigars this week Roy."

Loud applause.

"Now Captain Brent, nothing comes without a price. Effective with your promotion, you are appointed Officer-in-Charge of the section. So all ten enlisted and the four officers will report to you for administrative purposes. Everybody, including you, will maintain their existing work assignments for the time being."

Slight applause.

"Now, some other business," he continued.

He named two enlisted men as being appointed to Officer Candidate School. They would be leaving for San Antonio sometime in January.

Extended loud applause.

"Congratulations to both of you. In case the rest of you didn't know, these two guys went through a hell of a lot of aptitude testing and scored almost perfect grades. We're proud of both of you. Good luck with your officer careers."

Continued loud applause.

Sergeant Barney added, "I want to join the Major in congratulating you guys for all you've accomplished. I hope we can send more of you to OCS this year. Oh .... and don't forget about flight school. You're all highly qualified for the Aviation Cadet program."

"Thanks, Sergeant Barney. I have some more news," the Major continued.

"As you know, tomorrow is Christmas Day. Peggy Hickson and Ruby Barney invite you all to a drop-in at my house tomorrow from four until seven. Dress is casual. You can bring girls from the base if you care to. The wives are fixing some great food and I and Sergeant Barney will tend bar."

Loud applause, whistles, and cheers.

"OK, back to work. Thanks again for everything," the Major concluded his presentation.

It was back to serious Monday morning business in the room. Myles went back to reading his traffic. As he leafed through the pages, it was obvious that things were not slowing down in Vietnam just because of Christmas. Every day, truck convoys were bringing weapons and ammunition down from the North along the Ho Chi Minh trail. Decrypted intercepts revealed actual serial numbers of the moving equipment, their lead officers' names, departure points, and final destinations. After lunch he would summarize in an Emergency message to B26A.

There were also a number of intercepted telephone calls between South Vietnam government officials which indicated growing unrest with the Diem regime. Johnson was predicting Diem's eventual assassination.

"Hey Roy .... Johnson and I are having lunch at the snack bar. Would you like to join us?" Myles asked.

"I don't think so, thanks anyway. You guys go ahead. Some other time, I promise."

"Sure, and congratulations on your promotion. I think that's just fantastic", Myles said.

In the afternoon, Myles got off his messages and finished his daily traffic. He sent his Intelligence Brief on the Ho Chi Minh trail activities and the Diem Regime problem.

That night he wrote to his mom and dad wishing them a Merry Christmas and a Happy New Year. The thought of mentioning Yoshiko briefly crossed his mind but he decided to wait until his next letter .... or maybe the letter after that. He promised himself that he would tell them very soon.

Christmas Day

Myles awoke early and went for a long walk around the base. The snow had melted some yesterday but it had frozen over during the night. He was completely unaware of the twenty eight degree temperature. He occasionally kicked at snow piled up against the fence. After the thaw yesterday, it was still a little sticky and wouldn't go anywhere. It just piled up on his shoes.

Christmas Dinner in the officers' dining room was a tradition at Shiroi. Myles and the other four bachelor officers from the 21st had a reserved table at one o'clock. On their advice, he had skipped breakfast. It turned out to be good advice. The dining room was decked out in full Christmas regalia, lighted Christmas trees in every corner, white table clothes, red candles, and official Air Force China. Menus on green bordered white parchment were at each place setting. Japanese waitresses in white dresses with red sashes served tables. Christmas music played in the background.

Dinner was turkey with all the trimmings and there was a choice of wines. It was an unbelievable experience for a dining hall meal. Myles learned later that the enlisted men's dining room was a carbon copy.

After dinner they all adjourned to their rooms at BOQ for a short nap before the Hickson and Barney drop-in.

The Hickson house was small by homeland standards, but fairly large for Shiroi officers' housing. The party was laid out in the living room and den. The wives had set up an elegant buffet table and the Major and the Sergeant were tending bar as promised. Everybody from the 21st was there. It was a really nice party and it was evident the wives had put forth a lot of effort.

In spite of the Christmas dinner just a few hours ago, everybody was hungry and thirsty. The Major and the Sergeant had a hard time keeping with drink orders.

The party hummed on for an hour or so, when Peggy finally got a reprieve from the food table and cornered Myles near the front picture window.

"How are you doing, Myles? Having a good time?" she asked.

"Yes ma'am. This is a wonderful party. And the shrimp, I don't know where you got 'em but they are great. Can I get you a drink?"

"Yes, thank you. I would like a Scotch and soda."

He was back in a minute. The Major knew exactly what she wanted.

"Thank you Myles."

They both sipped their drinks for a minute or so.

"Myles, are we set up for our secret lunch tomorrow?"

"Tomorrow. Tomorrow I will see you at the snack bar at twelve-thirty. Nobody will know anything about it. What's the agenda, may I ask in advance?"

"Yes, of course. I was very impressed with Yoshiko at the party. She was so beautiful, sweet, and smart. I want to talk to you about her, if we can speak freely. So that's what I want to talk about."

"Is this going to be a serious talk?"

"Yes, it is. That's all I'm going to say right now. See you tomorrow."

With that said, she walked away and joined a group near the coffee table.

Myles stayed at the party until the very end. He spoke casually to Peggy a couple of times but that was all. He and Brent walked back to their quarters together.

"Roy, let me say one last time what a great Christmas Party that was. Thanks again. Uh .... Roy, how'd everything go while I was away? Anything unusual .... or anything like that?" Myles tried to sound casual.

"No. It was pretty much business as usual. I was busy getting the party set up .... but no, nothing. I promise."

Myles sensed that he was holding back.

Wednesday, December 26, 1956

Back in the office all the excitement was finally past ..... the party, the hotel, the announcements, the Christmas Dinner, and finally the Major's drop-in. It was a little bit of a letdown, naturally, but it didn't take long for everybody to get back into the swing of things.

On Monday, Myles and Johnson had worked furiously trying to catch up on the new Laos and Cambodia traffic. They had discussed Commander Banta's message over and over again, extracting every possible grain of information and meaning. They both agreed her next message would be loaded.

In the morning, Captain Brent spent a lot of time with Major Hickson and Sergeant Barney. They went over the new organization with Brent in a leadership role. Major Hickson didn't think a lot of changes were necessary in order to fit a new Captain into the chain of command. Myles was not included in the planning sessions and he wondered how the new organization might need to change once his and Johnson's reassignments took effect.

Around noon, Myles put a note on Brent's desk excusing himself to go the Base Exchange. He quietly slipped out on his way to his twelve-thirty lunch with Peggy.

"Here, Myles," Peggy called out.

Myles spotted her at a corner table.

"OK, you're early I see."

Myles took the chair next to hers, so they could keep their voices down.

"Yes, I went ahead and ordered soup and club sandwiches so you're not late getting back. I hope that's OK."

Peggy pressed her hand on his arm.

"Sure, that's fine. I do have a full hour though if we need it. They think I'm shopping at the Base Exchange."

"Good. We won't need that much time though. I just want to say a few things."

Just then the soup and sandwiches arrived and it took a couple of minutes to set the food around the table. Myles sipped on his Coke and watched Peggy work with the dishes.

"Well, dig in. This looks good," Peggy said, as she started on her soup. "You know, I've seen more of you in the past two weeks than in the past six months?"

"Yes, that's right, and it's really been nice. Thanks for that great party yesterday. I know you and Ruby Barney went to a lot of trouble. Now, Peggy, what do you want to talk about?"

"Well, first of all Myles, I'm talking to you as a close friend, and our conversation here, today, is totally private. There is no need for you to say anything to anybody else about this …… including the Major of course."

"OK. This sounds serious."

"Well, it is. I need to talk to you about Yoshiko. I'm concerned about you. I'd like you to share with me the whole story Myles. Can we start with you telling me how and when you met?"

"I can do that. It's not that much to tell really."

Myles told her about how he and Yoshiko met and how their relationship had grown over the past six weeks. He told her about the Ikebukuro apartment and how Uncle Masuda had provided the furniture. He finished his narrative with the Christmas Party.

"OK, that's exactly what I needed to know. Can you tell me a little more about her background, you know, family, where she went to that fashion school, and all that. I know you think it's none of my business but, believe me, I'm just trying to help you."

Myles filled in everything he could about Yoshiko. He described her severe father and her compassionate mother. He told her about the fashion school and everything he could think of about her work.

"OK. Now that's over. I know that was painful. Now we're in this together."

"In this .... in what, Peggy? Is there anything wrong?"

"Well, let me say one thing first and outright Myles. I've never had a child myself, but I am a woman. I want to tell you that I think that girl is pregnant."

Myles just about fell out of his chair. He pushed his dishes away and leaned his chair back on two legs. For a moment, he was speechless.

"Peggy, no that can't be. What makes you say that?"

"I watched her very carefully Saturday night and then again Sunday morning. Did you not notice, Myles, that she was feeling sick and could hardly eat Sunday morning .... and how tired she was the whole time?"

"Peggy, you got it all wrong. If that's all you're worried about you can relax. It was just a mild case of the flu. A couple of girls she worked with last week called in sick on Saturday for the Seibu show with the flu. So Yoshiko probably caught the bug and that's why she was feeling bad Saturday night and Sunday. I'm sure that's all it was. When I left her Sunday she was feeling fine ...... just like her old self."

"Well, Myles, I'd like to believe that and maybe there is some truth to it. But, I know pregnant when I see it. I could be wrong of course. I'm just telling you what I think. So tell me this. From what you've told me, I gather you've been sleeping together for the past four weekends. Have you used any birth control?"

"No, but we're going to start next weekend."

"Myles, what are you thinking? Do you know how girls get knocked up? Don't you know about the birds and the bees?"

Myles was taken back and embarrassed.

"I guess, we just weren't thinking. It all happened so fast. But I'm sure it was the flu."

"OK .... tell me this? Has she had a period in the past four weeks?"

"I don't know. She might have during the week. I only see her on weekends."

"OK. You know what I think now Myles. You might be right but I don't think so. Anyway, you start using birth control from now on. Will you promise me that?"

"Peggy, do you realize what you're saying here. You are telling me to use birth control with my girlfriend. You think that's right?"

"Under normal circumstances, that would be absolutely ridiculous. I would never do that. But anyway, just do it OK?"

"Damn, I promise. Is that what this conversation is all about Peggy. Don't get me wrong, I really appreciate your concern and being honest with me. That's what friends are for. Is that all?" Myles asked.

"No, there's more and it's a little more serious."

Myles straightened up in his chair.

"OK, what else?"

"Myles, I know from what the Major says that you are one of his brightest officers and you have a great future ahead of you in the Air Force. I don't know what goes on inside that building, but I believe you are very smart and a natural leader."

"Well, thanks, Peggy. I don't know about that, but I do like my work."

"In the Security Service and the NSA, that Top Secret Clearance is the whole thing, Myles. Nothing happens and you can't do anything or work anywhere without that clearance. Right?"

"That's true."

"Now, the rest of what I've got to say is simple and to the point. You cannot marry that girl and keep your clearance. If you so much as even ask about marriage, you will probably lose you clearance and be kicked out of the Security Service. So if you intend to stay in the Air Force in your line of work, your relationship with Yoshiko can go nowhere and it must end, and I mean soon. I guess that's all I need to say Myles. Please don't just be angry with me for saying all these things. We will continue to be best friends. OK?"

"We are and we will still be best friends. Thanks for your advice. You've given me a lot to think about and I'll take all that you said very seriously. I do think it was the flu though."

"Flu or not, just know that you can talk to me anytime about all this."

Myles thanked Peggy for everything. They hugged and left the snack bar.

Thursday, December 27, 1956

The next day Myles arranged to meet with Davison at ten o'clock to review his work on Chinese air defenses. They hadn't spent much time together since Myles' trip to the States. Earlier in the week, Davison had reassured him that all was going well and that some new ground had been broken.

Before that, however, Myles spent some time with Johnson to make sure he was keeping up with incoming traffic, especially intercepted phone calls between Saigon and the outlying Provincial capitals. For the first time, there was a reference to the Sea of Reeds.

"The Sea of Reeds, do you know what that is? Myles asked.

"Nope. I'll just keep watching for it though. Look here," Johnson handed Myles a short stack of intercepted phone calls.

"Diem's got things really stirred up. I suspect he's going to start rounding up folks for the firing squad," Johnson warned.

"Sounds like it. Get all your translating done this morning and make a list of his phone calls. And how about letting me know about any activity on the Sea of Reeds? I'm going to be tied up with Davison until noon and will probably skip lunch today. So, how about seeing me around two?"

"Sure thing."

Myles sat with Davison well past noon. He was amazed over his new attitude. He was especially pleased on how fast he had transitioned into his new Chinese assignment.

"Bob, you've done good work here. What do you make of all this traffic in and out of Shantou? This is more than just normal air defense drills and maintenance activity. Looks like the volume has tripled compared to a month ago," Myles asked.

"It is. We need to see more traffic, especially anything involving personnel transfers. I know Shantou is just about the upper limit of our responsibility but they could be staging troops up there for moving down to the South."

"You're right. This is your baby now, but I'd say you're on the right track. You know you can requisition airborne anytime you see the need? The 6922nd has six RB-

50s orbiting off the coast between Hong Kong and Shanghai. We can access them anytime. In fact, that would be a good idea. How about making an official request to put one of them on patrol up and down the South China coast? Johnson will show you how to process the request."

"Myles, you're amazing. I never thought of that. I do need more coastal traffic. I'll get one of those babies to start making sweeps up and down the coast at thirty miles out. At twelve thousand feet, that would give them an oblique angle of ……. let's see ….. about thirty degrees. The signals shouldn't be too diluted at that sweep. I'll get them going ASAP. Thanks pal."

"Don't mention it. I would like to know what's going on in Shantou though, so please keep me up to speed."

Myles stood up and arched his back and neck.

He finished up the day with Johnson and got updated on Diem. It did appear he might be rounding up firing squad candidates. Of course all this was giving the Vietminh a field day and helping them recruit more Vietcong.

Friday, December 28, 1956

Friday was a quiet work day for Myles and Johnson. There'd been no messages from the Commander since the one on Monday. Myles was expecting more to come at any time. After work, he and Brent went to the Officers Club for a couple of drinks.

"Myles, tell me about Yoshiko," Brent asked after his first Scotch.

"Well, there's not too much to tell. You already know we're staying together on weekends. And you saw her at the party, which by the way, for the hundredth time was fantastic. I'll be going to Ikebukuro in the morning so Yoshiko and I we'll have a nice quiet New Year's weekend."

"No, I mean, you guys gonna get married or what?"

"Gosh no, Roy. Sooner or later we'll break it off. You know there's no way I can even think of anything serious like that without getting kicked out of my job, and probably the Air Force. I want to make Captain like you some day."

"Well, if that's your plan I suggest you get along with it. From where I stand, I see her as being very much in love with you Myles, and not ever wanting to give you up. And, I'm not sure, but I think I see the same thing in you Myles."

"No, no, don't lose any sleep over it Roy. How about another drink and then I've got to go and pack a few things."

"One more drink would be fine."

"Roy, one last thing .... you said nothing unusual happened while I was gone. You sure you didn't forget anything?" Myles decided to go out on a limb. "Did anybody from the NSA call you or pay you a visit? Anybody, for that matter?"

"Myles, absolutely not. Is there something going on?"

"No, no, nothing like that."

Myles wasn't sure if he was getting the straight story. They had their second drink and Myles left for his quarters.

Later that night, Myles put down his pen and folded a letter to his parents. He lay back on his pillow and his mind was nearly racing out of control.

First there were those secret documents that Major Hickson had shown him before he left for Arlington. The Major hadn't mentioned them again since he'd gotten back to Shiroi. Then there was that strange encounter with Commander Banta about the encrypted message. Was his refusal to talk going to get him into trouble? Why had nobody contacted Brent as the Commander had promised? Was Brent lying? To add to all that, there was Peggy's confrontation about Yoshiko being pregnant. Could she be right? What would he do? And, if all of that wasn't enough, he was having growing concerns about the dangerous mission he and Johnson were getting into .... and The Sea of Reeds .... what was that?

For that matter, he'd almost forgotten where he'd first heard about The Sea of Reeds. With all the things going on .... he wasn't sure if it was in an intercept, or maybe in Major Hickson's secret papers. For some reason he couldn't get it out of his mind.

He lay awake for most of the night.

Spain relinquishes Morocco protectorate; Polish communist Andre Gromulka freed from prison; Six US Marine recruits drown in exercise at Parris Island, SC; Montreal defeats Detroit to take Stanley Cup; "Silk Stockings" closes after 461 performances at Imperial Theatre; Philips broadcasts first color TV in the Netherlands; Carroll Baker in "Baby Doll" by Tennessee Williams; Fats Domino's "My Blue Heaven" and Carl Perkins' "Blue Suede Shoes" high on charts.

Chapter Nine

Bebi-san

Saturday, December 29, 1956

Saturday morning was clear and cold. The Tokyo train was overloaded with skiers and shoppers as it wove its way into the city. As it slowed for its entry into the Tokyo Station complex, Myles could see sidewalks jammed with shoppers and vacationing school children. He'd never lived in New York but he imagined that's what it would look like.

It was still ten minutes or so to Ikebukuro. He leaned his head against the glass and began to think about his talk with Peggy on Wednesday and then with Brent last night. He'd meant what he said when he assured them he'd be breaking up with Yoshiko But now, if she were pregnant like Peggy thought, well that might change things. Anyway, he doubted that she was and there would be plenty of time to break up. He was startled out of his daydream when the train pulled to a stop in Ikebukuro Station.

It was a cold walk to the apartment and, more than ever, he hoped Yoshiko had the heater turned on. He slipped off his shoes and entered the hallway next to O-basan's apartment. The door was open and he spotted her bending over her stove. It was around eleven-thirty, so he figured she was starting to cook lunch ….. maybe some more of her great sukiyaki.

"God morning, O-basan," he called out.

"Good morning, Myru-san," she replied, as she hurried across the room toward the door.

"Myru-san, Yoshiko-san not here. She no come home last night. You know?"

She was obviously concerned.

Myles was taken aback. She was supposed to be there according to their plan.

"Did she not leave a message, or did Uncle Masuda-san call?"

He remembered there was no telephone in the building, so how could Masuda call, or even Yoshiko? I've got to do something about this telephone situation here … he thought. If I'm going to see Yoshiko for a while longer, we've got to have a way to talk on the phone. Phones were too expensive for O-basan so he'd have to convince Masuda to foot the bill.

"I am worried, O-basan. I will go upstairs now."

"Myru-san, I turn heater on for you so is warm now."

"Thank you. If Yoshiko-san comes, bring her to me right away please."

Upstairs, Myles unpacked his things and looked around the room. There was nothing unusual. There were clothes in the closet, the dishes in the sink were clean, and the bed was made. He was worried. It was Tokyo after all, the second largest city in the world, and there was crime …. and there were accidents. He'll wait a while, he thought, and then go over to Mitsukoshi and call Uncle Masuda at the camera store from a pay phone.

Around one o'clock, he started downstairs. As he walked out into the courtyard he spotted Yoshiko stepping out of a taxi.

"Yoshiko-san," he called out. "Come over here."

She turned and started running to where Myles was waiting.

"Oh Mai, I so sorry. I late."

With that, she threw the hat box to the ground and lunged toward Myles. She wrapped her arms around him so tightly he could scarcely move. He managed to push her back a little and they hugged and kissed.

"Come on inside," Myles urged. "It is so cold out here. Come in and warm up."

They stripped off their jackets and squatted on the straw floor next to the gas heater. Myles was the first to speak.

"Yoshiko, where have you been? I have been so worried and O-basan did not know where you were. She said you didn't come in last night."

She was obviously not herself. He could see she was not feeling well. As he waited for her answer, he placed his hands around her face and held them there. It might be from the heater, he thought, but it feels like she has fever. Besides that her face was a little puffy. He'd never seen her like that before. She held his hands in place for a minute or so, then pulled them away from her face.

"Mai, I am sick all week since you left. On Thursday, I go to Yokohama to see my Mama-san. I feel so bad. She tell my father and he take me to Doctor. Doctor say I might make baby and he very angry."

Myles' brain exploded. Oh my poor Yoshiko. I wish I could have been with her this week. I understand how bad her father is. I am so sorry .... and make baby .... so maybe Peggy was right after all. Now what?

"Oh Yoshiko, I am so sorry you have been sick. And so sorry you had to face your father. What did your mother say?"

"Mama say OK, she understand. She say who father so I tell her everything. She is happy for me and you. But my father very, very angry. He say never come home anymore."

"So where were you last night?"

"Last night I at Uncle Masuda-san apartment in Ginza. He understand everything. He not angry. He only want me be happy and feel good."

"OK, so then you came back here this morning. Tell me what the doctor said."

"Doctor, say I probably have baby. Next week he do some test but he pretty sure. What you think Mai?"

"Well, first of all, please don't worry about anything. I am very happy if we make a baby. I want you to feel better too. I think the doctor might be right."

As he spoke he glanced again at her swollen face. He couldn't help noticing that her ankles were swollen too. He pulled her legs up onto his lap and started massaging her calves and ankles. He wished Peggy were here now to help.

"When do you go back to Yokohama to see doctor?"

"I no go back Yokohama doctor. I afraid my father. Uncle Masuda take me to Tokyo doctor Wednesday. Can you come with me? Please?"

"Oh, I wish I could but I cannot. I have important work on that day. I will call Uncle Masuda today from Mitsukoshi and ask him if he can arrange to buy a telephone for us. If you make a baby, we need to talk on the phone during the week. Do you work next week?"

"I work on Tuesday, Thursday and Friday. On Friday I work at Seibu until six o'clock. After Wednesday, maybe I feel better ..... you think?"

"I think you will feel better soon, maybe tomorrow. Then you get tested at Tokyo doctor."

"I think so."

"And then, I guess you cannot go back home to your parents. I will talk to Uncle Masuda about that."

"OK, but what about baby?"

"Well, I will make a plan for you and me and the baby."

Myles reassured her but he had no idea what to do.

"Mai, I think we sleep a little and then go downstairs and tell O-basan everything. We will need her to help us, maybe. And then will you call Uncle Masuda about telephone, please?" Yoshiko reminded him.

"We will do that later when we go to get some supper. Let's change to our robes now and lie on the bed."

Myles put his head back on his pillow, then pulled her up half over him in their sleeping position. He wrapped his arm around her and she fell asleep. As he lay there, he tried to grasp the situation he'd gotten himself into. He's got a pregnant Japanese girl. He'd definitely need to see Peggy as soon as possible next week. He thought about marriage and what that would mean. It would be loss of clearance and discharge from the Air Force .... and definitely no NSA job. Beyond that, taking a pregnant Japanese bride back to the States would not be easy for either of them. Mom and Dad would be fine, but there's still a lot of resentment from Pearl Harbor. It'd been just eleven years since the end of World War II.

Abortion, yes that could be a solution. But he could never do that to her ...... never. Don't marry, just keep Yoshiko and the baby secret ..... that would be impossible. He didn't see any reasonable way out. He'd have to talk to Peggy. He fell asleep to Yoshiko's heartbeat and gentle breathing.

Saturday Evening

The sound of the door sliding open woke up Myles.

"Yoshiko-san, are you all right?" O-basan asked, as she stood in the open doorway.

It was nearly six o'clock and she was worried.

"We are OK," Myles replied.

Yoshiko moved and groaned slightly. They had slept for almost five hours. He knew she was exhausted from the past three days and desperately needed sleep.

"Yoshiko, time to wake up. O-basan is here and wants to see us."

They both managed to sit up in bed still partially coiled together from their sleeping position.

"O-basan, what time is it?" Yoshiko asked.

"It time to get up," O-basan spoke in choppy English.

"We very tired. We get dressed. OK?"

They took turns going down the hall and slowly dressed in the same clothes they had worn earlier in the day.

"Yoshiko, are you feeling better?" Myles asked.

She looked better .... he thought ...... all that sleep had done her some good.

"I feel better. I am hungry. We should go to Mitsukoshi now."

"Yes, we go and get something to eat and I need to make that phone call to Uncle Masuda. Will he still be at his store?"

"Saturday store stay open until eleven o'clock. So he be there."

"Good. Let's get on over to the store. I'm hungry too. You do look a lot better. I'm so happy."

He noticed her face didn't look swollen anymore. He cupped his hand on her cheek and it felt cool and normal.

It was cold and black outside and the walk up the gravel road and over to the Mitsukoshi was not fun. They kept their arms locked around each other as they walked.

In the store, they went to the public telephones first thing. Yoshiko sat a few feet away and watched as Myles dialed the camera store number. Uncle Masuda was there and they talked for nearly ten minutes.

"There, it is all OK. Uncle Masuda will try to get a telephone put into the apartment. He said to tell you hello and he hoped you feel better."

"I will be happy for telephone. Was he angry Mai?"

"No, not at all. He is a wise man. He is happy for us but he says it will be difficult time but he will help us all he can. He said he will take you to the Tokyo doctor Wednesday and wanted me to come. I said I cannot this time. He understood."

They made their way through the food bazaar to the tea room on the first floor and managed to get a small corner table. The sat across from each other and held hands as they looked over the menu. Myles noticed **Ladybug** perched high on her dress lapel. Good old **Ladybug** ..... he thought .... through thick and thin, she's always with us.

After the phone call to Uncle Masuda they were both feeling a lot better. Yoshiko was more like herself now and she devoured a huge dish of shrimp fried rice. Myles kept up with her all the way. Eventually, they made their way back through the food bazaar and out into the night.

It was another cold walk back to the apartment. The moonless sky was black as coal but the lights of downtown Tokyo lit up the horizon.

It was around nine o'clock when they neared O-basan's door.

"We see O'basan now, Mai?" she asked.

"I think we should. There are still lights."

Myles rattled her door, careful not to damage the paper and the fragile wood frame.

"Just a minute please," a voice from the inside called out.

O-basan slid open the door and invited them in. She gestured for them to sit at her sunken table.

"Tea please?" she said as she starting pouring the steaming green liquid.

They drank hot tea and chatted about the cold weather for a few minutes.

"Now, O-basan, thank you very much for this wonderful tea. If you have some time, Yoshiko would like to tell you something."

"Yoshiko-san, whenever you are ready ...." Myles said.

O-basan refilled their cups and settled back to listen. Yoshiko talked for almost thirty minutes. She even retold the story about how she and Myles first met that afternoon at the Victoria, and she called attention to **Ladybug**. O-basan was teary eyed, but took in the whole story.

"O-basan, now you know our story. Thank you for being such a good friend. Will you help me take care of Yoshiko-san whenever I am not here?" Myles asked.

"Yoshiko-san and I are fine. I take care. You not worry Myru-san."

She patted him on his arm and looked him straight in the face.

Myles held Yoshiko's arm and helped her up from the floor table. They all put their arms around each other and said good night over and over again before finally separating for the night.

The bedside lamp had been left on and the room was cozy and warm as they slid open their door. Inside, they quickly changed into their robes and climbed under the futon. It felt good over them and they cuddled up and kissed a few times. They fell asleep knowing that Uncle Masuda and O-basan would be there whenever they were called on.

Sunday and Monday, December 30 and 31, 1956

Sunday and Monday were happy days. They had long conversations about their experiences over the past seven weeks, including the wonderful Christmas Party. Yoshiko assured Myles that she liked his friends, especially Major Hickson and Peggy. They finally got around to looking at all the pictures they had taken that day on the Ginza. They took long walks both afternoons as the sun returned and it warmed up outside. They took Mr. Nikon with them on the walks and took pictures around Ikebukuro and Naka Park. They found a favorite bench in the park where they took long rests both days. They hugged and kissed openly much to the shock of passersby.

And they talked about the baby. There were all sorts of what ifs. What if a boy, what if a girl, what if ……. what if …… what if? After the shock of Saturday morning it turned out to be the quiet New Years Yoshiko had wanted.

Myles was sad when Monday came to an end. Yoshiko had to work Tuesday or else he would have stayed on New Year's Day. They changed plans for next weekend. Since Yoshiko had to work late at the Seibu on Friday, she would be in a taxi waiting for him at the South Gate of Tokyo Station at seven o'clock.

Myles stood at the door for a brief moment.

"Sayonara, until Friday."

He waved gently.

New Years Day, January 01, 1957

New Years day on the base was a lost day for Myles. Yoshiko and Uncle Masuda going to the Tokyo doctor on Wednesday stayed on his mind all day.

Once during the day, he wandered over to the compound and went over things in the office. He updated his wall chart of South Vietnam. There was new information on the Ha Tien area in the Mekong River Delta region. It looked like the Vietcong were setting up a new base at the south end of the Ho Chi Minh Trail. He scoured his maps looking for The Sea of Reeds. It was not to be found on any of his maps.

Tomorrow should be an interesting day, he thought with four days of intercepts to go through. No telling how Diem spent his New Years. Those celebrations sometimes ended up deadly with drunken firing squads going crazy.

Wednesday, January 2, 1957

Wednesday finally came and 21st Radio was back at work after the grand Christmas Party and the other holidays. One thing Myles had to take care was calling Uncle Masuda to see how the doctor appointment went.

"Roy, got a minute."

Myles sat down beside Brent's desk.

"Sure, Happy New Year again, and for the last time. What's up?"

"Well, I know in the past you've gone somewhere to make private phone calls. Where do you do that?" he asked.

"Oh that!" Brent said. "I go to the snack bar and ask the manager, Mark Patterson, if I can use the phone in his office. He's a great guy and he lets me use the phone. He calls vendors all the time in Tokyo, so it's just like a local phone call."

"Think he'd let me use his phone if I said I was your friend?"

"Absolutely, who do you need to call?" Brent was curious.

"It's private. You can probably guess. Thanks," Myles replied.

Myles worked at his desk for an hour or so to make it look like he wasn't too anxious. Then he went to the snack bar to see Mark and make his call.

"Is Mark around?" Myles asked one of the waitresses.

"That's his office over there. Just knock," she replied.

"Come in," a voice came from inside.

"Mark, I'm Myles Garrison. I'm a close friend of Captain Brent, I think you know him," Myles said.

"Sure, I know Captain Brent. What can I do for you?"

"Well, if you don't mind I'd like to use your phone for a short personal phone call to Tokyo."

"Tell you what. Just take my seat and I'll leave you alone in here 'till you're done. To call a Tokyo number, dial eight and then the number."

"That would be great, thanks a lot."

Myles took a the seat behind Mark's desk as Mark left the room and closed the door.

He dialed Masuda's camera shop number. There was no answer. Hmm .... he thought ...... this is a Wednesday at eleven o'clock. He must be seeing the doctor with Yoshiko. I'll try again tomorrow.

He left the office and found Mark sitting at the snack counter.

"Mark, I couldn't get an answer. Would you mind if I tried again tomorrow morning?" Myles asked.

"No, that'd be fine. Can I set you up with a cheeseburger or something. You guys do so much for us civilians, it's the least I can do."

"Thanks a lot, Mark, but I'll take a rain check. Maybe next time."

Myles went directly back to the office.

As he entered, Johnson spotted him and hurried over to his desk.

"Myles, we got a letter from Arlington a little while ago in the morning pouch," Johnson said as he handed the Top Secret Beehive envelope over to Myles.

"Here, sit down, let's see what this is. Feels like it might be a few pages. I will bet you it's from Commander Banta," Myles said, as he plopped the envelope on his desk and took a seat.

"I won't take that bet. I can guarantee it's from Sheila," Johnson replied.

Myles pulled out the three page message. They both scooted up their chairs and looked at the first page.

TOP SECRET BEEHIVE

TO: Chief Blue Cover; Chief Red Cover; Chief Brown Cover; Chief Green Cover; Chief DeSoto
FR: Commander Banta; Lieutenant Peabody

UPDATE BEEHIVE

FIRST FOUR VAN SHELLS SHIP TO CLARK AB PHILIPPINES WEEK OF FEBRUARY ONE.

DETACHMENTS AS FOLLOWS

BLUE COVER MIRV BLUE ALPHA DEPLOYMENT LONG MEI, MEKONG DELTA, CHIEF GARRISON

RED COVER MIRV RED ALPHA DEPLOYMENT DONG HA, NORTH COAST, CHIEF SMITHSON

BROWN COVER MIRV BROWN ALPHA DEPLOYMENT LOC NINH, HO CHI MINH TRAIL, CHIEF CLARKSON

GREEN COVER MIRV GREEN ALPHA DEPLOYMENT KON TOM, CENTRAL HIGH, CHIEF MORGANSON

DESOTO EAST COAST PATROL, CHIEF LT CMDR MOORE STARTUP DEFERRED.

ALL VANS TO BE EQUIPPED AT CLARK. EQUIPMENT INCLUDE NEW SCANNING

DEVICE ALL RECEIVERS, RANGE 250 MILE RAD, HF, VHF, UHF FREQ, KW6 ENCRYPTION DEVICE,, UHF VOICE RECORDERS ALL EQUIP, LOW FREQUENCY CRITICOM XMTTR.

AFTER OUTFIT, VANS AIR SHIP TO TAN SON NHUT EST WEEK OF FEBRUARY 21 NOT FIRM.

FIFTY MAN VAN CREWS TRAIN AT TAN SON NHUT FEBRUARY FIFTEEN THRU MARCH 15 ON MOCK UP.

ALL CHIEFS MEET AT ARLINGTON WEEK OF FEBRUARY EIGHTEEN THROUGH APRIL ONE.

EST CHIEFS DEPLOY TO MACV SAIGON WEEK OF MARCH ONE.

EST VANS DEPLOY TO GEO LOC WEEK OF MARCH FOUR.

EST START UP OPERATION BEEHIVE WEEK OF MARCH ELEVEN.

MORE TO FOLLOW REG TRAVEL AND OTHR DETAILS.

WELCOME BILL PEABODY AS LIAISON

COMMANDER BANTA

TOP SECRET BEEHIVE

Both men read the message together.

"Well, Johnson, guess that finally explains things pretty well. Even got the names of the chiefs. Isn't that a great name ..... the chief? And looks like we got slowed down to one van for each detachment, at least in the beginning. Guess the Navy boys will have to cool their heels."

"Yeah, and it looks like you'll be going alone to Arlington, this time for two weeks. Remember, Sheila promised chili the next time. Better be ready for that, if you know what I mean."

"I'll be ready. There was nothing in there about you and me rolling out of the Air Force, except it referred to me without any rank like the other civilians. Guess that means it's coming soon. You know we'll get a terrific pay raise when that happens," Myles said.

"Sure do, don't think I haven't been thinking about that. So we'll be setting up our van with fifty men in the middle of the Mekong Delta. That's pretty cool. That's the area where we've gotten a lot of stuff on Vietcong hideouts. Better get our life insurance paid up."

"I agree. It might be a little dangerous. But you and I will be based at MACV in Saigon, safely out of danger. Not that I especially want that, but I think that's the way it'll be. What say we go to the bowling alley tonight to celebrate?"

"I'm ready, how about right after work? But please refresh my memory .... MACV .... what is that exactly?" Johnson asked.

"Tell you what, I'd like to go change first and get a quick shower. Meet you there about six. MACV .... that's Military Assistance Command Vietnam," Myles said.

"Six o'clock is good."

Myles worked quietly at his desk the rest of the day. He decided to wait until the next morning to show Major Hickson the new message.

He walked silently back to BOQ a little after five. Everything was weighing heavily on his mind. No answer on the camera shop phone .... the doctor's appointment ...... the new schedule for Beehive and another trip to Arlington. Tomorrow, he thought, I'm going to see if Peggy can have lunch with me. I really need to talk to someone who understands all this.

Thursday, January 03, 1957

First thing next morning, Myles knocked on Major Hickson's door.

"Enter," came the quick response.

"Major may I speak with you for a minute please. I've got a message from NSA."

"Come on in Myles."

Myles handed the message to the Major.

"Why don't you look this over and I'll be back in a minute."

"Good", this won't take me long. "Hmm."

The Major started reading the message.

In a couple of minutes, the Major stepped outside his office and signaled to Myles to come back in.

"Well, looks like you'll be leaving us around the middle of February on Project Beehive. I'm glad for you Myles. Remember, I recommended you for this. One thing though, your rank wasn't given in the message. Is there anything you haven't told me?"

"Well, I actually thought I did. Anyway, Commander Banta is resigning me and Johnson from the Air Force and signing us up for government service. She needed to do that because the slots call for a higher rank than we have now."

"We'll hate to lose you guys but, anyway, good luck on your new assignment. When you leave, how about sending Sergeant Johnson in to see me. I want to wish him well too. I'm proud of you both," the Major concluded.

"OK. I'll see you later today, sir," Myles said.

Myles called Johnson over as he headed back to his desk.

"The Major would like to see you. Think he wants to congratulate you on your new job," Myles addressed Johnson.

Back at his desk, Myles hurriedly reviewed a fresh pile of intercepts. More and more it was looking serious in South Vietnam. Now that he'll be concentrating on the Mekong Delta, he looked at that traffic more carefully than before.

By eleven, he decided it was time to head over to the snack bar to make his next Masuda phone call. Then he would try to catch Peggy at home in time for a lunch meeting. He left the compound and headed out across the parade field.

"Mark, it's me again. I hate to bother you but could I possibly used your phone again. Yesterday I couldn't get anybody and I really need to try again if you don't mind," Myles asked Mark as he stood at his doorway.

"Sure Myles. I really don't mind. Come right in, I'm going back into the store room anyway. Have a seat."

Just like yesterday, the phone rang and rang at the camera shop with no answer. What in the heck's going on, he thought, maybe Yoshiko is sick. He thought about the situation for a few minutes but couldn't come up with any good explanations. Then he called Peggy.

She answered after the first ring.

"Peggy, this is Myles. I really need to talk with you. I'm calling from the snack bar. Is there any way you could meet me for lunch?"

"Well, sure. I can be there around a quarter after twelve if you can wait that long. That OK?"

"I'll wait right here. I'll be at our corner table. Thanks a lot."

Myles took a seat and glanced up at the clock. Fifteen more minutes until Peggy gets here, he thought, I can't wait to get her advice.

"Over here, Peggy," Myles called out as Peggy came through the door.

"Hey Myles, what's up? I couldn't pass up a free lunch."

Myles helped her with her jacket and hung it behind her chair. He gently helped her get seated at the table.

"Thanks for coming Peggy. Let me go to the counter and get some lunch. What would you like?"

"I'll have a chicken salad sandwich and a Coke. Thank you."

"Great, I'll be right back."

Myles went over to the counter and placed their order. In a minute he was back at the table.

"Now, Peggy, I want to talk seriously with you along the lines of our last meeting. I don't know if you can help but at least I'd like to share it with you."

"Oh Myles, I'm so sorry. I'm glad you called me."

"Thanks for listening. I think you were right about Yoshiko being pregnant. A doctor told her last week.

Yesterday her Uncle Masuda was supposed to take her to a different doctor for a second opinion."

"Wow, Myles, I'm sorry I was right. What did the new doctor say?"

"Well, that's another part of my story. I tried calling Masuda at his Ginza store yesterday and today and there was no answer. I can't imagine what's going on. I know I have the right number. Guess I'll try again tomorrow."

"Myles, there's probably a good explanation. Maybe he's closed the store for vacation. It is the week after the holidays, that just might be the simple answer."

"Peggy, you just might be right. Anyway, I'm meeting her in Tokyo tomorrow night at seven so I'll find out then what the new doctor said. I'm pretty sure she is pregnant."

"Myles, we do need to talk about this."

"Oh, there's more. I can't give you classified information Peggy, but it looks like I'll be leaving Shiroi in about six weeks and never coming back. I'll be in Arlington, Virginia, for two weeks and then I'll be going to Vietnam for at least a year."

"Well, Myles, I'm glad you called me. What takes place between you and me is strictly confidential so let's get that out front. OK?"

"Sure, I expected that."

"Now, Myles, I hear you've been telling people you expect to break up with Yoshiko. What's that all about?"

"Well, actually it's a bunch of bull. I love this girl and do not want to break up with her. I know she feels the same way about me. I've just been saying that to get people off my back."

"OK, I guess that's served its purpose. Anyway, I think people have been believing you, including my husband."

"I know, and I am so grateful to have you both as friends. Oh, there's one more thing that might be a little sensitive but I need to tell you. Navy Commander Sheila Banta is heading up the special unit in the National Security Agency that I'll be working for. Anyway, she is going to take me out of the Air Force and give me a high rank in government service."

"Does the Major know about this ….. the exit from the Air Force I mean?"

"Yes he does and he's all right with it because it's such a great move for me."

"Good. It's hard for me to believe he'd be selfish when it comes to your career."

"Now, Peggy, there are some issues here. If I were to ask for permission to marry Yoshiko I'd lose my clearance and get shipped back to the States within days. Yoshiko would be left all alone and helpless except for Uncle Masuda. Her father disowned her when the Yokohama family doctor said she was pregnant. She's not allowed to come home anymore. Now is that cruel or what?"

"That's awful."

"Now, since I'll be leaving the Air Force and joining government service I don't know what the issues would be if I applied for a marriage license. It might be that they would approve such a marriage and I could keep my clearance and my job. I'd just have to look into that once I get the NSA job."

"I have one suggestion for now, Myles. You'll be here for six weeks. So during these six weeks, you just do your job as normal and visit Yoshiko every weekend as you've been doing. But, during this period make discreet inquiries as to the rules about NSA civilians marrying foreign nationals. Maybe even talk with the the NSA liaison people."

"OK, good plan. I'll do that."

Myles was beginning to feel some relief.

"And Myles, could I possibly visit with you guys some weekend in Tokyo. The Major wouldn't have to know. I could just make an excuse like going in with the girls or something."

"That would be really, really great Peggy. Yoshiko likes you a lot from the Christmas party and you would be a good companion for her. Yeah, thanks, that's a great idea. Yes you can. We'll make plans for that soon."

"Now, I don't have many ideas beyond that for now, except that those two weeks in Arlington will give you more time to find out the ins and outs of getting married to a Japanese without getting fired. Now, we can talk more later about what your options are if you get kicked out of the NSA. Gosh, I hope it doesn't come to that. But, I'll be here to help you through it."

She reached her arm across the table and took his hand.

"Let's work this out Myles."

They had lunch and went their separate ways for the day. Both of them had a lot to think about after the lunchtime discussion.

Friday, January 04, 1957

The rest of Thursday and Friday, Myles worked hard. He and Johnson worked on intel from the Mekong Delta. It looked more and more like a scary place but they were looking forward to their adventure.

Around three o'clock on Friday Major Hickson called Myles into his office.

"Myles, do you remember the secret documents I showed you before you left for Arlington?"

"Yes, sir, I do. You said you would talk with me about them later but ordered me to keep them secret."

".... keep them secret .... that's what I want to talk to you about. I ...."

Myles interrupted, "You have more documents Major?"

"Myles, something came up during your last weekend at Arlington. An FBI man came to see me at home. He had orders to take me to Tokyo for questioning. I don't have to tell you how that affected Peggy. It was bad, very bad."

"Major, I can't imagine ....."

Now it was the Major who interrupted.

"I spent six hours in some building in Tokyo and didn't get back home until midnight. The bottom line is the NSA suspects you and I are involved in stealing secrets. I'm surprised you don't know anything about this. It was strange. They didn't even mention those documents that I showed you. The only thing they had was a short encrypted message that came from someone in our office. They weren't able to decrypt it and they locked me in a room for two hours to think about. Well, the message never came from me, so I tried to decrypt it. It was so short I wasn't able to. They finally took me to the train station and sent me back to Shiroi. Before they would let me go, I had to swear that I knew nothing about the message or any kind of conspiracy. I'm afraid this isn't the end of it. I don't know what to expect. Now let me ask you. What the hell went on back there in Arlington? Did you tell them anything about the documents? Do you know anything about the encrypted message?"

Myles heart was pounding and he started sweating.

"Major, I'm so sorry to hear about all that."

As he spoke, he was thinking a mile a minute. What should he say? He might be in trouble no matter what he said.

"I absolutely didn't reveal anything to anybody about those documents. I swear to it. It was a total misunderstanding and I can explain everything. It's late Friday. Can you wait until Monday morning? I'll explain everything then, I promise you."

"Well, it's a while since my FBI encounter and I haven't heard anything since. Yeah, I guess it can wait until Monday. I suggest you get your story straight by then. Dismissed."

"Thank you sir."

Myles turned and left the room. He sat at his desk for a while trying to regain his composure. He leafed through a tall stack of intercepts without reading them. He said goodbye to Johnson and left the office at five o'clock.

That night it seemed like the longest ride ever to Ikebukuro.

Hungary appeals to UN for assistance against USSR aggression; UN demands USSR leave Hungary; Brooklyn NYC discontinues streetcar service; Chet Huntley and David Brinkley team up on NBC-TV News; Elvis Presley's first film, "Love Me Tender" is released; Brooklyn Dodger pitcher Don Newcombe wins 1st ever "Cy Young Award"; "Pajama Game" closes at St. James Theatre in NYC after 1063 performances; "Bells are Ringing" opens at Shubert Theatre in NYC.

Chapter Ten

Hula

Friday Evening, January 04, 1957

Friday nights were something special in Tokyo Station. People occupied almost every block of space available. Skiers were jostling through the crowd jabbing innocent people with their ski poles. Business men in suits were scurrying to get home for the weekend and teenagers were grouping and shouting as if they owned the place. Myles was totally relieved when he finally made it through the South Gate.

His heart skipped a beat as he saw the taxi by the curb with the door open and Yoshiko waiting inside. She hadn't even seen him yet. The driver spotted him first and rushed over to meet him.

"Here sir."

The driver took his bag and led him to the open door.

Just then Yoshiko saw him. He felt like he just landed in Heaven as he saw that wonderful smile and her arms reaching to him.

"Mai, Mai, here," she called out.

Without a word, Myles scooted into the car beside her. They clamped their arms around each other so tightly that things went flying all over the back seat. She had two hat boxes this time and they ended up hanging over the front seat.

"Oh, Yoshiko, I've missed you so much. How are you my darling?"

"Mai, I miss you too. I love you too much. I am fine and the baby is fine too. Here feel."

Myles felt but of course there was nothing to feel except for her cute little belly. Yoshiko asked the driver to go on, instructing him to proceed to Ikebukuro.

"Yoshiko, tell me about the doctor and where has Uncle Masuda been. I've been calling his shop, but no answer."

"May, no worry. Tokyo doctor says we have fine baby here."

She pointed to her belly.

"I am busy working this week, and Mitsukoshi in Shimbashi today. Uncle Masuda has shop closed New Year week for vacation so no worry about him. He is OK. Everything is OK. I love you."

She kissed him hard again.

"You have an extra hat box. What is that?" Myles was curious.

"Oh, Mai, that secret. I tell you when we home. Just keep still," she insisted.

"Well, OK. Just let me hold it."

Myles reached for it with the hope of rattling it for tell tale sounds.

Yoshiko, grabbed it away.

"No, no. Please no."

She punched his arm.

"Ok, wait until we get home. Here"

He took her by the back of her neck and kissed her firmly on the lips.

"There, now I can wait," he said.

It was pitch black and bitter cold when the taxi pulled up to the front gate. He managed to pay this time. He was getting better at beating her to the draw.

They struggled out of the taxi with one bag and two hat boxes. They clumsily walked past O-basan's door, knocking bags and boxes against the wall as they went. O-basan slid open her door.

"Hey, what going on here?" O-basan joked.

"O-basan, we're just getting home late," Myles said.

"Yes, and O-basan, can Myru-san come down and sit with you for a few minutes?" Yoshiko asked.

"Oh yes. Just come down Myru-san," she replied.

They managed the stairs and the slippery hallway and plopped their things on the bed. Myles jumped on the bed and pulled Yoshiko over on top of him.

"Now, what about that hatbox?" he asked.

"OK, now you go down visit O-basan and come back room ten minutes."

Myles and O-basan talked about the weather, the new year, and Yoshiko for ten minutes, then he went upstairs.

He slid the paper door open and …. lo and behold …… there was Yoshiko standing there, in front of the bed in full Hawaiian grass skirt regalia. She had a huge gardenia in her hair, and a sky blue halter top was in place above a full billowing grass skirt.

"Mai, how you like?" she asked.

"Uh, uh, it's wonderful. It really is, but what.....?"

"Mai, I am going on Tokyo television in two weeks and will be hula dancer. What you think?" she asked, as she swished her hips back and forth.

"My, oh my. That's really exciting. Do you know how to do the hula dance?"

"No, I have records and instruction book. Tomorrow, we go to Mitsukoshi and buy record player. Then I practice dance here in apartment. You watch."

"Wow, that sounds great. I have always loved hula dancers and you are a beautiful hula girl in your grass skirt. What kind of television program will you be on?"

"It will be travel program for Hawaii and have all Hawaii things. It will be at two o'clock one week from next Wednesday. You will watch from base. OK?"

"Absolutely for sure."

He couldn't resist taking this hula girl up in his arms and hugging and kissing her.

"I think we should go to bed now and practice hula tomorrow."

"No, first I go downstairs and show O-basan grass skirt."

They went downstairs and rapped on O-basan's door.

"O-basan, what do you think of my hula dancer?" Myles asked.

O-basan was speechless.

"What you doing Yoshiko-san?"

Yoshiko explained as best as she could what it was all about. O-basan was excited and happy over the prospect of Yoshiko being on television. She immediately began thinking about where she could go to watch the program. Probably the television sales floor over at Mitsukoshi .... she thought. Yes, she would plan on seeing her good friend on television.

Myles helped Yoshiko undo her grass skirt and unwrap it from around her waist. He enjoyed every minute of it. Taking off a grass skirt was a pleasure he'd never, ever thought he would enjoy. But there he was undressing this beautiful hula dancer.

Saturday, January 05, 1957

They slept until nine the next morning. Yoshiko made her famous coffee and they lay back in bed drinking coffee and talking about hula dancing. Yoshiko had actually come to enjoy coffee as well as her beloved green tea. After a while, the coffee cups ended up back on the side table and they crawled under the covers until ten o'clock.

There was some coffee left over so they enjoyed a little bit more as they dressed for the day. They agreed a good plan was to go over to Mitsukoshi and buy a record player and then have a nice lunch somewhere. It would still be cold and breezy but the sky was clear so they might take some pictures.

They trudged up the gravel road turned right heading for the main street. Mitsukoshi was crowded, but this was the first Saturday after the New Year holiday. That meant there were plenty of exchanges and returns to be made.

"We go to radio department now."

Yoshiko guided him by the arm.

Myles was pleased at the selection of record players. They picked out a portable JVC player for about twenty-five dollars.

They had lunch at the noodle shop and enjoyed their favorite soba noodles with tempura vegetables. Hot green tea helped warm them up after their stint outdoors.

"Now, we walk home and place my record player, and then walk some in park, OK?" Yoshiko asked.

After a walk in the park and a lot of picture taking, they got back to the apartment around four. Yoshiko couldn't wait to set up the player and change into her grass skirt. Myles lay back on the bed enjoying the whole operation. The sight of her wrapping the grass skirt around her waist was most enjoyable. He couldn't wait for the Hawaiian music and a hula demonstration.

Fully wrapped in the grass skirt, she finally placed a record on the player and flipped the switch. Hawaiian music filled the little apartment and probably the rest of the second floor. She placed herself near the wall in front of Myles and gently started swaying her hips.

"Now, Mai, you must move hips one way and wave arms other way. See, how this look?"

She continued to sway to the music with her legs poking out through the dry grass and her bare feet twisting and turning in time with the rest of her body.

"Yoshiko, that is wonderful, did you just learn that?"

"Yes, the girl at agency teach me little, but I practice some before. I keep dancing now."

Myles was definitely impressed. She swayed her hips, waved her arms and moved her bare feet in time to the music. She even improvised a couple of slow spins. Myles wanted to jump up and grab her. His own hula dancer.... he thought, what could be better?

Before long, O-basan tapped on the door and Myles jumped up to let her in. She had a wide grin on her face and was holding a pot of something that smelled really good.

"I hear music and ...... oh, Yoshiko you hula dance. I like very much."

Yoshiko interrupted her dancing and turned off the record player.

"What you have in dish?" she asked.

"Oh, this favorite sukiyaki, you like before."

"We sure do, O-basan, thank you very, very much. Please sit down and join us in eating some," Myles joined in.

"No, no, I go downstairs now. You are welcome very much and I like music and dancing very much. Good night."

O-basan slipped out into the hall and quietly slid the door shut.

That night there was more hula dancing accompanied by an excellent batch of sukiyaki. It was a perfect Saturday evening. They didn't need to go out into the cold to get supper that night.

Sunday, January 06, 1957

Sunday was a good day. In the morning they had another nice walk in the park and around the neighborhood, with a brief stop for lunch at the noodle shop. After a short nap, Yoshiko told Myles she was going to the bath house and invited Myles to come along. He respectfully declined but promised next time.

From the back window, he watched her walk up the road toward the bathhouse in her robe and jacket. Her ever present hat box was filled with bath accessories and clean clothes. OK, maybe next time, he thought.

About an hour later, she came back to the apartment. Myles sighted her coming in the front entrance from the front window of O-basan's apartment. He'd taken that time to solidify his friendship with her and let her know Uncle Masuda might be arranging a phone for the building. He was surprised at her reaction. She really wasn't that interested in a phone. After all, she told him, she'd gotten along all these sixty years without one and why did she need one now?

"OK", she finally consented to some kind of phone arrangement.

"Yoshiko-san, we're in here," Myles called out.

The thoroughly bathed and refreshed Yoshiko came into the room.

"Mai, next time you come. You feel so good."

"OK, next weekend I promise. Now sit down for a minute."

"I just told O-basan that your uncle might arrange for a phone in the building and she said it would be OK. Now, I have a surprise for both of you."

Myles made sure everybody was comfortably settled.

"My good American friend Peggy has asked if she might spend a weekend with all of us here in Ikebukuro. Isn't that wonderful?"

"Mai, oh yes, yes, I love Peggy from Christmas Party. She very nice. She come stay with us? But where, we have only one bed. We sleep together? That your idea?" Yoshiko asked, a little alarmed at the thought.

"Yoshiko, please explain this to O-basan in Japanese and ask her if Peggy can stay in the empty room across the hall from us ….. and what would it cost?"

Yoshiko and O-basan spoke in mile-a-minute Japanese for a little while. Myles could tell O-basan was a little taken back by the prospect of an American woman in her apartment house. But eventually, they reached a conclusion.

"Mai, O-basan say Peggy-san can stay in room across the hall for no charge since she your friend. That very nice. When will she come?"

"Well, I don't know yet. Maybe next weekend or weekend after that. I'll have to see and let you both know. I think that will be exciting. Please thank O-basan very much for me."

"OK Mai, I hope next weekend," Yoshiko pleaded.

"If I know for sure I'll call Uncle Masuda on Wednesday. Can you find out from him if I do that?"

"Yes, that be fine," she replied.

With all that settled Myles and Yoshiko went upstairs for the rest of the day. Yoshiko stripped off her robe and showed her off her clean body. With only the slightest begging, Myles gladly rubbed her body all over with a glorious gardenia lotion. Then they lay silently in bed for a while before they began to stir for the Myles' ritualistic Sunday evening departure.

"So we have a plan. If you don't hear from me through Uncle Masuda, I will come Friday night as usual. If Peggy is coming for a visit, Uncle Masuda will tell you and you can tell O-basan to get ready. We come Friday night and leave Sunday as usual."

"Yes, Mai, and this week I work at the three stores and I practicing hula. I think I go TV studio this week to see stage and practice some dancing there. Will you work hard this week, Mai?"

"Well, there is a lot of important work to do. I have some new jobs to do for Washington that are pretty important. But I'll be thinking of you. I wish I could call you on the phone, but maybe sometime soon we can get that phone your uncle promised. So that is my plan. I must be going now. Can you get something to eat tonight?"

"Yes, I can walk to noodle shop or maybe eat supper with O-basan. She always happy for that. I hope you safe train ride tonight."

Myles went through all the preparations and then was finally standing at the doorway saying goodbye once more.

"Sayonara for now. See you next Friday. Please take care of baby. Have a good time at work this week. I love you very much. Sayonara."

"Sayonara Mai, I take care of everything and I love you very much too. I hope Friday come soon. Be careful and I love you. Sayonara."

Myles made sure he got one last glimpse of her lying back on double pillows bathed in the golden glow from the bedside table.

It was another cold dark night. The train was hot and Myles napped a little between Tokyo and Matsudo. He was back in his room by nine.

Monday, January 07, 1957

The week began with an impromptu meeting called by Major Hickson. It was barely nine o'clock when they all squeezed into the conference room to see what the Major had to say.

"Thanks for all of you getting together with me so early. Hope you've all had your first coffee by now."

The Major sipped on his own first cup.

"First thing. By now you probably all know about Lieutenant Garrison's and Sergeant Johnson's new assignment with the NSA. They will be staying on for a while, but I expect to be saying goodbye in not too many weeks. I guess that all depends on when they'll be ready for them in Saigon."

The Major looked around the room and nobody looked surprised.

"This morning, I'm asking Lieutenant Garrison to give you all a briefing on the nature of these assignments and what NSA is up to. Myles, I've gotten permission from Commander Banta to ask you to do this. She was very cooperative and said that so far there is nothing for you to hold back. I think she might be counting on some support from our group when you guys get set up down there. I don't like to put you on the spot but, here you go, you're on the spot."

"Sure, Major, I'll be glad to do this. I won't be speaking from notes, so I hope I don't leave anything out. Johnson, please chime in whenever you want."

Myles mind raced through the items on the Beehive message from last week.

He spoke for nearly forty five minutes and covered everything pretty well, he thought. Johnson helped him out a few times. He was pleased they could team up on this without any advance notice.

"That was great Lieutenant Garrison. Now, I have something to add from Commander Banta. Effective January 7, today, Lieutenant Garrison is on inactive Air

Force Reserve duty and is appointed Chief, Blue Cover, Operation Beehive. That will be an NSA GS12 position. Congratulations, Myles."

The Major walked over and shook Myles hand.

"Sergeant Harvest W. Johnson is retired from the Air Force and appointed Assistant Chief Blue Cover, Operation Beehive. That is an NSA GS9 position. Congratulations Sergeant Johnson," the Major repeated his congratulatory walk over to Johnson.

Everyone in the room applauded. Myles and Johnson stood for a few minutes.

"Any questions anybody?" the Major asked.

A couple of hands shot up.

"Yes?" the Major responded.

Lieutenant Davison asked, "Where will these new civilians be stationed and can Myles tell us any more about his job in Saigon?"

Myles stood up.

"Lieutenant Davison. As far as I know, we both will start out at Tan Son Nhut Air Base, or, maybe even the Grand Hotel in Saigon. Now, I have a feeling that if it is Tan Son, we will be transferred very shortly after that to MACV Headquarters in the Grand Hotel in downtown Saigon. MACV, that would be Military Assistance Command Vietnam."

Myles looked at Johnson.

"Johnson is that the way you see it?"

"Yeah, Myles, that's it exactly. Either place will be OK with me. They'll both be close to the Mekong Delta and where our first van will be placed."

"OK, now what was the rest of your question?"

"Can you tell us more about your duties?" Davison asked.

"Well, we now have about 600 military advisors in Vietnam. I don't know where they all are, but I expect to find out more about that soon. I can tell you this though, the Mekong Delta is a hot bed of Vietcong. They have secret hideouts all over the Delta and are killing ARVN troops left and right. They are experts at the ambush. One of our jobs with the first van will be locating VC radio transmitters and then intercepting all their traffic. The object here is obviously killing the VCs and wiping out their hideouts," Myles explained.

He went on.

"Now, besides the direction finding and intercept operation, we will also be intercepting all the other short, medium, and long range radio traffic we can pull in. We will be doing some traffic analysis but other than that all our traffic logs will go to Section B26A in Arlington. When NSA moves to Fort Meade later this year, they will maintain space in Arlington for derivatives such as B26A and Operation Beehive. Johnson and I spent over a week there before Christmas, and I'll be going there for a spell after I leave here. From there I go directly to Saigon."

"Will we ever see you guys again after you leave here?" Davison asked.

"Who knows? I certainly hope so. I'm hoping to have enough influence to be able to get hops to Tokyo once a month or so," Myles said, but then regretted his comment.

"What's that for Myles? You got NSA business in Tokyo?" Brent interrupted.

"Yes, I do. Any other questions?"

"All right men, that'll be it for now. Myles, are you and Johnson going to stay in uniform for a while?" Major Hicks asked.

"Well, Major that's a good question. Guess we will since we don't have enough civilian clothes to carry us through. Hope we won't be breaking any regulations."

"Hey, that'll be fine. I don't think I'd like the sight of coats and ties in my office anyway. Dismissed everybody."

The Major retired to his office and Sergeant Barney followed.

The group disbanded and slowly everybody migrated back to their desk areas.

"Johnson, can we talk for just a bit?" Myles asked.

Johnson and Myles walked over to the coffee pot and Myles poured two cups of steaming black liquid.

"You like it black today?" Myles asked.

"After that, I'd like it black with a little bourbon. That was a real surprise. Did you know anything about it before hand?"

"Nope, but I guess I'm glad it's over. Now there's no secrets about anything," Myles replied.

"Well, now, I don't think you can really say that Myles."

"Oh, right. Guess we do have some secrets. Thanks for reminding me. Let's go sit down."

"Now, Mr. Johnson, what we should do until we get new marching orders from the Commander, is concentrate real hard on our Vietnam traffic. You translate the hell out of everything you get your hands on, and I'll try to build up a file that will be the file to end all files. For our own sakes, we've got to know everything there is to know about the Delta. If we need to, we can request special frequencies and locations to monitor, to get more of the stuff we need. We just forward our request to Commander Banta or, I guess, Lieutenant Peabody. That should work for us," Myles said.

"OK, I've already got a few special requests. I'll give them to you later today. Anything else special, or is it just work away?"

"Guess that's about it. Oh, by the way, I guess we'll get a good pay raise starting today. I don't know how we'll get paid. Guess Peabody will be letting us know," Myles finished the conversation.

Around three o'clock, Myles decided it was time for a visit with Major Hickson. He was surprised that the Major hadn't called him in by this time. The door was standing open and Myles poked his head around the corner.

"Major, may I have a few minutes. I'd like to wrap up what we talked about on Friday."

Myles had carefully prepared his words and was only slightly nervous ..... nothing like the way he reacted the last time they talked.

"Come in Myles and sit down. You can relax. I think I got the whole story from Captain Brent a little while ago."

"You did, sir?"

Myles wasn't sure what the whole story might mean.

"Yes. I think he saw the state you were in when you left my office the other day. He just volunteered to talk. I didn't know it, but he'd been corralled by the FBI too. He told me how it was just a little joke between the two of you and how you refused to cooperate with Commander Banta. For a while there, the three of us were in deep trouble. Anyway, everything is fine now and I'm sorry I was so hard on you last Friday. Let me warn you though, don't ever pull anything like that again. Let this be a lesson learned. Unless you got anything to add, you can go back to work. That'll be all. Oh, one last thing, we all know about the girl now. Please get rid of that noose around your neck. Thanks."

The rest of the day passed by quickly. Myles sent Johnson's special request to Peabody and got an acknowledgement. There was no word yet on when they were getting paid.

He was relieved now that the issue was settled on the secret cryptogram between him and Brent. He was unsettled though about the Major's remarks about Yoshiko being a noose around his neck.

Tuesday, January 08, 1957

Tuesday was a good day. Myles was totally relieved that it was resolved without anybody getting into any real trouble. Both he and Brent found it incredible that none of the brightest minds in NSA's cryptology center had been able to solve their simple little cryptogram.

The volume of traffic coming in from the border regions of Laos and Cambodia had nearly tripled. The new frequencies were tapping into new networks and were highly productive.

Wednesday, January 09, 1957

First thing Wednesday morning, Myles excused himself for a trip to the credit union. He knew he could access a base phone there to make his call to Peggy. Anyway, he needed to withdraw a couple of hundred dollars to tide him over next weekend.

"Peggy, this is Myles. How've you been?"

"Well hello Myles. I've been fine. How was last weekend? Everything turn out all right after all?"

"It did, and I should have called you first thing Monday. I'm so sorry, but your husband had some surprises waiting for me first thing. As a matter of fact, things turned out just like you expected. Uncle Masuda was on vacation and his store was closed. That's why there was no answer on his phone."

"Good, I guess I must know some things after all. I'm so glad there wasn't anything bad. How was your weekend and how is Yoshiko?"

"Yoshiko couldn't be better. In fact, you won't believe this, but she's going to be a hula dancer on a television show. Can you believe that?"

"Oh, Myles that's so exciting. She must be OK with the baby and all I guess."

"She sure is. The Tokyo doctor confirmed she's pregnant and she's over her morning sickness now. I'd invite you to lunch today but I need to get back to the office. You can ask the Major about the announcement he made on Monday. I think you'll find it interesting."

"Can't you tell me about it now, Myles, or how about lunch tomorrow. On second thought, I can't make it tomorrow or Friday either. I'm so sorry. I want to hear all about Yoshiko's hula dancing and the announcement and everything."

"Well, we will have lunch next week for sure. But, can you come to Ikebukuro to stay with us the weekend after next? I got it all set up. I can get you a free room in our apartment building. Yoshiko is so excited. I hope you can. We will have a really great time."

"Yes, I think I can work it out, Myles. Now, this has to be strictly top secret between you, me, and Yoshiko."

"That's great. Let's say for now our plan is to have lunch next Wednesday to confirm everything and make plans. Then, you and I take the train to Tokyo late Friday afternoon. We will spend Saturday and Sunday in Ikebukuro and then come back to Shiroi late Sunday afternoon. How's that sound?"

"Myles, that sounds wonderful. I really need to do something like this …. get a change of scenery and all that. I'll make up a good story and the Major won't know the difference. Am I being a bad girl here Myles?"

"I don't see it that way, Peggy. This will do you a world of good and think of it as a good deed for some close friends."

"I'll work on not feeling guilty. But for now that will be our plan. Where are you calling from right now?"

"I'm over at the credit union but I need to get back to the compound right away. I'm over here on a flimsy excuse of needing cash."

"OK. I'll let you go. So next time I see you will be at our regular table at the snack bar next Wednesday. I'll be thinking about you and Yoshiko in the meantime. Bye for now."

"Bye, bye. See you."

Myles hung up.

The brown grass was frozen and crunched under his shoes. The snow was long gone but it was still cold.

"Myles, glad you're back," Brent called out, as Myles entered the office.

"I'm glad to be back. It's colder than a well digger's ass out there. Looks like snow," Myles replied, "What's up?"

"Oh, I just wanted to congratulate you on your promotion to GS12. You know that's like a promotion to

Major. You've done great. That will double your pay and then some. Congratulations buddy. One thing though, I'm worried about your well being. You're going from this soft cushy job here into hell's kitchen down there. That's some dangerous shit your getting into."

"I know that and I thought it over carefully before I took it on. Guess I thought about it for a full five minutes or so. Seriously, I know it's going to be dangerous in some ways, but I think I'll be all right."

"Another thing Myles, you and I are close, like brothers you might say. When you said you had a plan to get back to Tokyo once a month, I knew it had to do with Yoshiko. Would you like to share with me what's going on with you and her. A while back you told me you were expecting to break up. It don't sound like that to me now."

"Tell you what Roy, let me think about that. For now, I'll just say no comment with a promise to give you a comment tomorrow or Friday. Will you give me that courtesy as an old friend?"

"Sure Myles, whenever you're ready to talk, I'll be ready to listen. Better get back to work. Let's meet at the club for a beer tonight, or maybe tomorrow night."

"Let's have dinner at the club tomorrow night," Myles replied, as he went to his desk.

Myles felt good about his arrangements with Peggy next Wednesday for lunch and especially good about her coming to Ikebukuro for a visit.

Thursday, January 10, 1957

Thursday night around six, Myles stopped by Brent's room to pick him up for their dinner date.

"About ready Roy, I made a reservation for six-thirty?"

Inside the room, Kent was still in uniform.

"Myles, I just got in from the office. The Maj and I were working on some way to get more promotions. All right if I keep these on? After all, it is the officers' club."

"Oh yeah, no problem."

Myles noticed Brent's new Captain's bars glistening from the overhead light. He was nostalgic about leaving the Air Force.

Myles had been thinking for two days what to tell Brent about Yoshiko. He'd decided to tell him everything tonight and level with him that Peggy Hicks already knows the full story.

They had two drinks and ordered steaks.

"Roy, I need to talk seriously and confidentially about something. Can you handle it and pledge your secrecy, and maybe some help?" Myles asked.

"Myles, yes you can. You are my closest and dearest friend. I was waiting for this. I knew the time would come. Let's talk."

For thirty minutes Myles did most of the talking. He started with the Victoria Tea Room and finished up right up to last weekend. He felt good when he had finished. Now Brent knew the whole story.

"Wow. Myles, I'm so glad you shared all that with me. Please count on me to keep all this confidential …. and please ask me for any help you may need. And I know, I know, you will need some advice and help from both me and Peggy."

Friday, January 11, 1957

Myles was in a deep conversation with Johnson when Brent patted him on the shoulder.

"Myles, you need to answer this call in Barney's office. Better get in there, he's in a stew."

"I'm on my way."

Myles headed straight to the First Sergeant's Office.

"Lieutenant .... uh, Mister, you have a call."

Barney handed him the receiver.

"Yes, this is Garrison."

"Myles, just listen and don't say anything. This is Bill Peabody."

"Yes, go ahead. I understand. I'm listening."

"Good. I'm at the Okura Hotel in Tokyo. I got in last night. You need to meet me in the Okura lobby today at four o'clock. It's an emergency. I can't tell you anything over the phone. Commander Banta sent me here with one hour's notice. It's that important. Do you know where the Okura is? Just say yes."

"Yes."

Myles knew about the Okura. It was in central Tokyo just across the street from the American Embassy. It was the most prestigious hotel in Japan. It was where heads of state and celebrities stayed.

"Good. In the next hour or so you will receive a message from the Commander instructing you visit me in Tokyo on Beehive business. You can show it to the Major so your absence will be covered. You should not bring Johnson with you. Just tell him it's Beehive business that doesn't involve him. Just say yes if you understand and you will meet me here in the lobby at four."

"Yes."

"Good. One last thing. I don't know how long our meeting will last. There might be some other people here. Actually, we will probably have our meeting across the street. Please bring your passport and all your other passes and IDs. That includes your Shiroi badge.. Myles, I said this is an emergency. There might be lives at stake. That's all I can say. If you don't have any questions just say goodbye."

"Goodbye."

Friday Afternoon

Commander Banta's message arrived around eleven and Myles immediately took it in to Major Hickson. The Major quickly read it and handed it back.

"I guess we'll see you on Monday, Myles. I hope this is a good sign. When are you leaving?"

"Major, I'm skipping lunch and clearing my desk. I'll probably leave soon after that. I already told Johnson I'm leaving. I'm sure it's got to do with Beehive planning. I can't think of anything else. So, I will see you on Monday then."

Myles turned away and went back to his desk.

He had been thinking about Peabody's phone call and couldn't imagine what would prompt an emergency meeting. Like the Major, he hoped it was a good omen.

He walked through two inches of fresh snow on his way to Matsudo Station. The train was on time so he didn't expect any delays. On the way to Tokyo the countryside was beautiful in a new coat of fresh snow. It reminded him of a winter day back in Iowa.

Outside Tokyo Station, he hailed down a taxi.

"Okura Hotel please."

The drive acknowledged and push a lever on the side of the meter. Tokyo streets were covered with snow but were already scarred by hundreds of car tracks. The taxi skidded a few times but arrived safely at the hotel front entrance by a quarter to four.

Inside the hotel, Myles spotted the registration desk off to the left. He recognized Bill Peabody standing a few feet away, wearing a dark gray suit with a small leather attache case tucked under his arm.

"Bill, It's good to see you again. I missed you the last time I was in Arlington."

Myles extended his hand.

"Good to see you too, Myles. Just keep your coat on. We're walking across the street to the embassy."

After shaking hands, Peabody gestured Myles back to the front entrance.

It was only about a hundred yards to the embassy gate. Myles had never been inside the compound but had seen it many times from the outside. The embassy and the Okura were situated on top of a hill in the center of Tokyo. It was an ideal location. Besides a panoramic view of Tokyo, it offered excellent security from potential evil doers. In the twelve years since World War Two, there had been numerous unsuccessful attempts to breach the compound. Just a year ago somebody launched some fireworks out of the trunk of their car a few blocks away. Nothing struck the embassy or even came close.

"Myles, please show the guard your Shiroi badge and your military ID?" Peabody asked.

"Here you go."

Myles handed over the two items.

"Sir, do you have a passport?" the American MP asked.

"I do."

Myles started reaching inside his coat.

"Do you need to see it?"

"No, sir, but you might need it inside."

With admission taken care of, Peabody led Myles into the main lobby and stopped at a huge semi-circular desk. Two attractive American women sat behind the desk directly under a huge sculptured bronze eagle, suspended from the second floor ceiling. Myles was getting ready to show his passport, but Peabody pulled him past the desk in the direction of a bank of elevators.

From the time they left the Okura to the time they stepped off the elevator on the twelfth floor, Peabody had said very little and Myles had asked very little. Now Peabody led them down a long gray hallway with closed doors on either side. The doors were numbered but there were no names. Myles figured this must be the CIA floor.

Once again, Peabody led Myles past another reception desk. Then he took him into a small conference room. Two middle aged American men wearing black pin striped suits were seated at the table with coffee cups and papers in front of them.

"Myles Garrison, John Allen, Jim Allen."

Everybody shook hands as Peabody made the introductions.

"Please everybody have a seat," Peabody continued.

"Thanks for coming to Tokyo on so short a notice, Myles. John if you don't mind would you take over?" Peabody said.

Myles interrupted.

"That's OK. I was coming into town anyway later today. John and Jim .... are you guys brothers? I see a faint resemblance."

John answered, "No."

Myles tried to recover.

"Good. I didn't mean anything by that."

"Myles, I think you should listen to John," Peabody tried once more to get things started.

"Fine. First off, we know all there is to know about you Myles, and probably a little bit more. Just keep that in mind. We have a really bad situation going on in 21st Radio. Jim and I work for the CIA and we've been brought in to clear things up."

"What things?" Myles interrupted.

"Myles, please," Peabody stopped him again.

"One or more persons in your unit is passing secrets to Hanoi. We don't know much about it yet but we have confirmed that espionage is taking place in your office. Do you know anything about anything Myles?"

"No sir. Bill, these guys are CIA. Is NSA involved? Does Commander Banta know anything about this?" Myles asked.

"Yes to both questions Myles."

Now it was time for Jim to speak.

"May I talk now?" he asked.

"Go ahead," John gave his permission.

"Myles, we believe you are clean. We know all about Yoshiko and your silly prank. We are here today to ask you to help us. I can tell you right now that Major Hickson is a prime suspect. We don't know if he's getting help from any of the men in the 21st but he might be. Are you sure you don't know anything about such activity?"

"No sir. But I guess I'll be willing to help. Bill, will anything going on here affect our Beehive plans?" Myles asked.

"Myles, I'm sorry I just can't say. You've been picked for this because you have been so thoroughly vetted by

Commander Banta. Right now, you are the only person in 21st Radio who is not believed suspect."

"Well, please let the Commander know that I am cooperating."

"I will," Replied Peabody.

"John, just what exactly do you want Myles to do?"

"For now, all we want is for Myles to keep his eyes and ears open and pay special attention to Major Hickson ..... and I guess Sergeant Barney as well. Jim and I are leaving for Saigon tonight. Myles, I want you to coordinate everything with Lieutenant Peabody. We'll be in touch with him. He will be staying at the Okura at least for a week. We'll be working our resources in Hanoi to find out what we can. We know there is a pipeline connecting 21st Radio to some entity in Hanoi. The baton is probably being passed in Tokyo and then relayed to Hanoi. That's what we need to find out. Bill, you and Myles can leave now. Jim and I have some work to do and some phone calls to make. I'll be in touch with you this week at the Okura. Meanwhile, you have your orders."

"That'll be fine. So Myles and I will leave and I guess I'll hear from you then. Myles, let's head back to the hotel."

"That'll be fine. I guess nobody needed to see my passport after all. We ready to go?"

"Myles, we should go."

Peabody wanted Myles to quiet down so he could get the two of them out of the room.

Outside, Peabody led the way through the deep fresh snow back to the Okura. Once inside, they pulled off their coats and shook off a layer of heavy wet snow.

"Myles, sit with me for minute. We need to talk," Peabody said.

"We can talk over there where it's not so crowded. Do you want a drink or anything?"

"No thanks. I'm fine. There's an empty sofa."

Finally seated safely from prying ears, Peabody asked, "OK, Myles, what do you think?"

"Bill, I am in disbelief. I can imagine somebody spying in our group, but I just can't believe it's Major Hickson. He is the most patriotic guy I know. He is rock solid."

"Well, it's not him for certain. For some reason he is a suspect. You sure you don't know anything?"

"There is something, actually. Just before I left for Arlington a while back, the Major called me in and showed me a stack of documents. We were interrupted but I did get to see the top sheet. It was from a South Vietnam official. I think it was the Minister of Agriculture."

"Damn, I don't like the sound of that. What happened then?"

"Nothing. When we were interrupted he stuffed the papers back in his desk. Then, when it was clear he pulled the documents back out and ripped them up. He said he would talk with me later but he never did."

"Why didn't you say something to those CIA guys?"

"I didn't want them to take something out of context. By the way, were those fictitious names .... I mean John and Jim Allen?"

"Myles, welcome to the CIA. Sure you won't have that drink?"

"I'm sure. What should I do next Bill? What do you think?"

"Just go to work as usual. I'll call you on Tuesday and give you some specific instructions. I guess you'd like to leave now and go to Ikebukuro."

Without even thinking, Myles responded, "Yeah, I would like to leave now if that's OK."

"You go on and have a good weekend. Tell Yoshiko hello for me."

Peabody extended his arm and they shook hands.

"Bill, I guess you can take care of yourself in Tokyo. You going to be all right?"

"Don't worry about me Myles. I'm fine. I've got a lot of work to do. I'll talk to you Tuesday."

UN International Atomic Energy Agency is formed; Margaret Towner becomes first female Presbyterian minister; Largest iceberg spotted 60 x 208 miles; Syracuse fullback Jim Brown scores record 43 points; Boston Celtics Bill Sharman begins free throw streak of 55 games; Phil Rizzuto signs as NY Yankees radio and television announcer; "Fanny" closes at Majestic Theatre in NYC after 888 consecutive performances.

Chapter Eleven

Shimbashi

Friday Evening, January 11, 1957

Myles was in a taxi headed for Ikebukuro. He had plenty of new things to think about but promised himself he'd still have a nice weekend with Yoshiko. He'd try not to worry her.

When the taxi reached Ikebukuro the driver stopped where the gravel side road connected to the main street. He apologized but said he couldn't get through the layer of heavy snow.

He walked the last few blocks along the gravel road. It was getting colder by the minute and the snow was nearly six inches deep. There were drifts up to his knees in some places.

He finally reached the front entrance and carefully slid open the door. Inside, he slipped off his shoes and shook the snow from his pant legs. It was quiet and dark in O-basan's apartment and he didn't hear any sounds from upstairs. He carefully and silently crept up the stairs and down the hallway. There was light inside the apartment but still no sound.

He knocked gently on the wooden door frame.

"Mai, come in," Yoshiko called out.

He slid the door and low and behold, there was Yoshiko lying on the bed dressed in her grass skirt. He quickly put down his bag and jumped in bed beside her. He put his arms around her and they kissed for a couple of minutes.

"Yoshiko, why are you dressed in a grass skirt?"

"Mai, I am practice dancing two hours and so tired I lay down. I was looking beautiful snow on willow tree. Did you walk in the snow?"

"Yes I did. I walked a lot. Some at the base and some from the street over to here. It is really pretty. It is still cold too. I'm glad you have the heater working."

"Yes, it cold. Maybe snow more, you think?"

"Well, I don't know, but if it does we are all cozy here. Have you had anything to eat yet?"

"Oh, no. I wait for you Mai. O-basan not here. She go visit son in Mito. So I wait for you."

"Well, you can't go out in a grass skirt can you?"

"Yes I can, but grass might blow away?"

"No, no. We won't do that. Let's get some clothes on and maybe go to kushi katsu shop. Tempura sounds good to me tonight. Besides I went to the bank and I have some money to spend. Come on let's get going."

He helped her get out of her grass skirt and all the other parts of the costume. Then he helped her pick something to go out in. He was a little appalled that she didn't have a lot to choose from, only four dresses and about as many skirt and blouse outfits.

There weren't really any shoes fit for snow either. She only had one pair of low flat shoes, so that would be it for tonight.

They had a great time playing in the snow as they walked out of the neighborhood. He taught her how to make snowballs which he found was probably a mistake. She was a pretty good snowball thrower. He got peppered in the face a few times and he had snow down his collar.

They had their tempura dinner and it was just as great as the last time. They each had twelve sticks and one large beer.

They made it back through the snow and got into bed as quick as they could.

Saturday, January 12, 1957

The next morning the snow was still there. Yoshiko made coffee and offered Myles some little sweet rice cakes for breakfast. It was perfect for a snowy morning.

"Yoshiko, I have good news. Miss Peggy is going to visit us next weekend for sure. Won't that be fun?"

"Yes, yes. I'm so happy she will come see us. I make sure she has room across hall. We can do lots of things together. Go shopping and go sightseeing."

"I knew you'd be happy. Please promise to see me too sometime while she's here."

"No, you take care yourself Mai. Peggy and I have fun."

"I know you're kidding. Maybe you can take her to the bath house."

"Yes, I take you and Peggy to the bath house. That will be fun."

"Now, Yoshiko, I have a favor."

"What favor"

"Well, I'd like to take a taxi to Tokyo so I can order some clothes from my tailor shop in Shimbashi. Could we do that?"

"Yes, do you need new clothes?"

"I'd like to order two new suits. I only have three and one sports jacket. I need two more."

"Why you need five suits Mai? You not girl."

"Well, to look pretty for you. I need two more suits. OK."

"Mai, I buy you two suits. How much they cost?"

"Well, they cost too much for you to buy."

"That OK. I help pick out cloth. You know I am model. When you want to go?"

"I think maybe we should go just before lunch so we can order the suits and have lunch on the Ginza."

"OK. That good plan. I get ready soon."

Around eleven, they trudged out in the snow. She wore her only pair of flat shoes which were too low to keep the snow out. By the time they got to the street and squeezed into a yellow and red taxi she had cold wet feet. On the way to Tokyo, Myles pulled her feet up in his lap and removed her wet shoes. He rubbed her stocking feet all the way downtown until he finally felt some warmth coming back.

As the taxi approached downtown, Myles directed the driver to Yurakucho Station. From there, he could point out the side street where Morita-san's shop was situated.

"Morita-san, do you remember my friend Yoshiko-san from the Christmas Party?" Myles asked.

"Yes, oh yes."

Morita bowed deeply. Myles recognized most of his Japanese as he said he was pleased to see her again and inquired as to her health.

"I fine, thank you. And how is your friend from the party. He nice man," Yoshiko responded.

"Oh, thank you for asking," Morita replied, as he smiled at Myles.

"He is fine. I just saw him last night. I tell him you say hello. He was very impressed by you that night."

"Thank you Morita-san."

Yoshiko bowed.

"Now, Mr. Morita, I would like to order two business suits please. And I'd like to pick them up next Saturday. Can you do that?" Myles asked.

"Most certainly. You and Yoshiko-san sit here. I will bring you tea and then show you some of my new suit cloth."

Myles and Yoshiko settled down in two deep chairs. Myles could tell Yoshiko was really enjoying this. She was in her element for sure.

After a while, Myles, with a lot of help from Yoshiko picked out a gray tweed material and blue-gray herringbone pattern. He made sure they would be adequate for Washington, but probably still not too hot for Saigon, except in the hottest weather. It took about an hour for Morita-san to get all his measurements and write up the order.

"Myles, you still same weight and almost same measurements."

"Good. I must tell you this story. Last November 17, I picked up my last suit from you. It was the gray flannel. When I left your shop, I went over to the Victoria Tea

Room for a drink and some supper. Well, your suit brought me good luck, because that was when I met Yoshiko-san."

"Ah, so. How lucky my suits are. So happy for both of you."

"Yoshiko did you understand what I just told Morita-san about the day we met?" Myles asked.

"Yes, and what nice story. I lucky you buy suit from Morita-san that day."

"Well, we must be going Morita-san. We'll be back next Saturday about the same time. Do you need some money for a deposit?"

"No, not required. But don't forget you promised me a drink, remember?"

"Yes I did. Tell you what. How about joining us for lunch over on the Ginza today?"

"Thank you but I cannot. I have customers here, and I would not interrupt two lovers like you."

"Oh, Morita-san, you so polite and thoughtful. Thank you for being friend. Next time you join us OK?" Yoshiko said.

After leaving the shop, they walked a short distance in the snow and instead of heading over to the Ginza, they started out in the opposite direction toward Shimbashi. They found a really cute little soba shop a little more than a block away and had soba noodles with broccoli and asparagus tempura, and a small beaker of hot sake.

"This was a nice lunch for such a cold and snowy day," Myles said. "How about some more sake?"

"Oh no, thank you. Wait ….. maybe yes a little more for cold weather."

They had more sake, then decided to walk in the snow to downtown Shimbashi. An antique locomotive stood in the center of the square and it was beautiful in its coat of fresh snow.

"Mai, this very old train. It over one hundred years old. See the small wheels," Yoshiko told Myles.

"Yes. It looks the same as an American train that I remember from when I was a little boy. I'm glad we came to see it. What else would you like to do?"

Just then Myles remembered her skimpy selection of everyday shoes.

"Let's go to a shoe store and buy you some shoes for walking in the snow," Myles suggested.

"OK, thank you, Mai. That very nice."

Yoshiko spotted a store on the station side of the square just beyond the locomotive. She pointed it out and started pulling Myles in that direction.

"I see, I see, let's get on over there. The wind is starting tp pick up. Looks like more snow might be coming."

All of a sudden, Yoshiko stopped dead in tracks. Then she started walking slowly toward the locomotive as if in a hypnotic trance.

She stood alongside the engine and put both hands up against the boiler section. She just stood there, silently, not moving. Myles was concerned about what was going on and came up beside her. As they stood there, the wind was blowing sounds through the whistle.

"Yoshiko, come on it's getting cold out here. Let's get to the store."

She suddenly jumped back from the engine as if it were burning her hands.

"We go now Myles. Oh, where we go now?"

"We're going to that shoe store over there."

"Yes, shoe store."

They browsed around the warm shop for a few minutes. Later, they finished their shopping with two new pairs of shoes, a pair of lace up high tops, and a pair of brown penny loafers. Luckily, Myles had the cash from his trip to the bank earlier in the week. The two pair cost him nearly twenty dollars.

Yoshiko enjoyed her new high top shoes all the way back to the Ginza. . She barely stayed on the cleared sidewalk and sought out the highest banks to stomp through. She resumed her snowballing skills and plastered Myles a few times about the head. He didn't mind a bit.

Just before the Ginza, Myles noticed a little radio shop almost up against the Victoria Tea Room.

"Yoshiko, you know this place for sure don't you?"

"Mai, Victoria Tea Room is my best memory. We go again sometime, maybe?" she asked.

"Why not?" he said. "Maybe next week when Peggy-san is with us."

They went inside the radio shop and Myles bought a small Crosley table radio. He explained that they could listen to the Armed Forces Radio Service from their apartment. He realized she didn't understand what that was all about, but he would have a good time demonstrating it. He figured they would have a fine time listening to American music and news, and maybe even some soap operas.

They got back to the apartment around six and spent the rest of the evening in bed listening to AFRS on the new radio.

Sunday, January 13, 1957

Sunday was spent staying warm inside, listening to the radio, and practicing hula steps.

Late Sunday afternoon, O-basan brought up some rice and stir fried vegetables and they all sat on the bed eating and talking about O-basan's family and Yoshiko's hula dancing.

Myles reminded O-basan about the house guest next weekend and not to forget to save a room. O-basan was already on top of things and assured them that the room across the hall was reserved for Peggy-san. She was looking forward to Peggy's visit.

Around seven, Myles packed his bag and got ready to say goodbye.

"Yoshiko, I must be leaving," he said. "But before I go, I must ask you something. Please don't worry."

"Yes, Mai," she said soberly.

"Well, I have not seen *Ladybug* this weekend. Is she lost?"

"Oh, Mai, I cannot find *Ladybug*. I sorry. She not lost. I find her, you not worry. Next week she be here to visit with Peggy-san."

"Yoshiko, if she is lost, I will buy a new one. I hope you find her. Please don't worry though and I won't worry either," Myles reassured her.

Myles made his final preparations and stood by the door, looking over at Yoshiko lying back on the bed.

"Sayonara, my darling. Peggy-san and I will come Friday night."

"Wait, wait, Mai. I forget to tell you. I have appointment with Tokyo doctor on Wednesday. He check on baby-san."

"That will be great. I hope everything is OK. I wish I could be with you. I'll be going now. I love you. Sayonara."

Monday, January 14, 1957

"Man, I love Monday mornings," Davison shouted out, as he strutted over to his desk.

Cheers and boos arose from the rest of the staff, as the Lieutenant accomplished his purpose which was irritating the troops.

Myles shouted back, "Hey man, calm down. Not everybody here loves Monday morning. Just look around at those red eyeballs."

"Just getting everybody up and going my friend. How was your weekend in Tokyo, if I may ask?"

"Sure you may ask ..... but I may not answer. Anyway, it was nice in snow covered Tokyo. I even got by Morita-san's shop and ordered some clothes. What do you think of that?"

"Spend all your money did you?" Davison asked.

"Hell no, I'm loaded don't you know," answered Myles.

Just then Myles noticed Johnson coming over to his desk.

"Seriously, how'd it go this weekend?" he asked as he sat down in Myles' empty chair.

"It went real well in Ikebukuro," Myles replied.

"That's good. How's Yoshiko?"

"She's real fine thanks."

Myles couldn't remember if he'd told Johnson about the baby. Either way, he didn't think this was the time to talk about it.

"We got another message from Arlington," Johnson said.

He handed an envelope to Myles.

"Can we open it together? I noticed it was not addressed to Lieutenant Garrison, just Myles Garrison. How's that make you feel?"

"Truthfully, I don't like to see that. But we'll get used to it soon enough."

Myles opened the outer envelope and the inner TOP SECRET BEEHIVE envelope.

"Looks like it's from Commander Banta," Myles said.

TOP SECRET BEEHIVE

JANUARY 14, 1957

TO: MYLES GARRISON, CHIEF BLUE COVER

FROM: COMANDER BANTA, CHIEF B26A

UPDATE BEEHIVE

BEEHIVE TO START FIRST WITH BLUE COVER SAIGON. EXPEDITING COMPLETION YOUR VAN AND EXPECT DELIVERY AT CLARK EARLY AND THEN TAN SON NHUT ON OR ABOUT FEBRUARY 25. WANT YOU TO INSPECT AT TSH ON OR ABOUT MARCH 18. THEN DEPLOY TO DUAY BAH DEN. LONG MEI SITE CANCELLED. DBD SITE PREPARED ON 220 METER HILL AND READY FOR VAN. WILL INCLUDE SPACE FOR TWO TENT HALVES, GENERATOR, AND OTHER EQUIP.

URGENT YOU ARRIVE ARLINGTON BY FEB 6 FOR FINAL TRAINING. THEN HAVE TIME FOR SHORT LEAVE BEFORE DEPARTING FOR SAIGON ONE MONTH ON OR ABOUT MARCH 6. JOHNSON SHOULD DEPLOY TO ARRIVE SAIGON CONCURRENT YOUR ARRIVAL IF POSSIBLE.

YOU AND JOHNSON WILL PERMANENTLY LOCATE QUARTERS AND OFFICE GRAND HOTEL. ROOMS RESERVED 2ND FLOOR, WITH MACV HQ ON FLOOR THREE. WILL ADVISE FURTHER REDEPLOYMENT OF YOUR VAN. NEW LIST OF EQUIPMENT AND INFO ON FIFTY MAN CREW TO FOLLOW SOON.

YOUR RECENT INTEL EXCELLENT. VC GETTING STRONGER IN DELTA AND WILL BE DANGER WHEN YOU ARRIVE. KEEP ALERT ON DIEM STATUS. WILL ARRANGE CONTACT WITH MACV SOON.

THANKS FOR MEETING WITH PEABODY ON SITUATION.

DECISION MADE. B26A TO REMAIN ARLINGTON NOT MOVE FORT MEADE.

MY REGARDS TO JOHNSON. HIS REPORTING ON DIEM INDISPENSIBLE.

NEW PAY GRADE TO RETRO ON ANNOUNCEMENT DATE.

WILL ADVISE MORE IN FEW DAYS.

LOOK FOR YOU IN ARLINGTON FEBRUARY 6.

END MESSAGE

"OK," Myles said. "Today is January 14, That means I have three more weekends in Tokyo before I leave for Arlington. The weekends of January 19, January 26, and, I guess, February 2."

Myles realized he was thinking out loud in terms of weekends left with Yoshiko.

"Myles, that's pretty quick. What are you going to do about Yoshiko and all that?"

"Well, I guess I'll have to handle it somehow. It looks like I'll finish up in Arlington around March something or other. I can't even think that far ahead now. One thing for sure, looks like I'll be in Arlington for two or three weeks after February 6. I don't want any leave before Saigon. I just want to get the ball rolling."

"Myles, calm down. I don't see this as a big problem. Three more weekends with Yoshiko and then you let it go, right?"

"Right .... let it go."

He started thinking. Maybe I can get a few days off before I have to leave. That might help Yoshiko get used to the idea of me leaving. Man, I look forward to talking to Peggy on Wednesday. Hope the doctor's appointment turns out OK on Wednesday. Man, what a mess I've created.

"Johnson, I think I'll take the bull by the horns. Do you think we need some extra help here at Shiroi for the next couple of months, especially considering you'll be alone for a month?" Myles asked.

"We could really use some help. We're getting a ton of new stuff from the Saigon area. The commander's right. The VC are really stepping things up in the Delta. It's good news about our new site and all the equipment."

"OK, I'm going to send the commander a message today and ask for one analyst and one linguist to help us out. Don't know where she can get them, but we can't keep up without help. I'll make it a serious request," Myles said.

"Let's have lunch at the snack bar and a beer at the bowling alley tonight. What say?" Johnson suggested, realizing that Myles needed some relief.

"Great idea. Let's get out of here at a quarter to twelve."

They worked the rest of the morning on the heavy load of traffic that arrived in the morning courier pouch. One thing was shocking. Diem had rounded up thirty communists and assassinated them on New Year's Day. It was in front of a hoard of witnesses and the press. That should provide plenty of incentive for the Vietcong to get a lot of new recruits in the Saigon and Delta regions.

Later at lunch, they talked about the Diem situation, and the fact that they were going to be billeted just a few blocks from his headquarters building. They agreed they were both getting into a tense situation.

In the afternoon, Myles got his message off to Commander Banta, requesting two new people. He asked for an urgent reply.

That night, they had their Heinekens at the bowling alley, and for a brief time talked about other, less dangerous, things.

Lying in bed that night, Myles tried to review the whole situation in as rational a way as possible. He felt like he was lying under a ton of bricks. When and how to tell Yoshiko was first and foremost on his mind. He didn't want to do it over the weekend with Peggy there. That meant there would only be the weekend of January 28 and the weekend of February 1.

He didn't like that at all. Here's what he'll do, he thought. Tomorrow, he'll tell Major Hickson that he'll be going into Tokyo on Wednesday to see his tailor for suits.

He was certain the Major wouldn't mind that. Then he would go over to the snack bar and call Uncle Masuda. Surely he would be taking Yoshiko to her doctor's appointment on Wednesday.

He would ask Masuda to somehow contact Yoshiko to tell her he would be coming in Tuesday night, in order to go to the doctor with her on Wednesday. Yes, that's a good plan.

Then he could tell Yoshiko on Wednesday in the presence of Uncle Masuda. He would help stabilize the situation. Plus, he could hear what the doctor will have to say. Then, he could return to the base late Wednesday without going back to Ikebukuro. That will be his plan.

Of course, he will need to call Peggy tomorrow and change their lunch meeting from Wednesday to Thursday. If all this works out, a lot will be accomplished before he and Peggy go to Ikebukuro Friday night for the weekend.

He had one final worrisome thought. Bill Peabody was supposed to call him tomorrow.

He finally fell asleep, knowing at least what his plan would be for the next day or two.

Tuesday, January 15, 1957

It was not his best sleep and he finally got up around five thirty. He decided to go ahead and dress and have an early breakfast. He'd never eaten this early before, but he knew the dining hall opened at six.

After bacon, eggs, and lots of coffee, it was a cold dark walk through the snow over to the compound. He'd never been in the office at seven in the morning and possibly nobody else had either. Anyway, he was alone at his desk for nearly an hour before Major Hickson and a few others straggled in.

It was a good hour's work. He got off an Intelligence Brief to Commander Banta and the chain of command covering the Diem massacre. He also drafted an Intelligence Summary covering new suspected VC locations in the Delta. He included day and night radio frequencies for most of them, but could not pinpoint exact locations. He figured once the van is set up the new DF equipment would be able to pinpoint any transmitter within two hundred meters. As soon as Johnson arrived, he gave him drafts of the two documents for his comment and agreement.

Around eight-thirty he went in to see Major Hickson.

"Major Hickson, sir, may I speak with you for a minute."

"Sure Myles, come on in."

"Sir, I'll make it quick. Johnson and I are pretty current on our raw intel and all that's under control. Tomorrow I'll be going to Tokyo to pick up some civilian clothes I ordered. I'll be back in the office on Thursday."

"That's fine Myles, you're the boss. Can't you get clothes over at the base exchange?"

"Well, yes, sir, but there's this tailor near the Ginza that I and the other guys have ordered suits from in the past. It's a great deal, and he makes fine suits. I would recommend him to you, if and when you need a new suit."

"Sounds good. You going to leave in the morning or what?"

"Maybe, or I might leave this evening and stay in town overnight."

"You're all set then for your day off tomorrow."

"While I have your attention, Major, you should know that I've put in a formal request to Commander Banta to get some help for Johnson and me. This would be NSA funded help of course. I've asked for an analyst and a linguist to be placed here in 21st Radio. I don't think that will interfere with your operation, sir."

"Myles, that's fine. Only next time please talk with me about it first. Two extra people in this office is a concern of mine, if only for logistic purposes."

"I apologize sir. I just felt we needed the help as soon as possible. I will think of you next time. Oh, one other thing, I need to run over to the credit union and get some money."

"I thought you went over there last week for money. Of course, that's none of my business, just forget I said that. Go right ahead."

"Thank you sir. I'll be back in a little while."

Myles told Johnson his plan for today and tomorrow and the fact that Major Hickson now knows about their request for two people.

"How'd he take it boss?" Johnson asked.

"OK, I guess. He was a little miffed that I didn't get his permission first. I think he's confused about me no longer being one of his Lieutenants. I'll see you in a little while. I'm heading over to the snack bar for a few minutes to make a few phone calls. The Major thinks I'm going to the credit union."

"Sounds good. See you in a little while."

After another cold walk in the snow, Myles entered the front door of the snack bar. He went straight to Mark's office and knocked on his door.

"Come in."

"Mark, it's me again. I hate to bother you, but may I make two phone calls from your phone?" Myles asked.

"Absolutely, how's Peggy?"

"She is fine. I'll tell her you asked."

Mark cleared the front of his desk and pulled the phone over in front of his chair.

"Thanks, Mark."

Myles dialed Peggy first.

"Peggy, this is Myles."

"Myles, good to talk to you. See you tomorrow for lunch?"

"Well, no, that's why I'm calling. I can't talk long Peggy so I got to make it short this time. I'm sorry."

"That's fine, Myles. What's wrong?"

"Nothing really. First of all, can we meet on Thursday instead of tomorrow?"

"Sure, I'm open. Thursday at noon, right?"

"Thursday at noon. I'm going to Tokyo tomorrow to go to the doctor with Yoshiko for a check-up. That is, if I can get hold of Uncle Masuda and he can notify Yoshiko."

"Great, Myles. You definitely should do that."

"Then, Peggy, if it works out, I plan to tell Yoshiko about my having to leave Shiroi and go to Washington and then Vietnam. I'm not sure how I'll do it. It won't be easy."

"Myles, good luck. Guess that means she will know when I spend the weekend with you guys."

"Yes, if I get it done tomorrow. I got to go now Peggy and try to get Masuda on the phone. I apologize for such a short phone call. I look forward to Thursday."

Myles hung up and sat back in the swivel chair trying to regain his composure. For some reason, this was a difficult call to Peggy. Every call like this is crossing another bridge and it's not easy.

He pulled the phone back over in front of him and dialed Tokyo.

Thank goodness, Masuda answered the Camera Store phone right away.

Masuda was in good spirits and was glad Myles was coming to Tokyo for the doctor's appointment. He was certain he could get word to Yoshiko to expect him in Ikebukuro tonight.

"Thank you Uncle Masuda. You are a great uncle. I have to go now. I am on a borrowed phone."

"OK, bye for now. See you tomorrow at the doctor's office."

OK, it was done. The plan was now in place for tonight and tomorrow.

"Mark, thanks for your phone. Peggy and I will see you Thursday for lunch."

"Great, anytime. I look forward to Thursday," Mark answered.

Myles caught the four-thirty train from Matsudo on his journey through Tokyo and on to Ikebukuro. He had time to mull over his plan and put things on a good track. About half way into his trip it suddenly dawned on him that Bill Peabody hadn't called today as planned. He figured that could be good or it could be bad. Either way, he decided to call him at the Okura tomorrow after the doctor appointment.

Tuesday Evening

It was nearly six o'clock when the train pulled into Ikebukuro Station. There was still plenty of snow on the ground, but the streets, including their side street were clear. It was still cold enough to see your breadth, so it was definitely still winter.

Into the front door, up the stairs, and down the hall .... Myles was as quiet as possible. Yoshiko was stretched out on the bed, nearly asleep.

"Yoshiko, I'm here."

"Mai, come in and get on this bed please."

Once more like last Friday, Myles jumped onto the bed with his jacket still on and gave her some really big hugs and kisses.

"How are you tonight after dancing on television today?" he asked.

"I am wonderful Mai. I think my mother must have been Hawaiian. This was so easy for me. Want me to show you?"

"Not now sweetheart. First, let's go get some food. I'm starving."

"I starving too. Please help me with coat, if you don't mind," she said with a huge smile.

Somehow, they managed to get themselves ready and headed out into the cold darkness.

"Tonight, how about going to Mitsukoshi tea room for some really good food," Myles suggested.

"Good idea. You got money tonight Mai? We can eat soba you know."

"No, we can afford to go to Mitsukoshi."

After a great dinner of miso soup, steamed rice, and stir fried vegetables, they headed back to the apartment .... now fortified for the cold walk.

Inside the apartment once more, they undressed quickly and crawled under the futon on the bed.

"Yoshiko, Uncle Masuda told you today that I would be here tonight, right?"

"Yes, I got message at television station from agency. He say you go to doctor tomorrow with us. I so happy you will do that. We will get check-up and maybe listen to baby's heart."

"What time is your appointment?"

"It ten o'clock at doctor office."

"And where is the doctor's office?"

"It is third floor in New Kaijo building which is only two blocks from Tokyo Station. So it very close to Uncle Masuda-san camera shop."

"What is the plan? Do we meet him at the doctor's office?"

"Yes, we take train to Tokyo station and if not cold we walk to New Kaijo and meet Masuda-san there."

"Good. I think we should catch the train to Tokyo around nine o'clock so we won't be late," he suggested.

"Good plan, Mai. I set alarm for seven o'clock so we have coffee."

Myles rolled over and switched on the Crosley, hoping to find some soft music. Suddenly there was Elvis singing, "It's Now or Never". Not exactly soft music, but soft for Elvis.

"How do you like that Yoshiko?" he asked.

"Oh, you know I love Elvis."

She rolled him back over to her side and clamped her arms around him.

"I love you Mai. Tomorrow we might hear our baby. Are you happy?"

"I am very happy. You know we need to start talking about what we are going to do in the future. You know, get married or what."

"Yes, of course we get married. I already know that. Can we go to bed now?"

With her still in his arms, he knew what that meant and proceeded to comply with her request. They made love until midnight and it finished up a wonderful day for both of them.

Wednesday, January 16, 1957

In the morning they had coffee and rice cakes and after a trip or two down the hall, they got dressed and made themselves ready to go.

As she dressed, Myles noticed it was a new outfit and she looked absolutely elegant. Just like a true model, he thought, and there was *Ladybug* high on her collar.

"Yoshiko, who is that?" he said, as he pointed to her collar.

"Oh Mai, I find *Ladybug* and she fine."

"I'm so glad. You know in my country people believe *Ladybugs* bring good luck, so I believe we will have good luck today and hear the baby's heartbeat."

So they put on heavy clothes and shoes and started out on their cold walk over to Ikebukuro Station.

"Wait," exclaimed Myles. "What am I thinking? We will take a taxi to the doctor."

"Taxi, yes, thank you Mai."

She helped Myles hail down a taxi and they were off to see the doctor. They cuddled and held hands during the twenty minute taxi ride. Arriving at the New Kaijo, Myles paid the driver and helped her out of the car.

Inside, they took the elevator up to the third floor. Surprise, Uncle Masuda was waiting in the hallway near the elevator.

"Good morning," Uncle Masuda smiled as he greeted them.

Then he ushered them to Doctor Ishiyama's office, almost directly across from the elevator.

Uncle Masuda stepped up to the counter.

"I have Yoshiko Moryama here for an appointment," he addressed the receptionist.

"Yes, please have a seat."

Myles looked around the room and spotted three seats near the far corner. As he gazed around the room, he saw six or seven girls seated along the far wall, facing a huge butler's bench loaded down with magazines. Some had male escorts but most of them were alone. One thing they all had in common though, was their oversize bellies. He tried to envision Yoshiko with her belly poked out, but just couldn't construe the picture.

In about thirty minutes, they found themselves sitting in Dr. Ishiyama's examining room. Very shortly, a little round man in a white coat came in and introduced himself to Myles.

"You must be Mr. Garrison, the father. I am Doctor Ishiyama. I am pleased to meet you sir."

He bowed very deeply and slowly, then he extended his hand.

"Yes, I am the proud father. Please call me Myles."

"Now, if you gentlemen will wait back in the waiting room, I will call you back very soon," the doctor said. "Will that be all right, Miss Moryama?"

"Yes, I not shy but these men might faint, and please will you call me Yoshiko since this my second visit."

"OK …. out of here."

He waived the men out the door.

Myles and Uncle Masuda retreated to their original seats. They were both nervous and didn't know how to start a conversation. Then, they both spoke at once.

"Myles ......"

"Uncle Masuda ...."

"You first Uncle Masuda-san," Myles said politely.

"Thank you. I just want to thank you for coming today. This is very important to all three of us. Very soon we should all three get together and discuss future plans. You agree?"

"I do, I do. And today I plan on buying us lunch over at the Victoria Tea Room and starting our serious discussions. All right?"

"Very good, and especially since that is the place where you first met Yoshiko. I think that is nice idea."

Then the two men were silent until finally a nurse popped out of the door.

"Mr. Garrison, you and Mr. Masuda may come into the room now."

They almost knocked heads as they threw their magazines down and jumped up to get to the door.

"Now, first thing is for Mr. Garrison .... er ...... Myles to listen to the baby's heart. Here take these."

He handed Myles his stethoscope.

Yoshiko was now lying flat on the table with a huge grin on her face. She watched Myles put on the stethoscope and press the receptor against her exposed belly.

"Yes, yes, I hear the heartbeat," he cried out. "It sure is strong and healthy. Did you hear it Yoshiko?"

"Yes, it is good strong heart. I think it boy. Uncle Masuda, you should hear. Mai please give hearing thing to Uncle Masuda."

Uncle Masuda's reaction echoed that of Myles and Yoshiko. He was a happy man.

"That is a great sound. I think it is a good baby," he said.

"Now, said the doctor, I have given her a diet and some instructions, but only just eat correct and get exercise. Would you like to know when the baby is expected?"

"Yes, when will the baby be born?" Myles asked.

"Well, my best guess is early September. That is just my guess for now, but that would forty weeks. I have delivered over two thousand babies."

"Have you ever delivered a baby of Japanese and American parents?" Myles asked.

"Of course, many and all turn out very well. So no need to worry. Looking at you and Yoshiko, I predict a beautiful healthy fat baby. Now, she thinks it will be boy, but just have to be happy whatever it is."

They finally bid farewell to Dr. Ishiyama. He gave them another appointment in a month and reminded Yoshiko to take care of herself.

"The baby is fine, but one should always be careful," the doctor said as he saw them out of his office.

It was almost noon, and after the successful examination and the good news, they where all ready for lunch.

"We will now take a taxi to the Victoria Tea Room?" Myles said.

After a nice lunch and a few cups of green tea, Myles suggested they have the dishes cleared away and have some coffee.

With the table clear and the coffee set, Myles suggested that he would like to say a few important things about the future. Yoshiko straightened up like a little girl on her first day at school. Uncle Masuda got himself situated with his coffee cup and got ready to listen to Myles.

"Now, first of all, I must say I am very happy about everything I love Yoshiko very much and she is making me very happy with a baby. We will get married some day when I can work it out if I have your approval, Uncle Masuda."

"Yes, Myles, you have my approval. I assume you proposed to Yoshiko already."

"Well, I guess so, last night, and she didn't say no. Will you marry me Yoshiko?" he asked.

"Mai, I very pleased marry you," she replied.

"OK, Uncle Masuda, now you know we are in agreement. However, with my job with the Air Force it might be hard to work out the details. We won't be able to just go get married. It won't be that simple."

"Yoshiko, I haven't told you this yet, but they are sending me to Vietnam for a while."

Yoshiko looked startled.

"Vietnam, Mai, when, that is dangerous place?"

"Yes, maybe a little dangerous. But let me go on with my story," he continued.

"I will be here in Tokyo for three more weekends and then I will go to Washington for a while. Everybody understand so far?" he asked.

"Yes, three more weekends in Ikebukuro. I understand," Yoshiko said.

She suddenly turned to Uncle Masuda and started talking a mile a minute in Japanese. Too much and too fast for Myles, but he did understand something about how sad she was but she would be strong for the baby.

Then Uncle Masuda said, "But what after your time in Washington Myles?"

"Well, I'm pretty certain that I can come back to Tokyo for a full week with you and Yoshiko. That's the good part. But after that I will go to Saigon with a special assignment in intelligence. Actually, I will become a civilian for this job, which will make it easier to marry Yoshiko."

"And how long will you be in Vietnam?" Uncle Masuda asked.

Yoshiko was on the edge of her chair.

"Normally, this would be a one year job, but for this one I just don't know. Maybe less and maybe more. But, I'm pretty sure that once I get settled in Vietnam, I can arrange to fly to Tokyo about once a month for a visit with both of you. I think I can arrange for some business up here. I know this is going to be tough on Yoshiko but please ask her to consider this as just a small problem. Now that I am a civilian, I can leave the government work after Vietnam and go wherever I want. Please explain this to Yoshiko now."

Uncle Masuda spent the better part of ten minutes speaking with Yoshiko in slow, deliberate Japanese. She nodded periodically but didn't say anything. Myles had never seen her so sober and serious. He wasn't worried but it made him sad to put this burden on her.

Finally, Uncle Masuda finished.

"Now Myles, what about getting married?" Masuda asked.

"Well, here's what I think. Once I have been in Saigon for a month or two and gotten my work going, I will make a formal application for marriage. My new boss is a very reasonable person and I know she will help me every way she can."

"Will she help us to get married?" Yoshiko asked.

"I really think so. Please don't worry about her. She is a real good person."

"If you say, I no worry, Mai. Please try to marry me as soon you can."

"OK Myles, so you will be here for three more weekends and then you go to Washington for about three weeks. Then you spend one week with us here in Tokyo before leaving for Saigon. Then, you visit us once each month after that. And then you apply for marriage around, maybe October or November. Is that right? I will explain that to Yoshiko again," Masuda said.

"Yes, that's it exactly. Please tell Yoshiko again about this plan."

Uncle Masuda spent another few minutes summarizing Myles plan to Yoshiko.

"OK, Mai," she said, tears welling up in her eyes.

"Will you be all right here while I am gone so much?" Myles asked.

"Mai, baby and me will be strong for you. We only have to wait a few months, right? And baby come September. We be OK. I love you Mai."

Myles took her hand and placed both their hands over her stomach. For a moment he almost felt a heartbeat, then he realized it must be her rapid pulse. My poor baby, he thought.

Yoshiko wiped her eyes and seemed to regain her composure.

"Mai, you should go back to base now so you can come back Friday with Peggy-san," she said.

"Yes, Myles you go ahead now. Thanks for coming with us today and the nice lunch. If you bring Peggy to Tokyo this weekend please bring her to my shop," Masuda said.

"We sure will. In fact, I'll be picking up my new suits over at Morita-san's shop."

"Now, we should go, Yoshiko. I won't go to the base now. I will take you back to Ikebukuro by taxi, and then take the train from there," Myles said.

"No, no, Mai. You should go to base. I visit Uncle Masuda-san at his store and take taxi myself back."

"Thanks Yoshiko, I think that would be better for me if you don't mind. I look forward to Friday night."

"Before I leave, Uncle Masuda, please tell me about Yoshiko's parents in Yokohama."

"It same Myles. Father say she can never come home. She disgrace the family. Mother, my sister, tells me she is so sad and wants to see Yoshiko in secret some time soon. I will arrange that. It will help Yoshiko get through this to have her mother on her side and see her sometimes in private."

"That's really good news .... about her mother I mean. Thanks for taking care of all these things. I don't know what we would do without you."

"I am so happy for both of you and am pleased to help. You can count on me in future."

Myles gave Yoshiko another hug and then urged the three of them out of the booth. He left a comfortable amount of yen on the table to cover the bill and a nice tip. He took Yoshiko's hand and carefully led her down the stairs and into the lobby.

They walked together the two blocks to the Ginza. Then they split up and Myles headed over to Tokyo Station. He waived, as he turned and walked away.

"Sayonara. See you both this weekend."

Back at the Ginza Camera Shop, Uncle Masuda and Yoshiko spent almost an hour in the back office reviewing the situation and trying to come up with a reasonable plan. Yoshiko had totally regained her composure and had nearly as many ideas as her Uncle. Everything centered around how she would take care of herself until the baby came, and what to do thereafter largely depended on Myles' success at getting permission to marry from Commander Banta. By now Commander Banta was a central figure in their lives, even without her knowing anything about it.

After arriving at some reasonable expectations, Uncle Masuda said he would write up the minutes of their meeting for presentation to Myles. His approach took on a businesslike aspect, which probably should have been expected based on his twenty five years business on the Ginza. In all, he was basically pretty satisfied on his plan and so was Yoshiko.

Myles stopped at a pay phone in the main lobby at Tokyo Station and dialed up the Okura Hotel. He was relieved that the desk clerk spoke excellent English. He was not relieved, however, to hear that Bill Peabody had checked out on Sunday and left no messages. That was not good news. Bill checking out with no phone call as promised and no messages was a new complication. He'd need to look into that tomorrow but for now all he could think about was his good day with Yoshiko at the doctor.

He hoped she got back safely to Ikebukuro. He didn't like the idea of her traveling alone on the Tokyo rail system. Tokyo was one of the safest cities in the world but, still, here she was a beautiful well dressed young girl alone for hours every week on Tokyo trains and in busy stations. Not only that, there would be taxis to deal with and all the safety issues with that. Car traffic was horrendous in Tokyo and taxis were a dangerous way to travel. Accidents happened all the time.

Yoshiko got back to the apartment safe and sound. Once inside, she slipped into her robe and went downstairs to tell O-basan about her day at the doctor's office. She found it reassuring to have someone to share her personal thoughts with.

Myles got back to the base around seven and went directly to the club for supper. Wednesday nights were generally quiet and this one was no exception. Only three other tables were occupied in the dining room and, thankfully, none of the diners recognized him. He needed the quiet time to let down from the day at the doctor's and to think what to do next about Bill Peabody.

Thursday, January 17, 1957

In the morning, Myles got to work a little ahead of everybody else and he used the time to catch up on yesterday's traffic. He greeted everybody as they started filtering in around a quarter to eight. Around nine, Captain Brent stopped by Myles desk.

"Myles, the Major would like to see you and Johnson for a minute. I think he means right now,"

"Sure, we'll be right in."

Myles, Johnson, and Brent sat across the front of Major Hickson's desk.

"Well, Myles, I'm impressed with you and the Commander. Want to break the news, Captain Brent?" the Major said.

"Myles, yesterday we got word that Commander Banta succeeded in getting you the help you requested earlier this week."

"That will be great. I'm shocked. It's only been three days since my request. What help are we getting?" Myles asked, treading lightly on the subject.

He detected a little resentment in the Captain's attitude.

"OK, here's the deal. First, you're going to get Lieutenant Davison full time on project ..... what is it .... Beehive or something?"

That was it, Myles thought. There's the resentment. He should have gone through the chain of command on this.

"That will start next Monday, January 21. Now, the big news. You are also getting Army Sergeant Han DeMeur. She'll transfer from Camp Zama and report in on Monday."

Myles flashed a glance at the Major, who was looking down at the floor.

"What's her background?" Johnson asked.

"Glad you asked, Sergeant. She is twenty two years old. She was born and raised in Vietnam near Long Mei, where your van was going to be be located. Her father was a French plantation owner and her mother was a popular Vietnamese movie star. Her father and mother were killed in 1953 by the Vietminh. Guess she must have been sixteen or seventeen years."

The Major interrupted, suggesting they all take a break and bring some coffee back in. Myles was relieved to change the pace of things.

After the break, Brent continued.

"She is fluent in French, Vietnamese, and English. She attended the Army Security Agency school and studied cryptanalysis and traffic analysis. At Zama, she was a linguist and analyst with the Army Security Agency working on Vietnamese projects, of course. So she and Lieutenant Davison will be yours starting on Monday. For how long? Well I guess that depends on you, Myles?"

"Captain Brent, before you go on, I want to apologize for upsetting the apple cart here. I work for Commander Banta and I thought I was doing the right thing. Johnson and I will do our damnedest to make this transition as smooth as possible and try not to upset the rest of the troops."

"Myles, I appreciate your sensitivity here. This is a big deal for the Major and me. We've been working hard on our personnel situation, trying to get promotions and changing assignments. There's no permanent damage though. Just try to remember we are your landlord. OK, let's move on."

"Thanks Captain Brent. I'm already past this, if you are."

"I am. Now, there's more. Over the weekend, we'll move all four of your desks over in the far corner of the big room. We'll move your file cabinets and wall charts too, so you will have your own private work area. Don't worry about all this. You just enjoy your weekend and we'll take care of everything. Now, we expect Sergeant DeMeur to report on base sometime on Sunday. Major Hickson has secured billeting for her in one of the female civilian dorms. I think it's Building S24, right Major?"

"Yes. There are only female workers living there, school teachers, USO workers, nurses, and some retail clerks. They are all Americans. All the rooms are semi-private so the Sergeant should be comfortable. She will have orders to report to the compound first thing Monday morning."

"Thanks, Major. Now, Myles all the rest after that is up to you. You'll have to take care of getting her checked in around the base and a medical exam. Then, once all that is done, you and Johnson will need to start your orientation and training for her and Lieutenant Davison. Well, guess that's about it."

Everybody was silent for a minute or two. Then Brent got up and walked over to where Myles was sitting.

"Myles, I am so sorry for this little interruption."

He gave Myles a big bear hug.

"I'm all clear now, ole buddy. Maybe it's time for a few beers or something. How about next week? I'm busy tonight and I know you've got plans for tomorrow night," Brent said.

Brent glanced over at the Major. They made eye contact but didn't say anything. The Major re-crossed his legs.

Maybe I'm overly sensitive here, thought Myles, but what was that last statement all about? Could the Major know about Myles' plans with Peggy this weekend? Do he and Brent know more about Yoshiko than he thought? He was looking forward to lunch with Peggy in another two hours.

Myles and Johnson shuffled back to their desks.

"Whew, that was rough boss. I'm happy for the help, especially getting Han. She should be worth her weight in gold. I called her Han, guess that's all right? DeMeur is a little clumsy for me."

"Han is good. From now on, she will be Han, after we get her permission of course. Yeah, that was really rough. I haven't experienced anything like that for a long time. Let's not harbor any bad feelings though. Those two have been putting in a lot of long hours I know. I can just imagine how'd I feel if I got dumped on like that."

"You're right as usual. Did I hear you say something earlier about lunch at the snack bar?"

"Maybe you did, but this time I can't ask you to join me. I've got a little deal going here that I'll share with you but you must absolutely keep it secret."

"OK, what's up?"

"Well, I'm meeting Peggy Hickson for lunch to go over plans for this weekend. I am taking her to Ikebukuro Friday night to spend the weekend with Yoshiko and me. We'll be back Sunday night. This must be so secret that, well, just super secret. OK?"

"OK."

"Now, this afternoon, let's you and I get together and design a training program for Cameron and Han. So far, we don't have any specific instructions from the Commander, so we'll just do what we think is best. Between the four of us, we have a huge amount of talent and experience. Oh, I better ask Brent when he's going to announce all this to the rest of the troops. I'll go do that now. See you after lunch."

"Sounds good. Around one or a little after should be just about right."

Myles went over to Brent's desk.

"Roy, when are you going to announce all this to the rest of the office?"

"I'm putting it in a memo. I'll get it out sometime today."

On his way over to the snack bar, Myles started thinking about Bill Peabody. He figured the best thing to do was wait and see for a few days. Surely Bill would contact him somehow. The CIA worried him and he was concerned for Bill's safety.

Mark was sitting with Peggy at their favorite corner table. They didn't spot Myles when he came in, so he crept silently in their direction. Let's see what they're talking about so seriously, he thought. He realized Mark had a crush on Peggy. Who wouldn't after all? She was the cutest little blonde on the base. Married, or not, it didn't matter to Mark. He was so lonely. Myles felt sorry for him.

"Hey you guys, I hate to interrupt."

They were visibly startled. Mark jumped up.

"Just taking care of our girl here, Myles. I'll bring some menus. Cokes all right?"

"Cokes are great. Make it a cherry Coke," Peggy said.

Myles settled in next to her. No across the table seating today. This needed to be a private discussion.

"Myles, I can't wait to hear about yesterday. How'd it go?"

Myles spent the next twenty minutes explaining everything to Peggy. She was pleased as to how things were working out.

Then, he decided he needed to tell her about his encounter with the Major.

"The Major, I had a really bad experience with your husband and Roy Brent this morning."

"Myles, what?"

"Well, to make it brief, Brent called Johnson and me into the Major's office and told us we were getting two new helpers in our secret Vietnam project. I had requested two people earlier this week from my NSA boss, Commander Banta."

"OK?"

"On Tuesday, the Major called me into his office and chewed me out for going around his back requesting help from Commander Banta. OK, I guess I understood that, but technically I did the right thing."

"This morning, Brent and the Major announced we were getting two people, and one of them was Lieutenant Davison, one of their own. The other is an Army Sergeant transferring from Camp Zama. This really upset them. First, they were losing Davison which meant they'd be shorthanded by one man. They're already short on people so this really hurt. Then, getting an Army Sergeant was really insulting. To top it off, the Army Sergeant is a female. That means they will have to make all kinds of special arrangements for housing, eating, and all that stuff."

"Man, I guess, that was unpleasant."

"It was. Besides all that, they will have to rearrange the office over the weekend to make room for the new body. I guess I understand, but it was still a bad experience. Oh, one other thing, Peggy."

"What's that?"

"Well, as we were wrapping up and Brent announced having to work on the office arrangement over the weekend, he made a remark about my having plans for the weekend. He looked at the Major when he said it. And, I swear Peggy, it seemed like they both knew something. If they did, it could be about you coming with me to Ikebukuro."

"Oh, Myles, I think you're just over sensitive right now. I'm sure it's nothing."

"I hope so. Is there any way possible that the Major could have found out about our plans?"

"I just don't see how that could be. I haven't told anybody ... absolutely nobody. I think we can just discount that."

They agreed to put the issue behind them and finished their lunch. As they parted at the front door, they reminded each other about meeting at the main gate tomorrow afternoon. Peggy agreed to pack light and Myles agreed to be on time.

Myles met with Johnson shortly after arrival back at the office. Planning for next week's arrival of Han and assimilating Davison was pretty simple. They both agreed to make their own notes on what the best approach was and who would be responsible for what. It was a good discussion and the morning's events didn't even come up.

They broke up in an hour or so and agreed to meet again for a little while the next morning.

Around four o'clock, Davison stopped by Myles desk.

"Myles, if it's all right, I'd like to leave a little early today. I assume we'll talk some tomorrow. I read Brent's memo and I'm excited to be on the Vietnam team with you, Johnson, and DeMeur."

"Sure, take off. Something special?"

"Actually, I'm catching the train to Tokyo. It's Fumiko's birthday today and I'm meeting her at the Opal. She's getting off early and we're going to hit a few spots. Guess I'll catch the eleven o'clock back to the base."

"Fine, tell her hello for me. Make sure you don't miss that last train."

"Thanks. See you in the morning, boss," Davison sounded sincere in his thanks.

Man that's a quick turn around trip to Tokyo, Myles thought. An hour and a half in and an hour and a half back with maybe an hour and a half with Fumiko. Hope he's got his head straight on this, Myles wondered.

Friday, January 18, 1957

Myles and Johnson were busy reviewing their notes for Davison's and Han's training next week. It was nearly nine o'clock and Davison had not come into the office yet. Myles wondered about his plans for last night and whether or not he'd made that last train.

Sure enough, around nine thirty Davison sheepishly entered the room and quietly went to his desk. He was carrying a cup of coffee from the snack bar down the hall.

"Johnson, take a look over there," Myles said, as he gestured in Davison's direction.

"That guy's hung over, boss."

"That's exactly what I think. Tell you what. Let's you and I just not pay any attention or say anything. Let's give him the benefit of a doubt. Most of us have done stupid things before. Maybe he just celebrated Fumiko's birthday too hard last night."

Myles and Johnson finished their talk for the day and both spend the rest of their time working on traffic. Myles sent a few Intelligence Briefs to the chain of command disclosing a few new suspected VC transmitter sites and two new shipments coming the Ho Chi Minh Trail. By quitting time, there had not been any word from Bill Peabody.

Emergency crisis in Northern Ireland after IRA deadly strikes; Brooklyn Dodgers trade Jackie Robinson to the NY Giants for pitcher Dick Littlefield plus $35,000; Guy Mitchell's "Singin' the Blues" is high on the charts; Paul Hornung, Notre Dame, wins 22nd Heisman Trophy; Unofficial beginning of Rock and Roll music;

Chapter Twelve

Peggy's Weekend

Friday Evening, January 18, 1957

Myles got to the main gate a few minutes past five. It was already getting dark and the temperature was dropping fast. Peggy was inside the sentry house huddled around the little gas heater.

"Peggy, all set? It's getting cold out there. Not too late to change your mind."

"Myles, not for a minute would I consider that. I'm looking forward to this. Let's go if you're up to it."

It was a cold ten minute walk to the station and, luckily, the three car electric train had just arrived and was waiting.

"Hope it's warm in there. Let's get on," Peggy urged Myles on.

The two of them were like giddy teen agers on the hour and half ride to Tokyo and on to Ikebukuro. They made up fake characters for the strangely clad farmers, teen agers, and skiers as they paraded down the car aisles. Little did they know that those folks were doing the same thing about them. Two young Americans laughing and joking, and one wearing shoes with shiny brass coins stuffed in them. How funny!

Finally, Myles ushered Peggy off the train and out into the cold at Ikebukuro Station. As they approached the street, Myles pointed out the Mitsukoshi Department store and how big a role it had recently played in his and Yoshiko's lives. He pointed out the noodle shop and some of the other little shops that he and Yoshiko frequented.

"Now, Peggy, the going get's rough from here on," Myles cautioned as they turned off the paved street onto the gravel side road.

"Wow, Myles, this is pure country out here. I never realized ...."

"Right, this is just a rural neighborhood. Take my word for it, it will all be high rise buildings some day. Now down at the corner there, we'll turn left and you'll be able to see our little apartment building. Don't be expecting too much. I warn you."

"OK!"

"Well, there it is."

Myles pointed up the street.

"The light is on up there in the corner. That means Yoshiko is already there. Having fun?"

"Myles, I've been in Japan for almost a year, but now I realize I've never really been in Japan. This is where the people live."

"You got it, and that's where I live too, and that's where Yoshiko and our baby are right now, up there."

They finally made it through the front hall way, leaving their shoes behind at the front steps. It was dark in O-basan's room, but Myles was sure she had already made the room ready for Peggy.

"Now we go up the stairs, Peggy. Be careful the steps and the hallway are slippery."

At the door, Myles paused for a minute and listened. He heard some rustling inside so he went ahead and knocked softly on the door frame. Instantly, the door slid open.

Yoshiko was the first to scream out and reach her arms out to Peggy. Then Peggy screamed too and they both hugged.

"Yoshiko, you look terrific …. even prettier than at the Christmas Party."

"Oh, you too Peggy-san. So happy see you again. Come inside and warm up."

She took Peggy by the hand and pulled her inside, leaving Myles to fend for himself in the dark hallway.

"What you think of apartment? One room, one bed, one closet, one little chair, one little table, and little kitchen behind curtain in little window. Everything little!"

"Oh, Yoshiko, I think it's charming. I could live here. I can just see you and Myles having a wonderful time here. Do I sleep in this bed with the two of you?"

"Sure do, hope you don't mind," Myles joked.

"Mai, you stop. You have room just like this across hall. Only not much furniture. So sorry. You have heater and you sleep on floor rolled in futon. That way you feel like Japanese. Here I show you now."

She took Peggy's bag and led her across the hall.

"Hope you don't mind no lock, Peggy-san. We don't have lock on doors here."

"No locks are just fine, and this room will be perfect."

Meanwhile, Myles was unpacking his things in the other apartment. He switched on the Crosley and found some good Hit Parade music.

"Now, Peggy-san, I must show you the toilet. This not so good for Americans."

She carefully guided Peggy down the dim slippery hall to the toilet at the end. She slid the door open, revealing the floor level toilet.

"You know this?" Yoshiko asked.

"Yoshiko, I have never seen anything like this."

"Well, this is for both kinds of toilet. I show you later. Do you need to use it now?"

"No thanks."

For the better part of an hour, the three of them cuddled up on the big bed, talking about everything that was going on, including the baby.

"Peggy, I'm so glad we can share with you. As you see, we are both very happy, but very worried at the same time," Myles said.

"I can see that, Myles. Let's just work through this together. I'm sure that in a year or two we'll look back and be thankful it all worked out. By that time, there'll be another mouth to feed in this world."

Just about then, the door slid open. O-basan stood there with a huge grin on her face.

"Peggy-san, so pleased to have you as guest," she said.

"Thank you, and you are …. O-basan? Thank you for my wonderful room and taking such good care of my friends here. Join us on the bed."

"Wait a minute," interrupted Myles.

"I think we should all get ready to go celebrate with a nice dinner. "What do you think Yoshiko?"

"Yes, we should go kushi katsu, all four of us … and you pay."

"Great deal," Myles replied. "Let's get going."

So they dressed and headed off to kushi katsu for some tempura on sticks and draft beer.

That night was a perfect start for Peggy's weekend. They each had ten sticks and two beers. Myles paid the grand total of thirty dollars.

Afterword, they walked a few blocks window shopping and talking about plans for tomorrow, all the while Peggy in her penny loafers and Yoshiko in her high top shoes. O-basan, of course, wore traditional high step geta shoes.

Back on the big bed, they talked and giggled and finally decided to try to get some sleep. Peggy retired to her room across the hall.

Saturday, January 19, 1957

Peggy joined Yoshiko and Myles in the big bedroom for Yoshiko's famous percolated coffee and sweet rice cakes. The snow was all gone now but you could see the cold gray sky looming low out the side window.

"Myles, you really eat well around here. This is much better coffee than I make for my husband. Yoshiko, you do a good job."

"Thank you. Mai buy percolator."

".... and the kushi katsu was fabulous last night. I must admit I've never been to Japan like this before yesterday. Thank you both very much. What's on the agenda for today, Myles?"

"Here's the deal, Peggy. One errand I must run for sure is to pick up two new suits at my tailor in Tokyo. You met him at the party. You might remember, he had a male companion."

"Oh, yeah. What a delightful man. So what else?"

"Yoshiko, listen to this and see if it's a good plan."

"OK, Mai, what we do?"

"First, we take a taxi to Tokyo. We leave around ten o'clock. Then we go straight to Morita-san's shop and get my suits. Then we take a nice walk over to the Ginza, if it's not too cold. Both of you please wear your walking shoes, no high heels. OK, so far?"

"Good plan. Now what?" Yoshiko asked.

"Then we go down the right side of the Ginza and stop in at the Ginza Camera Shop to introduce Peggy to Uncle Masuda. I'd like to see him too. And then we walk down a little farther, all the way to the Kabuki Theatre. Peggy should see that. You haven't seen the Kabuki Theatre have you Peggy?"

"Myles, in my first full year at Shiroi, I've only been to Tokyo three times and even then I hardly saw anything. Everything you've mentioned so far is new to me. It sounds like fun."

"Good, then I thought we'd turn around and walk back up the other side of the Ginza and have some sushi at Sushi Oki. That's our favorite sushi in Tokyo. Yoshiko will order your sushi and make sure you get some good things. Right Yoshiko?"

"Good plan, Mai. I order sake too. It so cold today."

"Absolutely, sushi, sashimi, and sake. And then, we will walk back up the Ginza and stop at a pachinko parlor and play some pachinko. Then, finally the last thing on our Ginza tour will be to stop in and get a short tour of the Nichigeki Music Hall. Bet you've never been there, Peggy."

"No sir, but I have heard of it. It's like Radio City in New York, right?"

"That's it, only bigger and better. Oh, I forgot, after the Nichigeki we'll stop in at the Seibu Department Store. That's where Yoshiko does a lot of her modeling. Yoshiko, maybe we'll get to meet Kazuko-san there. That would be great for her to meet Peggy."

"Oh, yes, I hope she there. What after Seibu, Myles?" Yoshiko asked.

"Well, that's the last thing on my list, but I think that will take care of the whole day. After Seibu, we'll all be a little tired so we should go back to Ikebukuro and rest a little. What do you think?"

"I like plan. What you think, Peggy-san?"

"I am like putty in your hands, Yoshiko."

"What putty, what that?"

"I mean I agree with whatever you'd like to do. I guess that's what putty is."

"Nice recovery, Peggy. Putty is not an understandable word in Japanese," Myles said.

So they had a plan for the day. After breakfast, they dressed in warm clothes and comfortable shoes. Yoshiko was sure to attach *Ladybug* to her jacket lapel, now that she knew *Ladybug* would bring good luck.

"Peggy-san, what you think of *Ladybug*?"

She pointed to the small red and black cloisonné pin.

"I think it is precious. Does it have a special meaning?"

"Mai, buy for me first day we meet at the Victoria Tea Room and ..... oh, Mai, you forget Victoria Tea Room. We should take Peggy-san there too, since that where we first meet."

"Oh, my gosh, how could I forget. We'll drop by there right after seeing Morita-san about my suits."

They finished dressing and headed down the hall toward the stairs.

"Peggy, you need to stop here at the end of the hall for anything."

"No, I'm cool. And I want you to know, I had no trouble with the Japanese toilet. It must be a male thing with you Myles. Just where do you go anyway?"

"I usually go over to the Mitsukoshi Department Store. They have nice clean Western toilets on every floor. I think they're getting used to seeing me there. Anyway, I'm proud of your newly acquired skill. Let's get on down the stairs then."

On the way out, they stopped in to say hello to O-basan, and Peggy thanked her profusely for the nice room she had fixed for her. Then, it was back out on the gravel road, and a short walk over to the street. They caught a taxi and headed toward Tokyo on their big adventure.

The day worked out almost exactly as planned. Every venue was a successful new adventure for Peggy, and Yoshiko enjoyed everything as much as Peggy. The two girls couldn't have gotten along any better. Most of the time, they reminded Myles of two high school girls off on a field trip.

Morita-san was most gracious. He remembered Peggy from the party and served them up green tea and cookies. The new suits fit fine and the girls approved.

Peggy was spellbound by the Victoria Tea Room. She repeated over and over again how she must bring her girl friends to Tokyo and visit the Tea Room and all these other things Myles had planned.

Uncle Masuda couldn't have been nicer. Peggy had a hard time keeping the generous man from giving her an expensive camera. Finally, Myles had to come to the rescue and convince Masuda that Major Hickson might not understand.

Just as they were leaving the shop, Uncle Masuda pulled Myles aside and slipped an envelope into his jacket pocket.

"Myles, take this please and read it when you get some private time," he said with a shy smile.

Myles accepted the envelope without saying anything. With the envelope stashed in his pocket, he led everybody back out on the street and guided them to the right in the direction of the Kabuki Theatre.

They stood in front of the Kabuki for a good ten minutes taking in all the huge colorful pictures of famous Kabuki characters, many of them gaudily attired as princesses and warriors from the Samuri Period.

"Myles, have you been to see this yet?" Peggy asked.

"No, ma'am, and I guess I won't have a chance to. I think you and the Major should come in sometime and go. In fact, the Major should take you to a lot of things here in Tokyo. You're missing so much."

"Yes, Peggy-san, you come see me when Mai gone. I take you Kabuki," Yoshiko offered.

"You know, I think I will just do that. No reason why we shouldn't be friends after Myles leaves."

"Great idea. You girls get together a lot while I'm gone. If Uncle Masuda ever gets a phone put in the apartment, you'll be able to call each other. Glad you reminded me of that. I'll have to ask him to get the phone."

After Kabuki, they moved on to Sushi Oki. It was just as delicious and as much fun as Myles had expected. Yoshiko and Myles had loads of fun explaining all the different kinds of sushi and sashimi to Peggy. Most of all, she didn't understand raw blow fish, but she was a good sport about everything. Of course, being a good sport about sake was easy. The bill came to about forty dollars and Myles had to inventory his yen holdings.

Then they played pachinko as planned. Peggy had never even seen pachinko before, but she quickly got into the swing of things. The manager gave her and Yoshiko a starter supply of the shiny little balls. Myles, of course, didn't get any. They left after losing all their balls.

They finished their Ginza tour seeing the Nichigeki and then dropping by the Seibu. Fortunately, they hit the Seibu at a perfect time to hear the giant chimes. Unfortunately, Kazuko was off that day, so Peggy missed the opportunity of meeting her.

"Well, we take taxi home now. It four thirty," Yoshiko announced.

"I'll go along with that," volunteered Peggy. "How about you Myles?"

"I'm all for it. Let's get a taxi and I'll cuddle up in the middle."

The ride to Ikebukuro seemed much shorter than usual. The driver dropped them at the front entrance and they quickly went inside. O-basan was in, so they slid open her door without knocking to say hello. The four of them chatted for a few minutes about the events of the day. O-basan was pleased the girls had such a great time.

"I turn on heaters in rooms, so you be warm," she said.

"Oh, thank you O-basan," said Yoshiko. "We go upstairs now warm up."

Very carefully, the trio negotiated the dim slippery stairs and hallway, and went into Yoshiko and Myles' room. It was already warm and the three of them climbed up onto the high bed. Myles reached over and turned on the Crosley. He found some American music and turned up the volume slightly.

"Hey Peggy. Listen to this," he urged her.

"Somewhere Beyond the Sea," by Bobby Darrin was playing. It sounded so sweet to Myles and had such a special meaning.

"Oh, Myles, how perfect after today. I think it's prophetic. Turn it up just a little bit."

After the music, the three of them lay quietly on the bed under the futon and talked over the day's activities. Uncle Masuda's envelope was still in Myles' jacket pocket which was under the pile of coats over on the chair. I'll have to get to that later, he thought, when the girls are out of sight.

In a little while, they got up and trudged over to the noodle shop and Myles treated them to bowls of hot soba noodles. Later after more discussion about the day, Peggy retired to her room and Yoshiko and Myles crawled into their bed and fell asleep cradled in each other's arms.

Sunday, January 20, 1957

Everybody slept soundly that night. It had been a wonderful adventurous day. Before going to her room, Peggy had suggested a more relaxed day tomorrow, maybe a little shopping.

Coffee, pastry, and music was the program for breakfast. It took some doing, but all parties had managed to rustle out of bed and congregate in the big bedroom by nine o'clock.

"Today, Peggy-san, we will stay in Ikebukuro and go shopping and relaxing," Yoshiko reassured her.

"That sounds perfect. What will you do, Myles, while we go shopping?"

"Oh, I'll go along naturally, to carry the packages, plus make a stop at the Mitsukoshi rest room. What is our schedule Yoshiko?"

"I think we start go to stores around eleven o'clock. We have lunch somewhere. And I have another thought, Myles."

"What's that?" Myles asked suspiciously.

"In afternoon, I take you and Peggy-san to bath house."

"The bath house. That sounds like fun Myles. I've heard about that. Isn't that where the men and women all go naked in a hot swimming pool?"

"I think that's it. Yes, you and Yoshiko should definitely go. I'm just not sure about me. I need to think it over," Myles said, all the while thinking of some private time to read Uncle Masuda's letter.

"Oh, Mai, you sissy. If you no go, then we go anyway."

Suddenly, Peggy stopped. "I almost forgot. You were wonderful dancing the hula on television last Tuesday. Myles told me you would be on. You were really good."

"Thank you. Director say I might get more television parts. I will tell you when to watch."

They started to dress and get ready for the day. In a little while, they were all decked out in their finest shopping clothes and heading over to the business district. Peggy was definitely impressed with the Mitsukoshi, all eight floors of it. She bought sweaters for herself and the Major and some small gifts for all of her friends. Yoshiko, managed to find some nice scarves and some new jewelry, but nothing to compete with *Ladybug*.

Later, they walked through Naka Park and took a lot of pictures, Myles with Yoshiko, Myles with Peggy, Yoshiko with Peggy, and all three together. Naturally, Yoshiko drafted a couple of school girls to operate the Nikon for group pictures.

After lunch at the noodle shop they headed back to the apartment.

Inside, Yoshiko and Peggy proceeded to change and pack for the short trip up the road to the bath house.

"Now, I understand the penny loafers Myles. Good idea," Peggy said.

"See, sometimes I do think ahead Peggy," Myles said with a wink.

Myles positioned himself by the back window and watched the two girls trudging up the gravel road, hand bags in tow and towels draped over their shoulders. Finally, they were out of sight and Myles now had time to look at Uncle Masuda's letter.

It was neatly typed on Ginza Camera Shop stationary and had the appearance of a professional business letter.

Dear Mr. Garrison,

I am writing this letter to you with much pleasure and satisfaction. Since we first met some months ago, I have been very impressed with your sincerely and honesty. And I am filled with gratitude for the way you have taken care of my niece Yoshiko. Thank you so much, my friend, and future family member.

I know that after this weekend you will only have two more weekends in Tokyo with Yoshiko. Of course, after that you will return for one week vacation, and after that you expect

to visit us once every month. I also believe you when you say you will apply for marriage to Yoshiko in late summer. Maybe in time before the baby is born. I hope that happens. It will make Yoshiko very happy.

Now I want to speak to you like your true Uncle and almost like your true Father. First, I want to promise you that I will take very special care of Yoshiko while you are away. I will take to Dr. Ishiyama as often as needed. And, if you not here, I will take her to the hospital.

She cannot go home to her parents in Yokohama, so I will arrange for her to stay in the Ikebukuro place permanently until you can move her away. I will pay all of her expenses and give her an allowance for spending and maintenance. I will try to have a phone installed, but O-basan is trying to stop me from doing that.

Yoshiko and I talked about this last Wednesday after you went back to the base. She insists to keep working with the agency and will probably need to travel more around Tokyo area. I think this is dangerous and I have some ideas that might help in this situation. I tell you about my idea later.

Now, you should know that I am a very rich person, Myles. After the war, I bought the camera shop very cheap and started investing my profits in Tokyo stock market. Mainly, I own stock in Nickon camera company. My stocks and my Ginza store are worth about two million dollars. Of course, I have no need of this money. I have saved it for Yoshiko for such time as this.

Now, if you can resign from NSA sometime in a year, I will pay for you and Yoshiko to live in Tokyo and you to attend Sophia University to study Japanese language and Japanese business management.

If you are successful, I will offer you partnership in my Ginza Camera Shop. Then, you, Yoshiko, and the baby will be in very good shape for long and prosperous happy life in Japan. This will make me very happy.

Also, I will arrange for my sister, Yoshiko's mother, to visit her about one time a month in secret from her father.

Now, Yoshiko knows all about my plan and my offer. She hopes all of your plans work out and then you proceed with my plan.

If possible, I would like to see you and Yoshiko together one last time before you leave Tokyo. Maybe next weekend sometime sould be good.

With all my respect,

Uncle Masuda

Myles read the letter three times. Wow, he thought, they've got it all worked out for me. It's perfect. I don't deserve this.

He lay back on the bed and listened to the Crosley while he read the letter over and over again. He understood but at the same time it was hard to believe. He decided to share the letter with Peggy on the train ride back to the base.

"Myles, you really missed it. All these beautiful women parading around naked .... you would have gone crazy," Peggy said.

"Yes, Mai, and Peggy-san and I were no clothes too. You should be there."

"Well, I guess I'm not cut out for naked bathing in public, that's all there is too it. I'm so glad you both had a good time."

"We did, and now, I hate to tell you, but you're going to have to feed us again," Peggy added.

"Eat, eat, eat, that's all we do around here. What you got in mind Yoshiko?" Myles asked.

"It five o'clock, that mean Mitsukoshi box lunches be ready. Mai, you go Mitsukoshi and bring four lunches for our supper. That for O-basan too. I think we all like barbequed eel please. Peggy-san you like eel?"

"Eel, eel, I've never eaten it. I've seen them before in pictures. Look like snakes don't they?"

"No they are fish. Just long fish, Peggy-san. Very delicious."

"Myles, I have eel box lunch please," Peggy said with a giggle.

"Peggy, the proper word for box lunch is .... bento .... and the word for eel is .... unagi."

"Got it. Guess I'll have an unagi bento."

Myles hustled over to the Mitsukoshi and brought back four bentos. Yoshiko made tea and they invited O-basan to come upstairs and join them.

Later, the time had finally come for Myles and Peggy to leave for the base. It was a sad parting for the two girls. They had cemented a solid friendship over the weekend, being naked together, using a Japanese toilet, and all the other new and different things.

Now, for a change, it was Myles and Peggy standing at the sliding door saying goodbye to Yoshiko lying back on the bed in the low light, with the Crosley playing soft Hit Parade music.

"Sayonara, Yoshiko," Myles said.

"Goodbye Yoshiko, thank you so much for everything. I can't wait to see you again. Sayonara," Peggy said, waving goodbye.

On the train back to the base, Myles handed Peggy Masuda-san's letter. She read it intently, stopping occasionally to stave off a tear. Finally she passed it back to Myles.

"Myles, don't ever tell me there is no God in this Universe. This is the most marvelous act of friendship and generosity there could ever be. I can just see Yoshiko and Masuda putting their heads together and working this out. In a way, it's a little scary Myles, it's just too perfect."

On the short cold walk back to the main gate, Peggy did most of the talking. She relived all the events of this wonderful weekend, one that she would never forget as long as she would live.

Back on base, Myles walked Peggy to within a block from her house, just to be safe. She thanked him one last time for the weekend and they hugged and said goodbye.

Nelson Mandella and 156 other protesters arrested; First test firing of US Vanguard satellite program; "Candide" opens at Martin Beck Theatre in NYC; NY Giants beat Chicago Bears in NFL Championship game; Bobby Fisher, age 13, beats Chess Grandmaster Donald Byrne in "Game of the Century"; Elvis Presley enters charts with "Heartbreak Hotel; Popular movies are "The Ten Commandments", "Pal Joey", "Giant", and "The Tea House of the August Moon".

Chapter Thirteen

Peabody

Monday, January 21, 1957

Myles slept well that night and was ready for the day. Once again he headed over to the dining hall for an early breakfast. He wanted to get to the office before eight to see how Brent had arranged his new Beehive workspace.

He was pleased when he got there. The desks were two abreast with each having wall space behind it available for charts and maps. It was close quarters but actually that would be good. They could talk back and forth without disturbing the other folks nearby.

He straightened up his desk and arranged his work for the morning. Davison would need to relocate his own files and supplies. When Han arrives Johnson would need to help her set up her work space and get supplies from the storeroom.

"Guess this is my desk here, Myles," Johnson spoke up as he neared the corner arrangement.

"Well, looks like they put you next to the empty desk. So you'll be next to Sergeant DeMeur," Myles said

Next, Davison came back to his new spot.

"Well, ain't this cozy. Hope everybody has a good supply of deodorant."

Leave it to Davison, Myles thought. Hope he's used his.

"Bob, take your place next to me here. We'll be close enough to talk all day if necessary. Ready to start learning about Beehive?"

"Man, I'm ready. I want to know everything. I mean everything. When do we expect Sergeant Han?"

"Don't know .... anytime I expect. I don't even know if she made it to the base yesterday."

Just about that time Brent came back to pay a visit. He handed Myles a decrypted message from Arlington.

TOP SECRET BEEHIVE

DE BANTA, B26A, 21-1-57

GARRISON

FLASH FLASH FLASH

Urgent to Myles. Peabody checked out of Okura eight days ago and missing since. Understand meeting at Embassy went well. Expected Peabody remain in Tokyo for week on assignment or more. Have sent out alert all locations for search Peabody. Confirm your last sighting or contact with Peabody. Very concerned.

BANTA

TOP SECRET BEEHIVE

Myles immediately read the message and passed it Johnson.

"Take a look and pass this to Davison," Myles said with deep concern in a shaky voice.

After both men read the message Myles suddenly regretted showing it to them. His first instinct was to share it with them because of Beehive. Now he remembered what Peabody's mission was all about.

He quietly spoke to both of them.

"This is something very confidential. It's really not Beehive. It's more of a personnel thing. Just put the thought out of your minds. I'll be taking care of it."

Myles immediately penned out a reply to Commander Banta. He said he hadn't heard from Peabody on Tuesday as he had promised and hadn't had any contact since the CIA meeting at the Embassy a week ago Friday. He asked if the Ambassador and the Tokyo police had been put on alert.

Because of the time zone difference he hadn't expected a reply until tomorrow morning. He was surprised to get Commander Banta's reply in forty minutes

TOP SECRET BEEHIVE

DE BANTA, B26A, 21-1-57

GARRISON

FLASH FLASH FLASH

Thanks for response. Yes, Ambassador John Allison and Tokyo police alerted. Suggest you speak to Ambassador so he have real time contact. Same with Tokyo law enforcement. Allison to step down Feb 7 and Douglas MacArthur will step in Feb 25 so Embassy very

busy with transition. Please stay in contact. Extremely concerned for Peabody safety.

TOP SECRET BEEHIVE

This time Myles didn't let Johnson and Davison read the message. He decided to try to call the Embassy in the afternoon. The incident with Major Hickson and the top secret papers was still on his mind. He put both of Commander Banta's messages in his burn bag and settled down at his desk to review some new traffic.

"How's everything look Myles? We tried to give you as much space as we could. Hope we got everybody's wall charts up right. Once we started putting them back up we got some mixed up," Brent said.

"Roy, you did a great job. We can't thank you enough for coming in over the weekend," Myles answered.

"Great. Sergeant DeMeur should be getting in soon. How about joining me to greet her at the gate?"

"I'd like to, thanks. Did she get settled in all right yesterday?"

"Yeah. I met her at the main gate around four and got her settled in at her new quarters. On the way, I took her by supply and got her bed linens, towels, and stuff. I showed her where the NCO mess hall is and the NCO club."

"What's she like?" Johnson asked.

"Oh, well, she's an Army Sergeant. What more can I say?" Brent replied.

Just then Sergeant Barney joined in.

"Captain Brent, that was the guard shack calling. Sergeant DeMeur is there waiting for an escort."

"Ready Myles?" Brent asked.

"Let's go."

Myles jumped to his feet.

The two of them went out into the hall and started walking to the guard shack. As they walked across the clearing, Myles spotted her inside talking with one of the Air Police. She looked tall from that distance and appeared to be wearing her green Class A uniform. They went inside.

"Sergeant DeMeur this is Myles Garrison."

"Very pleased to meet you Sergeant," Myles said as they shook hands.

"And very pleased to meet you Lieutenant, I'm really happy to be here."

"Sergeant, I'm a civilian NSA employee now. I just don't have my civilian clothes assembled yet. This just happened last week."

"Sorry, guess I'll call you Mister Garrison."

"No, in the 21st and in our Beehive unit, we go by first names. Please call me Myles, unless you really want to get my attention."

"This will be new to me. From now on, you and Captain Brent can call me Han, please."

"And our informal names are Roy and Brent. I answer to both. Around Major Hickson and Sergeant Barney I guess you still should address the officers by their rank. Let's head back to our office."

As they left the guard house, Myles couldn't help but be impressed. She was strikingly beautiful as well as tall. Obviously she inherited her mother's looks and, most probably, her father's stature. Except for her height, she was definitely Vietnamese. She wore her shining black hair rolled up in a bun and tucked neatly beneath under her beret. Myles had never seen a female look so good in an Army uniform. Her regulation skirt stopped at mid-knee and revealed long shapely legs in regulation mid-height black heels. Even Army shoes looked good on her, Myles thought.

Everything went quiet as the three of them entered the big room. Brent briefly explained the layout. Then he escorted her and Myles into the Major's office.

"Major Hickson .... Sergeant Han DeMeur," Brent introduced them.

In a second Sergeant Barney came in and introduced himself.

"Sergeant DeMeur, we are happy to have you join us," the Major said. "We've been looking over your records and you're going to be a perfect fit for Myles' Beehive group. Do you really speak fluent Vietnamese?"

"Thanks for your warm welcome Major. Yes, as you probably saw in my file, I grew up and lived there until I was seventeen. I am a French citizen however, from my father's heritage. I am a linguist as well as a traffic analyst and even a part time cryptanalyst. Can't say how good I am at the latter two, but my language is definitely strong."

"Sergeant I'm sure you will be a great asset for Myles' Project Beehive. Myles, do you have a training program set up?"

"Yes sir. Johnson and I will be teaching Han, ... uh .... Sergeant DeMeur, all week. We've got a lot of work to do."

"Good, then I'll let you all go for now. Sergeant Barney will go over you records with you later today or, maybe tomorrow. You are our first Army person here and we need to learn something from you too."

"Thank you sir," Han replied.

The short meeting broke up and Myles took Han back to the Beehive section. Along the way, he introduced her to everybody, and very briefly explained their responsibilities.

"Sergeant Johnson and Lieutenant Davison, I'd like you to meet Sergeant Han DeMeur."

The two of them were nearly speechless. Johnson especially, could hardly contain himself. Wow, he thought, her desk will be next to mine and we'll be speaking Vietnamese.

They finally finished the hand shaking and Myles asked everybody to take a seat at their assigned desks. He asked Johnson to show Han around the base and take her to the hospital for her medical check-up. He suggested Johnson stay with her the rest of the day, including lunch at the NCO mess hall.

By the end of the day, Han had been fully base oriented and medically checked out. She'd gotten her stationary and other work supplies. She seemed to be comfortable at her new desk in the big room. In the meantime, Myles asked Johnson to assist her in any way possible to ease her transition to her new surroundings. Johnson was more than happy to oblige.

Myles decided to call the Embassy tomorrow.

Brent stopped by at the end of the day and invited Myles to the club for a beer. It worked out well for the two of them. Everything was back to normal now, as far as friendship and mutual respect was concerned.

Tuesday, January 22, 1957

The next morning, Johnson and Myles instructed Han and Davison on all aspects of Beehive. They both were quick learners. He had to slow Han and Johnson down several times when they relapsed into Vietnamese. Johnson was almost as fluent as Han. As to Davison, well, Myles was totally impressed with how well he picked up on things and his eagerness to take it all in. It was almost as if he was working against a timetable and needed to get it all as quickly as possible.

Around eleven o'clock, Myles remembered about his phone call. He excused himself from the group and headed over to the snack bar. He made it there in record time and asked permission to use Mark's phone.

"Peggy, I'm glad I caught you. I just wanted to thank you for visiting Yoshiko and me over the weekend."

"Oh Myles, that was a wonderful weekend. I enjoyed spending the time with Yoshiko, including the bath. We having lunch this week?"

"Peggy, I'm going to have to skip this week. I think I told you about Sergeant DeMeur. How about I call you next Monday and give you an update on Yoshiko, we can make some plans then?"

"OK that'll be fine. So call me next Monday."

It took some doing but Myles finally got a call through to the receptionist at the American Embassy. For a moment he wasn't sure what to say. Then he decided to follow the Commander's request just as she ordered.

"May I speak to the Ambassador please?"

"May I ask who's calling please?" a young female voice asked.

Myles identified himself as a civilian working for the NSA. He said it was urgent that he speak directly to the Ambassador.

"I'm sorry, sir, that would be impossible. He's in conference all day with the transition team. Would you like to leave a message?"

"Ma'am, I can't leave a message. It is NSA business. Is there a CIA person available?"

"We have no CIA persons working here at the Embassy. I can connect you with someone who might be able to help. Please stay on the line."

Momentarily a male voice came on line, "May I help you?"

Myles was elated that John Allen was on the phone.

"John, this is Myles Garrison. I met you a week ago Friday in a meeting with Lieutenant Peabody."

"I'm sorry, I don't know anybody by that name and I just arrived here yesterday from the States. What can I do for you?"

"John, are you CIA?"

"No."

"Is your name John Allen?"

"Yes."

"OK, whoever you are, maybe you can help. I am NSA. One of our people checked out of the Okura Hotel a week ago Sunday and has gone missing. His boss has notified the Ambassador and the Tokyo police but as of now, he's still missing. Have you heard anything about all this?"

"News to me. How can I help?" the man asked.

"Well, I guess all you can do is tell the Ambassador he can contact me at 21st Radio at Shiroi Air Base. Just one last question. Have you ever heard of Jim Allen?"

"Yes, Jim is here with me. We both just got here from the States yesterday."

"So now I do know you are John Allen. I met two guys named John and Jim Allen a week ago last Friday. We met in a conference room there along with Lieutenant Peabody.

This is really strange. Are you leveling with me. Weren't the two of you in Saigon last week?"

"No."

That was it. Myles was ready to give up. He was sure this was CIA crap.

"OK. If that's your story just tell the Ambassador about me, OK?"

Myles hung up and returned to the office. By the time he got there everybody had returned from lunch. Myles had completed forgotten to eat. All he could think about was Peabody missing and that futile call to Embassy.

Around four o'clock he decided to see the Major about the top secret papers. Johnson was completely in charge now teaching Han and Davison about Beehive and what their roles were going to be.

"Johnson, I'll be with the Major for a little while. Will you guys be all right."

"We're fine Myles. Go see the Maj."

Major Hickson invited Myles in and asked him to sit while he finished signing some documents.

"Thanks Myles. These are requests for some promotions. Captain Brent is doing a fine job. What's on your mind?"

"Well, a while back you showed me some top secret papers you had gotten from a source in Saigon. They looked really ominous. I think one was from the Minister of Agriculture. You told me this was all super secret. Then you tore them up and stuffed them in your burn bag. You said you would get back but you never did."

"OK, I guess this is a good time to talk about that. You know some folks like to use us as a conduit for secret stuff because we are trustworthy and cleared to the highest level.

This was a case of just that sort of thing. The South Vietnam Consulate in Tokyo is a key link in a special intelligence pipeline from assets in Hanoi. The Consulate folks needed a way to get the material to the State Department. Those documents represented some of that intel. I'd been receiving stuff from the Consulate and forwarding to State for a couple of months."

"But sir, you destroyed the documents."

"Yes, because as soon as I showed them to you, they were compromised. I realized immediately that I shouldn't have shown them to you. The reason I did was that I was going to ask you to carry them to Arlington with you so you could take them to State. It was a bad decision on my part. So you should please forget all about this. I guess that's an order."

"Thanks Major. Now I can see what this was all about. I've already forgotten about it."

"Good. Anything else?"

"No sir. I just thought you'd like to know how pleased we are to get Sergeant DeMeur. Please thank Captain Brent for finding her for us."

"I will and you can thank him personally as well."

Wednesday, January 23, 1957

Johnson and Myles spent most of Wednesday, Thursday, and Friday training Han and Davison. They had a lot to cover but the trainees were excellent students.

Myles spent a lot of time on the B26A organization and the overall Beehive mission. He explained about the five Beehive detachments, especially Blue Cover which was to be their future assignments. He told them he would be leaving for Arlington in about three weeks and from there he would be going to either Tan Son Nhut or Saigon. He said everything was high priority and even President Eisenhower was fully backing the operation. He explained how fluid everything was right now because of the worsening situation in the Delta. He couldn't say for sure exactly where Johnson would be and, for that matter, where they would be. They would all need to keep their noses to the grindstone and do a lot of talking between them.

Myles was extremely pleased with Han. She caught on to everything very quickly, and he seldom had to stop and explain anything a second time. It was the same way with Davison.

Johnson spent nearly twelve hours teaching Han and Davison the traffic analysis techniques he had developed in his Vietnam experience. It was an easy exercise and he felt they were nearly as proficient as him after they completed their final exam.

By Friday, both of the new recruits were deep into translation and traffic analysis of real time intercepts. Each of them had already written a couple of Intelligence Briefs which were quite good. By quitting time on Friday, Myles had not had any communication from the Embassy or the Tokyo police. Neither had he had any more messages from Commander Banta. His concern for Peabody was foremost on his mind. He was satisfied, however, that the intelligence leaks probably were not coming from Major Hickson. His explanation was perfectly believable. He felt he no longer needed to be concerned over the Major being implicated.

Now he wished Peabody would show up somewhere so that he could tell him about the Major. But for now, all he wished for was Peabody's well being.

Summer Olympics open in Melbourne; North Vietnam President Ho Chi Minh pumping vast amounts of munitions and supplies down the Ho Chi Minh Trail into the South Vietnam Mekong Delta; Rose Heilbron becomes first Britain female judge; Pipe bomb explodes in the Paramount Theatre in Brooklyn, NY; The Bell X-2 is the first aircraft to fly faster than Mach-3; John F. Kennedy's "Profile in Courage" is published; Kentucky Derby winner, "Needles" is put to stud; "The Bridge on the River Kwai" wins academy award Best Picture, and Alec Guiness wins Best Actor; Eugene O'Neill wins Pulitzer for "Long Day's Journey into Night".

Chapter Fourteen

Geisha

Friday Evening, January 25, 1957

Myles met Davison at the main gate around five-thirty.

"Hey man, you heading to town tonight, as if I didn't know," Davison spoke to Myles.

"Well, yes, matter of fact. What you up to? Going to town by yourself tonight? Another date with Fumiko?"

"Oh, yeah. Still celebrating my new job and my new boss. Going to meet her at the Opal as usual."

"Well, I wish I could join you but I've got other plans."

"I know, might as well enjoy our ride to Tokyo anyway."

And they did. Of course, there was absolutely no talk of work. So they covered everything else under the sun.

Several times Davison pushed Myles for information about his private life, but Myles stayed ahead of him and didn't volunteer anything.

At one point, Myles did get some information on Davison. He learned that he and Fumiko had been seeing each other regularly for about a month. Fumiko had a small apartment in Shinjuku and that's where they usually stayed. Somehow it just didn't sound like an honest loving relationship though, certainly nothing like between him and Yoshiko.

They split up after getting off the train in Tokyo, and Myles went on to his Ikebukuro connection. On the last leg of his trip, he couldn't get Davison and Fumiko off his mind. Why was he so secretive about it, he wondered? It just didn't seem like Davison. Normally he'd be bragging about his cohabitation. And why was that late night trip to Tokyo and then missing the last train and the huge hangover. Somehow, things just didn't add up. Anyway, he switched his thoughts to Ikebukuro and Yoshiko as the train neared Ikebukuro Station.

He got to the apartment around seven-thirty and didn't bother to stop to say hello to O-basan. He was eager to see his girl again since last weekend with Peggy.

Soft yellow light shown dimly through the paper walls and it looked cozy and inviting on a cold winter's eve. He rapped once on the wooden door frame.

"Mai, please come in. Be quiet please."

Myles slid the door open not expecting what he was about to see. Yoshiko was lying back on the bed fully dressed in an extravagant traditional kimono. Her hair was up in a tight bun with four ivory spikes jutting out in all directions. She had heavy white make up on her face and her eyes were heavy with long black lashes and black eye shadow. Her lips were over painted with crimson lipstick.

"Yoshiko, what, you are beautiful. Please stand up so I can see you. You are a geisha! Yoshiko, you are geisha!"

She managed to pull herself halfway up and then she held out her arm for help.

Myles pulled her up the rest of the way and stood her up like a stand-up doll. Once standing, she was fine.

"Yoshiko, you are magnificent. I've never seen a geisha up close and you are beautiful."

He continued to gaze and was at a loss for words. The kimono was in shades of blue, yellow, and red assembled to form trees, flowers, and birds. He'd never seen anything like it, or even known that such a beautiful thing could exist.

"Yoshiko, why are you a geisha tonight?"

"Mai, this afternoon we have show over at Mitsukoshi with models in kimono. This once every year we do. There many people and lots of pictures. I think be in Sunday paper. What you think?"

"I wish I could just squeeze you and make time stand still. This is wonderful. Can I kiss your white face and red lips?"

"Yes, please."

Without smearing anything too badly, Myles put his arms around her kimono clad body and kissed her gently on her over painted lips. It was awkward getting his arms around the obi and the huge heavy sleeves.

"I think we return Mitsukoshi tomorrow, Mai. What we do tonight?"

"Well, I just don't know. We should do something. Want to go out and show off a little as a geisha?"

"I think we do. Maybe this last time for kimono until we marry."

"How about we take a taxi to a fancy hotel and walk through the lobby? Maybe even eat in a dining room?"

"You got money tonight Mai?"

"I got enough for that. Do you know the Okura Hotel in Akasaka?"

"I know. Prime Minister stay there sometime, and President Eisenhower stay there last year. You remember?"

"You're right. It is the hotel of royalty and tonight I will take you there. Are you ready? Do you need to go down the hall for anything?" Myles asked, even though he knew she couldn't manage the toilet in a kimono.

"I ready now. We go. Help me please."

She handed him a short jacket that perfectly matched the kimono. It was full enough to cover over the top half of the kimono and the pattern and color exactly matched the top of the kimono. He helped her slide it on.

"Mai, this called hapi coat. It designed two hundred years ago to wear with kimono. I think it very beautiful."

"Yoshiko, it is beautiful just like the whole outfit. Let's get going."

Downstairs, Myles asked her to wait in O-basan's apartment until he could bring a taxi around to the front door. O-basan had already seen the kimono and sung it's praises.

It was the first time she'd ever seen one up close, just like Myles. Yoshiko couldn't sit. She stood by the door and watched outside.

Before long the taxi pulled up to the front gate. Myles jumped out and headed back inside. He took her arm and gently guided her down the gravel path and over the stone threshold. Walking was not easy in her geisha attire. She was wearing traditional kimono sandals called geta, which are always shorter that the foot causing the geisha's heel to overhang. This, plus the narrow hemline, causes the geisha to walk in short shuffling steps. Myles figured this was supposed to be sexy two hundred years ago and tonight it still is.

He finally managed to ease her into the waiting taxi and fold in the huge sleeves and all the heavy folds. The driver was in absolute awe at the sight. He said he'd never driven a geisha before.

At the Okura Hotel, Yoshiko asked the driver to drop them off at the main lobby. The driver accommodated. As the car pulled to a stop, two doormen rushed over to open the door and help her out onto the driveway. The driver told them all about picking her up and the ride from Ikebukuro.

The two doormen in their long green coats lead them into the lobby. It was the first time there for Yoshiko. It was a very special place, not like your usual big hotel lobby. Everywhere there was wood and lush carpet and subdued lighting. It was a large area with the low ceiling, wood columns and overstuffed antique sofas and chairs. it was a cozy place considering its size. One tended to speak in low tones in such a dignified place. In spite of guests, bellboys, and luggage carts, it was as quiet as a library. It was certainly intended for royalty, not the usual business traveler.

"Are you with the wedding party?" the taller doorman asked.

Before Myles could say anything, Yoshiko spoke up.

"Yes, with wedding party please?" she answered.

She poked Myles arm as she spoke.

Myles remained silent, a little stunned at unexpectedly being in a wedding party.

They were ushered across the lobby to a wide escalator. All the way to the escalator, guests stopped what they were doing and watched Yoshiko shuffle across the carpet. Myles held her arm tightly, not so much to help her, but more to reassure himself that he was in wedding party.

The ride down the wide escalator into the reception area was another experience. There were hundreds of guests and most of them stopped and gazed at the geisha on Myles arm. There were other kimono clad ladies in the crowd but none anywhere near as striking as Yoshiko. As they stepped off the escalator The attendant, clad in full morning coat and top hat, took Yoshiko's hand and led her from the escalator.

"Are you guests of the wedding sir?" he asked Myles.

Once again, Yoshiko spoke up.

"Yes, we are guests from Embassy. Mai, you have invitation?"

"Oh, my, I think I left it on the dresser. I'm so sorry, sir."

"Well, that's quite all right. We have some other folks from the Embassy here too. I assume you mean the British Embassy, right?"

"Yes. Thanks for your consideration," Myles said, trying to tack on a little English accent.

"Have an enjoyable time. The receiving line starts over there."

He gestured with his eyes.

"As you can see, it's going a little slow. I might suggest you have a cocktail and something to eat before you get in the line. And, may I say sir, your geisha is the most beautiful I've seen. May I touch her?"

Yoshiko stretched out both arms and gave him a very polite and proper geisha hug, not too tight and not to loose.

"So pleased to meet you sir," she said. "I am Yoshiko."

Myles guided her toward the cocktail table with people parting along the way. It reminded him of the Red Sea.

They had cold sake and began mingling with the crowd. Practically everyone spoke. Myles was glad he'd suggested coming to the Okura. After a while they had some of the delicious food from the sashimi table. The Beluga Caviar was magnificent, as was most of the raw fish.

"Mai, maybe we have reception like this. I tell Uncle Masuda-san."

"Yes, you tell Uncle Masuda-san to give us a reception at the Okura Hotel and see what he says. I'd like to be there when you tell him."

"Mai, let's have another drink."

So they wandered back over to the open bar. It was very crowded now and by the time Myles squeezed up to the counter he was separated from Yoshiko. Just as he was pulling away from the table he noticed Yoshiko standing near the end of the table talking with someone.

He joined back up with her in a few minutes and they sipped on their second drinks.

"Mai, I think we go now. We no need see pretty bride. She not know us anyway. OK?"

So they finished their drinks and walked back to the escalator.

Back on the first floor, they crossed the lobby and settled back in a waiting taxi.

"Ikebukuro Station please," Myles directed.

About ten minutes into the cab ride, Yoshiko took Myles arm and pulled it inside her kimono. At first Myles thought she was flirting as usual, but then his hand came against something cold and hard. What, he thought, he pulled his hand back.

Yoshiko extracted a nearly full bottle of Scotch Whisky from inside her kimono.

"What you think Mai? The barman give me for present."

"Yoshiko, you are amazing. You surprise me all the time. What do I think? Well, I think I will have a Scotch Whisky when we get home. Thank you for the present."

As the taxi neared Ikebukuro Station, Yoshiko completed the driving instructions back to the apartment.

They regaled in their geisha adventure at the Okura Hotel that night. Their final adventure before getting to bed was Myles disrobing Yoshiko from the cumbersome kimono and all its accessories. It took a nearly twenty minutes to complete the operation. Yoshiko instructed him on how to properly fold the huge T-shaped kimono. It took up most of the floor space.

In the bed they snuggled up under the futon and listened to Top Ten American music on the Crosley table radio. They fell asleep in each other's arms to the sounds of Chubby Checker and Bobby Darin.

Saturday, January 26, 1957

They slept until a little past nine in the process of recovering from their geisha adventure. Luckily, Yoshiko had stocked up on coffee and tea cakes so they were all set for breakfast. Her coffee had continually improved since her first percolated pot. Myles much preferred it to dining hall and O-Club coffee.

"What today we do, Mai?"

"Well, do you remember next weekend will be my last with you until I come back in a month?"

"Yes, so we should do special thing. Right?"

"Well, that or we can just enjoy each other like we always do."

"OK, but first you should know. Uncle Masuda will visit us today about two o'clock. He want say goodbye because next weekend he no see you."

"That sounds great. I always like to see Uncle Masuda. So let's listen to some music and we should go buy you some new records for your player. You no longer need Hawaiian music."

"Oh, Mai, I get one hundred dollars for hula dance on television. So I buy some clothes. In closet, I have two new suits. I wear today for you and save some money too."

"Very smart. I am proud of you."

They leisurely had coffee and cakes and then started dressing for the short trip over to Mitsukoshi. Yoshiko put on one of her new outfits, an earth tone two piece suit styled much like the pink suit she wore when they first met at the Victoria Tea Room. She slipped on a new pair of brown skin pumps and twirled around the room for Myles.

"Yoshiko that looks terrific, I mean really nice, beautiful. Wait, there's something missing."

"Here," she said as she opened her clenched fist revealing *Ladybug*. "Please put on."

Should have known, he thought, she would never forget *Ladybug*. He very carefully pinned the red and black cloisonné device on her jacket just above her heart.

"There, now everything is complete. I really like your new shoes but I think you should wear your penny loafers over to Mitsubishi. Those heels aren't good on the road."

"OK, I wear heels later today, but penny loafers now. You ready to take walk, Mai"

"Ready whenever you are."

She hastily straightened the bed and spread the futon smoothly over the full surface. Then she placed the kimono on the futon, and folded it five times, finishing up with a suitcase size bundle. After that she packed the other accessories into her hat box.

At the Mitsukoshi, shoppers stopped and stared as the couple walked through the ground floor carrying the huge kimono bundle. They went directly to the fashion floor and returned the kimono and accessories. Yoshiko thanked her friends over and over again and briefly recounted the Okura Hotel experience in Japanese.

From there, they went to the appliance floor and bought some new Ray Coniff and Mantavani records. Unfortunately all the Dave Brubeck albums were sold out.

They browsed around the store for more than hour, not buying anything, but talking a lot about how they would furnish their new apartment when they got married. Around noon, they decided to skip lunch and go back to the apartment. She was pretty sure Uncle Masuda would take them to a nice lunch when he got there in a little while.

In the apartment, they barely had started listening to Ray Coniff when they heard Uncle Masuda rapping on the door.

"Come in please," Yoshiko said.

Uncle Masuda was looking very smart in a dark blue suit, white shirt, and narrow knit necktie.

The three of them talked for thirty minutes or so updating each other on the status of things, everything from the baby to Myles going back to the States and then to Vietnam. Soon, Yoshiko indicated that some food would be nice since they were poor and hadn't eaten. Uncle Masuda apologized for not noticing that and invited them to lunch.

Yoshiko took them to a new place she'd discovered.

"We go shabu shabu place. You know Mai?"

"No, but you can surprise us. You always do," Myles replied.

At the restaurant, Yoshiko ordered the full course shabu shabu. The waitress placed a large open copper pot in the center of the table. It was filled with boiling water heated by an array of burners underneath. Each person was provided with a platter of razor thin sliced beef and vegetables and an assortment of sauces. Yoshiko demonstrated the proper way to eat shabu shabu.

She clamped several strands of raw vegetables with her chop sticks and proceeded to swish them around in the boiling water. Then she dipped the cooked vegetables in one of the sauces.

Myles caught on quickly and he was glad to have new Japanese experience.

"Now, I need to talk a little. Please give me your attention," Uncle Masuda declared.

Myles and Yoshiko nodded and straightened up in their chairs.

"Here is what my plan is for you two. Now, Myles, you go on to Washington the week after next, and then come back here in a month for a week vacation. Then, according to your plan, you will go to Vietnam as a civilian working for the NSA. I know what that is."

"Yes, so far so good," Myles assured him.

Masuda continued.

"Then you stay in Vietnam for a while. Then in September or October you apply to resign from NSA. Yoshiko have baby in early September and you arrange to come to Tokyo for that. Am I right so far?"

"Yes sir."

"OK, then when you are a civilian you come to Tokyo to marry Yoshiko. Is that right?"

"Yes sir."

Myles glanced at Yoshiko. Her eyes are as big a saucers and she was staring intently at Uncle Masuda.

"Now, I know the timing is not certain, but here is what I think. After baby is here and you are a civilian it might be in October or November. I hope so. You move to Tokyo and I pay for larger apartment for you and Yoshiko. I already told you I have much money and want to spend it on you and Yoshiko. You both are my life now. Follow so far?"

"Yes I do, but Yoshiko?"

"I explain all to Yoshiko later. Anyway, I think she does understand most of it."

Myles looked at Yoshiko. She definitely wasn't taking it all in. She was trying, that's for sure, but it was just too much and too fast.

"OK, please tell her you will explain later in Japanese."

"I will do that in just a minute. Anyway, to go on .... you come back and marry Yoshiko late in year. Then move into large apartment near Sophia University. I pay for one year at Sophia for you to be full time student studying Japanese language, Japanese culture, and Japanese business methods. I will buy you and Yoshiko a small car so you can travel back and forth to Sophia. You can also use the car to take Yoshiko to some of her modeling jobs."

"OK, but ...."

"Please don't interrupt Myles. That all finishes up in late 1958. Then, if you wish, I offer you partnership in my Ginza Camera Shop. Myles, my annual gross income is over a half million dollars so there is plenty of room for you in my business. But, main thing, you will be a valuable asset to my business. Just imagine a young good looking bi-lingual American in a Ginza camera store. I think we could pull in a lot of American and European customers. It will be fantastic. Don't you think?"

"Yes, I see your point. But that is just too generous of you to offer me all this. I haven't done anything to deserve it."

"Myles, you don't understand. This is all for Yoshiko, not you. About generosity, I already told you I am very rich and Yoshiko is my only family. Now do you see?"

"I guess so."

"So, by accepting all of these terms you will actually be doing me a great favor. So that is the plan. Later, I will explain to Yoshiko. She will be very pleased."

"Now, Yoshiko, when is your next appointment with Dr. Ishiyama?" Masuda asked.

"It is February sixth, I think. That is first week Mai will be gone so you will take me please."

"Yes, you and I will visit Dr. Ishiyama on Wednesday, February the sixth. Myles, you will be in Washington by then?"

"Yes, I will. By the way I will give mailing addresses for me in Washington and for my parents in Illinois to Yoshiko. I expect we will write a lot of letters starting right away."

"Yes, I will get the addresses from you. And don't you have a friend at the base who I can call?"

"Well, that would be Captain Brent. I think I'll ask him to call you at your store every couple of weeks to check on things. Will that be all right?"

"That is good idea."

"Now, you two, how about going back to the apartment. You probably need a nap after all that shabu shabu."

By this time, Yoshiko was numbed by the rapid fire English conversation. She didn't respond to Masuda's suggestion.

"Yoshiko, we go back home now? OK?" Myles said.

"Yes, we go home now. I ready."

After a short ride, the taxi pulled up in front of the apartment.

"Myles, I will leave you two now, but first please step outside with me. I have something private to say. Yoshiko, you go on upstairs. Myles will be right with you."

The two stepped out into the courtyard. It was cold and starting to drizzle a light rain.

"This will be quick Myles. It's pretty cold out here."

"What do you want to say Uncle Masuda?"

Masuda pulled a small box from his coat pocket. He flipped up the lid, exposing a beautiful solitaire diamond ring.

"Myles, you should give this to Yoshiko for a going away present. I know it is customary for American girls to have diamond rings for marriage engagement. Please don't argue."

"Now, Uncle Masuda-san, I can't afford a nice ring like that. I can't do this."

"Yes, you can and you will. It will be absolutely secret from Yoshiko. It would make me very happy."

Myles took the box and tucked it into his pants pocket.

"Uncle Masuda-san, you are so thoughtful and generous. I just can't thank you enough."

"Now, one last thing Myles. After Yoshiko was on television. I called the Sakura Agency to see how well she was doing. They said she is so talented that she has a very bright future. They said the television station will be calling her for more shows and maybe some commercials. The lady at the agency said she is a very talented model and is very much in demand by the big department stores and some special shows."

"Oh, that's wonderful. I'm not surprised. But Uncle Masuda-san don't you think she should slow down a little, what with the baby and all?"

"I think so. But I want her to be happy and successful. So, I will try to help her decide what jobs to take and I will always be there to watch out for her health and for the baby's health. I just wanted you to know you don't have to worry. She will be busy with her career and with the baby. She will miss you a lot, but your letters will be a great help and your visits to Tokyo will be a blessing. I hope it works out."

With that, Masuda stepped backward, bowed deeply and slowly, and extended his hand. They shook hands firmly.

"Myles, I will see you in about a month. I wish you great success in your new job and with your plan .... uh .... our plan."

"Thank you for everything Uncle Masuda-san."

Masuda turned and walked backed to the taxi. Myles watched the taxi pull away. Then he turned to go upstairs where Yoshiko was waiting.

Entering the room, Myles saw Yoshiko lying back on the bed still in her suit and partly covered by the futon. She seemed to be asleep. He slipped his suit jacket off and placed it over the chair. Then he crawled under the futon and placed himself against her quiet body. She didn't wake up. They slept that way, hardly moving, for two hours.

That night, Myles brought in box lunches for Yoshiko, O-basan, and himself. As usual, he got their favorites, unagi bento. The three of them ate while sitting in front of the gas heater in O-basan's apartment. They were in bed by nine.

Sunday, January 27, 1957

Sunday morning breakfast was sheer bliss. They put on the Ray Coniff album and snuggled up under the futon with hot coffee and pastries. It was another cold gray winter sky over Tokyo, so there probably would be no walk in Naka Park today.

"How about today, Mai? What we do?"

Myles thought for a minute.

"Well, let's put on your other new suit and go to the Ginza today. We can walk some if it's not too cold, and maybe visit some of our old places. Maybe we even go to a movie. How about that?"

"I like idea. Here I show you my other suit."

She leaped from the bed and pulled her other suit from the closet. She held it up against her as a model would do.

"You like?"

"Yoshiko, I like it very much. I think that that beige color will pull the brown out of our eyes. Yes, I'm taking my girl to town today. Let's leave around noon. Then we can have lunch somewhere on the Ginza."

So, that was the plan for the day. They dressed, said goodbye to O-basan, caught a taxi, and were standing on the Ginza opposite Seibu Department Store by one o'clock. They walked up and down the full length of the Ginza in spite of the cold. Around two, Yoshiko pulled Myles into a tiny soba shop and they ate a hearty lunch of spicy buckwheat noodles topped off with vegetables tempura. After that they went to a movie at the Nichigeki Music Hall and saw Elvis in "Blue Hawaii". It was a wonderful day on the Ginza.

By six, they were back in the apartment listening to the new Mantavani album.

Now is the time, thought Myles.

"Yoshiko, next weekend will be our last one together for a while but I want to give you something tonight."

He went over to the closet and extracted the ring box from his jacket pocket. Then he sat on the edge of the bed.

"Are you ready?" he asked.

"Mai, what you have?"

"Well, it's something sort of American but it's special for you. Here."

He flipped up the lid and showed her the ring. He tried to momentarily forget that the ring was all Uncle Masuda's idea so he could enjoy the moment with her.

"Oh, Mai, that beautiful. That for me, really? It is diamond? I never have diamond."

"Yes, it is for you. And it means that we are promised to be married and that you are mine and I am yours forever. I love you."

She put the ring, still in the box, on the bed and slung her arms around him. It was the hardest, sweetest embrace he could remember. Then they kissed and kissed until their lips were sore.

"Now, let's see how it looks on your finger."

Myles placed the ring on her third finger. It was a perfect fit. The diamond glistened with a thousand beautiful lights reflected from the bedside lamp.

"I love you so much, Mai, thank you very much. I will wear it always. And when I see it I see you. It help me when you gone. I love you. Thank you."

She kissed him again and with the ring now firmly on her finger, she pulled him down on the bed. They lay quietly for a while in each other's arms.

"Now, I must be going again for another week. Before I go, what do you think of Uncle Masuda's plan?" Myles asked, not knowing how much she was able to understand.

"Mai, I think it wonderful. You come back and go to Sophia and then be with me and baby and be business with Uncle Masuda-san. I think it wonderful."

"Well, I do too. Let me see that ring again."

Myles took her hand and kissed her fingers.

"It suits you just fine. I hope you have it forever and you will be with me always no matter what. I love you. Now, lay back on the bed while I get my stuff together."

She quickly jumped back and propped her head up on the pillows, her hand across her chest with the ring plainly in sight.

"Oh, I forgot, are you working this week?"

"Yes, I am at Mitsukoshi at Ginza tomorrow and Seibu on Ginza Tuesday. Maybe Wednesday, not sure. Then Seibu again Thursday and maybe a new job on Friday. So busy week. Oh, I forgot Mai, the television station want me come for interview someday next week. Maybe some more hula dancing. You think so?"

"I hope so. You are my favorite hula dancer. I hate to go, but I must go now. I will be here Friday night. Sayonara."

Myles slid the door closed with the vision of Yoshiko lying back on the bed lingering in his mind. He headed out for the station in the January cold.

Monday, January 28, 1957

Myles woke up around six and couldn't go back to sleep. He lay back on his pillow and thought about the weekend. What a great weekend it was. First there was the geisha adventure at the Okura Hotel. Really had them fooled. That was clever of Yoshiko to claim the Embassy. Then the record buying stint over at the Mitsukoshi. Of course, nothing could top Uncle Masuda's visit starting with the great shabu shabu and then his generous offer into the future. That brought his thoughts up to the diamond ring. He still felt wrong about taking it and accepting Yoshiko's gratitude like that.

Then there was the great Sunday afternoon on the ginza. He was glad they'd done that. It had to be one of their most fun days. Of course they forgot the Victoria Tea Room, but he'd make sure they visited it at least one more time before he left.

He heard some shuffling in the hallway.

"Is that you Roy," he called out.

"Good morning. Why are you awake so early Myles?"

"Couldn't sleep past six. I'm fine though. Get your shower and stuff. I'll catch up with you in the dining hall around seven."

"Good plan. Try to snooze a little. You still got a few minutes."

The two of them had breakfast around seven-thirty and then walked together across the parade field to the compound. It was definitely still winter. Myles hadn't seen the sun for almost a week and every day had been cold and damp. No snow though since that last good one a week or two ago.

Johnson spotted the two of them entering the office.

"Hey boss, got your coffee yet?"

"Well, no, was that an offer?" Myles answered back.

"Tell you what, I'll zip down the hall and bring back coffee for all four of us."

"Good morning everybody," Myles greeted Davison and Han.

Davison jumped up and offered his hand in a generous handshake. Han didn't stand, but gave Myles a really nice smile.

"Good morning Lieutenant Garrison," she said.

"Han, have you forgotten. I'm only wearing this uniform because I don't have enough civilian suits. Remember, I'm a civilian NSA employee now, so there's no more Lieutenant stuff, please. And I really prefer a first name basis between the four of us. That is except for Davison and Johnson, they want their last names. Got that?"

"Yes, Myles, that better?" Han replied.

"Definitely. I see you're both hard at work already. In a few minutes our fourth party will be bringing coffee."

"Myles, look at this."

Han jumped up and pointed to two new circles on her wall chart.

"I've got two new unloading points on the Trail. Looks like the 585th Transport Group is stepping up shipments. They've delivered stuff here and here."

She pointed to two new places that before had seen no activity.

"Han, good work. Get an Emergency message off to Lieutenant Peabody at B26A. He'll get that to the Air Force at Tan Son Nhut and the Ninth Infantry right away. They'll need to be alert to new ground activity, probably the VC or maybe even the Northern Army. Tan Son Nhut and the Ninth Infantry are two of our more important customers you know. We got to take care of them."

"I'll do that right away. Now do I sign my name or yours?"

"You sign yours. They know each of us by name and we are all equally important and reliable. Davison, did you hear that?"

"Yes. Use our own names from now on," Davison answered.

"OK. Davison, I don't see anything new on your chart. Any reason for that?"

"Well, I just haven't updated it yet. I've picked up two new VC transmitters in the Delta but without good direction finding equipment, I can't quite pinpoint the location. I'll be able to triangulate today and get it pretty close though. They do sound like VC. I do know that."

"Good, when you get those locations send that along to Peabody right away too. Here's Johnson with our coffee. I'll let everybody settle down to work now. I see a huge pile of intercepts on everybody's desk. Johnson, thanks."

Johnson passed the coffee around.

"Johnson, you and Han working together on translations?"

"We are. She's really teaching me a lot of Vietnamese that they didn't teach me at Harvard."

"Great. I have to speak to Captain Brent about something. I'll be back in a little bit."

Myles walked over to Brent's desk.

"Roy, Got a minute?"

"Sure."

"Just want to let you know about the Ikebukuro activity. When I leave for the States late next week, Uncle Masuda is going to step up big time and watch out for Yoshiko. Remember about the baby?"

"Yeah, how's that going?"

"Mother and baby are doing fine. Due date is early September. Anyway, we're not breaking up. Uncle Masuda is going to take care of everything. I haven't told you, but he is a very rich and generous man. He is like Yoshiko's father. I'm not worried at all. This is still strictly between you, Peggy Hicks, and Johnson, and me .... nobody else. Commander Banta and the NSA don't know anything, so my job is secure for now. I think I might tell my story to the Commander in a few months after I get to know her and the organization a little better."

"That's great Myles. Looks like you're handling things real well. Oh, what about your boy scout troop here on base?"

"I've turned them over to a friend so that's taken care of."

"Good. Now, you should count on me as your best friend. If now, or anytime in the future I can help in any way you can count on me. You know, I've already met

Yoshiko and Uncle Masuda. I could call him for you anytime when you're gone. Always, leave me your phone number and address wherever you are."

"Thanks pal."

They shook hands and Myles went back to his desk.

The rest of the day was all work. They each took an abbreviated lunch except for Han who needed to pick up some furnishings for her new quarters.

Throughout the day Myles couldn't get Bill Peabody off his mind. He was still miffed over that stupid conversation with the fictitious John Allen. He seriously doubted if he'd ever hear from the Ambassador.

That night they all met at the bowling alley and celebrated with a few Heinekens.

Tuesday, January 29, 1957

By nine on Tuesday morning, they were all once again deep into translating and working on wall charts. Davison had pinpointed the two new radio transmitters and sent the data along to Peabody.

Around eleven, the morning courier pouch arrived and Sergeant Wideman began sorting the packages. Before long, he walked back to Myles' desk.

"Myles, here's something with Banta's return address. It's Top Secret Beehive. Thought you might want to see it right away."

Myles opened the envelope and immediately called Johnson over to read it with him.

"Well, looks like we'll be doing a briefing tomorrow morning. Ever heard of Colonel Jack Giffers?" Myles asked Johnson.

"Matter of fact I have. He is the NSA Liaison Officer with the 9th Infantry. He's billeted in Tokyo someplace. Guess, the Commander wants us to score some points to help back her up on Beehive. You know they're giving her a hard time."

"Right. Well, we'll do our best with the Colonel. I thought I'd write out some notes and then review them with you, Davison, and Han. I think I should do the actual briefing. How about scheduling the conference room from nine to noon tomorrow morning?"

"I'll take care of that right away. What's a good time to review your notes? I'll let the other two know."

"Give me a little time. How about three this afternoon. I'll probably work through lunch today. How's the workload the last few days?"

"Heavy, you know we're getting about double the traffic than a month or two ago. I think your recommendations got some results."

"Good. I'm going to sequester myself in the conference room for a few hours with my notes. I'll do better without any interruptions."

Myles gathered up his papers and headed for the conference room, stopping by Brent's desk on the way.

"Roy, mind if I use your conference room for a few hours. I'm having a Colonel Giffers here in the morning from the 9th Infantry for a briefing. How about letting Hickson and Barney know about it. Sorry, this will be NSA business only this time."

"Go right ahead. Good luck with the briefing. I'll let the troops know about it," Brent replied.

By two o'clock, Myles finished assembling his notes and the result was a pretty good summary of his group's recent findings.

"Johnson, how about taking a look at this and add anything I've missed. Our objective is to make us look good for the sake of Beehive. Please review it with Han and Davison and then you and Han put it in presentation form. You might need to stay over to make charts and overlays if that's all right."

"No problem. I'm sure you've got everything covered really well. We'll just make it look pretty."

BRIEFING FOR COLONEL JACK GIFFERS
NSA LIAISON, 9TH INFANTRY

Wednesday, January 30, 1957; Shiroi AB, Japan

Intelligence Gleaned from Army Security Agency, Air Force Security Service, and Naval Security Group Intercepts. Analyzed and gisted by NSA B26A "Beehive", Fourth Qtr 1956. All intel xmitted Top Secret Beehive, Operational Immediate and Emergency over "Criticom" within forty eight hours.

Ho Chi Minh Trail

PAVN (Peoples Army of North Vietnam) established 559th Transportation Group late Fourth Quarter to manage shipments of personnel, arms, supplies, and equipment to South Vietnam and Mekong Delta. HQ in Hanoi with Colonel Vo Bam in charge. Strength divided between 70th and 71st Battalions, totaling neary 4000 personnel.

There is main transportation hub at Tchepone on Laotian Route 9. Main base areas along the trail are BA604, BA607, BA609, BA611, BA612, and BA619. These double as sanctuaries for PAVN and Vietcong troops. Hubs contain supply bunkers, barracks, hospitals, and munitions depots. All are cleverly concealed from the air.

Transportation hubs along the trail in the northern part of the delta are Loc Ninh, Tay Ninh and Vin Loh.

VC Radio transmitters in the delta are Can Tho, Moc Hoa, Cho Mai, Vinh Long, Cai Ly and Tra Vinh. We have call signs and day/night frequencies on all.

Vietcong 23rd River Brigade Mekong Delta, Kwang Tro

Twenty six gunboats, Khan Toa Class, thirty officers, eighty enlisted. Twelve torpedo boats, thirty officers, seventy enlisted. Concealed along waterways and tributaries emanating from Mekong in and around Long Xuen.

PAVN (Peoples Army of North Vietnam)

Infantry 80,000, Navy 20,000, Air 10,000, Special Ops 2500. Estimate 20% growth next six. Air compliment 19 J-5 (Mig 15). Weapons four 50 cal Machine Guns. 50% downtime for parts. Poorly trained NV pilots. Possible expect Mig 17 in less than year. Two Chicom Mig 17 squadrons now Hainan Island.

Vietminh Cadre, Mei Long Tran, Cambodia Thrust

Three hundred special forces embedded in various VC units scattered in delta region. Direct radio contact Hanoi trunk via repeaters in Highlands. Full list of officers available. Trunk and laterals continuously monitored by ARVN and Allied detachments.

Saigon Anti-Government Rebels

Two hundred civilian rebels led by Major Nhuen Lo embedded in secret locations within six hundred yards of capital. All communications UHF hand held phones continuously monitored by ARVN.

VC, Vietminh, and PAVN Personnel

List of three hundred field grade officers by name, unit, and specialty accumulated from plain language maintenance and personnel messages. List available in MACV, NSA Liaison, Grand Hotel, Saigon.

VC SIGINT Activity

Six VC remote VHF intercept sites identified in Mekong Delta and Saigon circle. Besides SIGINT (Signils Intelligence), two sites have transmitters sometimes used for decoy and deception on Allied frequencies. All units monitored twenty four hours. D and D stations JQ955X and JK454Y.

New NSA Thrust

Beehive intercept and analysis capability to be increased significantly next thirty days by deployment of Operation "Blue Cover" intercept van in vicinity of "Hook" region near Cambodian border. Unit commanded by Myles Garrison with fifty personnel. Capabilities include intercept, translation, direction finding, field analysis, message center with full encryption capability and connect to Criticom Net.

Johnson gave copies of Myles' information to Han and Davison. They liked what they saw and all agreed to work late into the night if necessary making charts and overlays. Johnson figured Commander Banta will be very pleased with this. The Colonel will publish and circulate within the Ninth Infantry and Seventh Air Force.

After passing his notes along to Johnson, Myles jotted down a draft message to Commander Banta regarding Peabody and his encounters with the CIA. He included his favorable conversation with Major Hickson regarding the top secret papers from Saigon. He also confirmed his diligence regarding possible espionage in 21st Radio.

He stayed over work long enough to send the Flash message.

Wednesday, January 30, 1957

In the morning Johnson greeted Myles coming into the office.

"Come on into the conference room boss."

He lead Myles to the conference room.

The podium was set up just to the right of set of elegant charts. On another easel there was a map of Vietnam with key featured identified and overlaid with six clear chart size plastic films. Each overlay featured a set of key locations coded with information from Myles' presentation.

"Johnson this is wonderful. Please thank Han and Davison. I know you all worked late last night on this."

"Yes, sir. Two AM to be exact. But you are most welcome. What time will the Colonel be here?"

"I haven't heard. I'll start looking for him a little before nine. I want you, Han, and Davison to be in attendance and participate wherever and whenever you feel you can contribute. OK?"

"Sure will. Thanks. We'll all be here," Johnson replied.

Colonel Giffers arrived at five till nine and after all the introductions Myles began his presentation.

The presentation and follow up questions lasted until nearly one o'clock. It was a huge success. Myles could tell the Colonel was very impressed. As he thanked everybody and was leaving, he said he would pass along a super well done to Commander Banta and B26A. He was very impressed with Beehive and especially the scheduled installation of an NSA van near the Hook. He was very familiar with that location.

Later in the day, Myles sent a message to Commander Banta reviewing the presentation he made to the Colonel Giffers along with the Colonel's comments.

Myles invited the team once again to celebrate over Heinekens at the bowling alley. This time he included a round of fried bologna sandwiches. Moral was high.

Thursday, January 31, 1957

Thursday morning Myles intended to brief Johnson, Han, and Davison and provide an update of some of Commander Banta's activities.

"Johnson, where is Davison this morning? Anybody seen him?" Myles asked.

"Han and I were just wondering. It's almost nine and he's usually not late, at least without calling in. How about having Brent call over at the BOQ and ask the Officer of the Day?" Johnson suggested.

"Good idea."

Myles walked over to Brent's desk and asked for his help.

About an hour later, Brent came back to the Beehive corner.

"Well, seems we have a mystery on our hands. Davison never slept in his bed last night and nobody has seen him this morning. I'm going over to the Provost's office and make out a missing person check."

"Good idea. I'm really concerned. We broke up about nine last night at the Bowling Alley, he might have been a little high but he was certainly in control of his senses and he was in an especially good mood."

"I'll tell them that," Brent said.

Myles, Johnson, and Han put their heads together but came up with nothing, except for one thing that Han said that was a little worrisome.

"Myles, you know lately he's been acting a little strange. Maybe since last Thursday. He's been asking a lot of questions that were a little puzzling, like exactly where were the other four Cover detachments going to be located, including the exact coordinates. That seemed a little unusual. Don't you think?"

Johnson added, "You know, I've had some strange feelings too. You don't suppose he's up to anything bad, do you?" Johnson asked.

"I don't think so," Myles said. "I've known him for over six months and except for being a loner I just wouldn't expect anything like that."

Friday, February 01, 1957

By Friday morning there was still no word on Davison. Around ten, Myles started getting his mind set on his trip to Ikebukuro that night. This was going to be his last weekend and it suddenly struck him that he didn't have a going away present for her.

"Johnson, how about looking out for things for a while? I've got to go the Base Exchange and the Snack Bar."

"OK. Go right on ahead."

First stop was the Snack Bar to use Mark's telephone to call Peggy. With the week being so busy, he'd completely forgotten to check in.

"Peggy, this is Myles. How've you been?"

"Well, I've been fine, but I've really missed seeing you this week. How's Yoshiko and the baby?"

"Everybody's fine, really fine. I'm so sorry for not calling this week. It's been real busy."

"I know, the Major has kept me up to date on things. Sounds like you had a great meeting with Colonel Giffers. Congratulations. And, I've heard about Davison gone missing. Any word on that?"

"Thanks. No word on Davison yet. I need to go the BX and get Yoshiko a going away present. This will be our last weekend before I go to Arlington late next week. Can I have lunch with you Monday or Tuesday and I'll fill you in on everything?"

"That'll be good. Let's meet at the Snack Bar at noon on Tuesday. That be OK?"

"That'll be great, I'll see you then. Got to go for now."

"See you Tuesday," Peggy replied.

Myles headed over to the BX. After a lot of consternation he settled on a beautiful gold bracelet. He had it engraved with Sunday's date and the words, "I love you always, Myles."

He had it gift wrapped and he was pleased with his purchase.

He made one more stop at the Credit Union to get some cash for the weekend.

It was nearly three by the time he got back to the office. Brent was watching the door waiting for him.

"Myles, how about stopping over here for a minute."

"Sure. Let me check in with Johnson first. I'll be right back."

Myles scooted a chair up beside Brent's desk.

"What's up?"

"Well, not much, really. We do know some more about Davison though. No answers, just more questions. Seems like one or more persons met Davison when he returned to his room Wednesday night. The Officer of the Day said they identified themselves as Army investigators. That's all they said and they wouldn't show any ID."

"That's strange. Why didn't the OD turn them in?"

"That's a good question. I intend to find out. Maybe he knew something in advance. Anyway, within a half hour they had packed up all of his clothes and other stuff and put him and his things in a van. All we know now is the van left the base. As of now, three o'clock, Friday afternoon, that's all we know."

"What in the hell?" Myles exclaimed.

"There's more. Major Hickson got a message today from Commander Banta. She said that an NSA investigation found problems with Davison and she had him pulled off his job with Beehive. She apologized to the Major for messing with his officers, but she said there was no alternative."

"Well, any ideas what we do now?"

"There might be something in here."

Brent handed an envelope to Myles.

"This just came in from the message center. Might be something about Davison."

"Thanks. Let me take it back to my desk and read it with Johnson and Han."

Back in the Beehive corner, Myles had Johnson and Han pull their chairs around his desk. He opened the envelope and read it quietly. Johnson and Han waited.

"OK, now we do know something about Davison. Commander Banta says that when NSA takes in new people they do a thorough background check in addition to any they've had in the past."

Looking at Johnson, Myles said, "She says you and I passed ours in flying colors before she appointed us to her group as NSA civilians. In the last couple of weeks, Davison and Han were investigated too."

Looking at Han, "Sergeant DeMeur, you did just fine, but she says Davison didn't pass muster. She doesn't say why, but he will be in Arlington shortly for debriefing and then discharge from the Air Force. That is, if there is no security problem or criminal activity. In that case, there could be a Court Martial and it would be real nasty."

"Damn," said Johnson. "I had no idea. I really liked the guy."

"Me too," added Han.

"I did too. We had some issues early on but I've come to really like the guy. Now we will need to double up on the work. Johnson and Han, will you please pick up Davison's work and try to share as best you can?"

"You can count on us boss," Johnson said.

"That's for sure Myles. Don't worry about a thing. I was pretty much up on Davison's work anyway. Especially his project on direction finding VC radio transmitters."

"I leave for Tokyo around five or maybe later today. I've got some important stuff to finish before I leave."

He managed to get away from the office around five-thirty. After a brief stop at the BOQ to get his things, he was out the gate at six-fifteen. He looked at his watch and estimated Ikebukuro station around seven forty-five. That would be a little later than usual, but he was sure Yoshiko would understand. He did regret getting in late on their last weekend together.

250 women and children massacred by Vietcong in South Vietnam Mekong Delta; Norma Jean Mortinson changes her name to Marylyn Monroe; Felix Wankel tests first prototype of rotary engine; World population is 2.833 billion; The Neutrino is first observed at Los Alamos Laboratory, New Mexico; Woodie Guthrie sings "This Land is Your Land"; "Tammy" by Debbie Reynolds, and "Teddy Bear" by Elvis Presley top charts.

Chapter Fifteen

Sayonara

Friday Evening, February 01, 1957

His estimate turned out pretty close. It was almost eight o'clock when he turned the corner and headed up the road to the apartment. He could see the light was on which meant she must be home for the night.

Inside, O-Basan's place was dark and all around the building it was dead quiet. He made as little noise as possible coming down the hall so as not to startle Yoshiko when he rapped on the door.

"Come on in Mai. I guess you work late. Everything OK? I so glad see you."

"Yes, I'm sorry. Some things came up late this afternoon and I couldn't get away on time. I'm fine. How are you?"

"I good too and baby fine too. I little tired from working this week. Have you eaten yet?"

"Well, no, but I'm really not hungry. How about you?"

"Me same. I had small food earlier Maybe we stay inside tonight?"

"That's a really good idea. You remember this is our last weekend before I go to Washington next week?"

"Yes .... but .... you come back in month, right?"

"I will .... for sure. What are you wearing under the futon?"

"Mai, I have my flower robe. You should put your bag down and take off your clothes. Your robe is over the chair, over there."

She gestured toward the straight chair.

Myles proceeded to slip off his clothes, eager to get into his robe and crawl under the warm futon. But first, he clicked on the Crosley and found some soft music.

"How do you like that, Yoshiko?"

"That very fine. Now you come into this bed please."

The table lamp was still on and he noticed her diamond ring glisten once or twice shooting out beams of reds, blues, and all the other colors of the spectrum.

Finally they both cuddled up under the futon. Yoshiko laid half way over his body with her leg and arm stretched over him and her head on his chest. This is the way it's supposed to be, he thought, your beautiful girl in your arms under a futon listening to soft music and the room aglow with golden light from the table lamp. Before long they both fell fast asleep. Around midnight Yoshiko got up to drink water from the tea kettle and turn off the radio and the lamp. She slowly slid the door open, thinking Myles was asleep, and quietly shuffled down the dim hallway to the end of the hall. She came back to the room as quietly as she left it.

"Yoshiko, I'm not asleep. I had some water too. I'll be right back," he said as he rolled out from under the futon and made his trip down the hall.

That night was the best sleep for both of them in a long time.

Saturday, February 02, 1957

They woke up around eight the next morning and Yoshiko fixed coffee. She apologized for not having any sweets but Myles reassured her that her excellent coffee didn't require any.

They talked for a while as they lay back in the bed sipping coffee.

"Yoshiko, what do you want to do this last weekend?"

She was ready for his question.

"Mai, I think today we go to Tokyo and visit all our old places to make some memories. What you think?"

"That's a really great idea. We should definitely include the Victoria, Uncle Masuda's shop, Sushi Oki, the Opal, the Seibu Department Store, the Albion, and the Shimbashi town square."

"Good plan. We should leave early so we eat early lunch in Tokyo. We have lot to do."

"I agree, and then tomorrow we do the same plan here in Ikebukuro. How about that?"

"Oh, Mai, you so smart. Now we have plan. We take Mr. Nikon with us too."

With the Saturday plan all set, they didn't waste any time getting themselves ready. They wore their favorite clothes. There was no snow but the cold reminded them that it was February.

Yoshiko finished dressing by pinning **Ladybug** to her coat lapel. Much to her displeasure, she yielded to Miles' insistence that she wear her penny loafers.

By ten-thirty they were in a taxi headed for the Ginza. They already agreed the first stop should be the Victoria Tea Room for lunch.

It was perfect. After a short wait they were seated in Yoshiko's favorite booth.

"We sit together here, Mai," Yoshiko said, as she slid to the side and made room for Myles.

Myles sat beside her. It was close quarters, but neither of them minded that at all. They both were so grateful to be together this last weekend. Myles took her left hand and kissed her fingers and her diamond ring.

"I want you be safe in America, Mai, and please come back to me."

They didn't talk much after that. After some hot sake and a quiet lunch, they decided to move on to the next destination.

"Now, Yoshiko, are you able to walk down the street to Shimbashi like we did a few weeks ago? Do you remember the snow that day and getting your new shoes?"

"Yes, it was perfect day. Thank you for my shoes. I wear them when you are gone, even these penny loafers."

They walked the short distance to the Shimbashi entertainment district next to Shimbashi Station. It was cold and they held hands during the entire time.

As they entered the central area, Yoshiko suddenly froze in her tracks. She shuddered and started to collapse. Luckily Myles was able to catch her and hold her up. She gradually seemed to regain her composure.

"Yoshiko, are you all right? What happened?"

"Mai, please take me somewhere away from here. The train, it scare me."

"Sure, let's walk back. Are you able to walk now? Do you think it is something to do with baby-san?"

"Yes, I walk back to Ginza. No, baby-san good. It that train. I don't know. I no understand. I so sorry."

Myles remembered the last time when she went into a trance at the sight of the antique locomotive. He could still see her silently standing alongside the engine touching the cold metal. He remembered she seemed totally unaware of her surroundings. Luckily, he'd managed to remove her from the scene and get her back over to the Ginza area. Now, today, he was doing the same thing. He had no idea what was going on.

"Yoshiko, we will walk down to Uncle Masuda's camera shop and get some rest. OK"

"Yes, we go there now. I feel better."

In the store, Masuda was overwhelmed by their surprise visit. The three of them bowed, shook hands, and hugged all around.

"Masuda-san, may we rest up a little bit in your back room? Yoshiko is fine, but she felt a little dizzy when we were over in Shimbashi. I think she is just a little tired."

Masuda ushered them to his lounge area in the rear of the store and helped Yoshiko lie down on a sofa.

"Thank you Uncle Masuda-san. I rest a little and then we go. We want to visit old places today since Mai will be gone for one month."

"Great idea, you just rest a little. Myles, are you all right?"

"I'm fine thanks. I'm just trying to give us a nice time before I leave tomorrow night. Looks like I might leave for the States on Tuesday or maybe Wednesday."

"Good. Remember we will write a lot of letters and we'll be looking forward to your return. I see Yoshiko is wearing her diamond ring. I'm glad you gave it to her. You didn't tell her it was from me did you?" Masuda asked.

"No, I didn't, I still thank you very much for that wonderful gift. Tomorrow, I will give her a gold bracelet as my going away present."

"I'm so glad you're doing that. Don't say anything, but she has something for you too. I helped her decide on something."

"Oh, no, you've done too much already."

"Stop, stop now. It's all proper and good. Anyway, it is all decided and done."

After twenty minutes or so, Yoshiko got herself off the sofa and declared herself all well and good. The two men checked her out and gave her a clean bill of health. Very shortly, they said goodbye and started walking down the Ginza to resume their odyssey.

That afternoon they stopped at all the places they had planned to visit. When they got to the Seibu Department Store, they toured the different departments but they were not able to see Kazuko. She had the day off.

After the day on the Ginza, there was just one more stop. They took a taxi to the Officers Club for one last drink and a little supper.

As usual, the doorman was extremely polite and attentive to Yoshiko. She thanked him over and over again.

Inside, they asked to be seated in the main dining room. Naturally, the attendants made a lot to do over them and took special care to escort Yoshiko and help her with her chair.

They had hot sake and a nice supper of poached salmon with risotto and snow peas. It was perfect for Yoshiko, although she would have preferred her salmon a little less poached. As they were sipping green tea, they checked Mr. Nikon and saw that they had taken thirty-two pictures today from up and down the Ginza and all their favorite places.

"Yoshiko, when you get these pictures please mail some to me in Arlington. I will be watching for them. Can you do that?"

"Oh yes, I will write you many letters and send pictures all the time. You should do the same please?"

"Absolutely, I will starting with the first day. How do you feel now? Are you ready to take a taxi back to Ikebukuro?"

"Yes, thank you very much for beautiful day. I think we go now."

In the taxi, they cuddled up in their standard taxi embrace to stay warm. The ride seemed a little shorter today, no doubt because they were totally enthralled with each other. They were back at the apartment by six o'clock. O-basan's door was open and her apartment lights were on as if she was waiting for them to return.

"O-basan, are you there?" Yoshiko called out.

O-basan came running to the door.

"Mai, you go upstairs now please. I explain to O-basan."

Following orders, Myles shuffled upstairs and then down the hall to the apartment. Meanwhile, Yoshiko sat cross legged with O-basan on her floor and explained how this was their last weekend for about a month. She told her how they had visited all the old places on the Ginza today and how they would stay close to home tomorrow.

O-basan did not take it well. She didn't cry but moaned repeatedly as Yoshiko unfolded her story. In the end, she regained her composure and assured Yoshiko that she would be there all the while that Myles was gone.

Yoshiko hurried upstairs. She heard music playing as she came up to the open door. Myles had already turned the heater on and had their robes laid out on top of the futon.

"Mai, I think we get in the bed and look at pictures from beginning last November. OK?"

"Great idea. We'll have music and look at pictures. Please get undressed now."

Myles lay back on the bed and watched her undress. He'd never seen her remove *Ladybug* so carefully before. She was being very careful to put it in a safe place in the little kitchen behind the curtain. He got up and helped her slip out of her dress and then unhooked her bra. He was making good memories of this, their last weekend.

They spent the next hour or so listening to music and looking at pictures. Finally, around nine o'clock they switched off the Crosley and turned off the lamp. They slept tightly clamped together under the futon.

Sunday, February 03, 1957

There was no alarm, but they both started waking up around eight o'clock. Yoshiko wasted no time getting the coffee made and spreading out some pastries for breakfast.

It was a totally lazy Sunday morning. Myles wondered if some day they would have lazy Sunday mornings like this in the States, having coffee, reading the paper, and maybe even kids running around. The thought pleased him and temporarily eased the sadness he was beginning to feel about leaving.

"Mai, look at my beautiful ring."

It occurred to him that this might be a good time to give her the present he'd brought. That way, he could see her enjoy it a whole day before he left.

"Yoshiko, please get a package out of my jacket pocket, over there in the closet."

She leaped from the bed sensing there might be a present in the offing. She dug deep in his pocket and extracted a small beautifully wrapped box.

"Mai, what this?"

She handed him the package.

"No, you open it please."

There was no hesitation. She tore off the ribbon and the rest of the wrappings and threw them on the floor. She held the box in front of her for a moment and then opened the lid.

"Oh, Mai, this beautiful. Why you do this?"

"Because you are my future wife with a beautiful baby, that's why, and also I am going away for a while. Here let me put it on."

He undid the clasp and placed the gold band around her left wrist. It was a perfect fit. Before he fastened the clasp, her showed her the back of one of the gold links.

It said, "I love you always, Myles."

She clasped the gold bracelet tightly in her fist and threw her arms around him. Then she pulled back and kissed him so hard and long that he gasped for breath.

Myles finally got untangled and managed to attach the bracelet.

"Now, Mai, please bring me little package from behind kitchen curtain. Be careful, it break."

Now it was Myles' turn to be excited. He retrieved the package from the kitchenette and held it in front of him, imitating her.

"Should I open?"

"Yes, please."

Inside the box was a gold wrist watch. Not just an ordinary watch, a special watch. It had a different face than anything he'd ever seen.

"Yoshiko, thank you very much," he said, as he examined the gold timepiece.

"Please Mai, look at back."

He turned it over and saw that it was beautifully engraved.

It said, "Mai, I love you always, Yoshiko."

"Yoshiko, this is wonderful. I thank you so much. I will wear it all the time I am away and be reminded of you."

Then he took her up in his arms and repeated her act of gratitude.

"Here, Mai, see this," she said, handing him the papers.

It was an electric Accutron watch. It worked on a tuning fork, and the front face was transparent to make the tuning fork visible. He had never heard of an electric watch, much less a tuning fork watch.

"Yoshiko, I think you spent all your money on this. You shouldn't ..."

"No, Mai, I spend only little. Uncle Masuda-san pay for most. It his gift too. He say this is from first shipment of this special watch to Japan. It very new, and he will start selling in his store. I want you have it and read message when you miss me."

"Well, thank you very, very much."

Myles couldn't help noticing how far she had come with her English. She was able to explain all this so well.

"Yoshiko, your message to me is the same as mine to you. That means our minds are the same and we love each other very much."

It was ironic, he thought, and maybe even a little prophetic.

So, she was now wearing her new bracelet and he, his new Accutron watch. It was a good start to a very important day.

"So now we get dressed and take a walk to Mitsukoshi. We wear our new jewelry. OK?" she said.

"Good plan."

Around eleven they started getting ready for their trip to Mitsukoshi.

Myles picked out Yoshiko's pink suit for the day. That was what she was wearing when they first met at Victoria's last November. He approved of the same high heels too, although they might do a lot of walking on this, their last day.

It was a wonderful day, full of memories and reliving a lot of good times. They had lunch at the noodle shop, a walk in Naka Park, a long time browsing at Mitsukoshi, and generally walking the length and breadth of Ikebukuro.

By four o'clock they were exhausted and decided to return home. By that time Mr. Nikon was loaded with a lot of new pictures. Myles was glad for the pictures. He would be looking forward to getting them in Yoshiko's mail.

After a short walk back to the apartment, they said hello to O-Basan and then went straight upstairs.

"Yoshiko, I will be leaving around seven. But promise me no crying please. If you won't cry then I won't cry. After all, this is just going to be a temporary separation."

"OK. No crying from me, Mai."

There was no plan for their last couple of hours so Myles suggested they lie back on the bed and talk about the future. They talked intimately as lovers do and covered everything from how they first met, the Christmas Party, and all the other wonderful things they had done. They talked a lot about the baby, and how Uncle Masuda was going to be such a great help. Yoshiko repeated the plan in which Myles was going to going to school at Sophia and then sharing in Uncle Masuda's camera shop business.

After a while, Myles rolled over and put his head on her belly.

"I think I hear a heartbeat. Don't breath," he said.

He did hear something, either the baby's heartbeat or maybe her pulse.

"Yes, I do hear our baby's heart beating. It's a good strong heart, and I agree it must be a boy."

She pulled him up and held his head against her breasts. They stayed that way, totally absorbed in the beauty and wonder of the moment.

Around seven, Myles said he must be getting ready to leave. Both of them grew silent as he packed his bag for the last time.

"Let me see your ring for the last time, Yoshiko-san."

She held out her hand and Myles put it against his cheek and held it there for a few minutes. She pulled it away and thrust her arms around his neck.

"Mai, I love you so much. Please come back to me."

"Yoshiko, I love you so much too. Please be careful with yourself and the baby so you will be here when I come back. OK?"

Myles placed his bag by the door. Then he went back to the bed and kissed her for last time. Then he propped her up against the pillows for his last sight of her. The golden glow from the lamp silhouetted her face and she was more beautiful than ever.

Myles stood at the door for a moment. Then he picked up his bag.

"Sayonara," he said, as he slid the door closed.

As he stepped back into the hallway he heard her softly call out, "Sayonara, Mai."

That last train ride back to Shiroi was very sad. He knew there was no real reason to feel that way. After all, he would be back in a month and all would be well. Just the same, it was tough. He would get over it though, he thought, once their plans start taking shape.

Monday, February 04, 1957

After a restless night, Myles got up early and had a six-thirty breakfast. He was in the office by seven thirty. He went through his late mail and notes from Friday. He remembered the revelation about Davison as he looked over at his empty desk. This all happened so fast, he hadn't even thought about how to carry on his work. For now, it would have to be Johnson and Han. Later this morning, he'd have to decide when to leave for Arlington.

Around eight, the office was filling up. Johnson and Han had arrived around ten to eight and brought Myles some coffee. He called a meeting at eight-thirty to make plans for the next few weeks. Meanwhile, he didn't do much other than sit back and think about the situation and what to do about it.

He was hoping for a message from Commander Banta with some perspective on the overall situation. One thing for certain though, the issue about espionage in 21st Radio was resolved. Davison must have been the only culprit. Major Hickson was now in the clear as far as he was concerned.

Just before eight-thirty, Brent came back to Myles' desk with a message from Commander Banta. It was addressed to Myles so it was unopened. Myles hurriedly opened the Top Secret Beehive envelope and retrieved a single page message. He quickly read it and folded it in half and tucked it into his pants pocket.

Johnson and Han pulled chairs up around Myles' desk. They each had a stack of documents and pads and pencils. Obviously they had prepared for this and were ready to go to work.

"Guys, before we start, I have something important to pass on. I want you to sit up and listen carefully. OK?"

They nodded and fidgeted a little in their chairs.

"Now, this is about Davison. I just found out there's a lot more to this than we suspected. As of today, he is in custody under armed guard somewhere in Washington. He wasn't just goofing off or anything like that. I don't know where to begin. First, he was having an affair with a girl at the Opal. You met her at the Christmas Party. Her name was Fumiko. I danced with her. Well, it seems Fumiko wasn't really a girl. She was a female impersonator or whatever you'd like to call it. Anyway Davison liked her …. uh …. him. If that's not bad enough, Fumiko was an agent for the North Vietnam Fuhn Dang. As you know, that's their version of our CIA. They will be interrogating Davison all this week. However, it looks like he might have been passing our secrets along to Fumiko. In that case, anything he passed on would go straight to Hanoi. Fumiko is in a prison in Tokyo and is in for a bad time with the Japanese and American governments."

"Holy cow, I'm speechless," said Johnson.

"Me too," said Han. "Is there any idea how much information he might have passed on?"

"We don't know much more than I just told you. I can tell you though that I'm worried about information on Blue Cover and the van operation. Even the timing and location of the van would be damaging. The Commander says she will stay in touch. Meanwhile, I am to leave for Arlington tomorrow."

"Man, we are in deep doo doo boss. What we gonna do?"

"First, I don't think we have time to talk just now. I've got to go pack my things and get my money and travel orders. I should get back here in a couple of hours. Meanwhile, you guys do your best at deciding how you're going to split up the work and keep things going."

"We will., count on us .... right Han?" Johnson said.

"We won't let you down Myles. If I might just say one thing more about Davison," Han added.

"Sure, but keep it short please," Myles replied.

"Well, this thing makes perfect sense to me now. I blame myself for not suspecting anything. From the very first day that I went to work with you guys, he was asking detailed questions about us and our operation. I mean these were not work questions. Myles have you considered the fact that he was taken away Wednesday night and so he heard your briefing for Colonel Giffers?"

"Yes, I have, but I can just hope they got him before he had a chance to pass it on to Fumiko. I think the only way he could have is if he called her and I don't think he did that. We went straight to the bowling alley that night. So we might have been spared on that. I'm just glad they got him Wednesday night and not a few days later."

"Myles, now that this has happened do you feel we will be in danger in Saigon? I'm so glad they changed our van location to Duay Bah Den. Did I pronounce that right? That is the new location for our van isn't it?" Han said.

"Yes, you said it right, and frankly I'm not a coward, but I must admit I feel a bit uneasy now. Anyway, I got to get going. Thanks for your thoughts Han. Don't feel bad about not spotting Davison earlier. That wasn't your job. I'll see you guys a little later."

They broke up and Myles hurried to the door. Before leaving he stopped at Brent's desk.

"Roy, I'm leaving tomorrow. Can you take care of letting everybody know? Please let's not have any goodbyes tonight. I just don't feel like it and anyway, I'll be plenty busy. I've got letters to write. I might be back in about a month for a short visit. I just don't know. Anyway, I want to thank you for your friendship these past few months. I don't know what I would have done without you."

"I'll take care of everything Myles. As for friendship, it's not over between us. We'll be friends for a long time. And, if I don't have time to talk later, you can count on me to check in with Uncle Masuda from time to time to see how Yoshiko is doing. Actually, if you ever need me to, I can go see him, or even go see Yoshiko."

"Roy, you've made me feel so much better. If all these people weren't around I'd give you a big hug."

"Hey, don't even say that. There is one last thing before you take off. I know the full story on Davison. Major Hickson shared a message with me that he got from the Tokyo FBI. I hope to hell he didn't do any damage to your program and your safety isn't affected."

"I don't think so. Anyway, I'll see you later. I got to go get all my travel stuff together. I leave early in the morning."

It was nearly one o'clock before Myles got his travel orders, tickets, and money. He made a stop at the Credit Union to close his account and withdraw his eight hundred dollar balance in US currency. On his way to the Credit Union, he stopped by the post office to leave his forwarding address. There was one letter from his Mom and Dad.

From there he headed to his room to start packing. He finished packing everything except for the things he'd need for that last night. He placed his open suitcase on the bed and sat down to open his mail.

He read the first few lines but couldn't quite believe what he was reading. His Mom said they had received a wooden crate from Japan last week. Inside, packed in straw, there was a Japanese tea set. There was a letter inside the tea pot but it was in Japanese and they couldn't read it. She and Dad had concluded it was a Christmas present. Mom said it was absolutely beautiful.

Myles chuckled. He remembered giving Yoshiko and Uncle Masuda his home address two weekends ago and now she's sent my Mom and Dad a tea set. He wondered why she hadn't written her letter in English though. .... maybe she was in a hurry.

He decided he would call them from Arlington and tell them who sent the tea set.

Just then something occurred to him. Peggy, what about Peggy, better go call her right now .... I can't leave without speaking with her. So he headed over to the snack bar for one last time.

Inside the snack bar, he spotted Mark just coming out of his office.

"Mark, I've got some news, not so good and not so bad .... I guess."

"Myles I don't like the sound of that. What's going on my friend?"

"Well, I've got to leave early in the morning for the States. I'll be there for maybe a month and then I'll be going to Vietnam. I hate to say goodbye like this but I just do what I'm told."

"Oh, man, I really hate to hear that. Have you told Peggy yet?"

"No, and that's why I want to borrow your phone. May I?"

"Of course, go on into my office. I'll give you all the time and privacy you want. Can I get you something to drink?"

"You know, actually, some coffee would be nice. Thanks."

"Go on in, I'll bring you some."

In the office, Myles scooted some piles of papers to the side and placed the phone directly in front of him. For some reason, he really hated to make this call. It was almost as bad as having to tell Yoshiko.

"Hello."

"Peggy, this is Myles. Is this a good time? Can you talk for a few minutes?"

"Sure. Haven't seen you for a few days. How's Yoshiko and the baby?"

"Everybody's fine. I had to say goodbye to them last night. It was tough, but she's taking it just fine. The train ride back to the base was hard."

"Myles, I'm so sorry."

"Now, Peggy, there's been a lot going on. You already know about Davison. I think I talked to you last week about that. Well, we found out today, he was in trouble with a girl in Tokyo and he's in jail in Washington as we speak. It looks like he might have been passing on secrets. He's really in big trouble. Commander Banta is afraid he might have compromised some important stuff about our new operation in Saigon. She is going ahead with everything though."

"I'm so sorry to hear that. The Major hasn't told me about that side of the story. I'll just keep quiet about it."

"Thanks. Now, I really hate to tell you this, but I'm rushing around today getting ready to leave at four in the morning. The Commander's called me to Arlington a little ahead of schedule. I had been hoping for using Tuesday for all my goodbyes and having lunch with you. Anyway, I'm sorry, but I can't see you before I leave."

"I'm so sorry too Myles. I don't like what's going on with any of this. Can I help in any way?"

"I don't think so. One thing though .... I think I can get back here for a week in a month or so. I think I can get a short leave in Tokyo on my way to Saigon. I've told Uncle Masuda and Yoshiko that, and I know they are looking forward to it. If that works out, I'll invite you to Tokyo. Think you can do that?"

"I'd love to. Just give me a heads up."

"Good. Now, in the meantime can I count on you to be here for me and check in on Yoshiko if I ask?"

"Myles, absolutely, whatever you need, I will do. I already have Masuda's phone number, and I think I could find my way to the Ikebukuro apartment if need be. How will you communicate with us back here?"

"Good. I think I can arrange something so that I can phone Brent directly from Arlington. So I guess Roy will be our go between. He's a good guy and he knows how to keep secrets. He knows my full story. I have your address and I'll send you a letter every week. I'll send you my mailing address first thing when I get to Suitland Hall."

"Wonderful, Myles, I think between Roy and me, you shouldn't have to worry. Maybe I'll start having lunch with Roy instead of you. That way we will both be in the loop. Gosh, Myles, I'll have to be careful with my husband. I'll just have to keep him totally in the dark. Don't worry, I can do this for you Myles."

"Thank you very much Peggy. I've got to be going now. You'll hear from me next week in a letter. By the way, when you go to the snack bar, please say hello to Mark. He's a great guy and awfully lonesome. I think he's got a crush on you."

"I know he does. I will speak to him when I can. Is this goodbye for now?"

"Yes, I guess this is sayonara. Thanks again, Peggy."

"Goodbye Myles, you take care of yourself and don't worry about anything back here. OK?"

"OK, bye."

It was another sad interlude, but he managed to shake off the sadness as he walked back to the compound.

"Boss, Han and I are ready to sit down and talk. Is this a good time."

"Yes, we've only got an hour or two. Let's have a go at it."

They pulled their chairs around Myles' desk. Some of the other men glanced over at the trio as they started to talk. By now, Brent had informed the whole staff, from Major Hickson on down, about the situation. All of the men had become dedicated close friends with Myles and his remaining two Beehive operatives and they were sorry to see him leave.

"Well, have you guys worked anything out?" Myles asked.

"Yes, Han and I are just going to split everything down the middle. We figure since we're both translators and analysts, we are kind of like four people. Of course, we'll have to put in the hours of four people, but after all, what else is there to do at Shiroi. You can only go to the bowling alley so many times."

"Very good, are you able to make the split or do I need to jump in."

"We don't think so. You taught us so well, we can manage," Han said.

Johnson spoke up. "Here's what we're going to do. I take the Mekong Delta and Han takes everything else. Anything to do with Diem and the Saigon situation we'll collaborate on. By the way, Diem assassinated twelve more people over the weekend. We picked that up a little while ago and I already sent a message to the Commander. This probably won't become public knowledge for a few days, if ever."

"Good. Thanks for your effort. Han, you got anything new?" Myles replied.

"Well, I've got two more Vietcong transmitters located. We really need to get more direction finding capability. We going to get DF equipment in our van?" she asked.

"Yes, plus a lot of other things. And you know our new location of top of Duay Bah Den is going to be terrific. It's way up high and we can triangulate our DF with at least two other stations. So you're going to get a lot of DF help," Myles reassured her.

Han handed Myles an intercepted phone call. "Great, one last thing .... just this morning Ho Chi Minh made a conference phone call to all of his units in the South. I think we're going to be able to identify his primary communication trunk lines before too long. It'll take just one more phone call like this. Johnson is helping me watch out for things."

"You guys are doing great. I won't worry about leaving the store with you. One last thing, I'll be staying in touch with you, using Beehive messages. I'll address everything to Johnson, but anything I send will be for the both of you. You can communicate with me the same way. I'll be expecting a lot of messages in Arlington."

"Sounds good. Myles do you know when you and I will meet up in Saigon?" Johnson asked.

"Not yet. You know, things are a little confusing right now. I think I'll be in Arlington for about a month, or maybe less if the van schedule picks up. Just a rough guess but I expect you and I will be at the Grand Hotel in about six weeks."

"Myles, what about me? Will I stay here at Shiroi, or what?" Han looked puzzled.

"Now that is a totally open question. Do you want to go to Saigon with us?"

"You bet I do. I have a lot of bad memories, but I really think I can be a lot of help. Can you put in a good word for me?"

"Not only that Han, right now I can almost guarantee I can get you transferred along with Johnson. I just don't know what the Commander wants to do with the Vietnam workload still going on here. Maybe she'll turn Major Hickson and his people loose from Vietnam altogether and let them concentrate on China. If that is the case, she might build up the Saigon office to centralize all Vietnam field work. Let's wait and see. But, yes, I'm pretty sure I can get you moved to Saigon, Han."

Myles looked carefully at both of them for a reaction.

"Speaking of teams," Myles added. "Is there anything going on between you beyond work?"

They were both silent for a moment.

"Myles, Han and I are actually sort of dating, if you can call it that. We eat together in the mess hall, we go to movies, and we go to the bowling alley."

"I'm not surprised. All the more reason to move you both to Saigon as a unit. Now, this is as good time as ever. I'll say goodbye for now."

He shook both their hands and they both came back with a good bear hug. Myles turned and went up to Brent's desk.

"Roy, this is it. I'll be in touch."

"Take care pal. You going to see the Major and the Sergeant one last time?"

"Yes, I'm headed in there right now."

As usual, the Major's office door was closed. Myles gently knocked.

"Come in," the Major answered.

"Major, I'm saying goodbye for now. The Commander and I will stay in touch. Take care of Johnson and Han for me please. Also, please say goodbye to Peggy for me."

"Will do, you take care, son."

The two of them stood and shook hands.

Myles spent a few minutes with Sergeant Barney, thanking him for all his cooperation and being a good first sergeant. He asked him to say goodbye to Ruby.

Myles headed up the hall for the last time and said goodbye to the guards on duty. He walked slowly across the parade field in the direction of his BOQ.

He spent the rest of Monday, busying himself around his room and packing and repacking his clothes. He'd picked up his laundry and that officially ended the last of his commitments to Shiroi. He was nervous and was anxious to get to sleep and then get up at three o'clock in the morning.

Tuesday, February 05, 1957

It was a different driver this time but the drive to Tachikawa seemed the same as last time. After making his presence known at the operations counter, he had a light breakfast at the snack bar and then proceeded to his gate. For the last time, he showed his orders and passport and then boarded his flight.

The flight went pretty much the same as the last two. There were stopovers at Wake Island, Honolulu, and San Francisco. He arrived tired and time lagged at Andrews around six-thirty Wednesday night. He got his car and drove to Suitland in a mental fog, eager to get to his bed at Suitland Hall.

Thursday, February 07 1957

The situation at Suitland was second nature to him by now. He had breakfast in the dining hall and stopped by the mail room on his way back to his bedroom. Much to his surprise, there was a letter from Japan. He recognized Yoshiko's English printing immediately. Before opening the envelope he decided to save the Japanese stamps for his little brother Matt.

Further back in his mail box, there was a plain white envelope addressed to him by name only, no address and not even a return address. Out of curiosity he opened that one first. Then he'd take a little more time with Yoshiko's.

Back in his room he opened the plain envelope. It was a one page handwritten letter. He quickly scanned to the bottom of the page. It was signed Sheila Banta. He was a little stunned and sat down on his bed to see what she had to say.

She had obviously written in a great hurry. The handwriting was more of a scrawl than what you'd expect in a lady's handwriting. She said things were helter skelter right now in Arlington and she just wanted to welcome him to Suitland and hoped he'd had a good trip. She suggested he sleep in until mid-morning and then show up at Arlington around one o'clock.

Myles was flabbergasted to say the least. This was not like the Commander Banta he knew. Things must be really messed up, probably something to do with Davison. But then, there might be some problems with Beehive. Asking him to sleep in like that made no sense at all. She must be tied up in the morning with something or somebody really important. Oh well, he thought, I'll just fool around here for a while and then maybe cruise around DC and do a little sightseeing.

He then went to Yoshiko's letter. He opened it carefully so he could save the stamps. Her letter was three pages of carefully printed English with a little Japanese mixed in. From the date, she must have written it Monday morning and then sent it Air Mail First Class. That was really quick, he thought, here it is only Thursday morning.

It was all good news. She was scheduled to work at Seibu all this week, but she'd be off Friday. She was feeling fine and the baby was fine too. She hoped he'd had a good trip. She went over some of their recent memories, and said she loved him over and over again. She loved her bracelet and her ring. It was a good letter and he would start saving them.

Instead of taking off in the car, he decided to go over to the little gift shop in the dormitory and buy stationary and stamps. He thought his time would be better spent this morning writing his first letter to Yoshiko.

It was an easy letter to write. After assuring her that he was fine and had a good trip, he gave her some information on what he would be doing for the next few days. He thanked her for the tea set that she sent to his Mom and Dad and scolded her a little for doing that without letting him know. Anyway, they really appreciated it and they said it was beautiful. He didn't tell her that they thought it was his Christmas present. He finished the letter and mentioned that he was enjoying his new Accutron wrist watch. He said to tell Uncle Masuda hello.

He pasted two dollars worth of stamps on the envelope and marked it Air Mail. On the way out to the parking lot he dropped it in the mail chute near the front door.

After a light lunch at his favorite Hot Shoppe, he drove on to Arlington taking a few scenic short cuts along the way. He drove by 1600 Pennsylvania Avenue but decided not to stop unannounced. Mamie and Ike probably wouldn't appreciate it, he joked to himself.

Inside Arlington Hall, he headed straight down the left hallway to Commander Banta's office. Petty Officer Davidson remembered him from his last visit and asked about Sergeant Johnson.

"Thank you for remembering us. Is the Commander in?"

"She is sir, but barely. She just got back from the Director's office. Should I let her know you're here?"

"Yes please, and tell her I can come back later if she's tied up."

"Commander Banta, sir, Myles Garrison is here from Japan. He says if you're busy he can wait or come back or .... yes sir."

The Commander interrupted.

"Mr. Garrison, she'll be right out."

No sooner had she gotten the words out of her mouth, than Commander Banta came out of the door.

"Myles, please come in," she said in a rather somber note.

"Yes ma'am."

Myles followed her into the office.

"Take a seat Myles."

"Commander, really, I can come back later today or even tomorrow if you're busy. That would be no problem at all."

"Now, Myles, let me speak."

"Yes ma'am."

Myles sat uncomfortably in the padded leather chair straight ahead of her.

"Myles, this Davison thing is about to kill Beehive. I've been in Director Samford's office all morning and gotten my ass chewed out royally. If that wasn't enough, Secretary of the Air Force Quarles and his deputy came in during the ass reaming and jumped right in. Myles, there's a lot of crap coming down the line. I mean real crap."

"Commander I'm so sorry. Guess he must have done a lot of damage, huh?"

"That's putting it mildly. He been spilling his guts all week and he might have compromised our entire Operation Beehive. I mean including all the intricate details. Samford is holding me responsible for not having cleared Davison well enough to have prevented this. Of course, he already had an Air Force Top Secret Crypto clearance, you would've thought that was good enough right there. Even so, I had the Tokyo FBI people investigate him real good. Nothing showed up."

"You know, after we got the word last Friday, Johnson and Han said they had been suspecting something might be going on. They should have told me but, unfortunately, they didn't. Are Captain Brent and Major Hickson going to be in trouble?"

"I wish I could say no, Myles, but at this point I'd have to say possibly. They're looking for scapegoats."

"Well, how do we stand on Beehive, now that you've had your twenty lashes?"

"As of now, we are still in the go ahead mode. But, and this is a big but, we are being told to slow down even more. I'll know some more tomorrow after the Director speaks to the President and the Secretary of Defense. You can see how big this is. One thing I do know is Blue Cover, that's you Myles, will be the only one activated in the beginning. That means your part of the project might go ahead, but all alone for a while. Looks like we'll have to prove our worth. I hate to do this to you Myles but the entire future of Beehive will depend on how good a job you do with your van on Duay Bah Den and your operations in the Grand Hotel."

"Commander, I'm ready to go and do whatever I have to do."

"I knew I could count on you."

"What you want me to do Commander?"

"Today, take the rest of the day off. I've got an appointment with the Deputy Secretary of the Navy at three o'clock. That'll be another chewing out I'm sure. Tell you what, just come to my office at nine tomorrow morning. I'll put you to work then. I'm really sorry for all this."

"Commander, how much of this is known outside this office and the higher ups? Am I free to talk about this with my people? I know I certainly can't talk to anybody in the 21st."

"Just keep it all to yourself," the Commander answered.

"One last question Commander? If Davison told everything, does that include details on our van, when and where it will be placed, and how I'm to set up my office in the Grand Hotel?"

"Myles, at this point we just have to assume Hanoi knows all that. If we do go ahead, and we'll find out for sure tomorrow morning, it means we'll have to double and triple all our security procedures. You and your people will be packing firepower wherever you go. Do you need to get more training in firearms?"

"I think I do, and don't forget Johnson and Sergeant DeMeur. By the way, I'm counting on both of them joining me in Saigon when I set up shop."

"Good, I was hoping you'd taken care of that. We won't send them down until you've been there for about a week and have the van in place and housekeeping set up in the hotel."

"Ok, I think I got the whole picture Commander. I'm sure sorry about Davison and all this. It's a shame, everything was looking so good up until now. Guess I'll leave and then see you in the morning."

"Yeah. Keep your chin up, we'll come through this together in better shape that before. One thing for sure, I'm so glad I have you Myles. Anybody else, and I think I'd consider closing up shop and going home. See you in the morning."

Myles saluted, even though it was indoors. He wanted to show some respect for the Commander. He decided to drive straight back to Suitland and beat the Washington rush hour traffic. After that, he'd decide later how to spend his evening.

That night he wrote Yoshiko another letter just to reassure her that he was OK and that things were going fine. He told her he met briefly with Commander Banta but didn't have much time to speak privately with her about personal things. Once again, he thanked her for her letter and asked for some pictures next time.

He wrote to his Mom and Dad and told them about his trip over and assured them he was fine. After a lot of thought he told them the source of the tea set and the rest of the story. He tried not to go on and on about it. He just wanted to let them know about Yoshiko and their plans. There would be plenty of time to provide more details and, eventually, about the baby. For now though, it was enough for them just to know that he was going to marry a Japanese girl.

He finished his letter and decided to walk up front and drop his two letters in the mail chute. He took his lined Air Force raincoat and planned to take a short walk around the grounds. As he pulled the coat from the closet memories of Yoshiko and Ikebukuro flooded his mind. He had worn that coat so often when he was with her it was almost like her being there with him at Suitland.

Friday, February 08, 1957

Friday morning was cold, very cold. He remembered Washington is on the same latitude as Tokyo so their climates are very similar. He wondered if it was cold this morning in Tokyo. There was no rush after breakfast. Most of the other officers were well on their way to their eight o'clock office calls. Myles didn't need to show up in Arlington until nine.

Washington traffic wasn't bad, so he got to Commander Banta's office right on time.

"Go right in Mr. Garrison," Petty Officer Davidson said. "She's been looking for you."

"Myles, come on in. How'd you do yesterday?"

"Well, the question is Commander is how'd you do? You still able to sit down?"

"Yes, but barely. I think all the ass chewing is done for now. I'm expecting a call from General Samford anytime.

There were meetings last night and I can tell you for sure the President was involved."

"Man, oh man. I can't wait to hear."

Just then the phone rang. The two of them looked at each other and the Commander picked up the phone.

"Sir, I have the Director on the phone. Line one," the Petty Officer said.

"You sit still Myles. I think this must be it."

Myles nodded and sat quietly waiting to hear the news.

"Yes, sir, Commander Banta here."

"Commander, I need to bring you up to date. I think you already how serious this situation is. You got a few minutes?" Director Samford said.

"Of course, sir."

"OK. I was in discussions last night with Defense, State, the President, Naval Security Group, and Air Force Security Service. The Vietnam situation is heating up real fast. For your information, Defense plans to raise the number of advisors to over two thousand in the next couple of months. The VC is hitting ARVN units real hard and the casualty rates are skyrocketing. CIA is going to assassinate Diem very shortly. Ho Chi Minh is pumping troops and supplies down the Ho Chi Minh Trail into the Delta like never before. Our intel is totally inadequate and outdated. Our intel assets need to be upgraded and expanded as soon as possible."

"Yes sir, you know we want to help any way we can," the Commander said.

"We know that and we're expecting good results from your Project Beehive. I was not pleased when the Navy postponed Gold Cover and put the Maddox and Turner Joy on hold. I'm sure we'll get them back though and move ahead with Gold Cover. We desperately need intercept coverage along the coastline from China to the tip of South Vietnam. Now, we've retrenched again because of Davison. That's the buzz word around here," he paused.

"I hate that sir. The Lieutenant was one of my people at Shiroi and we trusted him. Now we're going to get that rubbed in for a long time," the Commander said.

"I'm sorry too. But let's get over it. First the bad news! We are putting all your detachments on hold for six months, except for Blue Cover. We want you to get that one up and operating as soon as you can. Your proposed location of Duay Bah Den is perfect. It's right on the Cambodian border not far from Saigon. Actually just a short chopper ride. Get your van set up and operating as soon as you can, and set up your liaison office at the Grand Hotel as soon as possible. If you need any more people or any more money just let me know."

"Yes sir, I have Myles Garrison here with me in my office. He is chief of Blue Cover and he'll be setting up the whole operation as soon as possible. May I pass along the information you just gave me, sir?"

"Of course, may I speak with him?"

"Yes, sir."

She handed the phone over to Myles.

"Sir, this is Myles Garrison."

"Myles, may I call you by your first name?"

"Of course General."

"Myles, I want you to get over to Saigon and set up your office and staff ASAP. Commander Banta will get the van set up on top of that hill as quick as humanly possible. Ask her for any help you need. We need you to do a good job with Blue Cover to recover the prestige we lost over

Davison. More than that though, we need intel on the Trail and on the Delta. I can tell you personally son, we are headed for war with North Vietnam. There is no uncertainty about it. It's not a matter of if, it's a matter of when. My guess is within the next couple of years. The Department of Defense is counting on the NSA to provide swift, accurate intel on the VC and the Vietminh. How about putting the Commander back on?"

"General," Commander Banta was back on the phone.

"Commander, are you going to Saigon to help set things up?"

"I wasn't planning on it sir. I was going to wait until everything is up and going. But if you want me to ......"

"No, I'll leave that up to you. I won't bother you now for a few days so you can get on with it."

"Thank you sir. Is there anything you want to tell me about Davison?"

"No."

"Fine, I'll be in touch. Thank you General," she said.

She hung up the phone and looked over at Myles.

"Well, Myles, you got it straight from the horse's mouth. One thing, we should be able to move things along a lot quicker since we only have to deal with one detachment. Maybe this is a good thing."

"I hope so Commander. What should I do next?"

"Well, there's an empty desk just outside. Make it your desk while you're here. Get whatever you need from the supply room. I'll have a stack of manuals and stuff placed on your desk right away. I hate to put you off, but you're on your own today. I suggest you read all the manuals and all the correspondence and directives. You know how to use the message center to send things to Shiroi. I'll be gone the rest of the day out at Ft. Meade. I want to check on our new quarters."

"OK, sure. I'll do my homework. Is there any way I can use the phone link to call Shiroi or even a phone in Tokyo?"

"You can but it's a bit of a hassle. You'll need to do that at the message center. All calls are monitored of course and it is a secure line. And, yes, you can call a Tokyo number. Why would you want to do that?"

"No particular reason. I think I'm all set. Tomorrow is Saturday. Do I need to be here?"

"Yes. You've still got some reading to catch up on. You can come in around nine. I'll be leaving soon, so I'll see you in the morning."

"Take care Commander."

Myles was still in shock after his reception yesterday and what happened a little while ago.

British Prime Minister Anthony Eden resigns and is replaced by Harold McMillan; France intercepts Morroccan terrorist plane piloted by Ben Bella; US Congress issues final figure of 38,000 killed in Korea and promises Vietnam will "never be another Korea"; Cincinnati Manager Birdie Tebbits named National League "Manager of the Year"; Al Lopez becomes new Chicago White Sox Manager; Delhi becomes territory of Indian Union; Pope Pious XII publishes "Datis Nupperime"; "Blondie" premiers on NBC-TV; "Young Love" by Tab Hunter tops charts; "Gunsmoke" and "The Danny Thomas Show" popular on TV; John David Crow wins "Heisman" for Texas A&M with 1183 points.

Chapter Sixteen

Suitland

Saturday, February 09, 1957

Myles stopped by the Suitland mail room on his way out the front door. To his surprise there were two letters from Japan. One from Yoshiko and one from Peggy. He immediately retreated to his room.

He opened Yoshiko's letter first since it had pictures. Four were from their last weekend in Tokyo. But the best one was one of her lying back in bed, propped up on her pillow. Apparently O-basan had snapped the picture.

He checked the date on the letter and she had apparently written it Wednesday night. She had all good news. It was a cheerful letter to make him feel good. And it did, except for one thing. She said Uncle Masuda had met her over at the Seibu for lunch that day to deliver some good news. He was going to buy her a little car to get around in Tokyo. Oh no, he thought, no, no, no. Don't do that Masuda. He remembered Masuda saying he was worried about her taking trains and taxis all around Tokyo to her jobs. But a car, oh how he hated to hear that. He knew how treacherous Tokyo traffic was and a car would be far more dangerous that trains and taxis.

She went on to say that he was giving her a full week of driver training as soon as the car was delivered. She assured Myles everything would be all right. She was actually looking forward to driving a car. Myles slammed the letter down on his bed. He didn't know what else to do.

After a few minutes he opened Peggy's letter. She really didn't have much to say, just that she missed him a lot and her trips to the snack bar would never be the same. She said that the Major was in a terrible mood. He wouldn't talk to her about what his problem might be, but she suspected it had to do with Davison. In fact she was certain of it since Captain Brent had come over the night before for a private meeting. She knew Myles couldn't write her but she asked that he give any messages he might have to Brent. She asked if she could do anything for Yoshiko.

Myles was grateful for both letters but at the same time he was frustrated at what he'd read and that he couldn't do anything about it. He left for the office in a bad mood.

He got to Arlington around nine-thirty, late by thirty minutes but he really didn't care. He double parked in the back parking lot and didn't care about that either. After all, it was an Air Force staff car. Who would question that? Inside, he went straight to his desk and opened a manual in front of him. After a few minutes he seemed to get control of himself. This wasn't like him and he didn't like the feeling.

He was glancing over one of the van manuals when Commander Banta approached his desk.

"Myles how are you doing this morning? Have a big night last night?"

"No, I wrote some letters and then went to bed early. How do things look out at Fort Meade?"

"I'm satisfied. We could've gotten a little more space. We are on the first floor though .... which I like. You know B26A is going to stay here at Arlington don't you?"

"Yes ma'am. Where will you have your office?"

"I'll have a desk in both places. Guess I'll do a lot of running back and forth. It's good though to have B26A isolated from the main building. I see you're reading manuals. That's good. Tell you what, come into my office around eleven and I'll start you off on your program here in Arlington."

"I'll browse through some more of these things and see you then."

"Great. Oh by the way, remind me to tell you about Bill Peabody."

One document was of special interest to Myles. It was a restatement of the capabilities of his van. It was the way he remembered it but it was a good refresher.

Eleven o'clock rolled around and Myles hurried into the Commander's office.

"Take a seat Myles, I've got a few things to cover."

Myles took his usual seat and sat at his usual attention.

"First of all, you heard plenty yesterday about how important your mission is going to be. Now, let me give you a few reasons why. Some of them you will not have heard before."

"Thanks Commander. If I may interrupt .... what about Bill Peabody? Is he still missing? Is he all right?"

"Sure. I completely forgot to tell you about him the last few days. It's been so hectic. Bill is fine. He is still in Tokyo at the New Imperial Hotel. He is the one who exposed Davison. He did a fine job."

"I'm glad to hear that. How did all that go down?" Myles asked.

"Well, It's a long story but I can shorten it. Bill has been on the search for many weeks. When we learned about the leak, we used a lot of cover and deception. Have you ever heard of The Sea of Reeds?"

"Yes, I've seen it referred to a few times but I couldn't find out anything about it."

"Well, SR was a plant. In cover and deception work we would call it a girgle. Anyway it was imbedded in real intel in a way that we could watch it's movements. So SR was totally fictitious. Anyway, that was the key. We traced it from Saigon, to 21st Radio, to the Opal, to Red, and then on to Hanoi. Davison was the pivot from 21st Radio to the Opal. From the Opal to Red .... well, that was Fumiko."

"Commander, that was a great piece of work. Were those two CIA guys I met at the Embassy part of the sting? And, Bill, he must have been in on the whole thing from start to finish."

"Yes, the CIA guys were the Saigon part of the equation. They were the ones who planted the girgle. Bill Peabody was the overseer of the investigation."

"What about Red? Who was that?"

"Red was a very dangerous North Vietnam agent in Tokyo. He would transfer the baton from the Opal to Hanoi. Right after your meeting at the Embassy, we learned that Red knew about Peabody. That's why we secretly moved him to another hotel and declared him missing. It was for his own safety."

"Is the project over now Commander? Is Major Hickson cleared?"

"Yes, it's over and finished and the Major is cleared. Now, let's talk about Beehive."

"Is now a good time for you Commander?"

"Yes, we need to continue. I'm going to be referring to my notes. After we finish I'll give you the notes so all you need to do is just listen. We are certain now that supply convoys coming down the Ho Chi Minh Trail have increased over fifty percent in the last three months. That's not good news for the ARVN. They've been getting hit real hard in the Saigon area and down in the Delta, mostly by the VC's but some attacks are still being launched by the remnants of the Vietminh. The 559th Transport Regiment of Ho's army are in charge of all shipments down the Trail, plus it's maintenance and defense. Just recently Ho has started sending troops and supplies to coastal regions. That's being managed by the 579th Maritime Infiltration Regiment. Admiral Tran Van Guang is heading up that unit. So, troops and supplies are getting into the Delta along two routes. I guess some of this is new information, Myles."

"Yes, I didn't know about the coastal operation."

"There's more. In the Delta, the VC's are hitting small villages. They're beheading the officials and shooting the male villagers. Diem is very unhappy to be sure, but he won't accept any advice from General Williams at MACV.

The CIA is keeping tabs on Diem and the situation can't go on like this.'

"Yes ma'am."

"ARVN took a really bad hit last month in the Tay Ninh Province. The VC killed 61 ARVN troops from the 32nd Regiment at Ben Tre. They destroyed all buildings and property and stole an enormous amount of weapons. The number of Vietcong radio transmitters has quadrupled in the Nam Ben region. Without adequate direction finding equipment it's almost impossible to locate these transmitters. Myles you will have two DF consoles in your van. That will be a huge new asset for us."

She continued.

"Our intel is woefully inadequate. We need 2400 hours of daily intercept and we're only getting about 450. Most of that is coming from the Air Force's 29th Radio Squadron, the Army's 9th Radio Field Station, and the Navy's USN-27. All three of these are located on Luzon in the Philippines. We're also starting to get some good hours from the detachment on Monkey Mountain near Da Nang in Vietnam. Just hang on Myles. There's more."

"Commander, is there any way we can get Beehive moved up?"

"We're working on it. Anyway, you can see how important your NSA van is going to be. I figure you can give us a hundred-ninety-two daily hours once you get going. That's nearly a fifty percent bump over what we get now, plus you'll be giving us good direction finding. You should know that once we locate the transmitters, we only knock out the ones that are of no value to us. If we're getting good intel from a station we keep it alive and transmitting. One other thing, we've started getting good intel from Ground Control Intercept stations. Normally, these would be used to direct aircraft to targets. Now the bad guys are using GCI stations to direct ground forces to targets. So, we are desperately trying to locate the GCI stations and take them out. Your people will have to learn how to use your new DF equipment as soon as possible."

"I'm sure I'll have question during my visit here. Thanks for your notes."

"Oh, one other thing, you're still going into the Grand Hotel but we might be putting some assets of another kind in the Caravelle Hotel. That's directly across from one of Diem's headquarters. I won't say anything more about that, but you might keep that in the back of your mind."

"I think I know what that's all about."

Myles knew what she was referring to.

"One more thing I forgot. The VC's just recently pulled off a horrific raid on the Michelin and Minh Thanh Rubber Plantations. They destroyed half of the processing facilities and burned most of trees. There were a lot of casualties but I don't have any numbers. Now, Myles, you have been sufficiently briefed for now. Any questions?"

"I don't think so, not right now anyway. Oh, was there anything else about Lieutenant Peabody? You asked me to remind you."

"Yes, once you arrive in Saigon, I am sending Bill Peabody down there to work in your office. I figure you should have at least one Navy Officer on your staff. You and Bill are friends I believe."

"Yeah, I like Bill. I'll be glad to have him. That means we'll start up with Navy Lieutenant Peabody, Army Sergeant DeMeur, and civilians Johnson and myself. Do I get any more staff later?"

"Not in the immediate future. Before you leave here for Saigon, I'll give you the files on the people who'll be stationed in your van. There will be an Army Captain as Officer in Charge. You'll have two analysts on each shifts so they'll carry out first echelon reporting. I think very shortly after you start up, I'll put four linguist analysts in your office for second echelon reporting. Keep in mind this will be a big deal for the NSA, I mean setting up a remote site right in the middle of the VC with all that capability."

"Commander, I can't wait to get started."

"Now, you do what you want the rest of today, I mean here in the office. You're off tomorrow. Then we'll hit it hard on Monday."

"Thanks Commander. I'll work on manuals for a while and then leave around five."

That'll be fine, Myles. I'll see you on Monday."

Saturday Evening

Back in his room, Myles read Yoshiko's letter once again. This time he was able to put two and two together. Well, he thought, maybe it'll all turn out for the better. If she became a good driver, it certainly would be easier for her to get around Tokyo.

He decided he would use his Sunday to write a lot of letters and call his Mom and Dad.

Sunday, February 10, 1957

He used his Sunday as planned. He stayed in his room most of the day writing letters to Yoshiko, Uncle Masuda, Brent, Johnson, Han, and his Mom and Dad. He took his time and wrote really good letters, each one at least three or four pages long.

He had a lot to write about .... the trip, the sights around Washington, his boss Commander Banta, his Air Force staff car, and his expected schedule for the next couple of weeks.

In his letter to Brent, he enclosed another smaller envelope with a brief note to Peggy.

He was very upbeat with Yoshiko. He said he was happy for her getting a car although he did say he was a little worried and that she should be very careful. He thanked her again for sending the tea set to his Mom and Dad and he asked her about her last doctor's appointment. He said to give his regards to O-basan and to thank her for all her help over the past four months. He closed by saying how proud he was of her for being so brave. He told her how much he was looking forward to getting back to Ikebukuro in about three weeks.

In his letter to Uncle Masuda, he actually thanked him for ordering the car for Yoshiko. He said he was glad he was sending her to driver training and asked him to oversee the whole situation. Masuda, himself, was not a driver but surely he would do all he could to make sure she was safe. He told him he was still expecting to get to Tokyo in a few weeks.

As he closed Uncle Masuda's letter, he reminded himself that very soon he would need to get Commander Banta's approval for a short leave in Tokyo on his way to Saigon.

The other letters were a little shorter and a little easier. He stayed on the light side except he did get a little mushy in Peggy's letter. He thanked her over and over again for all that she'd done, and he reassured her that so far Yoshiko was all right.

He finished his letters and put them in the mail. In a little while he thought he'd call his Mom and Dad.

He talked with them for nearly an hour. He went into great detail about Yoshiko, how they met, how they lived together, and how they were going to get married later in the year.

He was so proud of them, especially his Mom. She accepted his decision totally and wished she could meet Yoshiko and even come to the wedding. She said Dad was happy too, and Matt, well, Mom would cover everything with him later but she was sure he would accept Yoshiko. She said she was proud of her two boys.

"OK. I got to go. It was nice talking with you. I'll talk to you all at least one more time before I leave for Vietnam. "OK. Bye"

"Goodbye son," his Mom said.

Monday, February 11, 1957

Myles spent Monday reading more reports and manuals. He had lunch with the Commander in the Arlington cafeteria. They talked past lunch for almost an hour about families, travel, food, and the future for both of them after Vietnam.

Near the end of the day, Myles sent one of his encrypted messages to Brent giving him an update on Arlington so far. He figured it was safe now to use their private encryption system. He asked him to check on Johnson and Han, and to call Peggy. He suggested he have lunch with Peggy at the snack bar sometime. He didn't mention Yoshiko.

Tuesday, February 12,1957

Commander Banta called Myles in first thing Tuesday morning.

"Myles, here's something remarkable from your team back at Shiroi. Take it back to your desk and put it on top of your stack."

"Thanks Commander. I knew they were capable of great things. I'll take it with me. But before I go, I have something to ask you. You mentioned I might take a leave before I go to Saigon. I thank you for that but I'd like to do something different."

"What do you have in mind, Myles?"

"Here's what I'd like to do. When I finish here, instead of taking a leave in the States, I'd like to spend a week in Tokyo on my way to Saigon. Do you think you could manage that?"

"I'll have to think about that but on the surface I think it's possible. Don't you need to spend some time with your family back in Iowa?"

"Well, I'll be talking with them a lot on the phone while I'm here. I think this would be OK with them."

"Fine. Just one thing, are you planning on spending that time with Yoshiko?"

Myles almost fell out of his chair.

"Commander, would that be all right?"

"Myles, we know everything there is to know about Yoshiko and her Uncle Masuda-san who owns the Ginza Camera Shop. All that is cleared with us."

"Thank you for looking out for me, Commander."

"When Lieutenant Peabody and I were in Tokyo last November, we met with the FBI for final clearances. That's when we kicked off our investigations of you, Johnson, and

Davison. We spent a lot of time and money trying to find out bad things about Yoshiko, but she is perfectly clean. In fact she and her Uncle were exemplary. They passed all our requirements."

"Well, I guess I'm relieved. So you know everything, right?"

"I think so."

"Commander, since we're on the subject I have a very delicate question."

"What's that Myles?"

"Is there any way that I could marry Yoshiko and still keep my clearance and my job.?"

"Myles, I expected that question. We'll tackle that whenever you make a formal request. There are a lot forms to fill out. I can tell you that it has been done before, but not under my watch. In the end, it might all boil down to my decision."

"I'm so relieved. I won't bother you with this again until the time is right."

"You can go back to work now. I'll see you later. I've got a meeting with some higher ups over at Bolling Field and the Pentagon."

Myles went back to his desk and started reading the report from Johnson.

He could hardly believe what he was reading. Johnson and Han reported in a Top Secret Beehive Emergency Priority message that fifty Swatow patrol boats were being sent to North Vietnam from China. It went on to say that twenty of them were torpedo boats and they were going to be deployed to a North Vietnam Navy base on the Gulf Tonkin. Also ten Swatow gunboats were to be sent to the same base. The exact base and location had not yet been learned. Twenty Swatow gunboats were to be deployed to various Vietcong bases on rivers and estuaries in the Mekong Delta. The exact landing point on the South China Sea had not yet been learned.

Nice going guys, I knew you could do it, he thought. I really need to discuss this with the Commander. He went to her office but she was out for the day with her meetings at Bolling and the Pentagon.

Myles left for Suitland around five-thirty hoping to get behind rush hour traffic. His plan didn't work out and traffic was jammed up on Key Bridge for nearly an hour. He got back to Suitland late that night.

Wednesday, February 13, 1957

Around nine o'clock the next morning, Myles managed to get a seating with the Commander.

"Commander, can we talk about that Beehive report on the fifty Swatow patrol boats from China?"

"Sure. In fact we need to. What do you think about that? What does it mean and what should we do about it?"

Myles recognized her challenge and felt up to it.

"Well, first thing is we can thank our friend Mr. Davison for this. I thinks this stinks to high heaven I believe he leaked all our Beehive deployments to Fumiko and Red. I think when they saw we were planning to picket two destroyers along their Gulf of Tonkin coastline, they told China and in return they got twenty torpedo boats and ten gun boats for their bases along the coast. I really think Davison did this to us."

"Myles you've got that right. The timing fits perfectly."

Myles continued.

"Now, the twenty gunboats for the Vietcong in the Delta, I don't think that is necessarily a Davison result. Of course it could be. They probably know about our van going in there and assumed ARVN troops might go in to protect it and expand their operations in the Delta."

"I think that is the case," the Commander replied.

"Furthermore, I think we should immediately get identification of the transmitters where USN-27 got their intercepts. Then we should inform ARVN through proper channels not to destroy these stations. I believe they might be a good source of intel."

"You're right. I do think it's unfortunate that Davison has created all that damage. Isn't it prophetic that Gold Cover got delayed and we aren't sending the Maddox and Turner Joy into harm's way?"

"Yes it is. I guess somehow Davison missed that point."

"Anyway, we aren't changing any other plans. We'll just have to operate like normal and keep in mind that what we're doing is known in advance. Be real careful, Myles."

"Yes ma'am. We will and I'll make sure we got plenty of weapons and protection from the ARVN. Anything else Commander?"

"Well, I'm going to let you go to Tokyo for a week on your way to Saigon. When that will be I'm not sure. One thing though, you won't be here for a full four weeks as planned. I personally feel you need to get to Saigon as soon as possible, even well in advance of your van. I'll make sure your office suite at the Grand will be ready when you arrive there. Let's see, today is Wednesday. I think by Friday I'll know when to release you for your Tokyo visit. Meanwhile, anything you want to do here? Want to go visit

Ft. Meade? Want to get a tour of the Pentagon? Want to meet with the Secretary of the Air Force? Anything, just let me know."

"OK. For now I've still got a lot of homework and I need to send some messages to Shiroi."

"Sure. Just let me know. I do think a Fort Meade visit would be good. Tell you what, I'll have somebody drive you out there in the morning. There's still construction going on but you can get a good tour."

"Great, I look forward to it."

Thursday, February 14, 1957

Myles spent most of the day at Fort Meade. Around four-thirty, he picked up his car at Arlington and headed back to Suitland. He was hoping for some letters from Japan.

Friday, February 15, 1957

There were no letters yesterday but surely something would come in today. He really missed Yoshiko's letters and had been looking forward to hearing from Peggy since his note to Brent a few days ago.

He spent Friday in the Arlington office and except for a few short sessions with the Commander, he spent most of his time at his desk. He did get off an encrypted message to Brent much like the one he'd sent earlier in the week. He included a note for Peggy asking her to look out for Johnson and Han.

He composed a fairly long message for Johnson complimenting him and Han for their intel on the Swatow boats. He urged him to continue their surveillance and to watch for exact details on the boats such as size, crew, speed, and armament.

Late in the day, Commander Banta stopped by to thank him for the message he had sent to Johnson. She said it was right on and hoped Johnson could get technical details on the boats. She urged Myles to enjoy himself over the weekend because it might be his last in the States for quite a while.

Friday night Myles stayed close to Suitland. He had a really nice dinner at the Cattlemen Steak House a few miles down the Suitland Parkway. He had some good Scotch and a great steak. What could be better, he thought, he wondered if there were any good steaks in Saigon.

Montgomery, Alabama, outlaws race-based bus seating assignments; Three B-52 bombers make non-stop around the world flights; International Geophysics Year begins; 1st electric watch is introduced; Elvis Presley makes 7th and final appearance on Ed Sullivan Show; The Wham-O Company produces the first Frisbee; Dean Martin's, "Memories are Made of This" tops charts; Southern Christian Leadership Council is formed.

Chapter Seventeen

Maryland

Saturday, February 16, 1957

Saturday morning and once again his mail box was empty. He was starting to feel neglected and even a little peeved at his friends. Yoshiko and Peggy .... Mom and Dad ... Matt ...... where in the heck were their letters?

He spent the morning writing letters to all of them. His main theme was please write more letters .... I need them desperately .... it's lonesome here.

After lunch he decided to go Arlington and bury himself in documents. He would make out a theoretical schedule for the next thirty days, finalizing with him and his crew in Saigon.

Late in the day he called the Commander to see if she wanted to take in a movie or something. She wasn't home. He wished he had Bill Peabody's phone number but it wasn't listed.

He finally decided he would go alone to the neighborhood movie theatre. He saw "Broken Arrow". Debra Paget was one of his favorites.

Sunday, February 17, 1957

Around noon, he got in his Staff car and drove all the way down to the southern tip of Maryland for some sightseeing.

In the town of Waldorf, he spotted a little seafood restaurant and had a dozen steamed crabs and a huge flagon of beer. What a deal .... a dollar for the crabs and a nickel for the beer .... maybe he should move there, he thought to himself.

Sunday night he wrote another letter to Yoshiko. He had to tell her about his crab feast. What a great time they would have had together.

Monday, February 18, 1957

Monday morning and still no mail. He was expecting to spend a lot of time with the Commander and wanted to go over the schedule he'd worked up a few days ago. Commander Banta was in early too. She was all work these days which suited Myles just fine. That meant things were starting to happen.

"Myles, Lieutenant Peabody left yesterday for Shiroi. Did I tell you I was sending him over there to work with Johnson and DeMeur? When the time comes, the three of them will go to Saigon together."

"Well .....," Myles paused.

"No matter. He's on his way. I was in yesterday and sent a message to Hickson, Brent, Johnson, and DeMeur. I told them Peabody would be joining them soon."

"Great. They will appreciate that. Thanks."

"By the way, Davison is going up for Court Martial in six weeks. Between now and then, he's in for some hard time. We don't use rubber hoses, but we do have some .... techniques."

"The lousy traitor," Myles mumbled to himself.

"Traitor is right. Now, take a look at this and you'll get a better picture of things. Johnson sent us this early yesterday morning."

The Commander held up a yellow document.

"Commander. why didn't you call me in yesterday? I wasn't doing anything anyway. All I did was eat crabs and drink beer."

"Good, that's exactly what you should have done. From now on Myles, there's not going to be much time off. You're going to be as busy as a one armed paper hanger."

"That's suits me fine."

Myles took the message and went to his desk.

What he saw blew his mind. Apparently, Johnson had gotten all the technical information on the fifty Swatow boats.

Detachment Two of 6925th Radio on Monkey Mountain had intercepted a bunch of transmissions between Hanoi and all North Vietnam and Vietcong coastal stations. Monkey Mountain was near DaNang, which was on the coast just below the seventeenth parallel in South Vietnam territory.

Somebody, somewhere in the Hanoi Navy command really screwed up and sent the messages unencrypted. That was a major blunder ..... but it happens sometimes ..... even on our side.

He read the details on the boats.

**Twenty Swatow Russian P6 Motor Torpedo Boats.
Displacement 76 tons, 88 feet by 21 feet x six feet, four
25 mm cannons, two 21 inch single torpedo tubes,
speed 45 knots, wooden hull, transferred from Russia
to China 1961.**

**Thirty Swatow Motor Gunboats. Displacement
unknown, 83 feet x 20 feet x 6 feet, two 37 mm cannon,
two 20 mm, eight 50 cal DCT, speed 30 knots, crew 27,
built in China in 1955. Wood hull. Pennant numbers
three digits in 600 series.**

**Twenty torpedo boats to deploy to south coast of
Gulf at Station Alpha. Ten gunboats to same port.
Twenty gunboats to Mekong Delta, Stations Zebra and
Tango.**

Myles, grabbed up the document and headed for
Commander Banta's office.

"Commander, you got to get that van ready and send
me over there now, today, or this week. This is bad news."

"Myles, hold your cool for a minute. Remember
we're not engaged in this civil war. We will be soon,
that's for sure, but for now we're just giving them advice.
I am getting the van ready and you'll be on your way in a
few days."

"Good, anything else going on?"

"Well, as you might guess, all this data is going all
around the system. I'm seeing stuff being passed around
CIA, NSA, USAFSS, ASA, NSG, and, of course, the White
House. There are secret Congressional hearings going on as
we speak."

"You testifying?"

"Yes, I'm just waiting for my call."

"Want me to go with you?"

"Maybe, I hope it won't be necessary. I think things will be perfectly clear. I just hope those agencies don't leak any of this to the media."

"Yeah, they are known for that."

"OK, I'll see you later. I'll see that you get to see everything that passes over my desk. If you need to talk to Johnson, use the secure phone in the message center. My charge code is 21-XX36. I should have given it to you before. Anyway, it is your charge code from now. Memorize it."

"Thanks. I will call him today. I'll leave you alone for now."

Myles went down to the coffee shop and brought back three coffees for the Commander, Petty Officer Davidson, and himself.

He worked all day on a fresh pile of classified documents and decided to wait until tomorrow to call Johnson.

That night, he wrote more letters. He wished he could tell everybody about all this stuff going on, but there was no way. He hit the sheets early and planned to get up early the next morning.

Tuesday, February 19, 1957

Finally, there was one letter. But that was OK, it was from Yoshiko. He held it close to his heart as he went back to his room. He sat on his bed and opened the letter. It was only one page and there were no pictures.

His first reaction was disappointment ….. one page and no pictures …. surely she could've done better than that. Then he unfolded the single page and started to read.

He instantly grabbed at the sheet of paper. My God, my God, he couldn't believe what was scribbled there. It was her printing, no doubt about that.

"Mai, I need you here. Please come right now. I in big trouble. I in apartment now sick in bed. I hit man with my new car. He under car and people push me down and there blood all over me. I go hospital. Bebi-san die. I so sad. Then I go jail. Then Uncle take me to Ikebukuro. I am big trouble Mai. O-basan here help me. You should come right now .Fast as you can. Please come help me. Yoshiko."

He sat motionless holding the letter just inches from his face. He kissed the letter. He held his breath. Suddenly. he couldn't breathe at all. His face felt puffy. His hands were sweaty. His temples were pounding.

Holding the letter in his hand, he pulled open his door and rushed up the hall, finally stopping at the Officer of the Day desk.

"Jack, glad you're on duty. I can't breath. I can't ......"

"Myles, you look terrible. I'll call the hospital at Bolling you just go lie down on the first bed you can find."

Next door, he found an empty bed and followed Jack's orders. After a while, he started breathing again and was beginning to feel better. He jumped up to go see Jack.

"Jack, don't call Bolling, I'm OK now. I just got some terrible news here."

He held up Yoshiko's single page letter.

"Too late Myles, they're sending an ambulance. Go lie down."

Once again he followed Lieutenant Jack's orders. About fifteen minutes later, he heard some commotion out in the hall.

"In here, men."

Jack pointed to the room where Myles was lying down.

Within minutes Myles was on a gurney in an Air Force ambulance screaming down the Suitland Parkway. It slowed after just a few minutes and careened into the Bolling off ramp.

Men in white rolled Myles off the ambulance and into the hospital emergency entrance. Myles was definitely feeling better, but the ceiling lights flashing by made him a little woozy. Doctors surrounded him and poked and listened to just about every place on his body.

This was Myles first ever experience with anything like this. Only once had he been to emergency. That was when he was eleven years old after his bicycle ran a red light and he hit a moving car. Anyway that's what he told his Dad ..... "My bike ran into a car, Dad."

That encounter cost him a busted collarbone .... not too bad considering the condition of his bike. He hoped this time there'd be nothing like this.

After his chest x-ray, EKG, blood pressure and oxygen check, the doctors pronounced him fit as a fiddle.

"You told the ambulance crew you just got some real bad news. This might have been a panic attack. Ever had this happen before?"

"No sir, never."

"Well, I must tell you that you're in excellent health. You know, I'm a flight surgeon. It says here you just turned twenty two. Ever think of applying for flight school Lieutenant?"

"No, sir."

He remembered they used his Air Force ID for admittance. He decided to leave things that way.

"No, I guess I've never considered that," Myles said.

.He was a little annoyed with the doctor. The only thing he wanted to think about right now was Yoshiko.

They kept him in a private room for observation and let him go around three. They assigned an Airman to drive him back to Suitland. All the while, he was thinking about the letter and what Yoshiko must be facing. He thought about their twelve week old baby and how he listened to his heart. In the car he didn't panic again. His reaction this time was tears.

"You OK Lieutenant?" the Airman asked.

"I'm OK thanks. I just got some bad news this morning."

"Somebody die or something?"

"No ..... well, yes actually. It's real bad. Thanks for asking. Thanks for the ride," Myles said as the car wheeled into the Suitland parking lot.

Myles immediately went to his car. Within minutes he was crossing the Anacostia River Bridge and heading up Pennsylvania Avenue. As he was driving, it occurred to him that he hadn't called the Commander, and he hadn't asked anybody to call for him. She must be wondering where he was. Right now, that was the least of his worries. He really didn't care about anything except Yoshiko. He started sobbing again and struggled to keep his eyes clear for driving.

It was nearly four-thirty as he brushed by Petty Officer Davidson and went straight to his desk. There was a stack of fresh documents and some traffic but no messages or notes. He hurried over to the Commander's door and knocked a few times.

"Come in Myles," the voice came back in an even tone.

"Commander, I'm real sorry I didn't call. I've been in the hospital at Bolling. I'm OK though."

"Hospital, Myles, what happened?"

Myles sat down without being invited.

"Commander, I got some terrible, terrible news in a letter from Yoshiko today. I think I had a panic attack and I would have been fine but they went ahead and called for an ambulance. I got checked out and I'm fine, really."

"What kind of news Myles?"

Myles pulled the folded letter from his pants pocket.

"Here, I think this explains everything."

He handed the letter to the Commander.

She quietly studied it for a few minutes, not moving or saying anything.

"Myles, this is terrible. I'm so sorry. I didn't know there was a baby."

Myles was trying hard to contain his emotions, but his voice was noticeably quivering every time to tried to get out some words.

"Yes, Commander, about twelve weeks. It was due in September. I feel awful Commander, and Yoshiko, I can't imagine. I've got to get over there right away."

"OK, we'll work on it. Myles, we didn't know she had a car either. When did she get that?"

"Well, she told me her Uncle was going to buy her a car so she could get around Tokyo better for her jobs. I would never had approved of that, but I guess he was sincerely trying to help. From her letters, I figure she got the car in the first week of February, maybe about two weeks ago …. I guess. I'm not sure."

"Damn, did she even know how to drive?"

"No, she'd never driven a car as far as I know. She said Masuda was going to send her to driver school."

"Myles, if this letter got here this morning, then she must have been driving only about a week. No wonder she had a wreck. Tokyo traffic is treacherous even for an experienced taxi driver. Oh, I hate to hear all this. What would you like to do?"

Myles was able to speak a little better now. His eyes were seriously bloodshot and his expression was one of fear and confusion. He was feeling terrible, sick, depressed, dizzy, everything …. all at the same time.

"First thing Commander, I'm going to try to get Brent on the phone. It's four-thirty in the morning over there, so I'll hang around here and place my call around eight-thirty tonight. I feel so helpless Commander. I love that girl so much …. and the baby …. my God."

"Myles I can only imagine how you feel. From this letter it sounds like it's been a nightmare for Yoshiko. I'm glad she's back at the apartment and has O-basan to take care of her. You going to call Masuda too? Go ahead and use the message center phone all you need too."

"Yeah, I'll call Brent first and then Masuda. Damn, I wish he'd gotten that phone put in at the apartment. He promised me he would."

"Myles, there hasn't been much time for that. I'm sure he was going to do that."

"Well, that doesn't help much now, does it! What I do after my phone calls, I guess, depends on what I find out."

"Just let me know. One good thing is you can go to Tokyo right away now. We got everything we needed out of you here and you need to get to Saigon as soon as possible. Let's talk early in the morning. I'd say you can leave for Tokyo early Thursday.

"I guess that's as quick as we can make it."

"…. and Myles, try to get word to Yoshiko that you'll see her Thursday night or early Friday morning. She really needs to know you're on your way. Maybe Brent can see that she gets the word through Masuda."

"Yeah, and you know Commander, Peggy Hickson is my good friend and she knows Yoshiko real well. She actually spent a weekend with us not long ago. I'll ask Brent to privately let her know. Maybe she can help me too."

"Good. We did know about Peggy, too, Myles and I'm glad you have her as a friend."

"My God, Commander, is there anything you don't know …… well, yes I guess the baby."

"Myles, we're only doing our job. I'm just so pissed off at myself that we let Davison slip by. Guess you're not much good today until tonight when you make your calls. Do whatever you like. Is there anything I can do?"

"No, not yet. Thanks for being so kind, Commander," Myles said, and then he added "….. Didn't Johnson and Han do good getting that intel on the Swatow boats? ….. And that Detachment on Monkey Mountain did good picking up those plain language messages?"

"Absolutely. We put the word out loud and clear not to destroy those radio stations. We are locked onto them now listening for more of the same."

"Good. I'll go back to my desk and try to get my mind off things for a while."

"Go ahead for now." The Commander turned her attention to a new stack of documents that Petty Officer Davidson had placed on her desk.

Tuesday Evening

Myles sat at the telephone desk in the message center with Yoshiko's letter spread out in front of him. He dialed Brent's extension at Shiroi.

"Captain Brent speaking."

"Roy, this is Myles in Arlington. Can you hear me OK? I hear you loud and clear."

"You're good. I hear you fine. What's up?"

"Roy, I got some terrible news. I got a letter from Yoshiko this morning …. it is Tuesday night here. Uncle Masuda bought her a car and gave her driving lessons last week. Sometime, I guess two or three days later, she hit and killed a man. She told me all about it in this letter I just got this morning."

"Myles how awful. Is she all right …. and the baby?"

"No, that's why I'm calling. From what I can make out, she didn't know the man was under her car and when she stopped the people around there must've pulled her out of the car and threw her down on the street. Anyway, that's what it sounds like."

"But ….."

Myles interrupted.

"Let me finish. She must have gotten hurt and she said there was blood all over. She said they took her to the hospital and she lost the baby."

"My God, Myles."

"Yes for sure. Then they must have put her in jail for a day or so until Masuda could bail her out and take her to the apartment. I think she is out on bail and there might be a trial. Anyway, that's what I figure putting two and two together. In her letter, she sounded so scared and sick and she is begging me to come over there right away."

"Can you do that?"

"Pretty much. Commander Banta is releasing me and I can get to Tokyo Thursday night. I'll go straight to her apartment. Now, can you help me Roy?"

"Absolutely. You know it's going on nine in the morning here. What can I do?"

"First thing is please call Masuda at the camera shop. Find out all you can and tell him I'll get to Tokyo late Thursday or, maybe, Friday morning. Tell him to let Yoshiko know this right away so she knows I'm on my way."

"OK, I got his number."

"Then, please call Peggy and take her to lunch at the snack bar and tell her everything. Now let's see ….."

"I'll do that. Should I call you at this number after I talk to Masuda?"

"Yeah, I guess I'll stay here until you call and, I guess, until you call me back after talking with Peggy. I want to know that she knows. She might have some ideas. I'll be near this for phone for the next five hours or so."

Myles looked at his Accutron watch. That would be around two in the morning for him. He stroked the watch and his thoughts shot back to that last weekend when they exchanged their presents. Oh how he missed Yoshiko just now. It's nine in the morning for her. I hope she's all right.

Before long the phone rang. It was Roy.

"Myles, you there?"

"I'm here, how'd you do?"

"Not too good. There was no answer at the camera store. I called Morita-san over at the tailor shop. He's going to walk over to the Ginza store and see if there is any sign of life. He promised to call me back right away and I'll call you back right away."

"OK. Wonder where Masuda is? Oh, I'll bet he's with Yoshiko. How about Peggy?"

"She's meeting me at the snack bar at twelve. I didn't tell her anything, just that you asked me to have lunch with her. So, she's all right so far. I'll get off now and wait to hear from Morita."

"OK. Call me back."

In an hour, the phone rang again.

"Myles, I just heard from Morita. He says the shop is dark and there is no sign or anything. He asked people in the adjoining stores if they knew anything and they didn't."

"OK. Call me back if you learn anything and for sure after your lunch with Peggy."

Around two-thirty in the morning, the phone rang again.

"Myles, Roy again."

"OK."

"Well, Peggy is devastated. She just broke down trembling and crying. Mark came over and brought a cold towel. I thought she was going to be sick. I stayed with her for a whole hour until she pulled herself together. What makes it worse for her is that she is tied up tomorrow with something she absolutely cannot cancel It has to do with the Major so she just cannot go to Ikebukuro. Myles, I feel so sorry for her. She took the news real hard."

"I was afraid of that. Thanks Roy. Stay close to her please. Now I think I'll go home and try to get some sleep

.... if I can. Oh, one more thing. For the time being please don't tell anybody in the office about this, including my two people. When I come in Thursday night, or Friday morning, I'll go straight to Ikebukuro and probably stay there for a week. I don't see how I can possibly come to the base for a visit. I guess I'll phone everybody early next week and discuss our Saigon plans. By the way has Lieutenant Peabody gotten there yet?"

"Yes he has, and he spent his first full work day yesterday. He's going to work out fine. I guess we'll have the three of them here for about another two or three weeks, right?"

"Probably, I just can't think right now. I'm leaving now and I'll call you again tomorrow. That would be Wednesday, right."

"Yeah, it is now Tuesday afternoon. Remember the date line."

"OK, thanks for our help Roy. I'll call you tomorrow then."

"That'll be fine. Early in the morning I'll start calling the camera shop again. Bye Myles."

"Bye."

The next twenty fours were awful for Myles. Roy had still not been able to contact Masuda and Morita still found the shop dark with no information from the neighbors. It was hard working or doing anything for Myles. He fidgeted around at his desk and stopped in to see the Commander a few times. He got his travel money and plane tickets and left early for Suitland to pack his things and do whatever he needed to do to get checked out early in the morning.

He decided not call his Mom and Dad and spare them the horrible news. Maybe things would get back to something like normal in a few weeks. He'll write them a letter then and go over things. Meanwhile he'd not received any more letters from Yoshiko or Peggy.

He would have thought Yoshiko could have written again but, he guessed she was feeling too sick to write.

Chapter Eighteen

Tokyo

Thursday, February 21, 1957

It was Thursday morning and Myles had accomplished all the rituals of departing Andrews for Japan. He'd turned his car in, cleared customs, checked his bag and was now seated on a chartered Northwest Orient Super Constellation.

As the plane climbed to altitude, he mentally reviewed his schedule. Let's see …. he thought ….. six hours to San Francisco ….. five hours to Honolulu ….. seven hours to Wake ….. and about six hours to Tokyo. With three refueling stops, that should get him to Tokyo Haneda, or maybe Tachikawa, ... around eleven Thursday night.

By that time ….. he thought …… Brent will have spoken to Masuda …. and Peggy might be in Ikebukuro with Yoshiko. For an instant, he felt like everything might be all right after all. But that feeling didn't last long and he relapsed into his melancholy.

He ate and drank sparingly on the long flight. He couldn't sleep. He watched the movies but he couldn't hear the sound. It was not a pleasant journey. His mind remained swept away by Yoshiko's letter and the horrid events which he could only imagine.

He picked up his bag and cleared Haneda customs. He was still in uniform so he experienced courtesy at every stop. It was cold outside, much the same as the way he left it in the early morning hours nearly two weeks ago.

Before long, he caught a shuttle bus to downtown Tokyo and settled down for the two hour ride. He was now counting on arriving at the Tokyo central bus terminal around three Friday morning. Mentally, he worked it out that he might get to Ikebukuro Station around four o'clock.

It was still dark and very, very cold. It was a long walk to the apartment carrying his overstuffed bag. It was a welcome sight when he finally rounded the corner and headed up the narrow gravel road. There was no light anywhere in the building .... probably everybody tucked in against the cold and in a deep sleep.

He'd practically forgotten the bad news and was now just looking forward to quietly slipping into the room. He'd try not to wake her .... he thought .... God knows she needs the rest ... he'll just keep his clothes on and lie down gently beside her on top of the futon.

Man oh man, is he ever going to take care of his girl. He'll pamper her like she's never been pampered before .... and no cars .... never, never again would she drive a car. He was starting to feel good and looking forward to a week with her.

The whole building was dark. He walked through the front doorway and O-Basan's place was absolutely dark and quiet. The hallway upstairs was just as dark. As he approached the apartment, he saw the door was half open.

Inside, he made his way over to the table lamp without making a sound, although by this time he believed the room to be empty. With the light on, his suspicion was confirmed. The room was empty. It looked perfectly normal except the bed was covered with her clothes all spread out neatly as if carefully arranged for a purpose.

He recognized all of her outfits. He was deeply disturbed by what he'd found. Where was she, and why were her clothes laid out like that. And where was O-Basan? Could the place have been vandalized? No, that would make no sense with her clothes laid out like that.

He began to rationalize just what could be happening. She must be wearing the pink suit. Then the clothes .... she must be in the process of moving into Uncle Masuda's place in Tokyo. She probably went to his place in her pink suit and then was planning to come back and pack her clothes. That's why she'd laid them all out like that .... and that's why she didn't close the door behind her .... probably left in a hurry. OK. That had to be it.

But O-Basan .... well, she must have gone to see her relatives in Mito. He knew she'd done that before. OK ..... so that must be what's going on. But what should he do now at four-thirty in the morning? He put down his bag and crawled into the bed under the futon and her neatly laid out clothes. Before long, he warmed up and fell asleep .... knowing that he'd figured everything out and that he'd see her at Uncle Masuda's in the morning.

Friday, February 22, 1957

He woke up around eight-thirty and quickly got his things together. With his suitcase in tow he caught a taxi to the Ginza. He stopped the taxi directly in front of Uncle Masuda's store. He paid the driver and turned to walk up to the front door.

The door was locked and the store was dark inside. His heart started pounding and he was getting the same feeling he had that bad day back at Suitland. Get hold of yourself Myles .... he tried to coax himself into believing that everything was still all right. But what to do now? He was at a dead end. He didn't know where Masuda lived ..... which was probably where both of them were .... and maybe waiting for him to show up .... but no, how could that be. Surely they knew he didn't know Masuda's home phone number or where he lived.

Suddenly he remembered Kazuko-san over at the Seibu. If anybody knew anything about Yoshiko and Masuda, she would. By now it was nearly ten-thirty, so she should be there by now. Ten-thirty on Friday morning would be a busy time at the store. So he took off walking the few blocks up to the Seibu Department Store lugging his heavy suitcase.

He managed the escalator up to the fashion floor and entered the show room area. He put his suitcase down near one of the overstuffed sofas.

"Ma'am is Kazuko-san here this morning?" he asked.

"Just a minute sir, I'll get her."

Myles sat near his suitcase and tried to be calm. He was definitely not feeling good about all this. He tried to remember the good times he and Yoshiko had there in the show room. He remembered seeing her on the platform in the center of the room last December in her white evening gown and her hair up in that luxurious French twist.

Just then Kazuko-san entered the room. She instantly stopped when she saw Myles, and then very slowly walked over to where he was sitting.

Seeing her, he stood up and was getting ready to bow and shake hands.

"Myles, oh Myles. You're here."

She broke into tears and started sobbing uncontrollably. Myles caught her as her body started sinking to the floor.

He moved her over to the sofa and sat beside her with his arm around her waist.

"Kazuko-san, what is it? What's the matter?"

"Oh, Myles, don't you know?" she could barely speak.

"I don't know anything. I flew in last night and there's nobody in our apartment and Masuda-san's camera store is closed. She wrote me about her car accident but ....."

Myles was beginning to tear up, and was having difficulty breathing.

"Oh, Myles. I must tell you bad news .... very bad news."

She was still crying and her voice was quivering and weak.

Just then, one of Kazuko's girls came over with two towels and placed them in their laps. Myles helped wipe Kazuko's tears then he put his towel over his face. He had a premonition of what she was about to tell him.

"Myles, it was a terrible accident. A policeman friend from Shinjuku told me about it. He say she hit a man and pulled him under her car when she didn't know it. Then people stopped her car and pulled out and pushed her down on the street. She was hurt and bleeding all over and she go to hospital in ambulance and ... Myles ... your baby was killed."

Myles stopped her from talking. It was too painful for her to remember all this and he was afraid to hear anymore.

"Then Myles, police take her to jail for one day, then Masuda-san take her to apartment in Ikebukuro. It was very, very bad Myles. She write you letter about it."

"And then what? Do you feel like talking, Kazuko-san? If you don't, I will understand."

She managed to continue. ".... and then Myles, she was feel so bad and she so ashamed .... she jumped in front of train coming into Ikebukuro. She die Myles and is in heaven now with baby. I am sure of that."

Myles sank to his knees in front of the sofa. With the towel over his face he started trembling and sobbing. He couldn't stop. He couldn't get the image of Yoshiko dying like that out of his head. Why, why, oh why did she do that? Why couldn't she wait a little longer. My love Yoshiko. I love you Yoshiko.

The two of them stayed like that for almost a half hour. Finally they slowly started to regain some composure. Kazuko hugged him and kissed him on his cheek. Myles pulled back.

"Kazuko-san, we should be strong now. This is so terrible. I can't …..," he didn't know what to say or what to do.

"Masuda-san …. Kazuko-san do you know where he is?"

"Oh, Myles, I guess when he hear about Yoshiko dying, he couldn't live any longer. He take poison and die in back of his store."

"Oh, Myles, all this is so terrible and sad. What can you do Myles? Where can you go? You go back to Ikebukuro today?"

Myles thought for a minute. At first …. he thought …. no, I will never, ever go back there again. No …. he couldn't do that ….. if Yoshiko were here, she would say go back one more time …. you should thank O-Basan and say goodbye …. you should do that Myles.

"Kazuko, thank you for being such a good friend to Yoshiko and for talking with me today. I know it was hard to do. Sayonara."

Once again Myles piled himself and his suitcase into a taxi. This time he directed the driver to the Dai Ichi Hotel which was only a few blocks in the direction of Shimbashi.

He had the driver go past the Victoria Tea Room on the way. He didn't cry. He was through with that for now.

By now it was almost one o'clock on this fateful Friday afternoon. He went through the motions of unpacking and taking a shower as if in a trance. Around four o'clock he walked out of the lobby and took a taxi back to Ikebukuro. Every landmark along the way bombarded his senses as memories of trips past flooded his consciousness. This was his last trip to Ikebukuro .... his last ..... his last forever.

It was getting dark as he stepped from the taxi in front of the apartment building. The building was dark and quiet, just the way he left it earlier in the day. Inside, O-basan's quarters were still empty. Sadness began to overtake him again as he quietly went up the stairs and down the hall, as he'd done so many times before. He knew what to expect when he slid open the door.

There was still enough light so that he could see her clothes laid out across the bed. When he left earlier in the day, he straightened out the futon and her clothes the way they were when he got there. He switched on the table lamp.

Without thinking he began moving about the room gently touching things as he went. He put his mouth on the teakettle where her lips had been so many times. He touched everything in the little kitchen. He touched the Crosley, the side table, and the lamp. He rubbed his hands over the walls and the straight chair.

Then he started folding her clothes. He neatly folded all her dresses and blouses as if packing them in a suitcase. He didn't know why he was doing this. It was just something he had to do. He placed her shoes on the stacks of folded clothes.

Then it struck him. Her pink suit was missing. Besides that, all the things he'd bought her were missing too. Her penny loafers, her high top shoes, and her jacket, all were missing. Still worse, where was her hat box .... her ever present hat box?

Then the thought of **Ladybug** crossed his mind. Their treasured little pin was missing. Suddenly, he knew. **Ladybug** was with her. Yoshiko, in her pink suit, with her hat box in hand, and **Ladybug** high on her lapel, was gone forever.

He fell onto the bed and cried with his hands over his face. He couldn't push the thoughts back. She must have packed all his things in her hat box when she left for the station and then, finally, pinned **Ladybug** to her jacket for the very last time. He began trembling as he couldn't erase the picture from his mind.

By this time, it was pitch black outside and the cold night air began filtering into the room. He hardly knew where he was anymore. All he could think about was how he was responsible for all that had happened. Because of his intervention at the Victoria Tea Room on that cold November afternoon, one fine young beautiful girl with a brilliant future ahead of her was dead. Not only that, one kind gentleman with a thriving business and a wonderful life was also dead.

Why, oh why, did he ever go to that tea room that day. He should have stayed away and minded his own business. He'd actually killed these two people.

He looked around the room for one last time. Her clothes were all folded and neatly stacked. The room was neatly arranged with everything in its place, including the Crosley, the JVC record player, and the stack of hula records. He didn't know which way to turn and what to do. Without thinking, he simply turned out the light and stood by the door for a few seconds looking at the bed.

"Sayonara," he said for the last time.

He left the building for the short walk over to the main street.

He arrived back at the Dai Ichi around eight-thirty. He hadn't eaten all day and was not the least bit hungry. Back in his room, he sat down in an overstuffed chair and stared at the opposite wall.

None o'clock Friday night .... he thought ..... there was no rush to get to Saigon. He actually had arranged for the week off. Tomorrow, he would go to Shiroi and visit Brent and his old friends .... certainly Johnson and Han would be happy to see him .... and Peggy .... he could see Peggy.

Suddenly, without explanation, he completely changed his mind.

He picked up the phone and called the concierge.

"This is Myles Garrison in 212. Can you get me Northwest Orient Airlines on the phone please?"

"Yes sir? Please hang up and I'll have them call you."

"Thanks."

A few minutes later, the phone rang.

"Yes."

A pleasant American female voice answered.

"This is Northwest Orient, are you Mr. Myles Garrison?"

"Yes, I know it's very late but I need your help."

"Yes, sir, it is not too late."

"I have an open ticket from Tokyo to Saigon. Can I catch the first plane in the morning?"

"Hold on please."

A short pause.

"Sir we have an early morning departure. Flight Zero Two departs Tokyo Haneda at zero eight hundred in the morning, that would be Saturday, February the 23rd, or course. I can get you on that flight, but you'd have to leave your hotel real early to make that flight. I show you're booked coach. What do you think?"

"Thank you ma'am. I think that's just fine. Make that reservation for me then. I'll be there."

"Yes, sir," she repeated the details of his reservation and his flight which included changing planes in Manila.

"Thank you."

He hung up and called the concierge once again.

"This is Mr. Garrison, I'm checking out around four in the morning. Please have my bill ready, and I need a shuttle to Haneda. Can you do that?"

"Yes sir, will that be all?"

"Yes, that'll be fine. Oh, wait, I need a wakeup call at three. Now don't let me down. I need that wake up call for sure.

Chapter Nineteen

Northwest Orient Zero Two

Saturday, February 23, 1957

"Sir, we're coming into Taipei."

Myles didn't move.

"Sir, sir, you asked to be awakened at Taipei."

The stewardess started shaking his shoulders.

Myles emerged from a deep, deep sleep. He had trouble getting his eyes open and clearing his head. He hadn't slept like that since he didn't know when …. and the dream …. he had dreamed the last four months in amazing detail. It was like reliving that time all over again. It was a beautiful dream …. the wonderful time spent with Yoshiko …. the happy times ….. from their meeting up until it ended in a horrible nightmare. He was glad to be awake once again.

"Sir, would you like a drink or anything? We land in about twenty minutes."

She handed him a hot towel.

"Thanks, Nancy. I'd like some orange juice please and thanks for the hot towel."

In spite of his long nap, he was still able to remember her name.

The Taipei refueling stop was over in thirty minutes and Northwest Flight Zero Two was back at altitude heading for Manila. This time Myles decided to have a drink and some dinner. He didn't want to get to Saigon sick and dehydrated.

Manila was a quick turnaround. There was no plane change as had been scheduled, instead the same plane and crew went on to Saigon.

After that one incident on the Tokyo to Taipei leg, the dark Oriental had not reappeared. It was as if he vanished in the middle of the flight.

Myles sensed the engines cutting back as the Connie began a long slow approach to Saigon. Nancy made the landing announcements as the other stewardesses went up and down the aisle collecting customs declarations. Myles felt refreshed after his dinner and hot towels and was relieved to be finally arriving in Vietnam.

The Saigon airport was hot and humid and outside it was pouring rain. People were shoulder to shoulder going through customs and throngs of people awaited arriving passengers with signs and placards. There was no one meeting Myles. In fact, no one in the world knew exactly where he was at this very moment. He barely even knew himself where he was.

Somehow, he got through customs and found himself in a taxi headed to the Grand Hotel. It wasn't a nice clean taxi like he'd gotten accustomed to in Japan. It was filthy dirty with the headliner shredded and hanging down in his face. The driver was just as dirty and his clothes were just as tattered.

So this is Vietnam …. he thought to himself. Take me back to Tokyo anytime please …. what have I gotten myself into?

"Driver, how long to the hotel?"

"Sir, two hour."

"No, no, no way. It's only supposed to be five miles from the airport. You get me there in a half hour. OK?"

"Yes, sir, but it might be dangerous way. You understand?"

"Dangerous? What are you talking about?"

He didn't like the sound of the ominous warning.

"If I go quick way, we go through VC check point. You an American in Air Force uniform, they not like."

"OK, take the long safe way."

He didn't argue.

The deeper they got into the city, the more he realized this was the place he and his Shiroi team had been working on for the past two months. Some places, just names in the past, were now becoming real. The taxi passed the Caravelle Hotel which they had determined to be an anti-Diem hideout where his assassination was probably being plotted.

Very shortly they came up on the Hotel Continental which was another rebel stronghold. He could vividly remember writing about the Caravelle and the Continental in intelligence briefs. It had stopped raining now and the air was like a steam bath. Motor scooters were everywhere. One intersection had three lanes jammed with scooters in all directions. The sound was deafening, like a giant monster hornet.

It had been dark now for a couple of hours and the city was totally lit up by colored signs and neon lights. Along the streets, hookers loitered everywhere grabbing at passersby, men and women both, it made no difference to them. Soldiers sat at outside bar tables chatting, drinking, and smoking. So that's what the ARVN looks like, he thought He was not impressed.

The driver continued on to the Grand Hotel. So far, they had avoided the VC so the trip from the airport had been safe, although twice as long. He did get a good glimpse of the city on the way through and there was absolutely no resemblance to Tokyo.

Finally, there was the Grand Hotel. What a misnomer, he thought, nothing grand about it. This was going to be his new home, so might as well accept it for what it is.

First thing at the hotel would be to get this Air Force uniform off and burn it.

"You have dollar mister?" the driver asked.

"Yes."

As a matter of fact that was all he had. In his daze he hadn't even thought of changing money. He didn't even know what they called money in Vietnam. All he had was a huge wad of unused travel dollars.

"Twenty dollars."

"Here, here's ten dollars. That's all I got."

The driver didn't argue, which meant he probably overpaid by a goodly amount. He exited the taxi, not looking back at the monstrosity.

He dragged his overstuffed bag past a double row of sandbags and entered the lobby.

Inside it was a fairly large area. Its once elegant furnishings and decor had turned old and ugly from four years of civil war. Paint was peeling from the walls and four huge ceiling fans were silent with missing blades. A massive central chandelier was dark with missing parts.

Myles approached the desk clerk, a small dark Vietnamese man in a soiled white suite, yellow shirt, and blue necktie.

"I am Lieutenant Myles Garrison."

Although he was now legally a civilian, he didn't want to confuse matters. He was still using his Air Force ID card.

"Yes sir, I know your name, let me see now."

He retrieved what looked like a large tattered scrapbook.

"You are in room two twenty two sir, how will you be paying?"

"I am with the United States government …."

"Of course, I know how to charge. So that will be fine. Front."

A bell hop, strangely looking like the desk clerk, escorted Myles to the elevator and up to his second floor room. By now it was nearly nine o'clock.

"Hmm … let's see," he said to the porter. "What is there to do on a Saturday night in Saigon?"

"Well, first thing Myles, is get a shower put on civilian clothes and meet me in the lobby bar for a drink. I'll see you down there in thirty minutes."

"Wait, wait, why would I have drink with a porter, and why did you call me by my first name?"

"I am not a porter, Myles. I am Raul. Commander Banta arranged for me to meet you here tonight. I work for the Commander too. I've trained in Arlington like you, even though I am Vietnamese."

"Damn, I've been outsmarted Raul. How'd you know I was arriving tonight?"

"Myles, we know everything about you all the time. We know how bad your situation was in Ikebukuro and what you went through yesterday. Actually, we thought you would spend a few more days up there and visit with Johnson and Han, but we understand."

"Raul, I'm so glad to meet you. Will you be working with me? I hope so."

"Yes all the way, but we'll discuss that tomorrow morning in the office. See you downstairs."

"OK, I'll shower and put on a suit. Should I throw away all my Air Force uniforms?"

"Yes."

With that, Raul quietly left the room.

Myles piled his Air Force uniforms into a corner and decided to have them shredded or burned as soon as possible. He unpacked and hung up his Morita-san suits, pants, and jackets. After he cleaned up he changed into his gray flannel suit.

As he looked in the mirror to straighten his tie, it all came back again. That was the suit he had picked up at Morita-san's shop the day he met Yoshiko at the Victoria. He felt like calling down to the lobby and cancelling his meeting with Raul, but somehow he managed to pull himself together. He spent a few minutes in the bathroom mopping his face and fixing his tie. Then he headed downstairs to meet with Raul.

As he stepped off the elevator, he glanced around the lobby looking for Raul. In a far corner of the room, there was a small bar which he hadn't noticed when he came in. It was a cozy setting with four bar stools and a bamboo trimmed mahogany bar. A wicker fan oscillated slowly overhead, gently flooding the area with warm humid air.

The bartender busied himself drying glasses and chatting softly with an attractive young girl standing near the end of the bar. Myles noticed that he was not Asian and looked more like an American than anything else. He was overweight by quite a lot of pounds, and was totally bald. Judging by his tanned leathery skin and baggy eyes, Myles guessed he must be sixty years old. He had tatoos on both arms from his wrists to his shoulders. He was sweating profusely and his orange tank top was soaked half way down to his waist.

"Myles .... over here."

Myles recognized Raul's voice coming from a small table near the bar.

"Raul, I'm sorry I'm late. It took me a few extra minutes to look decent."

Raul pushed out a chair.

"That's fine. You'll get used to the heat and humidity before long. I ordered you a Scotch and soda."

"Thanks. You even know what I drink. I am impressed," Myles said.

Just then the attractive young girl arrived at the table with Myles' drink. Unlike the bartender, she was definitely Asian. Myles couldn't help noticing how her low cut sarong showed off her figure.

She placed the drink in front of Myles.

"Magandang gabi," she said.

Myles glanced over at Raul.

"Myles, this is Ludi. She is Filipino. She just said "Good evening."

"Good evening and thank you," Myles said.

"And Myles, believe it or not, the bartender is her husband. His name is Lenny and he's an expatriate from Brooklyn. This is a weird place .... you'll soon find out. Now, take a sip of your drink and follow me into the men's room over there."

It was getting stranger by the minute, but Myles nodded and took a sip of his drink.

Raul reached under the table and retrieved a large paper bag. Together, they walked across the lobby and entered the men's room.

Once inside, Raul reached into the bag and pulled out a small handgun. Myles jumped back for an instant.

"It's OK, Myles. This is for you."

He handed Myles the pistol and then recovered a shoulder holster from the package.

"Commander Banta ordered me to fit you out with this as soon as you got here. This a Walthers PPK 38 with a loaded eight cartridge magazine. You are to carry this with you everywhere you go. Because of Davison, you could be in a lot of danger. Here let me strap on the holster."

Myles fiddled with the leather straps and slipped the pistol in and out of the holster a few times.

"This feels good. Thanks Raul."

"Good. On Monday, I'll get you a box of ammo. Oh, I forgot, here is your passport."

Raul reached inside his jacket and handed Myles a brand new American Passport.

Myles leafed through the first few pages, expecting nothing but blank paper. To his surprise, the first ten or twelve pages had Japan and Vietnam Visas and were stamped with dozens of entry-exit stamps.

"When you get back to your room, you need to burn your Air Force ID. That will be your last connection with the military. Right?"

"That's right. But what about my uniforms? They're up in my room."

"I forgot. Tomorrow I will take them upstairs and turn them over to MACV. They have an incinerator up there for burning documents. Anything else?"

"No, that'll be all."

"Good. Now let's go back and finish our drinks," Raul said.

As they exited the men's room, Myles was jolted by another surprise. There, sitting at the Bamboo Bar was the tall dark Oriental from the plane. He was still in his black suit and appeared to be in a serious conversation with Lenny.

Myles stopped in his tracks.

"Raul, that guy over there ....."

"It's OK Myles. I know all about him. Commander Banta assigned him to be your shadow bodyguard. He rode the jump seat on your flight down here from Tokyo. I know he made a pest of himself on the plane. He shouldn't have done that but, anyway, there you are. Actually, he's been with you ever since you left Arlington.

"Raul, I'm so relieved. But why is he here now?" Myles asked.

"Myles, he will be staying here at the hotel but you probably will hardly ever see him ..... unless he is needed of course. There is one last thing. Lennie and Ludi work for the Commander too. That's just a little extra security. They won't bother you and please don't bother them. Now let's have another drink."

They used the next hour to get acquainted with each other. Myles filled in the missing blanks for Raul, including some personal things from his relationship with Yoshiko.

Myles learned Raul was quite a guy. During the war with the French, his parents sent him to the States for his personal safety and to go to college. He graduated from the University of Wisconsin in 1955 with degrees in political science and languages. He was fluent in French, English, and almost all the Vietnamese dialects. His parents had been killed by the French, so he was happy to see them run out of Vietnam. He had no love for Ho Chi Minh either, and joined the NSA to offer his services against the North. He'd been in Saigon for about a year and has been Commander Banta's liaison with MACV during that time.

Beyond that, there wasn't anything else left to talk about that was unclassified. Raul did say, however, that he was unmarried but had a cute Vietnamese girl friend. Myles liked him.

Sunday, February 24, 1957

The two of them had breakfast together the next morning in the hotel coffee shop. Around nine o'clock, they met at the second floor suite of rooms that was to be Blue Cover headquarters. Raul had leased Rooms 231 through 234 so they would be convenient to Myles' Room 222. With the Commander's money, he had the connecting walls removed and replaced with columns. He had bars installed on the windows and double lock bolts put on the four doors opening into the suite.

Myles was impressed as he walked into the new suite. With the walls removed, it was roughly sixteen feet by sixty five feet. There were eight empty desks neatly arranged in two rows, with one large desk front and center. Except for windows, there were large maps of Vietnam provinces on all the walls.

Each desk had a phone and the main desk had three phones, one white, one red, and one black.

"Raul, this is fantastic. I see nine desks. I guess that would be me, you, Johnson, DeMeur, and Lieutenant Peabody. That leaves four empty desks."

"Yes, and I can tell you for sure they will be occupied in the next few weeks. The Commander will be in touch with us by late in the week. I'm going downstairs now to get a crate of office supplies that I ordered yesterday. Anything you want from downstairs?"

"No thanks, but when you get back, let's sit down and go over everything."

"Sure. We need to. I'll be back in ten minutes."

Raul headed out the door.

Myles sat back in his swivel chair and savored the quiet moment. Yoshiko was somewhere in the middle of his consciousness but he managed to apply his thoughts to his present situation. He looked forward to hearing the latest from Raul in a few minutes.

There was a loud banging on the door and Myles jumped up to let his new partner in. Raul struggled through the doorway with a huge paper box.

"Here, let me help you with that."

"Good, let's just put it on that desk over here. We'll stock all the desks with supplies later," Raul said.

"One thing missing, Raul, where's the coffee pot?"

"Hey, you're right. For the next day or so, we'll just have to use room service. I don't think the Commander will object. Do you?"

"No, I'm sure it will be all right. So let's order up some coffee and then let's sit down and talk."

"OK. Coffee and pastry on the way."

Raul picked up the phone. Coffee and Danish arrived in a matter of minutes.

"Raul, after we talked last night, I took a little walk to get some fresh air. Are the hookers always out there like that?"

"Oh yeah, man, they are everywhere all the time. My advice is stay away. They'll grab at you but just push them away. You know, some of them aren't what they appear to be, if you know what I mean."

"I do. Anyway don't worry about me. I can take care of myself. Oh, and I noticed the sand bags by the front entrance and a couple of other places down the street."

"Myles, they've been putting sand bags everywhere for the past couple of months. Usually the VC stay out of town, but sometimes they sneak in a patrol or two and it can get pretty messy. My advice is don't ever forget to wear your pistol. This is a dangerous place."

"OK. Now, what can you tell me about Blue Cover and the latest from the Commander?" Myles asked.

"Blue Cover now has the highest priority from the NSA. I guess you knew that. General Samford is taking a personal interest in us since the Davison affair. I guess that's a good thing. Now, here's our deal. Today is yours to write messages to all your people, including the Commander, and give them your condition. The message center is one floor up inside the MACV office. Here is your clearance badge for our offices and MACV's offices."

He handed Myles a plastic badge on a bead chain much like the standard issue at Arlington.

"Tomorrow, go upstairs and get your picture taken. They'll laminate it onto your badge. Also, tomorrow, I'll drive us out to Tan Son Nhut to inspect our van. It's supposed to be fully equipped and ready."

"Great, that's a little ahead of schedule," Myles replied.

"I told you we got priority. Then on Tuesday, we'll get an Army chopper to fly us out to our site. Remember, we're going to be on top of Duay Bah Den."

"Yes, I do. I know it is higher and has much better listening capacity than our old site. Anything there to see yet?" Myles asked.

"There's a small Army radio transmitter up there, but that's about all. ARVN sentries have been guarding the site while bulldozers have been grading an area to place our van and two half tents …. and I guess a latrine and a cooking area. It won't be ready for the van until Friday. When it's ready, we've arranged for a Sikorsky Sky Crane to hoist up the van and transport it to our mountain top. That should be a sight to behold."

"Yes, we need to be there," Myles replied.

"We will. On Tuesday, though, we'll have a chopper drop us off at the base of the hill and we'll have an ARVN jeep drive us up to the top. It's a real narrow dirt road to get up there so it'll be a bumpy ride."

"What's the schedule on that?" Myles asked.

"An Army chopper will pick us up on the roof around zero eight hundred. It's only a thirty minute flight to Duay Bah Den. I guess the Jeep ride to the top might take an hour or two. When we get there all we can do is walk around and look, and try to stay out of the way of the bulldozers."

"Good plan. What about the rest of the week?" Myles asked.

"On Wednesday and Thursday we'll be having meetings with people from the Air Force, Army, and Navy intel to set up communications and a chain of command."

"Busy week. Anything else?"

"I guess that's it. Then next week we'll meet our crew out at Tan Son Nhut. We're getting fifty four people. Army Captain Jack Matthews will be in charge on top of the hill. He'll be there."

"And I guess week after that we'll put our people on top of the hill and build the tents. Guess we should put everything else up there later in the week, or maybe, the next week," Myles said.

"So that's about it. Anything else?" Raul replied.

"How about moving our Shiroi people, when do we do that? They already have their orders. They'll be working hard this week packing up files and their personal belongings. When will they move down here?"

"They fly down here on Sunday. We'll have rooms for all three of them here in the hotel," Raul answered.

"Man, this is going to be great. They'll love this arrangement. Will we continue to eat our meals in the hotel dining room?"

"Yes, until further notice. Food's pretty good I'd say," Raul replied.

"OK now, Raul, I'd like a little quiet time to compose some messages if that's OK."

"Sure. I've got some things to do around town. Tell you what, I'll see you in the dining room at six," Raul said as he left the suite.

Myles went back to his room for a short break and then took a short walk outside.

The street was teeming with people and every variety of conveyance imaginable. Bicycles and motor scooters were the preferred vehicles. Hookers were out, even on a Sunday afternoon. The air was hot and steamy and the smell of burning charcoal filled the air. Vendors peddled their wares along the street curbs selling everything from porn magazines to barbequed ducklings.

Back at his desk Myles wrote messages to Commander Banta, Johnson, Han, and Brent. They weren't work messages. They were really letters telling about Yoshiko and all the sadness of the last week. He described his last day in Tokyo when he discovered all the details from Kazuko and what he found in Ikebukuro. It was hard to write these things but it had to be done.

He asked Brent to give the information to Peggy and to tell her that he would write soon. He took the messages upstairs to the message center for encryption and transmission. In his message to Commander Banta, he was very explicit in thanking her for her understanding and generosity. He also thanked her for setting up Raul to help him.

Back in his room, he sat down and wrote a long letter to his Mom and Dad. That was just as hard, or even harder, than writing to his peers. He didn't mention the baby, but he did feel it necessary to describe those last few days. He put the letter in the mail drop in the hotel lobby.

He didn't return to the suite. Instead he took a short nap before having dinner with Raul. As he rested his head on his pillow, he felt at peace now that he'd brought all his friends and family up to date on his relationship with Yoshiko and how it had ended. He was teary eyed for a brief spell, but it didn't last long. He couldn't help having a feeling of finality. Some things were finished now and some things were just beginning.

He and Raul had a drink in the lobby bar and a nice dinner in the hotel dining room. The dining room and the food were the only nice things he'd experienced so far in Saigon.

He talked to Raul about Saigon, and Raul promised him that the city was really a beautiful place once you got away from the downtown hustle, bustle, and sandbags. There was a wonderful zoo and a world famous botanical garden. There was also a really nice theatre district where players from all over the world would perform. He promised to take Myles on a sightseeing tour after they got back from the mountain on Tuesday.

Chapter Twenty

Raul

Monday, February 25, 1957

"Raul, I'm really going to enjoy this dining room. This is a tremendous breakfast buffet. I know the Shiroi people will love it."

"Glad you like it Myles. If you're finishing up, we need to get going. I've got a Jeep ready for our drive out to the air base. They'll be expecting us between nine and ten. There'll be some people from the manufacturing team to give us a tour and explain all the equipment."

"Good. I guess I'm ready."

"Fine. Let's go."

It was an interesting Jeep ride. Myles was amazed at this ancient modern city. It was a paradox in so many ways. Three wheeled bicycles pulling rickshaws up and down the crowded streets, careening in out of traffic. The drivers were stereotype …. barefoot skinny old men with ragged shorts and shirts, topped off with straw cone hats. Somebody told him they peddled two hundred miles a day.

The hookers were everywhere, even at nine in the morning. Not far from the hotel he spotted one of those snake shops he'd heard about. Raul slowed down and pointed it out to Myles. They were close enough so that Myles could see stacks of cages with all sizes and colors of snakes imaginable. Raul said, the locals loved to eat snakes every way possible, from skinned and raw, to barbequed, to soup. It was traditional to drink snake bile mixed with rice wine as a powerful aphrodisiac. Raul said he, personally, didn't care for snakes.

By nine-thirty the air was hot and humid and Myles was perspiring heavily in his Morita sports jacket. The tight shoulder holster didn't help much either.

Around ten, they drove through the first of three mandatory Air Force check points. In thirty minutes Raul pulled the Jeep up alongside the van. It was just as he'd visualized from the mock-up in Arlington, only bigger than he'd remembered. In an instant, the Jeep was surrounded by a dozen Army Green Berets armed with M16s and loaded down with ammo belts and grenades.

The leader ordered Myles and Raul to step away from the Jeep and hand over their ID's. Once properly identified and authorized, they were cleared to approach the van. Just then another Jeep pulled up with an Air Force driver and two men in civilian clothes. After introductions all around, Myles learned the two had been with the van ever since it left the factory. Now they were ready to turn it over to its new owners.

The van was fully equipped with radio intercept positions, communications and encoding equipment, weapons, explosives, and even a coffee machine. It was ready to go and Myles signed enough papers to choke a horse. This was a big day. He had his first van, Van Alpha. He locked the door and stuffed the huge key ring in his jacket pocket.

"Now, Raul, don't we need to touch base with the engineers and the helicopter people?"

"We'll do all that downtown at MACV headquarters. We have a meeting there at three o'clock. We can go back to town now. I'm real pleased with our van. It's awesome."

"I agree. Captain Matthews and his people are going to be real happy and I know the Commander will be real pleased with our products. How about lunch? Any place special?"

"Hey, good idea. While we're on base, let's go to the O-Club. I haven't been but I hear they have great food."

So that was how the rest of the day went for Myles .... a great lunch at the Tan Son Nhut Officers Club ..... a nice ride back to the hotel .... a little office time .... and the meeting with the engineers and the helicopter people.

Everything was looking good. The site would be ready for the van on Friday. Work crews were scheduled over the weekend to set up the generator, the half tents, and the out buildings. Myles was looking forward to the helicopter ride in the morning..

Their meeting with MACV went well and everything seemed to be on schedule.

Around five, the courier from the Embassy dropped off a sack of mail. This was going to be the regular courier run, he learned. Everything else in the form of messages would be brought down from the message center the instant of arrival. There was no personal mail for Myles, but he really didn't expect any.

Before long, a messenger from upstairs came down with a short stack of decrypted messages. Raul sorted them out and passed one of them to Myles.

"Myles, this one's for you. I'll take care of the rest of the business."

"Thanks. If you don't mind, I'll take this down the hall and read it in my room."

"Sure, good idea. How are you holding up today. I've noticed you drifting off into a sort of trance a few times.

Guess all those memories are heavy on your mind. I can sure understand that. Tell you what, when you're finished in your room, how about coming back to the suite? I'll be here until you get here. Take your time."

"I will. Raul, I can't thank you enough for being such great help, but mostly for being such an understanding friend. See you in a little bit."

Raul, leafed through his stack of messages. There were several from Commander Banta, mainly dealing with the lease and some housekeeping matters. There was no intel, so he put the stack in his in tray thinking he'd read them later in the evening."

Back in his room, Myles opened his message. It was from Brent. He started out by comforting him over his great loss. He said he'd only met Yoshiko two times .... once coming out of the Tokyo O-Club and the other time at the Christmas Party. He said he'd told everybody in the section about Myles' loss and his current situation in Saigon. He said Johnson and Han were especially broken up by the news about Yoshiko. He said Lieutenant Peabody had fit right in and was liked by everybody ... including Major Hickson. He went on to say he'd given Peggy the whole story.

He finished the message and then he put his head down on his pillow for a few minutes. Then he remembered about Raul.

He picked up the phone.

"Raul, I'll be over in a little while. Think I'll grab a quick shower. Give me ten minutes. You OK over there?"

"Sure, I've been putting pads and pencils in all the desks and sticking pins in the wall charts. Take your time. I'll meet you down at the bar."

In a little while, Myles sidled up to Raul on one of the bar stools. They had drinks but didn't engage Lonny or Ludi in small talk. After drinks they enjoyed another nice dinner in the dining room. Myles liked this part of his assignment more than anything. The service and the food were wonderful and Myles especially enjoyed the pressed duck. Duck seemed to be a favorite food here in Saigon. He watched Raul enjoy his oysters on the half shell and thought maybe he'd try some tomorrow night.

"I'll see you on the roof at eight in the morning," Myles bid goodnight to Raul as they headed for their rooms.

Back in his room, he found himself totally exhausted. He stretched out on the bed for a while before undressing and getting ready for sleep. Almost instinctively, he went to the dresser and started looking through pictures and letters from Yoshiko like he'd done so many times before. Only this time there was no sorrow and grief. He felt closure and peace as if she were there standing beside him.

He fell asleep and dreamed of happy times with Yoshiko in Ikebukuro.

Morning in Arlington

"Commander, are you not worried about how much information Davison passed on to Hanoi?" the Director asked.

"Yes sir, in fact I am extremely worried. All of us are. But General, we've decided we have no choice but to go ahead. We're beefing up our defenses as much as we can."

"I hope that will be good enough Commander. How's it all going?"

"I've got Myles Garrison billeted in the Grand Hotel now, along with Raul. You don't know about Raul yet sir.

He's been with me for about a year. I'll send you his file later today."

"Good, I'd like to know more about Raul."

"So they both have rooms at the hotel and we've leased four rooms and knocked out the walls to make a good sized suite for Blue Cover. We've got desk space for nine people."

"Sounds good, go ahead, I won't interrupt," the Director said.

"On Tuesday, Myles and Raul will go out to see our new hill. You know we've switched to Duay Bah Den. It's a much better location. It's near the Cambodian border in an area known as The Hook. It's higher, and it's in a better reception zone for low and middle frequencies. Not only that, our advanced direction finding equipment should be extremely accurate from that location. Tomorrow, Myles and Raul are going to inspect our first van out at Tan Son Nhut. It's supposed to be finished and ready to go. Then, if it passes our inspection, we'll place it on top of our hill with a Sikorsky Sky Crane, courtesy of the 9th Infantry Aviation Battalion."

"Sounds like a good plan. How about after that? the Director asked.

"Next week, were bringing our Shiroi crew down to Saigon and will billet them in the hotel along with Myles and Raul. Then, next week Myles will meet his crew out at Tan San Nhut. Right after that, they'll convoy down to Duay Bah Den. I estimate we'll be up and running with our first Blue Cover van in two to three weeks."

"That's great Commander. We really need more intel and your project should help, at least we're counting on it. The three services are still in the dark ages as far as Sigint is concerned. We're only getting about a third of the intercept hours we need and even that is practically useless. They're short on analysts and linguists."

"We're going to try like hell to make up for that, General. Once we start up we've got a whole encyclopedia of frequencies and networks to work on. I'm looking forward to when we can go ahead with our other four detachments and start deploying their vans."

"Commander, that depends on what we get out of Blue Cover. One thing though, your Gold Cover might get transferred to Naval Security Group. The Navy is getting nervous about turning two of their tin cans over to the NSA. If that happens, I think you can still manage them the same as if they were yours."

"I guess so, General. Main thing is to get started. Having two destroyers patrolling off the coast of North Vietnam with our vans on board will be an extremely valuable asset."

"I think that will be all for today Commander. Good luck with Blue Cover."

"Thank you sir."

That night back in her apartment Sheila couldn't stop thinking about Myles. What a terrible tragedy he'd endured .... and his baby ..... my God ..... the baby. She just couldn't imagine what he must be going through, just having arrived in Saigon. Yoshiko must be heavy on his mind and, if that wasn't enough, there was the shock of being in Saigon for the first time. She'd been there and knew what it was like.

Her thoughts went back to when she had him and Johnson at her place for spaghetti. What a happy time that was.

Now she was worried about his safety. They were never able to learn fully the extent of Davison's compromise to Hanoi. There were ARVN guards for sure at the hotel, but the confidence level with them was not high. She'd have to think over what more security she could order. She was relieved that she'd put three undercover people in the hotel. In the meantime, she would send him a message first thing in the morning ordering him to postpone his inspection trip out to Duay Bah Den.

Then it suddenly occurred to her it was already Tuesday morning in Saigon. Damn .... she thought .... too late to stop them. By now they're either on their way, or already on the mountain.

It was nearly nine o'clock, but she decided to go back to Arlington and get a message off anyway. Just a chance .... she thought .... maybe they got held up and I can still stop them. Let's see ... nine o'clock Monday night here is nine o'clock Tuesday morning in Saigon .... it's worth a try.

Traffic was light going up Pennsylvania Avenue and once past the White House there were practically no cars.

Back in her office she scribbled her message to Myles ordering him to abort the trip to Duay Bah Den until further notice.

She didn't bother to put the message in a classified envelope. Instead, she folded it over once and headed upstairs to the message center.

"What priority ma'am?" the clerk asked.

"What .... I didn't get that?"

"What priority ma'am? You didn't fill out the priority space."

"Make it Emergency," she blurted out.

An hour later she was home. All she could do was hope now that for some reason Myles' trip was delayed. Oh damn .... she thought .... let the helicopter have engine trouble.

In the morning she read the first message on top of her morning stack. Its Emergency priority caught her eye immediately. It was from Myles and it was his full story about his visit to Tokyo and finding out about Yoshiko's tragic death. She couldn't bear to think about what Myles was going through. She'd never met Yoshiko but felt a deep sorrow for her and, of course, Myles.

Chapter Twenty One

Chopper

Tuesday, February 26, 1957

Myles walked out onto the roof of the hotel. Raul and the pilot were waiting alongside the chopper. The rotor was not turning.

"Myles, I'd like you to meet Captain Dave Bishop. He's going to fly this OH13 off the roof and drop you at the base of Duay Bah Den."

Myles extended his arm and the two shook hands.

"Wait, Raul, you said me. What about you? You're not going?"

"Well, Myles, those oysters really did not like me. I was sick all night. I'm just not up to a helicopter ride this morning. Anyway, Dave will keep you company during the ride. It'll all be OK."

"If you say so. I wish you were coming along though."

"Myles, may I call you Myles?" the Captain said.

"Sure. I'll call you Dave, or should I say Captain Dave?"

"Very funny. I hear you were just recently an Air Force officer. Any problems flying in an Army airplane Myles?"

"Oh, no, I like it. Raul called it an OH13. Are there any guns?"

"No, sorry, no guns. Most of my flying is observation and taxi service like today."

"Good for you Dave. That's kind of dangerous sometimes, right? I mean observation without any guns to defend yourself."

"Well, yes, but I just dodge the bullets. Haven't been hit yet. Some of my buddies have though. Yes it is dangerous, but today should be a piece of cake once I get this dude off the roof."

"Dave, you trying to scare me?"

"No, not really. You should be ready for some excitement though when I pull up and push her over the edge. I'll warn you ahead the nose is going to drop fast so hold on. As soon as I get her up to twenty three knots or so I'll climb out and we'll head straight for your mountain. Should only take about twenty minutes or so."

"Thanks for the warning. I'm so glad you told me. I'll be all right. We ready to go?"

"We're all set. You want to climb up into this bubble and strap in? Here, take this step up."

Myles turned to Raul.

"Well ole buddy, it's been real nice. You know where to send the body."

"Myles, this will be a cool ride. You'll be all right. Mark my words. See you later today."

Up in the cabin, Dave handed Myles a pair of headphones and showed him how to operate the volume control.

With headphones on and tested, Dave made a twirling motion with his right hand and started the engine. First slowly, then picking up speed, the rotor started to turn. He revved it up to twenty five hundred RPM and checked all his gauges. Then he dropped it back to a slow idle.

"Everything looks good Myles, ready to go?"

"I'm ready," Myles said.

Just like he said, when the ship lifted up five feet or so and moved over the edge the nose dropped like a rock.

Myles held on to both sides of his bucket seat as he stared fifteen stories down to the street.

Then, just as Dave had promised, the nose picked up a little and the helicopter started accelerating and climbing. Myles began to relax as roof tops slid away under them faster and faster. Gradually, Dave got them up to fifteen hundred feet and they started cruising at sixty knots in the direction of Duay Bah Den.

"Dave, you're a great pilot. How long you been flying?"

"Well, I started flying little airplanes when I was at Clemson and then I got my commission and went to helicopter school at Fort Rucker. Guess that was four years ago now."

"I'm impressed. You can fly my chopper any day."

Before long Dave pointed directly ahead.

"There's your mountain Myles. I'll be letting down and putting you on the ground near the south base. There's supposed to be an ARVN Jeep there to meet you and take you to the top. Want to take a look at the top before I put you down?"

"I don't think so since I'll be taking the land route up there. Thanks anyway."

"Your choice. Make sure your seat belt is tight."

"I'm good."

Dave backed the engine down to two thousand RPM and circled the landing zone. Myles could see the altimeter needle slowly moving counterclockwise as they approached the surface. Before long the ship bounced a couple of times and Dave shut down the engine.

"Well, here we are, and there's your Jeep waiting over there. I see twin M-60s mounted on the back. That should scare off the flys. I'm staying inside Myles, can you manage yourself out? Be careful going down the steps."

"OK. When you coming back to pick me up?"

"They have a radio in the Jeep and they know how to call me. Otherwise, I plan to be back in two hours on the button. That long enough on the ground?"

"I think two hours is just about right. See you then. Thanks again."

Myles managed the steps and planted his feet on the hard clay surface. He stood back and watched Dave restart the power train and gently lift the ship into the air. Just as when they pulled away from the hotel roof, the nose dipped down as is started moving forward. Myles was actually looking forward to his return trip.

One of the two ARVN soldiers pulled himself out of the back compartment and out from under the twin machine guns.

"Over here sir," he directed Myles to the front seat.

"Thank you," Myles replied.

As he looked ahead and up toward the top all he could make out was a narrow dirt road running straight ahead for maybe fifty feet or so and then snaking a turn to the left and disappearing into the thick overgrowth. This is going to be some ride ..... he thought ..... maybe as exciting as the helicopter ride.

"Let's go," he ordered, as he pounded his hand on the ledge over the Jeep dashboard.

The driver spun all four wheels and the Jeep jerked forward.

Dave was off the ground in a couple of minutes, anxious to leave the dangerous area. He was in the first rotation of his climbing circle when suddenly his tiny OH13 was hit by a massive sonic boom.

Instinctively, he grabbed the collective and pushed the throttle full forward as he was blown over sideways. He jammed down the right rudder pedal when he found himself looking through the Plexiglas bubble straight down at the trees below. Somehow he managed a glimpse back at the landing site. All he could see was a monstrous orange fireball in the spot where the Jeep had been and a black mushroom cloud rising into the sky.

He only had seven hundred feet to work with as he started trying to right the ship and regain control. Blood was streaming down the left side of his face and his head felt like it had been hit with a sledge hammer. He wiped the blood from his face . He continued to work the controls until he got the ship rolled back to nearly horizontal but it was still losing altitude fast. He remembered encountering a situation like this in the simulator back at Rucker.

Airspeed .... that was the main thing right now ..... he thought as he pushed the nose down and the throttle full forward. Finally, just above the trees, he passed twenty three knots and pulled the nose up and the collective full forward. He was no longer worried about VC snipers. All he was concerned about now was getting safely back to Saigon.

"Birdcage Seven this is Redbird Two," he called on UHF radio.

"Redbird, Birdcage, go ahead," a female voice responded.

"Birdcage, Redbird at one thousand two miles southwest for emergency landing. I am declaring an emergency. Over."

"Redbird, copy emergency. You are cleared straight in. Do you need equipment?"

"Roger, Redbird, request fire trucks."

"Roger, fire trucks."

"Birdcage, Redbird …. contact Blue Cover at Grand Hotel. Contact information in my flight plan. You copy over?"

"Roger, contact Blue Cover. What message?"

"Birdcage, my passenger is casualty at mountain. Possible land mine. Request Blue Cover meet Redbird on arrival. ETA ten minutes. Redbird over."

"Roger Redbird, contact approach on two two decimal fiver when field in site."

"Roger Redbird."

An ambulance dropped Dave at the operations shack. He wasn't seriously hurt except for a lump and a cut on the left side of his head. His helicopter was damaged but it did get him back safely. Raul was waiting as he entered the building.

"Captain Bishop I'm so sorry about what happened. You all right?"

"I'm fine, but your friend Myles, I'm afraid won't be coming back."

"What happened?"

"Well, I had just lifted off and was starting a climbing turn to Saigon when a huge blast knocked me over sideways. I could only get a glimpse back there, I was trying like hell to get control of my ship. It looked to me like maybe just as the Jeep pulled away it might have driven over an incendiary land mine. The VC just started using those things. As near as I could see there wasn't much left of the Jeep. Everything was on fire for maybe a hundred yards around. Man I'm so sorry to have to tell you the bad news."

"That's OK. Nothing you could do about it. Thanks for your help today. I need to get going back downtown. Thanks again."

Chapter Twenty Two

Top Secret Beehive

Tuesday Evening, February 26, 1957

Raul sat at his desk, staring up front where Myles should have been. He was still stunned by what had happened this morning and wasn't sure just what to do. He thought back and couldn't believe he was so cool and detached a little while ago when Captain Bishop told him Myles was killed. He went to his typewriter and started a message to Commander Banta.

TOP SECRET BEEHIVE

Operational Immediate

26/2/57

To: Commander S. Banta, NSA, B26A

Fr: Raul, NSA, Blue Cover

With much regret I inform you that your Chief of Blue Cover, Myles Garrison, was killed today when his Jeep struck land mine at base of Duay Bah Den. Await your instructions.

AR

TOP SECRET BEEHIVE

He rolled the document out of his Smith Corona and slipped it into a Top Secret message center envelope. He double bolted the door behind him and walked up one flight to MACV and the message center.

He was through for the day, there was nothing else he could or wanted to do. He walked past Myles' room on the way back and stared straight ahead. Tomorrow he'd start taking care of things.

Chapter Twenty Three

Shiroi

Wednesday, February 27, 1957

Captain Roy Brent placed his first cup of coffee on his desk and pulled a stack of early morning courier messages in front of him. First on the stack was a high priority message from Commander Banta.

He started reading, and then he put the page down and looked at the wall map beside his desk. His eyes were drawn to South Vietnam. Just where in the hell is Duay Bah Den he asked himself?

He picked up the document and finished reading. He was not one to cry but tears started to well up in his eyes. He walked into Major Hickson's office and told him the news.

"Better get his people in here right away and then draft a memo for the rest of the staff. Let's talk again after all this is done."

Brent went to the rear of the room where Johnson, Han, and Peabody were already going through the morning logs.

"You guys want to come into the Major's office for a few minutes?"

Johnson's intuition was kicking in big time. From the look on Brent's face he knew something bad must have happened but he was thinking about cancelled funding or something like that.

"Here, you all sit down for a minute," the Major said.

"Roy?" he asked.

Brent could hardly speak. Tears clouded over his eyes .

"It was a land mine," he got the words out in a quivering voice.

Johnson was the first to react.

"Land mine ….. you mean Myles. What happened?" his voice was beginning to quiver.

"All we know Sergeant, is what I got from Commander Banta this morning," he held up her message.

"What happened?" Johnson repeated.

"Well, it says here, his Jeep hit a land mine at the base of Duay Bah Den. That's all it says ….. except he was killed. I guess it was bad and he must have died instantly ….. a Jeep and a land mine is a terrible combination."

"What are we supposed to do? We still going down there over the weekend? Will there be a funeral? Captain we all loved Myles so much and to have this happen …… especially now right after …..," his voice stopped.

"Sergeant, all I can say is what I just told you. I'll get a note out to the rest of the office in a few minutes, and Major Hickson will inform all the proper people around here."

"You going to call Mrs. Hickson Captain?" Han asked.

"I'll let the Major take care of that."

"I guess, you all can go back to work. If you want to take the day off, we'll understand," Brent concluded.

"No, we'll be working as usual. I'm sure we will be hearing from Arlington later today," Lieutenant Peabody replied.

The small group broke up and returned to their desks and their Beehive work.

Brent decided to call Peggy.

"Peggy, this is Roy."

"Hey, Roy, any news about Myles?"

"Peggy, I've got some terrible, terrible news. You might want to sit down."

"What? OK, I'm sitting."

"Myles is dead. His Jeep hit a land mine and he was killed instantly."

There was total silence on the other end of the line. Then Roy could hear gentle sobbing.

"Peggy, if you need me, call me here at the office or in my quarters. You'll probably be getting a call from your husband."

Still …. nothing but silence.

"Peggy, you there, can I do anything?"

"Oh, Roy, thanks for calling me. I got to go. Bye"

Brent put the phone down. Man, oh man ….. he thought …. how terrible this must be for her. She must be in shock. She just learned her best friend died yesterday in tragic circumstances. He figured that up until his phone call she had already been grieving for her other best friend who took her own life so horribly two weeks ago. Now she knew Myles was gone forever. She's in shock for sure …. he thought. He didn't know what to do.

Did he do right by handling this over the phone …. he wondered to himself … there was just no easy way he could have done this. At least …. he thought …. she was alone at home and not in a public place like the snack bar. Yes …. he comforted himself …. the telephone was OK in this circumstance. It is best to let the Major see about his wife.

Back at his desk, he stared at some papers and occasionally glimpsed around the room. How could all of this have happened in just four or five months, he thought. He remembered it all started when Myles met Yoshiko last November. Myles had told him all about their first meeting the night they ate steaks at the O-Club. It just was not that long ago.

Then there was the Christmas Party. It was the perfect occasion for everybody. In a way, it was Myles presentation of Yoshiko to his culture. It was probably sometime that weekend that Myles realized his future would revolve around her.

Now this ….. up until just a couple of weeks ago Myles and Yoshiko had such a beautiful and exciting future together. Now there was nothing …. no future ….. no future at all.

Chapter Twenty Four

Commander Banta

Dear Mr. and Mrs. Garrison and Brother Matthew,

By now, you have been officially informed of Myles' death in Saigon, Vietnam. I know how impersonal these notices are and I apologize for our bureaucracy. Unfortunately I can't do anything about that. It's just the way they've done things for many, many years. I think Myles would have been appalled at this way of doing things, and if he were here standing beside me he would say, "Commander Banta, how about writing to my Mom and Dad and Brother?"

So, in keeping with Myles' request, I'm writing to the three of you.

My name is Sheila Banta and I was Myles's supervisor for the past four months. I'm sure he must have told you about "Commander Banta" in his letters. Knowing Myles as I did, I'm certain he only had kind things to say about me, not that I deserved them of course …. that's just the kind of young man he was.

I want you to know how proud I am to have served with Myles these past few months. Last November I personally selected him for an extremely important and dangerous assignment from a long list of candidates. He had such exemplary credentials and accomplishments that he stood out from all the rest of the candidates. Picking him was probably the easiest job I've ever had. He wasn't required to accept the assignment but he did so without any hesitation. It meant resigning his Air Force commission, which was difficult for him.

He was looked up to and highly respected by his work associates and had developed friendships and loyalties with many of the Japanese people with whom he had contact. In short, he was loved by all and we will miss him greatly.

You should know that he was killed while performing a very dangerous mission for his country. He was in charge of four officers and more than fifty enlisted men whose mission was to operate a radio van on top of a mountain in dangerous VietCong controlled territory. On the day he was killed, he was flown from the roof top of his Saigon headquarters to his mountain in a small unarmed helicopter. The van was going to be air lifted to the top of the mountain in a few days and he was going out there to inspect the site. He knew it was very dangerous to fly out there that way but he felt it necessary to insure the safety of his men when they arrived there later.

Within seconds after leaving the helicopter, his Jeep struck a Vietcong land mine. The explosion seriously damaged the helicopter which had just gotten airborne. Fortunately, the helicopter pilot was able to fly his damaged plane back to Saigon in spite of a massive head injury. Myles wasn't so fortunate however, as he was killed instantly by the explosion. The helicopter pilot reported later that Myles had spotted some dangerous activity near the landing site and ordered him to land a few hundred yards from the intended landing zone. Apparently he was concerned for the pilot's safety but felt he urgently needed to complete his mission that day. I have applied for a Bronze Star for Myles.

Normally, I would not give such detail on casualties. In this case, however, I feel compelled to tell you about the heroism of these two people. There are many more men like Miles and his helicopter pilot now serving in Vietnam. They serve their country with pride and honor and we should all be proud of them.

I can tell you that Myles' radio van was successfully placed on the mountain top a few days after his tragic death, and has been in operation now for several weeks. Because of Myles' work and leadership resulting in the successful van deployment, American and South Vietnam lives are being saved every day. Without him, I can honestly say, this mission would have been seriously delayed and perhaps might never had happened at all.

Once again, you should be very proud of your son, Myles. Thank you for giving him up to his country.

Very truly yours,

Commander Sheila Banta, USN
National Security Agency
Arlington, Virginia

Postlude

In the months following the tragic death of Myles Garrison, the team of Johnson, Peabody, and DeMeur successfully started up the Blue Cover command center at the Grand Hotel. Van Alpha was successfully put into service at Duay Bah Den and provided nearly 150 hours of daily intercept hours. Raul continued to serve as liaison between Blue Cover and MACV.

By the end of 1957, three more vans were deployed and operating at three inland sites near the 17th parallel. At the same time, the uniformed services had upgraded their land based intercept sites and increased their airborne intercept sorties. The total output of all these facilities was close to reaching General Samford's goal of 2000 daily intercept hours and was providing timely, actionable intelligence. Battles were being won and lives were being saved.

The Commander in Chief Pacific Fleet continued to resist turning over the USS Maddox and the USS C. Turner Joy to the NSA for Beehive missions.

ARVN forces, assisted by US and Canadian advisors, continued to fight VC and PAVN forces in the South and Central regions through 1957 and 1958. MACV set up a training facility for ARVN troops at Nha Trang under the supervision of US Green Berets.

Hostilities continued to accelerate unabated. By the end of 1962, there were 11,300 US military combatants in Vietnam and 243,000 ARVN troops. Over 300 US soldiers had been killed since 1957.

In 1963, NSA had a total of twelve intercept vans throughout South Vietnam and increased its intercept capabilities at the San Miguel and Clark Air Base facilities in the Philippines. The Air Force and Navy were averaging over fifty sorties a day over South Vietnam and the Gulf of Tonkin. Sigint had become a huge operation and was heavily relied on to provide intel to all US and ARVN forces in the South. The NSA expansion and the combined military operation were yielding nearly three thousand intercept hours a day.

President Kennedy placed great value on the South Vietnamese being able to repel the Northern incursion and prevent a communist takeover of the country. It was obvious that he was prepared to apply whatever military resources necessary to insure the South's success.

In early 1963, the Navy finally agreed to put the USS Maddox and the USS C. Turner Joy into service for the NSA in the Gulf of Tonkin along the North Vietnam coast. They were reluctant however to transfer operational control to the NSA. They designated the Navy mission Project DeSoto. Each of the destroyers were equipped with a Beehive van welded to its foredeck. They were put into twenty hour service patrolling the North Vietnam coastline just inside the North's territorial limits.

President Kennedy was assassinated in November 1963 and was replaced by Lyndon Johnson. When Johnson became Commander in Chief, there were 16,300 US combatants in South Vietnam.

On August 2, 1964, Walter Cronkite reported on CBS Nightly News that North Vietnamese Navy torpedo boats had attacked the US destroyer Maddox in the Gulf of Tonkin. The Maddox returned fire and requested help from the carrier Ticonderoga which was steaming north in the South China Sea. Carrier jets strafed the three PT boats, damaging two and crippling the other. The Maddox only sustained minor damage.

Two days later on August 4th, the Maddox and her companion ship, the C. Turner Joy were attacked by North Vietnamese PT boats in the same area as two days earlier. Neither of them suffered damage.

After both attacks, Hanoi claimed our ships were inside their territorial waters and were conducting intelligence missions. On national television President Johnson categorically denied both allegations.

On August 5th, fighter bombers from the carrier Ticonderoga bombed coastal North Vietnam fuel and petroleum storage facilities at the coastal city of Vinh and attacked four North Vietnamese PT boat bases.

On August 6th, Secretary of Defense Robert McNamara went before Congress to testify on the attacks on our ships in the Tonkin Gulf. He stated that the Maddox and Turner Joy were on routine patrol and the attacks were unprovoked and deliberate.

The next day Congress unanimously passed the Gulf of Tonkin resolution, giving President Johnson the authority to "take all necessary measures to repel any armed attacks against US Forces and to prevent any further aggression". This resolution provided President Johnson with the necessary authority for military action in Vietnam without the need for a declaration of war.

On that day, the seventh of August, 1964, the United States went to war in Vietnam. By the end of the year, there were 23,300 US combatants in Vietnam.

The conflict accelerated rapidly as the US built up ground forces and established Army, Navy, and Air Forces bases throughout South Vietnam. In March 1965, President Johnson approved "Operation Rolling Thunder", a sustained bombing campaign against North Vietnam. The Ho Chi Minh trail was a primary target, as well as major fuel and ammunition depots, and troop staging areas. By the end of the year there were 184,300 US combatants in Vietnam.

In January 1966, President Johnson announced that US troop level in Vietnam would be gradually increased to 205,000. South Korea decided to send in an additional 20,000 troops bringing their commitment to 25,570. The US 25th Infantry, the 196th Light Infantry Brigade, the 1st Aviation Brigade, the 199th Infantry Brigade, and the 9th Infantry Division were deployed to Vietnam by the end of the year.

Bombing continued throughout 1966 as B-52s strike the Ho Chi Minh trail and fuel storage and troop emplacements in North Vietnam. Total US troops in Vietnam reached 385,300 by the end of the year, in stark contrast to Johnson's prediction of 205,000.

In January 1967, 1st, 25th, and 173rd Infantry Brigades, and the 11th Armored Cavalry took on 90,000 VC in "Operation Triangle".

By the end of the year, the US had sent an additional $150 million in aid to South Vietnam, bringing the total aid since the start of the war to $700 million. Late in 1967, the 101st Airborne Division is deployed to Vietnam. At the end of 1967, the US troop level is 485,600. General Westmoreland announced the allied forces were winning the Vietnam War.

On January 30th, 1968, the VC and the North Vietnamese Army launched the "Tet" offensive across most of the country. The US embassy in Saigon was attacked by the VC. Soviet tanks were used on the battlefield for the first time.

The My Lei massacre occurred killing 500 civilians at the hands of the 1st Battalion, 20th Infantry Regiment.

The Paris Peace Talks continued and for the first time, South Vietnam representatives were allowed to sit at the table. In October, 1968, President Johnson ordered a cessation of bombing in North Vietnam.

By the end of 1968, there were over 546,000 US troops stationed in Vietnam with over 36,000 killed in action since 1557.

In January, 1969, Richard Nixon became president after a humiliating defeat of Lyndon Johnson. Henry Kissinger became the new Secretary of State.

On January 26th, 1970, US Navy pilot Lt. Everett Alvarez, Jr. spent his 2000th day as a POW. Lt. Alvarez was shot down during the air strikes launched against North Vietnam in retaliation for the Gulf of Tonkin attacks on the Maddox and Turner Joy.

In 1971, the US began drawing down forces in Vietnam as peace talks continued and anti-war demonstrations take place across the US. By December 31, US forces declined to 156,800.

In March 1972, the North launched the "Easter Offensive". Equipped with Soviet tanks, the North Army launched a full scale offensive across the DMZ into Quang Tri province. In response, President Nixon ordered US bombing of North Vietnam up to the 18th parallel. The "Easter Offensive" continued into May. Nixon *ordered the mining of North Vietnamese ports to cut their supply lines. He escalated bombing raids to strike all Northern military bases, supply depots, and transportation networks.*

In June 1972, five burglars were arrested breaking into Democratic Committee offices at the Watergate building in Wasington, DC.

In July 1972, Jane Fonda delivered an anti-US war message on Hanoi radio.

Peace talks continued unsuccessfully through 1972. On December 18, the US launched the most intense bombing campaign of the Vietnam War. "Operation Linebacker" was intended to drive North Vietnam back to the bargaining table. On December 28th, Hanoi agreed to reopen negotiations and Nixon suspended "Operation Linebacker". US troop level was at 24,200.

On January 15th, 1973, Nixon announced a total halt to all US offensive military action against the North.

Withdrawal of US military forces continued during 1973, By December 31, only fifty US military remained in Vietnam.

On August 9th, 1974, President Nixon resigned and Gerald Ford took over as president. By December 31st, there were still only fifty US military left in Vietnam.

On August 29th, 1975, the North attacked Saigon and the US Navy began evacuating all US civilian and military personnel from the rooftop of the US Embassy. The few Marines who were sent in to help evacuate the Embassy left on the last helicopter.

By the end of the conflict, over 58,000 American servicemen had been killed. It was a horrible bloody war and believed by most to have been totally unnecessary.

Throughout the Vietnam War, Signals Intelligence operations conducted by the NSA, the Air Force Security Service, the Naval Security Group, and the Army Security Agency played a major role in providing timely high quality intelligence to the US and South Vietnam military. Thousands of analysts and linguists operating in remote sites in VC and North Vietnam Army controlled territories unquestionably contributed to saving tens of thousands of military and civilian lives during the Vietnam War.

Author's Afterward

In 1961, Major Hickson was killed in an Air Force plane crash on a flight from Tachikawa Air Base in Japan to Osan Air Base in Korea. After the Major's untimely death, Peggy Hickson moved to Chicago and became active in local charities.

In August 1975, Raul braved heavy gunfire and exploding shells as he transported Lieutenant Peabody, Sergeant Johnson, and Sergeant DeMeur for evacuation from the American Embassy roof. He swung his Jeep around and headed back to the Grand Hotel to finish destroying Blue Cover documents. He was never heard from again.

John Johnson served nine years in Saigon as Chief of Station, National Security Agency. He retired from the NSA in 1980 to Beaumont, Texas, where he is a high school teacher and basketball coach.

In 1978, Major Roy Brent retired to his family farm in rural Georgia. He died of cancer in 1982.

After the Vietnam War, Sergeant Han DeMeur served with the Army Security Group assigned to the National Security Agency at Fort Meade, Maryland. She retired as a Senior Master Sergeant and now lives in Ho Chi Minh City, Vietnam.

Lieutenant William Peabody resigned from the Navy one day after the final armistice in Vietnam. He served as an analyst with the Central Intelligence Agency for twenty years and now lives in Washington, DC.

Commander Sheila Banta rose to the rank of Captain and retired as Deputy Director of the National Security Agency. She retired in 1985 and now serves as a councilor to disabled Vietnam veterans at Walter Reed Hospital in Bethesda, Maryland. She never married.

Matthew Garrison followed in his brother's footsteps, earning a Master's Degree in Mathematics at Notre Dame University in 1963. He went to work at the National Security Agency and currently is on assignment at Clark Air Base in the Philippines.

Kasuko-san was promoted to Vice President, Fashion Merchandising, for the Seibu Department Store Corporation.

Shortly after Yoshiko's death, O-Basan gave up her landlady job and moved in with her grandson and his family in Mito, Japan.

Morita-san died from Auto Immune Deficiency Syndrome in 1962.

Lieutenant Robert Davison was convicted of treason and sentenced to twenty years at the US Military Prison, in Fort Leavenworth, Kansas. He died there as a prisoner under strange circumstances.

Fumiko-san, alias Akito Isabi, was hanged by the Tokyo Ministry of Justice in a secret location in Tokyo.

"Red" disappeared after the arrest of Fumiko-san and is presumed to be an operative for the post-war Vietnam Government.

In 1982, the Ikebukuro neighborhood was bulldozed over and replaced by a high rise office building.